PRAISE FOR
KAREN KINGSBURY'S BOOKS

When Joy Came to Stay

"Kingsbury confronts hard issues with truth and sensitivity."

FRANCINE RIVERS, BESTSELLING AUTHOR OF *LEOTA'S GARDEN*

"Kingsbury's poignant tale of a lost and broken family and how they experience God's miraculous healing is a sure guarantee to bring hope and joy to her readers."

MELODY CARLSON, AUTHOR OF *DIARY OF A TEENAGE GIRL*

"A thought-provoking account of the battle of depression in a believer's life. It leaves no doubt that God is loving, merciful, and faithful."

NANCY MOSER, AUTHOR OF *THE SEAT BESIDE ME*

A Moment of Weakness

"With the careful pacing of a seasoned storyteller, Karen Kingsbury spins a tale of love and loss, lies and betrayal, that sent me breathlessly turning pages to discover what might become of Jade and Tanner. These flawed characters are easy to sympathize with...and celebrate with by the story's end! Contemporary issues of faith and the First Amendment add to the timely message in *A Moment of Weakness*."

LIZ CURTIS HIGGS, BESTSELLING AUTHOR OF *BOOKENDS* AND
BAD GIRLS OF THE BIBLE

"Karen Kingsbury has written a heart-gripping love story. *A Moment of Weakness* demonstrates the devastating consequences of wrong choices and the long shadows deception casts over the lives of God's children. It also shows the even longer reach of God's providence, grace, and forgiveness."

RANDY ALCORN, BESTSELLING AUTHOR OF *SAFELY HOME* AND *THE ISHBANE CONSPIRACY*

"One message shines clear and strong through Karen Kingsbury's *A Moment of Weakness*: Our loving God is a God of second chances."

ANGELA ELWELL HUNT, BESTSELLING AUTHOR OF *THE JUSTICE*

Waiting for Morning

"What a talent! I love her work."

GARY SMALLEY, BESTSELLING AUTHOR

"Kingsbury not only entertains but goes a step further and confronts readers with situations that are all too common, even for Christians. At the same time, *Waiting for Morning* will remind believers of God's mercy and challenge them to pray for America. The book...reveals God's awesome love and His amazing ability to turn moments of weakness into times of strengthening."

CHRISTAIN RETAILING, SPOTLIGHT REVIEW

WHEN JOY CAME TO STAY

KAREN KINGSBURY

Multnomah Publishers

WHEN JOY CAME TO STAY
published by Multnomah Publishers
A division of Random House, Inc.

Published in association with the literary agency of Alive Communications, Inc.
7680 Goddard St., Suite 200, Colorado Springs, CO 80920

© 2000 by Karen Kingsbury

International Standard Book Number: 1-59052-751-8

Cover design by Kirk DouPonce, DogEaredDesign.com

All Scripture quotations are taken from
The Holy Bible, New International Version © 1973, 1984 by International Bible
Society, used by permission of Zondervan Publishing House
The Holy Bible, New King James Version © 1984 by Thomas Nelson, Inc.
Excerpts from the hymn GREAT IS THEY FAITHFULNESS by Thomas O. Chisholm
© 1923, Ren. 1951 Hope Publishing Company, Carol Stream, IL 60188.
All rights reserved. International copyright secured. Used by permission.

For information:
Multnomah Publishers
12265 Oracle Boulevard, Suite 200
Colorado Springs, CO 80921

Library of Congress Cataloging-in-Publication Data
Kingsbury, Karen.
  When Joy came to stay/by Karen Kingsbury.
    p. cm.
ISBN 1-57673-746-2 (pbk.)
    1-59052-751-8(pbk.)
1. Women—Fiction. 2. Identity (Psychology)—Fiction. I. Title.
PS3561.I483 W48 2000
813'.54—dc21   00-009451

06 07 08 09 10—19 18 17 16

Donald, who is and has been my very best friend regardless of the storms of life. Thank you for believing in me, loving me, and praying for me as if your life depended on it. Persecution is a promise in the kingdom of God, but with you by my side the lessons we have learned this past year are both vivid and welcomed. My greatest joy is knowing you are by my side, now and forever.

Kelsey, caught somewhere between the oh-so-cute little girl and the tenderly precious young woman whose image grows clearer with each passing season. Whether kicking a soccer ball, mastering a math test, or seeking God's heart on the daily dilemmas of growing up, you are proving yourself to be intensely committed, deeply devoted, sincere, genuine, and true. I am the most blessed mom in the world to have the privilege of calling you my daughter, my little Norm, my song.

Tyler, tall, strong, and handsome—in the days of becoming, it is clear the type of man you'll be. And yet now, for a short while, you're still a little boy, remembering to pick a dandelion for me on family walks. Kind and compassionate, always ready to share, thinking of others. When I look at you, so often I see your daddy. And on many wonderful moments I see your Father, too. If I could bottle your zest for life, your sincerity, and share them with others, the world would be a different place.

Keep your eyes on the goal, son; God has great plans for you. I love you always.

Austin, no longer making baby steps but running through our house and our hearts. It's marvelous to see the way God has made you focused—gifted with the ability to master an action regardless of the time and energy involved. Even more amazing are the glimpses of a tender heart beneath the toughness—"Daddy, I'm going to kiss your wife…"

Mingled with your three-year-old laughter are words that will ring through the decades. I remain always in awe of the miracle of your life.

And to my loving Lord and Savior, who has, for now, blessed me with these.

Acknowledgments

As with all my books, this one was written with the help of many friends and professionals who made it ring true literally and sing true spiritually. Writing about depression is not something I've done before; although I've wrestled with testing and persecutions, battling depression has never been one of my trials. For that reason I did extensive research on what I came to understand as an illness and drew heavily from the results God brought my way.

In this light I especially want to thank my dear friend, Sylvia Wallgren—a Christian counselor and licensed psychiatrist—for giving me understanding. In a way that was both miraculous and timely, the Lord ordained that Sylvia and I meet. She also is a prayer warrior and lifted me up to heaven's throne daily as I wrote this book. I strongly suspect Sylvia will be a treasured friend—part of my close, close circle—throughout our journey here and on into eternity. Sylvia, I can't tell you strongly enough how much your daily encouragement and e-mailed prayers meant to me, still mean to me. I thank God for you.

Again, thanks go to my amazing editor, Karen Ball, who takes my work and fine-tunes it so that the music you hear is truly a thing of beauty. Karen, you're a gifted editor, and I am blessed for knowing you, working with you.

To the Multnomah family, from my dear friends in sales to those in publicity, marketing, editorial, management, cover design, endorsements, and everyone in between—you are the most amazing people to work for. Every now and then, in the quiet moments before dawn, I find myself in awe that this is my job and you are my coworkers. I believe God is taking our books someplace we've never imagined before! Thank you, a million times over.

Like last year, thanks to Kristy and Jeff Blake for taking care of my precious angel child during those hours when I absolutely needed a moment to write.

Also a special thanks to my niece Shannon Kane, to Jan Adams, and to Joan Westfall for always being the first in line to read my books and give me valuable feedback. Also to my other family and friends for your love, support, and encouragement in every aspect of my writing. Especially my mom and dad, who have been there since my first stapled, colored-in book at age five.

With every book I write there are people who pray for me and lend an ear while I talk plots and character traits. These are my special, oh-so-close friends and sisters in Christ, the golden ones who will never change or leave regardless of the passing of days. You know who you are and how precious each of you are to me and my family. May God continue to richly bless our friendships.

There are nights in the midst of writing a book when leftovers are the best thing going at dinnertime and the laundry is piled to the ceiling. For those times and any others when I might have been just a tad preoccupied, I thank my incredible husband and sweethearted children—I couldn't do this without the combined efforts from each of you.

And thanks to the Skyview basketball team, for always giving me a reason to cheer, even on deadline.

The Descent

Weeping may endure for a night,
but joy comes in the morning.

PSALM 30:5

Prologue

SIX DAYS HAD PASSED SINCE LAURA THOMPSON'S JOB AS A MOTHER had officially ended.

The wedding had gone off without a hitch, and the last of Laura's four babies was out of the house, ready—like his siblings—to build a life of his own. She would always be their mom, of course, and in time she and Larry would welcome grandbabies and opportunities to visit with their grown children.

But for all intents and purposes, Laura was out of a job—and that was the primary reason for today's meeting.

She let her gaze fall on the circle of women gathered that Friday morning at Cleveland Community Church—women she'd known most of her life—and she was struck by the realization that they'd arrived at this place together. Houses quiet, children gone, grandchildren still years away...

Only their Friday morning Bible study remained the same.

The chattering among the women diminished and Emma Lou, women's president for the past year cast a tender smile their way. "Pastor gave me the names this morning."

A hush of expectancy settled over the group, and several of the women crossed their legs or tilted their heads, shifting their attention to the bowl in Emma Lou's hand. Inside were the names of younger women, women who felt the need for prayer, women who were diapering babies and solving multiplication problems over dinner dishes and wondering how to make laughter and love last even in a Christian marriage.

Laura swallowed hard, surprised to feel tears in her eyes. Women like she and her friends once had been.

"Before we open our Bibles, let's everyone draw a name. And remember, these are women who want your prayer and support, possibly even your mentoring. We may be finished raising our families, but these young gals are just starting out." Emma Lou's eyes shone with the memories of days gone by. "Draw a name, keep it confidential, and take the responsibility of praying for that one as seriously as you once took the job of mothering. I believe the Lord would find our work in this task every bit as important."

Laura dabbed at a tear and sucked in a quick breath. She wouldn't cry, not here, not now. She had a wonderful family and a million happy memories. There was nothing she could do to change the fact that her family was grown. But this—this role of praying for a young mother in their church fellowship—was something she could do today. Something that would give her life purpose, meaning, and direction.

Laura intended to carry out the assignment with all her heart.

The bowl was passed around the circle, and when it came to her she reached in, moving her fingers through the papers. *Who, Lord? Who would You have me pray for?*

She clasped a small slip and plucked it from the others. Would it be a mother overwrought with financial challenges? One burdened with the daily demands of mothering? Or perhaps a sweet daughter of the Lord whose husband didn't share her faith? Whoever she was, Laura knew the power of lifting a sister directly to the throne room of God. She could hardly imagine the results of praying for such a one over time.

Laura waited until Emma Lou asked them to read the names they had drawn, then her eyes fell to her hands as she unfolded the piece of paper and saw the bold writing inside. For a moment, a sharp pang of disappointment stabbed at her. *What's this? I must have grabbed the wrong slip.*

Maggie Stovall?

Of all the women in the church, God wanted her to pray for

Maggie Stovall? What special needs could an exemplary woman like Maggie possibly have? How could she require daily prayer? Surely there was someone who needed her support more than Maggie Stovall.

Laura settled back in her chair, surprised Maggie had even gone to the trouble of requesting prayer. The young woman was a regular at church. Each week without exception, she and her husband volunteered in the Sunday school wing to lead the children in song. As far as Laura knew, Maggie was a successful newspaper columnist, her husband an established attorney. For the past few years, they'd even opened their home to foster children.

In need of prayer? The Stovalls were part of the blessed crowd—popular, well-liked people who cast a favorable impression on the entire church body, people the pastor and elders were proud to have in their midst.

Never, not even once, had Laura seen Maggie Stovall look anything but radiantly happy and perfectly put together.

Maggie Stovall? Am I hearing you right, Lord?

The answer was clear and quick: **Pray, dear one. Maggie needs prayer.**

Immediately an image filled Laura's mind. The image of a woman wearing a mask.

Laura couldn't make out the woman's features, nor were the details of the mask clear. Still the image remained, and though Laura had no idea what to make of the mental picture she was instantly seized with remorse. *I'm sorry, Lord. Really. I'll pray…maybe there's something I don't know about Maggie.*

Laura ran her finger gently over the young woman's name, then folded the slip of paper and tucked it inside her Bible.

The vision of the masked woman came to mind again, and a sadness covered Laura's heart. Was it Maggie? Was there something she was hiding? *What is it, Lord? Tell me?*

Silence.

Laura sighed and her resolve grew. She might no longer be

needed in the daily tasks of mothering, but clearly she was needed in this. God had spoken that much to her months ago when she had first suggested the idea of praying for the young women in their midst. And if this woman was the one she was to pray for, so be it.

She would pray for Maggie Stovall as though it were the most important job in the world.

And maybe one day God would let her understand.

One

THE MOMENTS OF LUCIDITY WERE FEW AND FAR BETWEEN ANYMORE.

Thankfully, this was one of them. Aware of the fact, Maggie Stovall worked her fingers over the computer keyboard as though they might somehow propel her ahead of the darkness, keep her inches in front of whatever it was that hungered after her mind, her sanity.

Despite all that was uncertain that fall, Maggie was absolutely sure of one thing: She was losing it. And the little blond girl—whoever she might be—was only partly to blame.

Maggie's desk in the newsroom of the *Cleveland Gazette* was one of the remaining places where, most of the time, she still felt normal. The twenty or forty minutes a day she spent there were an oasis of peace and clarity bordered by a desert of hours, all dark, barren, and borderline crazy. The newsroom deadlines and demands left no room for fear and trembling, no time for worrying whether the darkness was about to consume her.

Maggie drew a steadying breath, glanced around the newsroom, and saw that the office was full of more reporters than usual for a Wednesday. *Slow news day. Great.* When news was slow her column got front-page billing, and the one she was writing for tomorrow's paper was bound to gain attention: "The Real Abuse of Abused Children." She let her eyes run down the page. This column would be clipped out of papers around the city, tacked to office walls, and mailed to the Social Services department by irate citizens. She would receive dozens of letters, and the paper would receive more, but none of that bothered Maggie.

15

She'd gotten the job at the *Gazette* more than two years earlier and she'd been churning out her column, "Maggie's Mind," five days a week since. She'd developed a reputation, a persona, that a segment of the public hated and a greater segment couldn't seem to get enough of. People said she put words to the thoughts and conversations that took place in a majority of homes in their area and around the country. The conservative homes. The people who voted against tax hikes and partial-birth abortions; people who wanted tougher prisons and longer sentences, and prayer in public schools. The segment of the population who wanted a return to family-friendly governing.

For those people, she was a welcome voice. The voice of morality in a time and place where few in the paper, or anywhere in the media for that matter, seemed committed to speaking on their behalf. Most *Gazette* readers loved Maggie. From the beginning they had applauded her, and a few months after starting at the paper the editorial staff had been forced to hire an assistant simply to weed through the mail generated by Maggie's efforts.

"You know, Maggie girl, I think you've really got something with that column of yours," her editor had told her more than once. "It's disconcerting, really. Like the rest of us are writing for some small special interest group, but you…ah, Maggie, you're writing for them. The moral majority."

Maggie knew the paper's editorial board was glad to have her on staff, even if many of her peers disagreed with her political views. But no one was more proud than her husband, Ben, an assistant district attorney who was also president of the Cleveland Chamber of Commerce. After nearly seven years of marriage, Ben was still in love with her; she had no doubts. Even now, when they had to search awkwardly for things to talk about and her attitude toward him was vastly different than a year ago, he would still walk over burning coals to prove his love.

Because he doesn't know the truth.

No. Not now, Maggie thought. *Not with a column to finish.*

Among the silent voices that taunted her these days was her own, and at times like this she was her worst enemy. If Ben knew the truth about her past, if he knew the real person he'd married, he would do what Joseph set out to do to Mary two thousand years ago: divorce her quietly and leave town on the first passing donkey.

"How's it coming, Mag?" It was Ron Kendall, managing editor, and he shouted the question from twenty feet away where the editors' desks formed an imposing island in the middle of the newsroom.

"Fine. I'll file in ten minutes."

"I might need it for page one. Give me a liner." Ron leaned back in his chair for a clearer view of Maggie's face.

She glanced at her screen and summed up her column. "Woman's lawsuit demands changes in the way abused children are handled by Social Services."

"Good. Got it." Ron returned to the task at hand—planning the paper's front page.

There were those at the paper who disliked Ron, but Maggie wasn't among them. Built like a linebacker with a mass of unkempt white hair and a perpetual two-day beard, the man's voice rang through the newsroom whenever a deadline was missed or an untruth reported in print. But deep down, beneath his work face, Ron Kendall was the last of a dying breed of editors, a churchgoing conservative who cherished his role in shaping and reporting the news of Cleveland.

Once Maggie ran into Ron at a dinner raising money for the city's rescue mission. Near the end of the evening, he pulled her aside.

"Someday you're going to get offers to leave us." The flint was missing from his eyes and in its place was a sparkle that couldn't be contrived. "Just remember this: Losing you would be like losing one of my arms." He patted her shoulder. "Don't

WHEN JOY CAME TO STAY   17

ever leave us, Maggie. We need you."

That was a year ago, and Maggie was surprised to find Ron had been right. Offers had come from Los Angeles, Dallas, even New York. Editors might have enjoyed staffing their papers with liberal-minded news seekers, but nothing met the readers' appetite like a conservative columnist—and those who were well liked were in high demand.

Maggie had done what Ron asked and stayed. She liked Cleveland and their church friends at Cleveland Community. Besides, Ben's job was there.

If they knew the truth about me… Maggie closed her eyes. *They'd fire me in a heartbeat. I'd have no marriage, no column…*

Stop it! Stay focused! That was seven years ago, Maggie.

But Maggie knew it didn't matter how many years had slipped by. She would never get past the truth. And there would never be any way she could tell Ben.

Let no falsehood come from your mouth, but only that which is…

There it was again. The familiar calm, still voice…and with it a strange feeling of impending doom so great Maggie had to fight the urge to take cover. Her eyes flew open and she moved her hands into position at her keyboard. "Let's get this thing done," she hissed through clenched teeth. This was no time for strange, scriptural warnings about lie telling. She had a deadline to meet.

What was done was done.

Help me concentrate, God. Help me forget about what's behind; help me look ahead without this…whatever it is that wants to consume me.

Her head cleared, and she studied her computer screen once more.

Her column that day was based on a lawsuit filed against the city's Social Services department by a Cleveland woman contesting that the department was to blame for destroying her son. She'd adopted the boy when he was five years old. Over the next four years he'd been diagnosed with a host of disorders all attesting to the fact that he was unmanageable, unable to attach emotionally, and inappropriately aggressive toward her other children. Finally, the woman felt forced to turn the then nine-year-old back over to Social Services.

The lawsuit shone a flashlight of concern on the Social Services department, which still held to the notion that children should be raised by their parents whenever possible, regardless of the situation in the home. The woman contended that if Social Services had removed the boy from his birth mother sooner, he wouldn't have been so badly scarred emotionally.

Maggie's heart ached with understanding.

She and Ben were foster parents, currently of seven-year-old twin boys. Their mother was an alcoholic, their father dangerously violent. Still, Maggie knew that one day, long after the boys had bonded with her and Ben, they would be returned to their birth mother. Stories like the one she was writing about were tragically common, and Maggie hoped her words might touch a nerve across the city. Perhaps if enough people demanded change...

She scanned what she'd just written.

The way the department operates today, a child may be kept hostage in closets while Mom sells herself for drugs; he can be beaten, mocked, and left to sleep in urine-soaked rags, yet that type of home life is deemed best for the child. The solution is obvious. We must fight to see the system changed and demand that such children be removed from the home the first time harmful circumstances come to light—while the child is still young enough to find an adoption placement.

The statistics tell the story. With each passing year, the odds of a troubled child finding an adoptive home diminish by 20 percent. In the first year, the chances of adoption are brilliantly high. Even at age two most children will find permanent, loving homes. But many children removed from abusive homes are not released for adoption until age five, and often much later. What happens to these children?

Too often they are left to squander their baby years in abusive situations and temporary foster homes, moving every few months while Mom and Dad dry out or serve jail time. In the process, they become emotionally "damaged goods": children too old and too jaded ever to fit into a loving, adoptive family. In cases like these, we have only one place to point the finger for the tragic consequences: The archaic rules of the Social Services department.

I thank God for people like Mrs. Werdemeir, whose lawsuit finally exposes the type of tragedy that has gone on far too long. The tragedy of thinking that no matter the situation, a child belongs with his mother.

Tonight when you kneel beside the bed of your little one, remember those babies out there sleeping in closets. And pray that God will change the minds of those who might make a difference.

Suddenly Maggie's mind drifted, and her eyes jumped back a sentence: *Your little ones…little ones…little ones…kneel beside the bed of your little ones…*

Her eyes grew wet and the words faded. *What about us, Lord? Where are the little ones we've prayed for? Haven't we tried? Haven't we?* She remembered the testing, the experimental procedures they'd participated in, the drug therapy and nutrition programs that were supposed to help her get pregnant. A single tear slid down her cheek into her mouth. It tasted bitter, like it had come from some place deep and forbidden in her soul, and she wiped at it in frustration.

Nothing had worked.

Even now her arms ached for the children they didn't have. Foster kids, yes...but no babies to pray over, no little ones to be thankful for. *Why, Lord? It's been seven years...*

You had your chance. You don't deserve a child of your own.

The truth hit hard, and her breath caught in her throat. ·

Maggie blinked twice, and the taunting voice faded. She quickly included a footnote at the bottom of her column advising readers that there would be more information in the coming weeks and months on the issue of abused and forgotten children in the Social Services system. She saved her changes and sent the file to Ron's computer.

"It's in." She spoke loudly, and when she saw her editor nod, she turned her attention back to the now blank computer screen. Seconds passed, and a face began taking shape. The newsroom noise faded as the picture on the screen grew clearer, and suddenly Maggie could make out the girl's features...her pretty, innocent face; her lovely, questioning eyes.

Do you know where my mama is? the girl seemed to ask.

Maggie wanted to shout at the image, but she blinked twice and before her mind could give her mouth permission to speak, the girl disappeared.

It was her of course—the same girl every time, every day. She saw the child everywhere, even in her dreams.

The girl's presence had been a constant for nearly a year, making it difficult for Maggie to think of anything else. As a result, the days were no longer consumed with her work as a columnist, her role as a foster mother, or her duties as the wife of an important lawyer and civic leader. No, each day had become consumed with the idea that one day—perhaps not too far off—the little girl would not fade into air.

One day, the girl would be real.

The visions of the blond child had pushed Maggie to the edge of insanity. And with them came something else that filled Maggie's mind even now, a darkness that threatened to destroy her, to leave her locked in a padded cell, wrapped in a straight jacket. Or worse.

The problem wasn't so much that she was misplacing her car keys more often than usual or forgetting dentist appointments or leaving cold milk in the pantry by mistake or seeing imaginary little girls every time she turned around. It was all of that, yes, but it was something more that made her truly question her sanity. It was the certain feeling that something hideously dark and possibly deadly—something that now seemed closely linked to her secret—was closing in on her.

Something from which she couldn't escape.

A chill ran down Maggie's spine; the secret was no longer something she could ignore, something she might pretend had never happened. It didn't matter whether she acknowledged it or opened it and laid it on the floor for everyone to look at.

It simply was.

Indeed, its presence had become a living, breathing entity. It was the embodiment of darkness that lay beside her at night and followed her through the making of beds and breakfast and daily appointments in the morning. It sat next to her in the car, breathing threats of destruction should anyone find out the truth—

Stop this! You're making yourself crazy!

Maggie pushed away from her desk and gathered her things. Fresh air, that's what she needed. Maybe a walk through the park. She glanced at a stack of magazines on her desk and did a double take. There she was again! Gracing the cover, looking directly at Maggie...the same little girl.

Then in an instant, she was gone.

Air released from Maggie's lungs like a withering party balloon.

Yes, she was losing it—free-falling over the canyon's edge—and there was nothing she could do to prevent the coming crash. She wanted help, truly she did, but there wasn't anywhere she could turn, no one to talk to.

No one who would believe that Maggie Stovall was having a problem she couldn't handle by herself.

Finally, desperate, she'd placed her name in the offering bucket when the pastor had asked which women would like prayer from an older, senior Christian. Maggie didn't know if it would help, but it couldn't hurt. And it was better than facing someone with the truth.

She headed for her car.

How had things gotten so bad? Years ago she would have had two or three days a month like this and called it depression. Not that she told anyone how she was feeling, even back then. She was a Christian after all, and Christians—good Christians like her and Ben—did not suffer from depression. At least not as far as Maggie could tell. But this...this *thing* that haunted her now was beyond depression.

Far beyond it.

This was the kind of thing that sent people packing to psychiatric wards.

Two

AMANDA JOY SAT HUDDLED ON A NARROW BED, LEANING AGAINST the chilly wall of the third house she'd lived in that month. The silence was scary, like in the movies before something bad happened…but then she was only seven, and lots of things seemed scary. Especially since coming to the Graystone house.

Footsteps echoed in the distance, and Amanda gulped. Mrs. Graystone was awake, and that meant she'd be coming to check on her. Pushing herself off the bed, Amanda yanked on the covers and straightened the sheets. Beds had to be neat or…

Amanda didn't want to think about it.

Maybe there was another place she could go, some other foster family who wanted a little girl for a while. She tugged on the bedspread as she remembered the house she'd stayed at just after summer. Her social worker had called it a mistake, a bad placement. Five days later Amanda was packed and sent to a home five miles south, a working farm with three teenage boys.

She shuddered at the memory.

The boys' parents wanted a foster girl to give the missus a hand with laundry and indoor chores. But while she did up dishes or folded laundry the boys teased her until she was afraid to get dressed or take a shower. Two weeks later the mister found her in the barn, hands tied behind her back with baling twine. Her shirt lay in a rumpled heap on the ground, and the boys were taking turns poking at her, threatening to do terrible things to her if she screamed.

The boys received a whipping from their pa, and she escaped with her social worker before dinnertime.

She didn't know what she would have done without her social worker. For a moment, Amanda forgot about the chores and sat slowly on the corner of her bed. Kathy Garrett.

In some ways Kathy was more like a mother than anyone she'd ever known. Anyone except the Brownells.

The Brownells had been Amanda's only real parents. They adopted her as a baby and gave her a wonderful life for five short years.

The house was quiet again, and Amanda wondered if Mrs. Graystone had fallen back asleep. There had been an empty liquor bottle on the table when Amanda got home from school. Alcohol made Mrs. Graystone very tired, so maybe she would sleep for a long time.

Amanda slipped off the mattress and lifted the plain, gray bedskirt, poking her head under the bed. There it was. Gently she pulled out a brown paper bag, opened it, and sat cross-legged on the floor, staring at the contents inside. A photograph of her with the Brownells, three folded-up awards she'd won in school, a bracelet she'd found in the lunchroom the year before. She plucked out the picture and stared hard at it. The checkered dress she'd worn that year was a hand-me-down from the neighbors. All the girls in kindergarten had laughed at it, but Amanda figured out how to make them stop. She prayed for them.

She'd knelt beside her bed at the Brownells and prayed. "Dear Jesus, help those girls in my class be nice. Because they don't have happy hearts, at least I don't think so."

Neither did Mrs. Graystone. Which was why Amanda had been praying for her, too. She sighed and set the photograph back in the sack. As she peered inside, her eyes fell on the yellowish newspaper article.

Amanda pulled it out and opened it carefully.

She couldn't read very well, but she'd read the article often enough to know what it said. It was a news report of the accident that killed the Brownells.

"Icy tree limb lands on car, kills Woodland couple," the big words on top yelled out.

Amanda felt tears stinging her eyes. The smaller letters said how the Brownells had a five-year-old daughter. But they didn't say there was no one for her to live with once the Brownells were gone.

She remembered meeting Kathy Garrett for the first time at school that afternoon—the day of the accident. Kathy told Amanda that she had known her as a little baby and that she had helped the Brownells with the adoption. At first it had been nice, sitting in the office talking with the pretty lady. But then Kathy told her about the accident and after that her tummy had felt sick inside.

Sick and scared.

"You can stay with us tonight, sweetheart," Kathy said. "But after that we'll find you a foster home. A place where you can stay until another family adopts you."

They'd found a home. A foster home, like Kathy had talked about. And then another one. And another one. But the best times of all were when Amanda was between foster parents and got to spend a night or two with Kathy and her family.

Amanda closed her eyes and pictured Kathy Garrett's home. Warm, with lots of light and laughter and good smells from the kitchen. Someone was always talking or telling a story or singing or dancing. When Amanda was there she didn't feel like her name was Brownell at all. She felt like it was Garrett. Like she belonged there. Like she was one of them. She even had her own chair at the kitchen table.

At times like this she wondered if they left her empty chair at the table when she wasn't there, if the Garretts missed her as much as she missed them.

She opened her eyes again, folded the article, and slipped it back inside the bag. It was the same bag she'd had for two years, and she was careful not to rip it as she folded the top down and slid it back under the bed.

Kathy Garrett was married to a happy man named Bill. He would lay on the floor and wrestle with the kids until they were laughing so hard they couldn't breathe. He always laughed. But one time…

One time Bill didn't laugh. When he brought everyone together in a circle once to pray for Amanda. During the prayer, when he thought she wasn't looking, Amanda caught him crying. Not loud tears like kids cry, but quiet ones that rolled off his face and didn't make his nose sound stuffy.

Amanda stared at the barren walls in the chilly room, but in her mind she could see Bill and Kathy, laughing, playing with their children. Lots and lots of children. The Garretts had more kids than anyone Amanda knew. Seven altogether, all squeezed into three happy bedrooms. Kathy liked to say it wasn't the size of the house that mattered, it was what the house was made of. After living in a dozen different houses in two years Amanda was sure of one thing: Kathy wasn't talking about bricks and carpet and stuff.

She was talking about feelings. So as far as Amanda was concerned, the Garrett house was made of all love and sunshine.

There were footsteps again and Amanda's heart quickened. Mrs. Graystone had four other foster children living with her, all of them crammed into two small bedrooms. Her husband drove a truck for a living and was hardly ever home. The other kids liked to tell secrets about Mrs. Graystone, and the first day Amanda arrived they told her what they thought of their foster mother.

"Old Graystone uses all our money to buy her smelly cigarettes," one of the kids told her that first day.

Amanda frowned. "What money?"

An older girl laughed out loud. "The gov'ment money, goofball. She's supposed to use it to buy us food and clothes and stuff."

"Yeah, but she never does," the first boy poked Amanda on

the shoulder. "You'll see soon enough. Two meals a day if you're lucky. And if you're hungry at night then too bad for you."

The kids had been right; Mrs. Graystone's house was made of scary sounds and hungry nights. Lots of hunger.

There was a sharp knock at the bedroom door, and Mrs. Graystone burst inside. She was a big woman with an angry mouth and rolls of stomach pushing against her flowered dress. Amanda jumped to her feet and backed up against the farthest wall as Mrs. Graystone waddled toward her.

"Why aren't you cleaning your room?"

Amanda looked about and saw nothing out of place. "I made the bed and picked up the clothes like you said."

"Anyone could do that." She came closer and shook a finger at her. "Do you think I brought you here so you could live like a princess?" The woman's voice rattled like windows in an old house when the wind blew hard outside.

"What else do you want me—"

"Don't be impertinent with me, young lady." Mrs. Graystone's face was red, and Amanda was scared. The woman had never hit her, but that didn't mean she wouldn't. Other foster parents had done it. Not all of them, of course. Some of Amanda's foster placements had been wonderful homes like Kathy's. But her stay at those homes was never permanent. They were something called short-term or crisis-care stays. Something like that. After a little while in those places, Amanda always got packed up and sent to the next foster home.

Since she was not sure what *impertinent* meant she squirmed toward the corner of her bed and remained silent.

Mrs. Graystone lowered herself over Amanda and glared at her. "I don't need no insolent brat living with me. I can make the same money with someone who'll do as I say. Do you hear me?"

"Yes, ma'am."

The woman raised her hand, and before Amanda could

take cover it came crashing down across her cheek. The blow made her fall to her knees, and she gasped for breath. *I'm scared, God, help me!*

Amanda covered her face with her hands and felt her body shaking with fear. *Don't let her hit me again, please...*

"Don't you 'yes, ma'am,' me, missy. Now get up and get to work."

Amanda separated her fingers so she could see Mrs. Graystone again.

"Move your hands from your face!"

Amanda's cheek felt hot and sore but she did as she was told. The woman pointed to a broom that stood in the corner of the room. "I want that hardwood floor swept and polished. And when you're finished you can take a rag to those awful walls. I swear the last brat who had this room didn't do any better than you."

She was still on her knees, afraid to move. *Kathy's coming today. It won't be long. Just a few more hours and I can leave. Kathy won't let me—*

"Move it!" Mrs. Graystone grabbed Amanda's arm and yanked her to her feet. Then she pulled a rag and a bottle of floor polish from her apron and tossed it on the floor. "I want this place clean in an hour or you can forget dinner."

The woman took slow steps toward the hallway, then slammed the door shut as she left.

Why does she hate me? Are You there, God? Don't You hear me? All I want is a mom and a dad. I'll clean my room perfect every day, I promise. But please, God, please give me a mom and dad. Someone like Bill and Kathy.

Tears stung at the girl's eyes as she took the broom and worked it across the floor in long strokes. She would be eight in six months and though she was small for her age, she'd been sweeping floors for as long as she could remember, so she had the task finished in a few minutes. Her mind began to drift back to when she was little, before her adoptive parents were killed. As she took the rag and began working polish into the floor, she started to cry harder.

Even if she were going to see Kathy later, it wouldn't solve anything. She'd still be a ward of the court, a foster child looking for a family. She wandered tentatively over to the brown sack and the photograph of her with her adoptive parents, the Brownells. They had been wonderful people, but they hadn't been like real family.

She closed her eyes and she could hear herself asking the familiar question:

"If you adopted me, how come I can't call you Momma and Daddy?"

Mrs. Brownell's answer was as clear now as it had been that spring day all those years ago. "Child, we will always think of you as our daughter, but Mr. Brownell and I never planned to have children and we don't think it proper for a child to call us by so familiar a term. Mr. and Mrs. Brownell suits us better. But it doesn't mean we love you any less."

Even back when she was five the answer had felt uncomfortable, like a shrunken sweater. She studied the picture once more and as she went back to work on the floor she thought of her mother. Her real mother.

The Brownells had told her about a young woman who had been unable to care for her new baby and so, out of love, had given her to them to raise. But ever since God had taken the Brownells home, Amanda had kept a secret wish that somewhere out in the big world her real Momma was missing her.

And that one day God would bring them back together again.

Three

MAGGIE STOOD IN THE PARKING LOT OUTSIDE THE NEWSPAPER building, pulled her running shoes from the trunk of her car, and slipped them on. Just then her cell phone rang, and she exhaled in frustration. *What now? I only have an hour to finish my run and get the boys.* If she didn't burn off some of the anxiety coursing through her she wouldn't make it through the day. She grabbed her purse and yanked the phone from inside.

"Hello?"

There was a hesitation on the other end that almost made Maggie hang up. Then the voice of an older woman cut the silence. "Maggie Stovall?"

"Yes?" *Great. Now I'm getting sales calls on my—*

"Maggie, this is Laura Thompson. From church. I'm sorry to bother you…"

As the woman's voice trailed off, Maggie pictured her: late sixties, gray hair, soft face, always involved in one committee or another. Concern transcended Laura Thompson's voice, and Maggie felt herself tense up. What would Laura Thompson want with her? "No, that's fine. What's going on?"

The woman cleared her throat. "Well, dear…we picked names last week, and I wanted you to know I got yours."

Maggie's mind was blank. *Names?* What was Laura talking about? "I'm not sure I'm following you."

"The prayer team, remember? You put your name in the basket so one of us would pray for you."

Maggie's concentration was waning and without reason her heart began to race. "Prayer?" Then it hit her. Laura was right; she'd written her name on a slip of paper requesting one of the older women in the church to pray for her. She'd never expected a phone call from one of them. Silent, anonymous prayer was one thing, but this… She felt her cheeks grow hot. "I remember now. So, uh, thanks for letting me know."

"Yes, I'll be praying. And I'm here for you, dear. If you need anything, anytime. You can call me. We'll pray on the phone, or I can meet with you. Whatever you'd like. Whatever's on your heart."

Pray with Laura Thompson about what was on her heart? The idea was so terrifying it was ludicrous. Impossible. If Laura knew her secret everyone at Cleveland Community would know, too. And they would never look at her the same. Maggie's heart beat faster still, and she managed a polite laugh. *Control, Maggie. Show her you're in control.* "Thanks for the offer, Laura. But really, everything's fine. I only asked for prayer because…well, you know…it can't hurt." She laughed again, forcing her voice to sound upbeat.

Silence.

She knows. Oh no, it can't be. How did she find out about me, Lord? Maggie closed her eyes and forced her trembling knees together. "Laura?"

"Yes, dear, I'm here. It's just—"

Maggie cut her off. "Don't get me wrong. I'd still like you to pray. But there's no crisis or anything, that's all."

"Okay." Laura didn't seem convinced. "I'll let you go, dear. But I'll be praying all the same. My number's in the church directory."

She knows. I know she knows. Maggie hung up and slipped the phone back in her purse. Who had told her? Why else would she have called? Wasn't the prayer team supposed to do things in private, secretly?

Her hands were shaking, and perspiration ran down her arms and neck. She glanced at the running shoes. Why did she have them on? Oh yes, her run. She frowned glancing about the parking lot and across the street to the park. *Think, Maggie, come on.* Had she finished her run already? So quickly? She barely remembered a moment of it.

Remembering to breathe, she slipped her shoes off and froze. She felt the breath of something evil on the back of her neck, something close enough to touch. Tossing her shoes back in the trunk she hurried into the driver's seat, slammed the door shut and hit the lock.

It was no use.

The invisible darkness had followed her into the car and now was locked inside with her. *How did I finish my run so fast?* She looked across the street once more at the familiar park and its asphalt jogging trail that ran the circumference. *I did run, didn't I?* Her body was sweaty, her heart beating hard. She must have run.

Maggie started the car and again felt the presence of evil beside her. "Get out!" Despite her shouted command, the feeling didn't ease. *All I want is peace, Lord, what's it going to take?*

Confess your sins and you will be clean.… The prayers of a righteous person are powerful and effective.…

Maggie shook her head. No. She wouldn't confess to anyone. Not after years of building the life she had, her marriage with Ben, the career she loved. She wouldn't throw it all away now by admitting the truth.

Not even to one whose prayers might be powerful and effective.

One like Laura Thompson.

Maggie pulled out of the parking lot and realized she had never been so tired in all her life. *I must have overdone it on the run.* She needed to pick up groceries and stop at the post office before getting the boys, but in that moment every breath required a conscious effort.

As she drove, the darkness closed in around her. If only there were a hole she could crawl into, a place where she could sleep for ten years or twenty, she would have gone there without hesitating. She forced herself to regain control, summoning the strength to keep the car on the road. Things began to look familiar, and she knew she'd be home in a few minutes. *Maybe I'll take a nap.*

Other drivers were passing her, and Maggie wondered why they were speeding. She let her eyes fall to her speedometer. *What? Twenty miles an hour?* How long had she been driving that slowly? She stared at the road ahead of her, concentrating, frowning. *I need to pick up something…buy something…*

Up ahead, a store sign caught her eye, and she made a sudden turn into the parking lot. That was it; she needed food. They were out of milk and eggs and cheddar cheese. But she was so tired. The idea of climbing out of her car and grocery shopping right now felt as impossible as attempting the Boston Marathon on two hours' sleep. *You can do it, Maggie. It's not that hard.*

She parked, climbed out of the car, and pulled herself across the parking lot. For what seemed like an hour she wandered through the produce section, staring at row after row of vegetables, fruits…round, even, orderly rows…

What food did she have back at home? Ben liked apples, green apples mostly. Or was it red apples? She ripped a plastic bag from the roll, opened it, and began placing apples inside. *Five, six, seven apples, that ought to do it. One a day.*

She dropped the bag into her cart and made her way deeper into the store. Vegetables. Canned vegetables. She had a casserole to make for the weekend. A church function. What was it? A potluck? A reception? Maggie stopped walking and pulled her cell phone from her purse. She scanned the numbers programmed into the directory and pushed connect when she saw "C.C. Church."

"Hello, Cleveland Community Church, can I help you?"

Maggie started at the voice, then froze in place. *Why am I standing in the middle of the grocery store calling church?* "Uh…never mind. Wrong number."

She put the cell phone back and stared at the shelves. What did she need here, anyway? Why couldn't she remember what she was doing and how come she was so tired? If it wouldn't seem a little crazy, she would just as soon lie down right where she was standing—smack in the middle of the canned vegetable aisle—and take a nap. An hour of sleep, that was all she needed. Maybe then she'd feel better. But of course people would notice if she took a nap in the middle of the grocery store, wouldn't they?

They would, Maggie was fairly sure. She'd have to wait and sleep at home. What was it she needed? Tomato sauce. That was it. She pulled four cans from the shelf and moved on to the next row of food products.

At that moment a woman entered the aisle from the other direction and beside her was—

Maggie gasped and her hand flew to her mouth. It was her! The blond girl. She was six, maybe seven, and her blue eyes took up most of her face. Cascades of curls spilled over her shoulders, and she had that questioning look in her eyes, the same one she always had, like she wanted Maggie to help her find her mama.

Other times Maggie knew she'd imagined the little girl, but not this time. This time it was really her. Maggie dropped all four cans of tomato sauce on the floor and pushed her cart straight for the child. When she got close enough, she left her food and knelt in front of the girl. Moving slowly so as not to frighten the child, Maggie took her small, warm hand—but before she could speak she heard someone talking above her.

"Excuse me, ma'am? Do I know you?"

Maggie blinked. An Hispanic woman in a tailored business suit was peering down at her, and though the woman's tone was polite, her face was lined with concern.

Where did she come from? Maggie blinked again. "Yes...I mean, I thought your little girl..." She glanced back at the child and inhaled sharply. The girl whose hand she held had short brown hair and brown-skinned features.

The little blond girl was gone.

Maggie dropped the child's hand and uttered a nervous laugh as she stood and faced the girl's mother. "I'm sorry. I thought she was someone…" Maggie's mind raced. "Someone I knew from church. Sunday school, actually."

The woman smiled coolly and reached for her daughter's hand. "I don't think so." She pointed to the other end of the aisle. "I think you forgot your tomato sauce."

Tomato sauce? Maggie saw the cans lying on the floor and forced another laugh. "Right. Thanks."

She pushed her cart back down the aisle, retrieved the cans, and dropped them in the cart. *Why did I need tomato sauce?* She stared at the bottom of her cart and squinted in confusion. There was a bag of onions where her apples had been. Did she have the wrong cart? Had someone taken her apples and replaced them with onions?

The girl and her mother had moved to a different aisle, and Maggie hoped they didn't think she was crazy. She wasn't, after all. Tired maybe, worn out. But not crazy. It wasn't her fault the little blond girl followed her everywhere she went.

Maggie wandered the aisles. Later on she would look back and know that the breakdown truly began in frozen foods, somewhere between the boxed pizzas and bagged tropical fruit. But now…now she didn't know what was happening, only that tears were coming quickly, filling Maggie's eyes and making her mind a jumble of thoughts. Why had she married Ben in the first place? How had she survived so many years living a lie? Why was she so tired and what was she doing with tears streaming down her face and a cart full of tomato sauce and an overstuffed bag of onions, paralyzed by something she couldn't see or understand?

A white-haired man with a cardigan sweater and a concerned look tapped her gently on the shoulder. "Are you all right, ma'am?" He waited for an answer.

Maggie dried her eyes. *I'll be lucky if he doesn't call a doctor and have me committed.* "I'm fine." She nodded tersely at the man. "Just…it's been a long day. I'm tired."

"Okay." The older gentleman hesitated a moment longer, then continued shopping.

Collect yourself, Maggie. Get it together. You're bigger than this; you've been bigger than it for years. Why should things be any different now? She thought of the little girl and how sure she'd been that this time—finally—it was really her and…

Help me, Lord… Please.

I'm here, daughter. Come into the light.

But there was no way out, no light to come toward.

Maggie began to tremble again. She was on the edge of the darkest, deepest canyon that had ever bordered her path, and the only thing stopping her from tumbling over was a threadbare rope of memories. Even that was fraying badly.

She forced herself to take deep breaths and suddenly she was at the checkstand, falling asleep on her feet. The ground seemed to shift as her eyes flew open and her head jerked back into an alert position. What was that in her cart? Onions? Tomato sauce? Where were the apples? The milk? She had forgotten every item she'd come for.

She stared over her shoulder into the store. The thought of turning around and heading back for milk was overwhelming. Too many aisles and food displays stacked high above her. Too many colors and people and sales signs fought for her attention. Suddenly the store seemed like a sinister maze, one from which she might never come out alive if she ventured back inside. She exhaled slowly. *Help me, God. I need You.* The words felt empty, much as they had often felt lately. Maggie waited for an answer. Silence. *Okay, Maggie, concentrate. You can do this on your own.*

Over the next thirty minutes she forced herself back through the store where she painstakingly collected the three necessities and several canned goods and packaged food that would help get her family through the week.

As she pushed her cart out of the store toward her Chevy

Tahoe, she congratulated herself on having survived. Whatever it was that wanted so badly to consume her, she would simply have to be tougher, think things through, and gather her determination. It was merely a matter of trying harder.

The darkness isn't going to get me. Not ever again. I don't need to wait for an answer to prayer; I need to believe in myself. I'm stronger than I think.

She unloaded her groceries, slipped the cart back into the nearby rack, and climbed into her vehicle. Only then, as she glanced into the rearview mirror and saw her face in the reflection, did she realize things were worse than she'd thought.

How long had she looked like this? Why hadn't anyone said something more to her?

If the mirror was right, she was weeping without her knowing it; tears streaming down her face. Minutes passed, and suddenly she was jolted awake by the honking of a horn behind her. Two cars vying for a parking space.

I've been sleeping…

The realization shook her. *The boys! What time is it?* She glanced at her watch and her heart sank. She'd lost almost an hour. She was still tired, but she forced herself to stay awake.

Casey and Cameron needed her.

Four

MAGGIE SLIPPED ON A PAIR OF DARK GLASSES, THEN RACED TO GET the boys. Since her eyes seemed bent on shedding tears, she kept her glasses on even after she and the boys got home, wearing them during snack time and while she made dinner. Everything inside her cried out for the warmth of her bed. Now, before the sun sank and the nighttime demons refused to let her sleep.

She searched the cupboards. *Macaroni and cheese, that'll work. It's been months since we've had that.*

Maggie opened a box of noodles and poured it into a cold pan of water. She began slowly stirring the mixture. Ten minutes passed…twenty…and suddenly one of the boys was at her side, tugging on her sleeve.

"Aren't you going to cook it, Maggie?" He dipped his finger into the water and Maggie pushed him back.

"Don't! It's hot…can't you see it's boil—" She blinked twice. The water was not boiling; the macaroni inside was no closer to being ready to eat than it had been half an hour earlier.

She dropped the spoon on the countertop and pulled Cameron into a hug. "I'm sorry, honey. I didn't mean to push you. I thought—"

"It's okay. You thought it was boiling. You were just trying to protect me." His eyes raised to meet hers. "Right, Maggie?"

There was fear in his face. Her strange behavior was probably worrying both boys even though they'd only been living with her and Ben for a month.

"Right, honey. Maggie has a lot on her mind, that's all."

"I like macaroni and cheese. We had it last night, too."

Last night? Maggie thought hard, but she had no memory

whatsoever of the night before. She watched Cameron return to the table and then she switched on the burner beneath the pan. At the same time she heard the door swing open.

"Hey, Maggie, I'm home."

It was Ben. Maybe he could cook dinner and she could get some sleep. That was all this was, this darkness and desperation. A simple lack of sleep. Ben tossed his briefcase and overcoat onto a living room chair and came up behind her.

"Hi." Maggie knew she didn't sound very enthusiastic, but she could no longer force herself. Everything about their marriage, about who she was when she was with him, all of it was a lie. What was the point of making small talk?

Ben kissed her neck tenderly and glanced over her shoulder. "Good thing we all like macaroni and cheese."

She could hear the teasing in his tone, but she bristled anyway. "You don't like it, *you* cook for once."

He stepped back, his expression changing. "We had it last night, Maggie. I'm fine with that, but don't get defensive with me. I'm only trying to make you laugh."

His eyes searched hers. "How was your day?"

Maggie thought about the desperate feeling of doom that had followed her from the keyboard at work, to her jogging, to the frozen food section of the grocery store. She thought about how—without knowing it—she had wept while paying for her groceries and how she had stirred a pan of cold water and hard macaroni noodles for thirty minutes before realizing she'd forgotten to turn on the burner.

She looked at Ben and forced a smile. "My day was fine. You?"

He walked toward the boys, keeping his eyes trained on her. "Things are coming along with the Jenson murder trial. The evidence is in, and I think we'll get a conviction." Leaning over, he studied the boys' homework sheets and smiled broadly. "You boys are going to be scientists one day, mark my words."

He looked back at Maggie. "Brightest boys in Cleveland, Mag, wouldn't you say?"

Why am I here? Why are we going through the motions when it's all a big lie? "Yep," she mumbled.

Dinner was uneventful, and Maggie maneuvered her fork through the pile of cheese-covered macaroni trying to figure out how she'd made the same meal two nights in a row without remembering it.

When they were finished eating, the boys went upstairs to their room to get ready for baths. Maggie dropped her fork on top of the now cold noodles and stared at her husband. "I'm not hungry." Her voice was flat as she stood and moved toward the kitchen, aware that Ben's eyes followed her.

"Sit down, Maggie."

His voice was not angry, but neither did it leave room for negotiation. Maggie set her plate in the sink and returned to face her husband. There was nothing she could think to say, so she waited.

"What's wrong with you, Mag?"

She sighed and studied her fingernails for a moment. "Nothing."

Ben shook his head. "There's something wrong. Either something with you or something with me or something with both of us. But I'm tired of walking around here acting like everything's okay."

Why didn't I tell him the truth from the beginning? Then he never would have married me, and we wouldn't be in this mess. "Okay." She leveled her gaze at him. Her voice sounded tired as she continued. "You want to know what's wrong with me, I'll tell you."

Ben waited expectantly. There was love in his eyes, so much so it pained Maggie to know she was hurting him. But sooner or later he would have to know that she wasn't the sweet, Christian girl he thought he'd married. Maybe if she told him now, at least part of the truth…

Not too much, Maggie. Don't tell him too much.

She drew a deep breath. "I'm tired of pretending."

Ben couldn't have looked more dazed if she had just announced she might like to dye her hair pink. "Pretending?"

"Yes." Maggie crossed her arms. "All day long I pretend. I pretend to be this wonderful Christian woman worthy of handing out advice to half the people in Cleveland, then I pretend that managing foster children is a satisfying substitute for having babies of my own. And when *you* get home…" Her voice trailed off and she saw his eyes fill with fresh pain.

"What, Mag? When I get home, what?"

The walls of the dining room began to close in on her. *Why, God? What's happening to me? How come I can't leave it alone and let it go?* She gripped the edges of her chair.

Come on, tell him. He's waiting. Tell him the truth about how you feel. At least give him that. This isn't someone you love, remember? He's hurt you; he's the enemy.

"Ben, it's just—" Her voice was barely a whisper and this time she could feel the tears gathering in her eyes. "What I'm trying to say is, well…I pretend with you, too."

He hesitated, and a flash of fear skittered across his eyes. "Come on, Maggie. You're overreacting, having a bad day or something. I mean, there's nothing here that can't—"

"No! You're wrong." She was trembling now, crying openly and raising her voice. "I'm telling you how I *feel*. Don't you understand?"

Ben was silent, and Maggie saw his eyes were wet, too. **Tell him, Maggie. You've lied to protect him long enough. It's your turn to hurt him for a change.**

She closed her eyes for a moment and when she opened them she felt stronger than before. He had done this to her, after all. Forced her to live a lie, to pretend she was the perfect Christian girl, and then later, the ideal wife. What choice had she ever had but to lie to him?

Maggie exhaled and steadied her voice. "The truth is…you

don't know me, Ben." She leveled her gaze at him and held it there. "You never have."

His face grew pale, then flushed—all in a matter of seconds. He stood and turned away. Maggie gazed out the window where the sun had not quite settled beyond the nearly bare tree line. *I hate this; all of it.* Her arms ached, and she recognized the feeling as familiar. Aching, empty arms. The same way they'd been that May morning so many years ago…

Stop! The order echoed in her heart and stopped all other thoughts. She shifted her gaze to Ben and then, without saying another word, without stopping and doing up the dinner dishes or looking in on Casey and Cameron, she stood and dragged her feet up the stairs. It took the rest of her energy to tear back the comforter that lay twisted on her unmade bed and bury herself beneath.

There, still wearing her clothes and shoes, with visions of the little blond girl filling her mind and the sun not quite set in the evening sky, Maggie Stovall willed herself to sleep.

Five

THE COLUMN WAS FAIRLY SCATHING, AT LEAST THAT'S WHAT KATHY Garrett's coworkers at the Social Services department were saying. Kathy found that hard to believe. Now, after going nonstop through lunch, she finally had a moment to read it for herself.

"Okay, where is it?" she muttered as she pulled the paper out of its plastic sleeve and spread it on the table. Kathy was a fan of "Maggie's Mind" and figured that if the columnist had taken on the department there was probably some merit to her argument. She opened the paper and saw the headline at the top right side of the front page: "Maggie's Mind: The Real Abuse of Abused Children." Kathy studied the columnist's picture that accompanied the article and was struck by a familiar thought. Something about the reporter's eyes was more than a little familiar.

She dismissed the idea and delved into the article, immediately swept up by the picture Maggie painted. Children shuffled from one home to another, experiencing enough trauma to destroy their psyches and change them forever into societal misfits. Maggie's view was simple: Social Services was a system desperately understaffed and far too quick to place kids back in a dangerous environment because of some noble idea that children are better off with their birth parents.

Kathy closed her eyes and pictured the children she'd seen pass through the system in just that manner. Maggie was right. Many times the department's good intentions to keep children with their biological families only made matters worse. And there was nothing anyone at Social Services could do to prevent it from happening again, not until laws governing parental rights were changed.

Kathy could see why the column upset the staff at the department, but she silently applauded Maggie for having the courage to take on a federal agency and illuminate an issue that was every bit as troubling as the columnist had described it.

Of course there was the other problem with the system—one Kathy was sure Maggie would inevitably tackle in future columns: the lack of quality foster homes. Sometimes, it seemed, the need for foster homes throughout the state was so great only a cursory safety check was done on the applicants. Motives certainly could not be checked, and since Social Services provided foster parents with a stipend to provide for the child's food and clothing, there would always be those who provided substandard care as a way to make money.

She thought of her appointment later that night—pictured the lonely little girl—and her eyes burned with the beginning of tears. Amanda Joy Brownell. The child had been in the system so long she had only a very slim chance of ever being adopted. Foster care was also difficult. The better foster homes tended to take young children; not seven-year-old girls with a history of removals.

It isn't her fault, Lord. Kathy hung her head as two tears splashed onto the newsprint and worked their way into the layers of paper beneath. Kathy remembered the day she was called to the hospital to talk with the girl's biological mother, a wide-eyed twenty-three-year-old who had been convinced that being a single mom would ruin her life. At least before the delivery. But that day at the hospital the young mother had broken down and wept, so distraught over giving up her baby that Kathy had asked her to reconsider. Instead the girl had been adamant, repeating over and over that giving up the baby was something she had to do.

Kathy stared out her window across the tree-lined parking lot. The sky was slate gray, and most of the leaves had fallen from the maples. Thanksgiving was coming, and Christmas. Another year gone by, and still Amanda Joy had no place to call home. The situation—like so many others Kathy worked with—was enough to break her heart.

Where's her birth mother today, Lord? Kathy released a slow breath and wondered like she had a dozen times before about the girl's young mother. Did she regret her choice to give the baby up for adoption? Kathy still remembered her hesitation as she'd signed the paperwork that day at the hospital, and again as she took the newborn girl from the trembling arms of her mother and whisked her into the waiting arms of Stan and Tammy Brownell. Most babies were placed through private adoption agencies housed in decorated suites on the fifteenth floor of a corporate high-rise in downtown Cleveland. Kathy remembered thinking it unusual that the young mother chose to come to Cincinnati's Social Services Department to give the baby up.

At first Kathy had been happy for the Brownells—a couple without the means to adopt privately but with a great desire to have a child. Her opinion changed after she met with them. The couple seemed so serious and somber... Kathy had a very real feeling that although their home study was complete, the placement wasn't right for the baby girl. Either way—as with most of her cases—there was nothing Kathy could do but pray about the situation.

She hadn't expected to see the little girl again.

Kathy cringed like she always did when she thought of the accident, the frozen tree limb that had fallen on the Brownells' car, killing them both instantly. Since the Brownells had no extended family, Amanda Joy was made a ward of the court and again Kathy was called in to help. She had met the child at her kindergarten class that day and escorted her to the office, where together with the school counselor they revealed the awful news.

Amanda's reaction had confirmed Kathy's fears from years earlier. The child had stared at her nailbitten fingers and scuffled her feet nervously. "Will I still be living at their house?"

Kathy had been confused. "Whose house, honey?"

"Mr. and Mrs. Brownell's." The girl's eyes were dry.

The words had hung in the air a few moments. "You mean your house, your mom and dad's house?"

Amanda shook her head. "I'm not allowed to call them Mom and Dad. They said it wasn't formal."

Looking back Kathy wasn't sure which realization hurt more, the fact that Amanda Joy was once again without parents or the fact that she'd been little more than a favorite guest in her home for all of her five years. Since then Amanda had spoken kindly of the Brownells, so Kathy knew they had not been harmful in any way. They just hadn't given her the love and acceptance a child deserves.

Kathy noticed a squirrel scurrying down the trunk of a tree just outside the office window. *Even he has a home, Lord...*

Her eyes welled up again. *The Brownells were better than anything she's been dealt since then. We'd take her in a minute if we could, God. You know that.* She and Bill had brainstormed several times ideas for buying a bigger house. They knew no judge in the county would award them another child until they had more room. They'd already petitioned for an exception, and been denied. *Dear God, there has to be someone for her...somewhere out there. Please...* Another tear fell. *She's a good girl, Lord, but every month, every year that goes by...it'll take a miracle to find her a family now.*

Amanda had been shy before the death of her adoptive parents. Now she had slight learning disabilities and trouble attaching to people. When she was scared or anxious she stuttered, so in addition to weekly counseling and special education courses, the child was mandated to receive speech therapy.

Kathy closed her eyes and loosed two more tears. It wasn't fair. The child's file was full of "problem areas," tarnished judgments that in all likelihood would scare off potential adoptive parents and send them hurrying to private agencies for younger children without the baggage Amanda carried.

She wiped her tears and gazed out the dining room window once more. *I'm not a miracle worker, God. But You are. Please...please help me find someone who'll give her a home.*

Then because she knew too well the department's statistics, she added one more thing. *And hurry, Lord.* She thought of the children who started out sweet and anxious for love only to become jaded and antisocial after too many transfers to different foster homes, too many years waiting for a family that never came. Despite her file, Amanda Joy was not yet one of those. But she could be if something didn't change soon.

Kathy sighed softly and folded up the newspaper. Yes, God would have to speed things up if He was going to work a miracle this time. The child needed a home and parents who loved her, and she needed it now.

Before it was too late.

Six

BEN STOVALL STARED OUT THE WINDOW OF HIS FOURTH-STORY office and wondered exactly when his life had started falling apart.

Days like this it was difficult to concentrate on establishing motives or gathering depositions. A death penalty case couldn't have mattered less to him now that it seemed clear his marriage was crumbling. And no matter how long or hard he thought about it, he couldn't come up with a single reason why.

Everything about his life with Maggie had seemed literally plucked from a storybook. They were married young, both strong believers bent on putting God first in their relationship. And though there hadn't been any children, Ben believed there would be one day. Whenever God deemed it right. And if not, then he believed it was because the Lord had a different plan. Adoption, maybe. Or more years of foster children.

Ben loved the idea of affecting the lives of a different set of children every year or so. Besides, things were going well at work and he figured the coming spring might be a great time to initiate a private adoption. Live right and experience the rewards. That had always been his motto.

For that reason, Ben knew there'd be children one day. After all, he and Maggie had done everything right in their relationship. They had been pure when they came together on their wedding night and had remained faithful to each other since. They tithed at church, prayed daily, and read their Bibles— usually cover to cover in any given year.

Ben thought about that for a moment. Well, maybe not daily. But for the most part he and Maggie lived a godly life.

Even at work they did whatever they could to please the Lord, and He had always rewarded their efforts. After all, blessings didn't come any bigger than Maggie having her own column. Not in the newspaper business, anyway.

Between her job and his, they pulled in a steady six-figure salary, and because they were in their early thirties they had plenty of time for children.

Outside his window a sparrow appeared from nowhere and began attacking a much larger crow. *Probably protecting his nest.* Ben watched them for a few minutes, thinking.

What was it Maggie had said? *"You don't know me…you never have."* He could see her face, the way it was cloaked in discouragement, as though she were holding back a very deep, dark secret. What did she mean he didn't know her? Of *course* he knew her.

Didn't he?

Now, alone in his office, he wasn't so sure.

He remembered the first time he saw Maggie, when their churches had joined a handful of others in Cleveland for a statewide prayer rally. The event had lasted all weekend and had included numerous activities. It was during the tug-of-war competition, when his church's college group was about to beat the group on the other end of the rope, that Ben spotted her.

She was without a doubt the most gorgeous woman he'd ever seen. He would never forget the way she'd made him feel that day, all tingly inside as if something magical had happened. Both hands securely on his team's end of the rope, Ben had leaned to the side for a better view of her. In the process, the rope slipped and he fell to the ground. He could still close his eyes and see Maggie grinning at him as she and her team doubled their efforts and won the event before Ben could get up.

His attraction for her increased daily after that, despite the fact that he was dating someone else at the time. Ben sighed. Those first years for he and Maggie were rough. They wrote and talked on the phone, and in his heart he knew there was no one else he could spend the rest of his life with. But the girl he was dating came from a family that his parents had known all their lives. There was no easy way to break things off—especially after the accident.

If I could do one thing over again...

Ben let the thought hang there. When he had been unable to end things with his girlfriend, he and Maggie agreed to go on with their separate lives. Of course after only eighteen months apart, they had found each other again and began dating exclusively. But somehow Maggie had seemed different than before, older than her years, less willing to share...

He frowned. Was it possible she could have held that time against him? Harbored anger because he had chosen another girl for that period in his life?

Ben shook his head. *Ridiculous.* Whatever was happening to Maggie now it was a phase, nothing more. All that had ever mattered was how he felt about her when they found each other again. How he'd felt about her ever since. If he could do anything over again he would have broken things off with the other girl immediately. Maggie had to know that. But he'd been so young, so confused. After the accident it seemed that staying with his old girlfriend was the right thing to do.

Ben turned his attention toward the work on his desk. *Impossible.* Whatever was troubling Maggie couldn't be rooted in something that had happened so long ago.

Still, as he set about dealing with the tasks at hand, trying to put Maggie's hurtful words out of his heart and head, Ben was troubled by one very serious suspicion: *What if...*

What if, despite living a pure life and being devoted to God, Maggie had turned into someone else, someone who had hidden her real feelings from him for months or years. Ben hated himself for even entertaining the thought, but it was possible that Maggie was right. Maybe she *was* pretending around him. And maybe somehow, no matter how much he had always loved her, Maggie had changed, become someone Ben didn't even know.

He glanced at his watch and saw that it was four o'clock. One more hour and he would wrap things up. He picked up the telephone receiver and dialed a number he'd long since memorized. "Hi, this is Ben Stovall."

A woman answered on the third ring. "Hello, Ben." He could hear the smile in her voice. "What can I help you with today?"

He grinned, sure this was the answer he was looking for. "I need a dozen long-stemmed red roses for this evening."

"Very good, and a white ribbon like usual?"

"Yes, like usual."

Ben felt better when he hung up the receiver. Maggie was wrong; of course he knew her. She was his soul mate, his best friend. And whatever was troubling her yesterday, why it was nothing that couldn't be made better with a bouquet of flowers. She loved red roses, especially when there wasn't any special occasion.

"It's a celebration of our love," Ben liked to tell her. And it was. She was the perfect woman, handpicked for him by God above. He loved her more than life itself.

He thought of the roses again and grinned. He could hardly wait to see the expression on her face when he brought them home.

Maggie had the strangest feeling...

It was as if she were single again.

As if by being even somewhat honest she had severed ties to Ben, to the man she married, the man to whom she been lying for nearly eight years.

For that reason—or maybe because the little blond girl hadn't yet made her daily appearance—Maggie was looking forward to her run in the park. For months it had been her favorite way to spend the hour between finishing up at work and picking up the boys at their bus stop. The first lap was effortless, and as she ran Maggie thought about her columns, how they might help children caught in the foster system. They were a good influence on society, good for her career. Even if her personal life was falling apart, even if there were times when the darkness seemed overwhelming, she was still doing something useful. Helping in some small way.

Maggie picked up her pace and as she rounded the corner of the trail, she saw a blur of motion near the playground, a hundred yards away. From this distance it was hard to make her out, but then…

Maggie pushed herself faster, her eyes trained on the child. Her view was better now. The child was swinging, while a teenager—a baby-sitter or older sister—sat with a teenage boy at a nearby picnic table. *Closer, Maggie. Get closer.* With only fifty yards between them she spotted the hair.

Long blond curls. It was her! This time it wasn't a mirage or a figment of her imagination or any other such thing. It was a living, breathing child, and Maggie was almost certain it was the same girl she'd been seeing. *Who is she, God? Why is she here?*

Maggie was sprinting now. She wouldn't approach the girl, not yet. Not until she was absolutely sure it was her. Even then she didn't want to scare the girl. Maggie kept running until she was parallel with the child. Glancing over her left shoulder she saw the girl's face. Yes! It was her; there was no doubt in Maggie's mind.

Not sure what to do next, Maggie kept moving. Whatever terrible force desired her, it wouldn't catch her here—not with the little girl so close. *If only I could talk to the child, ask her who her mother is, learn more about her. Then maybe I'd understand why my thoughts are so filled with her image…* Especially now, nearly eight years after—

Run, Maggie! Faster…faster!

Three laps around the park equaled a mile, and usually Maggie did no more than six laps. But as long as the little girl stayed on the swing, moving back and forth, smiling and unaware of her presence, Maggie kept running. Twelve laps, fourteen...sixteen...

Finally, on the eighteenth lap, Maggie realized her heart was pounding erratically, and her vision was blurred. She clutched her side, dropped her pace to an unsteady walk, and headed for the little girl.

Without saying a word, Maggie dropped into the swing beside the child and smiled at her. "Hi. My name's Maggie."

Before the girl could respond, Maggie felt a hand take hold of her upper arm and she spun around, jerking free from the grip. Fear sliced through her gut like a hacksaw. *God, please, no...*

The man standing beside her wore a police uniform and a badge that glistened in the midafternoon sun. "Ma'am, I'd like to have a word with you, please." He motioned toward a grassy area several feet away.

"Nicky! Nicky!"

At the sound of the child's cries, Maggie turned back to her at once. The girl had jumped from the swing and was running toward an older boy and girl seated at a nearby table. Then the child glanced back at Maggie...and Maggie's whole body went cold.

This wasn't a blond little girl. Instead, the child running away from the swings had red hair and a freckled face. *But...where did she go? Why is this happening again? What's wrong with my eyes? Am I that far gone, Lord?* Maggie stared at the child and then directed her attention back to the officer. She was sweaty and rumpled and desperately in need of a water fountain. She had never run six miles in her life, and now she was about to be interrogated by a policeman.

"I think I'm going to faint." Maggie slipped her head between her knees and urged herself to breathe slowly. After several seconds, she raised her head and looked over her shoulder. The officer was waiting.

"I'm serious, ma'am. Get up. I need to talk to you."

"Sorry, I just…I don't feel very well." Maggie rose up off the swing and followed him, terrified that she would collapse and be taken away in an ambulance or worse, be arrested in the park adjacent to the office where she worked. If her peers got hold of the story…

Help me, God…please!

When they were a distance away from the playground the policeman turned and faced her. "I'm Officer Andrew Starmer. Got a call from one of the neighbors in the condominiums across the street that a female jogger was stalking a child on the playground."

Maggie saw black spots dance before her eyes. *Breathe. Breathe, Maggie. Don't faint now.* "A female jogger?"

The officer glanced at her sweatsuit and nodded. "Did you know that child, ma'am?"

"Child?"

Officer Starmer sighed. "Yes, the one you were talking to."

"Oh, her. I, uh…I thought she was my niece. My niece lives near here and plays at the park all the time."

The officer raised an eyebrow. "Tell you what, why don't you follow me to the car, and I'll make a report. Just to be sure."

Panic coursed through Maggie's veins. "An arrest report?" She did her best to sound indignant. *What have I done, Lord? Help me.*

"No. Just informational. Take down your name, that kind of thing."

Maggie wiped her hands on her pants legs and released a laugh that said there must have been a mistake. "Officer, I work across the street. I jog at this park every day at this time. I thought the girl was my niece. Isn't that enough information?"

Officer Starmer eyed her for a long moment. *Let him believe me, please...* "You work at the newspaper?"

"Yes. My car's parked there right now."

His eyes narrowed. "Okay. Just be aware that people are sensitive about strangers getting too close to kids. You read your paper, right?"

"Sure." *Oh, thank You, God. He doesn't recognize me, doesn't know I'm a columnist.* "Right. Definitely. I'll keep that in mind."

The officer glanced once more at the redheaded girl then back to Maggie. "If you've finished your jog, why don't you make your way back to the office."

"I'm on my way." Maggie smiled at him and nodded as she and the officer headed in different directions. She was ten steps away before she remembered to exhale.

That was too close. What if he'd taken my name? What if he'd arrested me or taken me in for questioning? What was I doing there anyway? And why does the child keep disappearing? Who is she?

Come into the light, child.

What light? Maggie argued with the still, silent whisper. *There hasn't been light for years.*

She had the strangest feeling she was forgetting something but she could hardly stop and think about it. Not with the officer watching her from his squad car across the park. She opened her car door just as her cell phone began to ring inside her purse on the front seat. Instantly her eyes flew to the watch on her wrist.

The boys! That was it! She had forgotten the boys.

Maggie tore open her purse and grabbed the phone, speaking in a voice that sounded half-crazed even to her. "Hello?" Her heart raced and she was assaulted by a wave of nausea.

"Mrs. Stovall?"

"Yes, I'm late to get the boys. Are they okay?" Her words spilled out in a panicky blur.

"Uh...yes. They're back at school. They waited at the bus stop for thirty minutes, and apparently one of your neighbors verified you weren't home. She contacted the school, and we sent the bus back out."

This was crazy. She was losing her mind. Everything she was doing proved that. She needed to be honest, ask for help. Maggie's mind raced.

"I...my car..." She cast a frustrated glance upward, grasping at anything that might sound logical. "It...my car broke down and I...I was just going to call and see...make sure they were okay."

The school secretary hesitated. "I had to contact Social Services, Mrs. Stovall. These children are wards of the state and anytime something like this happens..."

What was she insinuating? That Maggie was an abusive foster mother? That she and Ben were no better than the foster parents she referred to in her column? Maggie thought of how she'd failed even to tuck the boys in the night before, and a murky cloud of fear suffocated her. *Get a grip, Maggie. Come on.* Her racing pulse was causing her body to tremble, making it difficult for her to speak.

How could I have forgotten the boys?

"What did...what did Social Services say?"

"They said these kinds of things happen and they made a note of it." The woman paused again, and Maggie could hear disapproval in her tone, almost see the indignation on her face. And if the officer had taken her name... She couldn't bring herself to think about it.

"I'll be there in ten minutes. Please tell them I'm coming." Maggie hung up the phone and steadied herself. *How could I forget them? I love those boys. They may not be worth much in the eyes of society, but right now I'm all they have. And I let them down.*

You're a wretch! Worthless. The voice in her head had changed from doubt and discouragement to a devilish hiss. **No one would notice if you drove off a cliff, Maggie Stovall.**

Forget about it, Maggie. Think about something else.

Images shot through her mind—the blond girl, the onions in her shopping cart, the policeman—as Maggie pulled into the school parking lot, she was horrifyingly aware that the sense of approaching doom was worse. It clawed at her with every step, making it nearly impossible for her to breathe as she found her way inside the school, comforted the crying twin boys, and led them back to the car.

When they were buckled in, Maggie rested her head on the steering wheel and began to cry, too. At first the sobs were muffled, but within a few minutes she was wailing, terrified by the despair that seemed to be sucking the life from her.

Where am I? Why am I weeping in the school parking lot and why can't I think clearly?

"Mrs. Stovall, what's wrong?" It was Casey and he'd stopped his own crying.

Oh no…I've scared him.

She straightened in her seat and quickly wiped her eyes. The child's question cleared the fog and brought everything into focus again. She was crying because she'd been so busy looking for a little girl that didn't exist she'd forgotten her foster boys at the bus stop. She was crying because thirty minutes ago she'd been on the verge of being arrested and losing everything she had ever worked for over the past seven years.

And she couldn't think clearly because she was going crazy. What other explanation could there be?

"I'm fine, honey." Her voice was still trembling, but she glanced in the rearview mirror and saw a relieved look cross the twins' faces. *They believe me. Good. Now we can go home and have a normal night.*

Maggie pulled out of the parking lot and headed east toward their neighborhood, fighting off another bout of tears. Normal? It had been months since she had felt anything close to normal. Most likely, she'd spend the evening barely tolerating her husband's probing glances and tidying a house that never seemed to be clean. Then she would stumble into bed and lie awake under the watchful eyes of whatever demons had taken up residence in her home.

The thought of it made her want to turn around and drive

west, maybe until she reached California or the ocean. Maybe drive the car into the ocean until it swallowed her up—along with whatever was trying to destroy her. However far it took to get away from it all. The tears came again, and though Maggie willed herself to drive home, forced herself to battle the desperation, she couldn't still the one thought screaming through her mind...

Maybe it really was time to check herself into a mental hospital.

Seven

MAGGIE REMAINED AN EMOTIONAL HURRICANE THROUGH A LONG night of ignoring Ben and his roses and on into the next morning as she tapped out a column decrying the standards in many foster homes. She could barely concentrate for the voices waging war in her head.

She focused on the computer screen and the task at hand. *Come on, Maggie. You can do this.* She began typing.

Something is terribly wrong with our system when we place the abused children of our state in homes where, at least on occasion, they'll be abused again. What type of safety net is that for a child who's falling through the cracks? The time has come to toughen the standard by which we judge people worthy of taking in foster children.

Her fingers refused to move, and she pictured the boys, alone and scared at the bus stop.

Hypocrite. Hypocrite, hypocrite, hypocrite. You're the worst foster mother of all. Leaving those boys out at the bus stop while you…

"Lots of good feedback on the Social Services column, Mag." Ron Kendall leaned against her desk so he could face her. "This the final one in the series?"

Maggie gulped. She was having trouble understanding him. Something about Social Services and a series. "Yeah…it's a series, Ron."

His face reflected his confusion.

What? Why's he looking like that? What did I say? Everything about who she was seemed to be disconnecting. As if nothing she was thinking or hearing or doing made any sense at all.

Ron frowned. "Hey, Mag, you feeling all right?"

The way his eyes narrowed told Maggie he was genuinely concerned, and she felt a rush of panic. If Ron was worried, then maybe she really was losing her mind; maybe it wasn't only a couple of bad days or the fallout from having forgotten her foster boys and nearly having been arrested the day before. "I...I feel fine, if that's what you mean." Maggie stared back at the computer screen, hoping Ron would get the hint and leave her alone. She had just thirty minutes before deadline.

"Okay." Ron angled his head and waited until he had her attention again. "You just haven't seemed like yourself lately." He chewed on his lip and gazed at the ceiling, and she had the strong sense he was searching for the right words to say. "I'm here for you, Maggie. That's all. If something's wrong let me know, okay?"

She forced a smile. "Thanks, Ron. I'm fine. Really."

He walked away, and she stared at her column. *Everyone knows. It might as well be written on my forehead: "Maggie Stovall is going crazy."*

Over the next fifteen minutes she finished her column and for the first time since working for a newspaper, she didn't bother to read it through again. Instead she filed it, pulled her things together, and headed home.

It was time to get to the bus stop. She would not forget again.

Five after three.

That's when the bus arrived. Five minutes after three. 3:05 P.M. 3:05 in the afternoon.

The number sounded in her mind like the words to an unforgettable song: *3:05, 3:05, 3:05. The boys' bus comes at 3:05.*

Maggie had rushed through every activity since early that morning, everything from getting dressed to writing her column. She would not be late this time.

It was 1:45 when Maggie shut the door of her home behind her and set out on the five-minute walk to the bus stop.

The walk involved crossing a very busy street, one that gave mothers nightmares about children getting knocked under the wheels of a speeding car or being struck by a menacing tractor-trailer. The twins—like other foster children Maggie and Ben had cared for—were absolutely forbidden to cross it alone.

Maggie moved quickly, doing her best to ignore the haunting feeling that something was chasing her, closing in on her. When she arrived at the stop she checked her watch again: 1:50. Her shoulders eased downward, and she allowed herself to exhale. She didn't mind the wait; her feet could take it. They would have to. She could never be like those foster parents she'd written about earlier, the type who gave a child more trouble, more pain and heartbreak. More insecurity. No, Maggie would never do that again. Even if she had to stand in place for an hour or more, she would be there when the boys got off the bus.

The temperature was dropping, and a cloud layer had taken its position in the sky above her. Maggie couldn't help herself. She kept looking over her shoulder, sure someone was there, waiting with a hunting knife poised above her head.

Help me, God. Clear my mind so I can think again. Please.

She rocked back and forth…back and forth, licking her lips nervously as the minutes trickled by…3:05, 3:05, 3:05. It became a rhythm that surrounded her, kept her company.

At one point she thought she saw the bus and she straightened. Yes, it was the bus all right. But…

Maggie inhaled sharply. Every face beyond the bus driver's was that of the little girl! Ten or twenty girls with curly blond hair filled the bus, and Maggie didn't know whether to run away or flag the vehicle down before it could get away. She moved further into the road, her eyes locked onto the busload of little blond—

The sound of a blaring car horn jarred her from her thoughts, and she reeled backwards, tripping over the curb and falling onto the sidewalk behind her. Her head smacked the concrete, and for a moment she lay there unmoving. She heard a car slow down and someone shout, "Hey, lady, you all right?"

Instantly she sat up and was assaulted by the urge to vomit. She waved weakly at the man in the car and smiled. "I'm fine."

He looked doubtful but drove off anyway. When he was out of sight, Maggie ran her hand over the bump that was forming on the back of her head; something warm and wet met her probing fingers. *Dear God, help me! I'm bleeding...*

How far out in the road had she been when the car honked at her? She had thought it was a bus full of little girls, blond girls...all with the same face...

Where had the speeding car come from, anyway? There ought to be a law against driving so fast on a residential street! It was downright dangerous. Maggie fixed her hair over the wound so that the blood wouldn't drip onto her white jacket. Did she need stitches, or would her hair be enough to stop the bleeding?

While she was trying to decide if her headache was from the fall or the anxiety that consumed her, the bus pulled up. Immediately Maggie saw the shocked look on the face of the bus driver and she realized she was still sprawled on the side-walk. The driver opened the door and shouted above the sound of the engine. "Mrs. Stovall? You okay?"

She was on her feet, brushing off her jeans and fixing her hair again so that the driver couldn't see any signs of blood. "Fine. I tripped."

His expression grew slightly less concerned. "I was afraid you'd been hit by a car."

The children were making their way out of the bus, and Maggie choked out a laugh. "No...nothing like that. Weak ankles. Happens all the time."

How long have I been rambling? Five minutes? Ten? Where are the little girls who were on the bus a few minutes ago? Or was that a different bus?

The bus driver was still staring at her.

"I'm okay, really. Just clumsy, I guess. Don't know why I wasn't more care—"

Cameron and Casey appeared at the top of the stairs. *Thank, God...* The boys were all right and she was there, on time. They made their way to her. "Mrs. Stovall!" Their voices rang as one as they ran the remaining few feet and threw their arms around her.

"We were scared you might not be here." Cameron flung his backpack over his shoulder and grinned at her.

"I told him you'd come." Casey cast her a confident smile. "You never missed us before."

Maggie put her arms around the boys and hugged them close. *If only they were my own children...*

You don't deserve children of your own. Not after what you—

"Boys, let's go home and have some hot chocolate. Sound good?" She forced herself to be clear minded. If the darkness wanted to hound her it would have to take a backseat. This was her time with the boys, and there was no room for delusional voices. She'd waited all day to hold the twins in her arms and reassure them that she would never, never again forget them.

The bus pulled away, and Maggie looked at the boys with a frown. *What are they doing? Why aren't they sitting down?* Maybe they wanted to talk first, before she made them their snack. She plopped herself down and sat cross-legged on the hard surface. "Come on, sit down at the table. I want to hear about your day."

The boys stared at her, an odd fear and uncertainty clouding their eyes.

"What?" Maggie felt a stabbing sense of terror. Had they

seen her bloody head? Her fingers poked at her hair once more, and she made a mental note to turn up the heater. The house had never felt so drafty. "Come on, boys, sit down. I'll get your snack as soon as you tell me about your day."

Other children who had been let off at the stop had already walked home, and Casey and Cameron looked at each other. "Mrs. Stovall, why are we gonna sit here in the middle of the sidewalk?"

Maggie's eyes widened, and she shot furtive glances about her surroundings. *What am I doing?* Cameron was right. A moment ago she had been certain she was back home at the dining room table. She hadn't heard the passing traffic or realized that she was sitting cross-legged on the cold cement.

I'm crazy, God. What's wrong with me?

She said nothing, only rose slowly and took the boys' hands in hers. She was suddenly so tired she didn't know if she could make it across the street.

Just go, Maggie. The boys are hungry. Squaring her shoulders and tightening her grip on the boys' hands, she stepped off the curb.

It was Casey's screams that caught her attention first, and then the horrifying realization that they were in the middle of the road, with cars coming at them from every angle. Seeing no way out, Maggie clutched the boys to herself and shielded them with her arms.

The sound of the crash was so deafening Maggie was certain they were all going to die. *Please, God, take me but not the boys...*

And in that moment—believing her death was imminent and knowing she wouldn't have to battle the demons another day—Maggie finally felt at peace.

The blow never came.

Maggie didn't know how much time passed before she realized it, how long it had been since the screams of brakes and grinding metal and breaking glass all came to a stop. She just knew, for whatever reason, it was strangely silent around her.

Was this death? This silence and stillness?

She opened her eyes. She and the boys were fine, but two cars had collided head on—Maggie guessed in an effort to avoid hitting them. From where she stood, frozen in place, she could see that both vehicles' airbags had inflated.

Let them be okay, God. I didn't mean to…

There was a wailing coming from the wreckage, and Maggie wondered which car contained people who were crying. Then she looked down and saw that it was Cameron and Casey. The boys were shaking badly, crying and clinging to her in desperate fear.

My God, what have I done? I could have killed us all! What's wrong with me?

She knelt between the boys and stroked their backs, keeping her eyes trained on the damaged vehicles and the host of people running toward them to help. "I'm sorry…" She whispered the words over and over until in the distance she heard sirens, then not long afterward, a man's voice behind her.

"Ma'am, I'm Officer Boe. You and the boys all right?"

Maggie looked over her shoulder and saw a policeman. "It was…it was an accident."

The man's face was filled with kindness. "We know that, ma'am. There were several witnesses who saw it happen. Looked like you and the boys were talking and accidentally walked into traffic."

Maggie's entire body was vibrating and she thought for a moment she might be sick. *No, not here.* She swallowed hard. "I'm so sorry."

The officer came closer and put his hand on the top of her head, moving it so he could get a better look. "You're bleeding."

At this news another flash of fear tore across the twins' still-stricken faces, and Maggie tightened her grip on them. "It's okay, boys." She turned to the officer once more. "I banged my head earlier. Twisted my ankle and took a fall."

A knowing look filled the officer's eyes. "Ma'am, I think you might have a concussion. Could be why you walked into traffic."

Maggie ignored him and stared at the broken vehicles. "Are the people...is everyone okay?"

The officer nodded. "Only one person in each car. Both had airbags, so it looks like they'll be fine." He ran his finger over her skull and around the tender area, making her wince slightly. "Right now we need to take care of you."

Officer Derek Boe stayed with the woman until paramedics lifted her onto a stretcher. He'd worked accident scenes for more than ten years and he knew a concussion when he saw one. Whatever else might be wrong with the woman's ankle, one thing was sure: Her brains had been scrambled in the fall.

She had the dress and demeanor of a gentle suburban housewife, but when he ordered paramedics to load her on the stretcher, she was almost combative.

"No! Let me go! I'm okay, really, I don't want to go to the hospital. The boys need a snack...hot chocolate..."

The officer took the boys' hands in his and directed his words at the woman. "Now, don't worry about a thing. The boys and I will be right behind you. We'll just get you in and have you checked out, then you can go home and have hot chocolate, okay?"

The woman shook her head and for a moment she looked like some of the drug overdose victims they found on the streets of downtown Cleveland. Wide-eyed and frantic, shaking from head to toe. Almost crazed. "Ma'am, you need to relax. Everything's going to be fine. We just want to get you checked out."

The paramedics were ready to roll when the officer realized he didn't have her name. "Ma'am." He raised his voice so she could hear him above the commotion and traffic. "Could you tell us your name?"

The woman stopped shaking and stared at him blankly without blinking. "My name?"

Seconds passed, and Officer Boe tried to conceal his concern as one of the paramedics jotted something down on his notepad. "Never mind, ma'am. We'll get it later."

Loss of memory was further proof of a concussion.

"It's Mrs. Stovall." One of the twin boys tugged on Derek's arm so he would be heard. "Her name's Mrs. Stovall."

The officer looked down at the boy. "But I thought she was your mom?"

The woman tried to sit up, but the paramedics eased her back down. "I'm...I'm their foster mother," she managed.

The officer sighed. That would complicate things. Whenever victims in an accident were wards of the state, the Social Services department had to be notified. He looked back to the woman. "What's your first name, Mrs. Stovall?"

Again the woman hesitated. And then as if someone flicked on a light switch in her brain, she said, "Maggie. Maggie Stovall."

She rattled off her phone number, and Officer Boe wrote it down quickly as the paramedics whisked her into the ambulance. "Wait!" she screamed. "I don't want to go to the hospital. What about the boys? Wait! Isn't anyone listening to me? Isn't anyone—"

Her voice echoed in the roadway as they slammed the doors shut and sped off.

Officer Boe shook his head and walked back to his car, the young boys still at his side. There he telephoned Social Services and reported that two of their charges had very nearly been killed in a traffic accident.

Ben arrived at the hospital and rushed to Maggie's side just as the doctor was explaining to her the severity of her head injury. Her heart soared at the sound of his voice.

"Doctor…I'm sorry, I couldn't get here until now. I'm her husband. What happened? How bad is it?" Ben was breathless and looked several shades paler than he'd that morning. He stood next to Maggie's bed and intertwined his fingers with hers.

Warmth washed over her, surprising in its strength. *I still love him, Lord…really. Help me understand what's happening, why I'm acting so strangely.*

For the first time in days, Maggie felt safe. Ben was with her, his hand warm and big enough to cover hers.

But nothing is big enough to cover the way you lied to him all those years ago. You're a liar, a hypocrite. A sickening excuse for a wife.

Maggie closed her eyes. Nothing could make her shake the feeling of dark desperation that seemed to be tightening its grip on her with each passing hour.

The doctor nodded at Ben and turned his attention back to Maggie. "It isn't as bad as we first thought." He seemed to be choosing his words carefully, and Maggie forced herself to listen. If it wasn't bad, then there was no reasonable explanation for her behavior. She had sat down with the boys in the middle of the sidewalk thinking that they were at the dining room table. Then she had taken hold of the twin boys who had been trusted to her care and walked directly into oncoming traffic.

"Do I have a concussion?"

The doctor glanced down at the X rays in his hands. "No. Doesn't appear so." He approached her and ran his hand over a bandage on the back of her head. "The bleeding's stopped, no stitches needed."

Ben's sigh rattled around the examining room. "Thank God."

The doctor shifted his weight and stared first at Maggie, then at Ben. He obviously had something important to say, but instead he slid his hands into the pockets of his white coat and studied Maggie once more. "Officer Boe will be in to see you both in a minute."

When they were alone in the examining room, Ben leaned over the bed and kissed Maggie's forehead. "Honey, I was so afraid…I got the call as soon as I walked in the door. All they said was you'd been in an accident and you had a head injury. I thought…"

Maggie saw tears form in his eyes, felt his love, his relief, his fear…

How can I love him so completely and hate him all at the same time?

"I thought…I was worried that if something happened to your head you might never be the same." His voice fell to a whisper. "I thought I might have lost you."

Maggie stared at him, not sure what she felt. *It's all your fault. You wanted perfection, and I gave it to you…*

Ben bent over and put his face against hers. "I couldn't bear it if I lost you, Maggie."

She waited until he straightened up. "You never had me." As soon as the bleak, flat words escaped, she chided herself. Ben didn't need to hear that. He had no idea what she was talking about.

His eyes clouded and he set his jaw, but before he could speak, Officer Boe entered the room. There was something foreboding in his expression and he waited until he had both their attention. "Mr. and Mrs. Stovall, I need to talk with you about something serious."

"Where are the boys?" Maggie's voice was suddenly shrill with concern. "I thought they were with you." How could she be a foster mother if she couldn't even keep track of two well-behaved boys? *Weren't we just about to have hot chocolate?*

The officer nodded toward the hallway. "They're safe; they're just outside."

Ben crossed his arms and leveled his gaze at the officer. "Go ahead."

"It's about the boys. Social Services is sending someone over to pick them up."

Ben cocked his head, his face a mask of confusion. "That won't be necessary, Officer. I'll be driving my wife and the boys home as soon as they discharge her."

The officer frowned. "Well, that's just it. The caseworker is concerned, what with Mrs. Stovall's accident and, well, apparently there've been several incidents lately…"

"What incidents?" Ben turned his focus on Maggie. "What're you talking about? The boys are fine at our house, right, Maggie?"

She felt herself breaking into a sweat and she wanted desperately to escape, to run out of the hospital and keep running until she dropped. Keep running until she died from exhaustion. Anything to avoid the scene that was unfolding before her.

Officer Boe glanced at his notes. "Apparently the school reported that the boys were sent to school without lunches three times last week. Then yesterday the boys were left at the bus stop. Someone, a neighbor most likely, called the school, and the boys were picked up again and brought to the principal's office where—" he looked up at Ben—"your wife picked them up nearly an hour late."

Ben's eyes grew wide and he stared at her. "Maggie?"

She had the unnerving feeling that something was crawling on her face and she realized it was her perspiration forming drops and rolling off her forehead. Ben was waiting for an answer, but she had no idea what to say. The conversation was headed someplace that terrified her. *They can't take the boys, God, no. Please, no!* She closed her eyes and nodded.

"Yes? You forgot the boys at the bus stop?"

Opening her eyes, she nodded again. Officer Boe closed his notebook and stared at them, making eye contact only occasionally, as though he were uncomfortable with the awkwardness of the moment.

Maggie realized with surprise that her eyes were dry. What had happened to her ability to cry? Didn't she care about this?

Wasn't she upset that the boys weren't coming home with her? She noticed her legs stretched out on the hospital bed and she bit her lip. *What am I doing here?*

When the officer saw that neither of them was going to speak, he continued. "Either way…" He paused and appeared to be searching for the right words. "Either way someone from the department is coming to take the boys." He looked at Ben. "If you could go home and collect their things, that'd make the transition a lot easier for the children."

"No!" Maggie screamed the word and threw the hospital sheets off her body. Before anyone could stop her, she was out in the hallway. "Casey! Cameron!" Everything seemed to be tilting. "Where are my children?" She turned on the nurses who had stopped working and were now staring at her. "What have you done with them?"

Officer Boe was there almost instantly. He shot the nurses an apologetic look and forcefully took Maggie's arm. "Mrs. Stovall, if you don't come with me I'm going to have to place you under arrest."

Ben appeared at her other side, and together the men led her back to the hospital bed. A minute later, a nurse gave her a shot and she felt herself losing consciousness.

They've killed me. Good. I don't want to live anyway. I want my boys. "Casey…Cameron…" Her voice was weak, and she could no longer open her eyelids.

Then there was nothing but all-consuming silence and deep, utter darkness.

When Maggie woke up she was in her own bed, and Ben was asleep beside her. Images flashed in her mind. She had banged her head on the sidewalk and walked into traffic with the boys and gone to the hospital and someone had taken the boys and…

She sat straight up in bed. The boys! Were they really gone

or had the entire ordeal been a crazy nightmare? She moved slowly out of bed and crept down the hallway until she reached the boys' room. *They're here; of course they're here.* She looked inside and let her eyes adjust to the darkness. The bunkbeds were empty; everything that had belonged to Cameron and Casey was gone.

Maggie collapsed slowly onto the floor outside their room. So it was true, all of it. They were gone; her boys were gone. She felt her shoulders hunch forward with the weight of the truth. The nightmare was real, and it wasn't her dreams that were crazy.

It was her.

Minutes passed until she formed a plan. Moving quietly she made her way back to bed and crawled in next to Ben, where she pretended to sleep until he left for work. When she was sure he was gone, she got up, packed a suitcase, and wrote her husband a letter.

Then, at eleven o'clock that morning she did something she never in all her life thought she'd do. Something she was sure her Christian friends would consider shameful, a sure sign that perhaps she wasn't a believer after all. Or if she was, the sin in her life was so severe that God had abandoned her.

Maggie drove to Orchards Psychiatric Hospital.

Refusing to think or feel or do anything more than survive moment by moment, Maggie stared at the building. It was over now: her life with Ben, her dreams of being a mother. No need to run from the darkness anymore. She went over her game plan and refused to give in to her desire to flee. It was this or…

She shook off the thought. No, she would not flee. She would check herself in, and when the admitting nurse asked her to describe her current mental status, Maggie Stovall, popular columnist and formerly sane person, would have just one word:

Suicidal.

Eight

ORCHARDS PSYCHIATRIC HOSPITAL WAS A PRIVATELY RUN FACILITY supported almost entirely by donations and money paid out by insurance companies. The building was set back from the road and was difficult to see because of an imposing brick wall and a row of elm trees that lined the front of the property. The arch that ran over the paved roadway leading into the facility said only Orchards. As though the grounds might house a stately bed-and-breakfast or perhaps a fine dining establishment.

Red brick made up much of the exterior of the three-story structure, and a covered walkway led to heavy French doors and an impressive foyer filled with old English furnishings and, in one corner, a Steinway baby grand piano. Only the white uniformed nurse stationed behind the admitting desk gave visitors any indication that the nature of business conducted at Orchards might somehow pertain to the field of medicine.

Maggie waited for the woman to complete her paperwork and a sense of devastating shame washed over her. How had things gotten so bad? Why had it come to this?

"What religious preference are you, Mrs. Stovall?" The nurse's voice was soothing, like honey melting into hot lemon tea.

"Does it matter?" Maggie knew the nurse meant well, but she was terrified of making this decision. What would the people at the *Gazette* say? What would her readers think? She couldn't *do* this!

She started to stand up.

"Sit down, Mrs. Stovall."

Maggie did as she was told.

"Orchards is a Christian-based hospital. We need to know for the records if that is something you're okay with."

"What? I thought it was for anyone…" She had to force herself to stay in her seat. A Christian facility? They would kick her out as soon as they learned the truth. How could she bare her soul to a hospital full of Christian counselors and expect to get any real answers?

The nurse smiled patiently. "Orchards is for anyone. We can make a note that you don't want any Christian counseling if that's the case—"

"No!" Maggie's heart was pounding again. *And He shall be called Wonderful Counselor…* "I mean, yes. Christian counseling is okay. I just…that's not what I expected here."

"Are you a Christian, Mrs. Stovall?" Somehow Maggie knew in that moment that the nurse was a believer.

"Yes…but not a very good one." She muttered the last part, and the nurse put a comforting hand over hers.

"That's okay. None of us is, really."

Another nurse appeared and smiled down at Maggie. "Ready?"

Run! Get out of here before they lock you up and throw away the key…

My peace I give you, My peace I leave you…do not let your heart be troubled, daughter. Do not be afraid.

Run! Leave now before—

The warring voices echoed loudly in her mind, and Maggie gulped, not sure what to say. Not sure even what the nurse had asked her.

The admitting nurse patted Maggie's hand again. "My name is Tani, and I can answer any questions you have now or later." She hesitated. "Do you have any questions, Mrs. Stovall?"

Maggie shook her head and looked from Tani to the new nurse, still waiting expectantly beside her. "What's going to happen to me?" Her voice sounded different, like a lost child's, and Maggie felt the now familiar confusion clouding her thinking. The new nurse leaned down and gently took her arm.

Don't arrest me, please! Maggie flinched at the woman's

touch and then realized it was time to go.

"We've got your room ready, Mrs. Stovall. Everything's going to be okay."

Everything's going to be okay, everything's going to be okay, everything's going to be...

Maggie repeated the words to herself as she allowed the nurse to lead her down the hallway. In her free hand, Maggie carried her suitcase, which was stuffed with all that she had left of the life she once lived.

The life that was over now.

The nurse escorted Maggie down a series of halls and into a room. "This is where you'll stay. We'll be notifying your insurance carrier later today and seeking approval. Generally, we get permission for a two-month inpatient stay if that much time is required.

Panic pulsed through Maggie's veins. *What if I need three months? What if I can never live on my own again?* The questions assaulted her like so many hand grenades but she nodded helplessly at the nurse.

"Here..." She handed Maggie a glass of water and two capsules.

Maggie took tiny steps backwards, shaking her head at the nurse. "No. I don't want to sleep." *The nightmares will be too much tonight.*

"They're not sleeping pills, Mrs. Stovall. They're relaxants. To help ease your anxiety."

What's wrong with me, God? What happened to the days when Your Word was all I needed to feel peace? She took stock of her trembling legs and clammy hands and the way her heart bounced about in irregular patterns. Then without another word she reached out and took the water and pills. She swallowed them quickly before she could change her mind.

"Very good, you should feel better in no time." The nurse glanced at Maggie's belongings on the bed. "Why don't you open your suitcase? We like to check the belongings when a patient is first admitted. Certain items are not allowed in the private rooms."

Maggie stepped back and watched in horror as the nurse removed a blow-dryer and a leather belt from her things. "Very well." The nurse's tone was cheerful, as if there were nothing out of the ordinary about sifting through someone's suitcase and taking away various personal items. "Go ahead and put the other things away. After that you can take a nap for an hour or so. Your first session will be an evaluation with Dr. Camas at two o'clock."

The nurse left, and Maggie felt the darkness close in around her like a shroud. She was dead, wrapped in grave clothes made up of the very blackest doom, and there was no way out. She was no longer the proud Maggie Stovall, author of "Maggie's Mind," conservative columnist and local celebrity.

She was just another mental patient.

Maggie stared at what was left of her things and it dawned on her why the nurse had taken the blow-dryer and belt.

Both items could be used to kill herself.

Two o'clock came quickly, and a nurse appeared to escort Maggie to her appointment with Dr. Camas. Maggie sat up and stretched. For a moment she wasn't sure whether she was at a hotel or in the hospital. Then she remembered. It was the middle of the day, the first day of the rest of her life. And she had an appointment with a psychiatrist.

She moved slowly down the hallway to Dr. Camas's office. The moment she stepped inside Maggie knew she was going to like him. He had a warm glow about his face, short white hair, and a neatly trimmed beard. He smiled with his eyes when she walked in and sat down.

"Mrs. Stovall?" He rose and held his hand out to her. His handshake was firm and something about it made her feel safe. Maggie relished the feeling. How long had it been since she'd felt that way? *Not long, really. She'd felt safe in the hospital, with Ben at her side, holding her hand...*

"Dr. Camas, I'm...it's just...I'm sorry to bother you..." Maggie stumbled over her words, apologetic and relieved at the same time. At least she wasn't like the typical patient at a hospital like this. Whatever was wrong with her probably didn't require a lobotomy or a straight jacket, and Maggie didn't want the doctor to think she was wasting his time. After all, she wasn't really crazy.

Her mind filled with the image of herself sitting on the sidewalk by the bus stop. Who was she kidding? The doctor had probably never counseled anyone as crazy as she was.

"No apology needed." He paused, and Maggie relaxed into her chair. *The pills must still be working.* Dr. Camas looked calm and unhurried. "Now why don't you tell me what's been going on?"

She closed her eyes and drew a deep breath. When she opened them, she saw the unmistakable look of Christ in Dr. Camas's eyes. "It's sort of a long story."

He leaned back and folded his fingers over his waist. "I've got time, Mrs. Stovall. Go ahead."

Where to begin? Yesterday? The day before? Eight years ago? Her eyes grew wet and her vision blurred with unshed tears. She blinked, and several tumbled onto her cheeks. Maggie studied Dr. Camas and somehow knew she could trust him. "One thing first..."

"Very well."

"I don't want my husband to see me. I...he isn't welcome here."

A troubled look crossed Dr. Camas's face. "Are you in danger, Mrs. Stovall? Has he hurt you or threatened you?"

Maggie shook her head, remembering again the warmth of Ben's hand the day before. "Nothing like that. It's just...our marriage is finished and I need to go forward. Seeing him would only make matters worse."

Dr. Camas jotted something down on a pad of paper. "Very well, I'll inform the desk of your wishes. We can intercept phone calls and personal visits, but I'm afraid there's nothing we can do about written correspondence. Perhaps you can tell him yourself if he writes."

Maggie nodded and imagined Ben's reaction when he got home from work later that day and found her letter. She winced, and her heart felt gripped by pain for what he would suffer when he found out. The air was beginning to feel stuffy, and Maggie drew a deep breath. Their marriage was over—she had no choice in the matter. If she were going to survive, it was time for both of them to let go and move forward. *I still love him, though. I'll always love him...*

"Mrs. Stovall, you were about to tell me what's been happening in your life..."

Maggie snapped to attention and suddenly knew there was only one place to start, only one that made any sense at all. She would start where it all began: nine years ago at the Cleveland Community Church Annual Prayer and Picnic.

The first time she ever laid eyes on Ben Stovall and knew she would never—as long as she lived—love anyone else. It was as true then as it was now. And even though her marriage was over, it would be true until the day she died.

Maggie drew a steadying breath and allowed herself to remember.

Deep in the heart of the city, Ben spent the afternoon meeting with three different judges and a host of attorneys establishing court dates for coming trials. It was the type of work that didn't require much concentration but made the time pass quickly all the same. Ben was thankful. There was no way he could have done anything more taxing; there hadn't been a spare moment all day that he wasn't been thinking about Maggie.

He'd considered staying home and talking it out, insisting

that she tell him what was wrong. But the doctor had said she might sleep most of the day, and Ben wanted her to get rest.

Of course, that wasn't all the doctor had said. He'd confided in Ben that he suspected Maggie had suffered a nervous breakdown. There was medicine she could take for a while, pills that would stabilize her anxiety and help her cope. But there would not likely be improvement in her outlook until she got real help.

Psychiatric help.

Just the sound of the word—*psychiatric*—sent shivers of fear down Ben's spine. Psychiatrists were for people who battled emotional problems, weren't they? Medical doctors helped people fight illness. But psych doctors—everyone knew *their* role. They worked with people who were crazy, people for whom life held no hope. Non-Christians, basically.

Ben had pondered these thoughts continuously throughout his day and now that it was finally almost time to go home, he could hardly wait to talk to Maggie. He had called her several times but she hadn't answered. That was understandable, especially if she were tired. But tiredness was not a sign of mental breakdown. Surely the doctors were wrong. His faith-filled wife had not suffered a nervous breakdown and she was not in need of psychiatric help. He had been her covering, after all, the one who prayed for her and took his role as spiritual leader of their home as seriously as he took his need for a Savior.

She had to be okay, didn't she?

What have I done to her, Lord? Wasn't I good enough? Didn't I pray for her as often as I should have?

He left the office half an hour early and a feeling of peace came over him as he pulled into the driveway. He had done all those things; of course she would be okay. As hard as she worked, wasn't it normal for her to have some kind of letdown now and then? Maybe her column was getting to her; maybe writing about children was making the fact that she didn't have any of her own more painful than usual.

Of course! That must be the problem. Maggie was desperate for a child. Ben allowed the relief to wash over him as he made his way into the house. He would sit down with her tonight and they would make a plan, figure out a time when they could try the in vitro fertilization again. Or if Maggie wasn't up for that, they could discuss adoption. If she wanted a baby, then by God's grace they would find her one. Whatever it took to bring back the smile that had all but disappeared from her face over the last two years.

"Maggie, honey, I'm home."

He had decided the best way to handle her was to downplay the events of the day before. She was bound to feel terrible now that Cameron and Casey had been taken from her. There was no reason to make her feel worse. He thought about yesterday's accident and thanked God again that no one had been seriously hurt. Maggie would have been devastated if her carelessness had caused anyone to be injured or…

He couldn't bring himself to think about it.

And we know that in all things God works for the good of those who love him, who have been called according to his purpose.

The verse from Romans flashed in his mind, and he allowed it to bathe him in peace. Of course they did. All things, even this. The fact that Cameron and Casey were gone was sad, but perhaps that meant it was time to have a baby of their own. He would share that with Maggie and help her believe it was so.

"Maggie?" Ben tossed his coat and briefcase on the stairs and bounded up. *Those must have been some drugs. Maggie's never slept all day long before.* He rounded the corner into their bedroom and jerked to a stop. The bed was made, and Maggie was nowhere to be seen. On his pillow lay a white envelope with his name scrawled across the front.

"Maggie, honey?" He moved quickly toward their bathroom, then glanced inside the closet. No one. He made his way to the different rooms of the house, one by one, until he was sure she wasn't there. Panic began building deep in his gut. Where had she gone? Was it safe for her to be out on the streets if she really was having a breakdown?

He dashed back up to their bedroom and snatched the envelope from his pillow. Sitting on the edge of the bed, he tore it open and pulled out the letter inside. His heart pounded loud and erratically as he unfolded it and began reading:

Dear Ben,

I'm sorry you have to learn the truth this way. But things are what they are and I can't run from them any longer. I don't know what's happening to me, why I'm so confused and tired and forgetting things. Yesterday I couldn't remember where I was or even who I was half the time. I really think I might be losing my mind.

Because of that I have packed some things and moved out…

Ben felt his insides tighten and he closed his eyes for a moment. *No, God! This isn't happening. Everything has always been perfect between us. Why? Why would she leave me?*

As though in response, another Scripture banged about inside his head: **In this world you will have trouble, but be of good cheer…I have overcome the—**

No. He couldn't handle this type of trouble, not now. Not with his wife packed and gone to who-knew-where. He opened his eyes and continued reading.

I'm checking myself into Orchards Psychiatric Hospital but I don't want you to come looking for me. You need to understand that no matter what help I can find for myself, things are over between us. When I am able to think more clearly, I will hire a divorce attorney who will contact you at that time.

Until then, please pray for me. I feel like I'm suffocating in darkness and I know for certain this is my last hope. I love you, Ben. I'm sorry I lied to you about everything. I'm sorry it's brought us to this. I hope you'll move on and meet someone else so that one day you can have the life you always dreamed of. And I hope in time you will forgive me.

Love, Maggie

The shock was more than Ben could imagine. A strange tingling sensation made its way down his spine and over the tops of his arms. *This can't be happening; it's a bad dream, a joke.* He felt as though he'd fallen into some sort of strange dream world. There was no way Maggie would leave him and ask him not to follow her! She was a woman of faith, and never in a million nervous breakdowns would she hire an attorney and sue him for divorce. It wasn't happening.

He moved toward the telephone, working to convince himself the news wasn't real. Then he called information. "The number for Orchards Psychiatric Hospital, please?" It felt strange hearing himself speak the words. *Psychiatric Hospital.* When was he going to wake up? Surely Maggie would laugh at him for having such a strange dream.

He dialed the number and waited.

"Orchards, may I help you?"

With his free hand, Ben rubbed his temple and tried to concentrate. "Uh, I'm looking for a patient. Maggie Stovall...was she admitted today?"

There was a pause. "Who's calling, please? Our patient information is highly confidential."

Ben felt himself beginning to shake. "This is...I'm her husband. I'm trying to find her."

The nurse's tone changed and she seemed almost apologetic when she spoke. "Your wife is a patient here, yes."

He took two steps backward from the blow, his mind reeling. *It was true.* His wife was in a psychiatric hospital. Ben paced the bedroom floor, desperately searching for a solution. "What kind of place is Orchards, anyway?" He was buying time, trying to think of a way to get Maggie home where she belonged.

"We're a private Christian hospital for patients suffering with mental illness."

Mental illness? Maggie? It wasn't possible. "All right, when will she be released? This evening? Tomorrow morning?"

The nurse hesitated. "Sir, the inpatient program can last up to two or even three months."

Ben couldn't breathe; pain wracked his body as though someone had sucker punched him in the gut. The blow forced him to sit down on the edge of the bed. "Three months?"

"Yes, sir."

"Can you put me through to her, please?"

"Your wife is very ill, and I hope you understand what I'm about to say." She paused again. "I'm afraid she's requested no contact with you, Mr. Stovall."

This time the shock of her words sent him to his knees. *"What?"*

"She has advised us that she will not accept your phone calls, letters, or visits."

Ben struggled to breathe. *God...help me.* "She said that?"

"Yes. But understand that her feelings could change once she's had time to talk with the doctor."

"Does she...is she in a private room?"

The nurse seemed to consider whether this was information she should share. "Yes, but we have her in a special unit."

Ben's head was pounding, and he didn't know what to say, how to respond. "Special unit? What...what special unit?"

"Suicide watch, Mr. Stovall. I'm sorry."

Ben hung up the phone and, still on the floor, hunched over his knees.

It couldn't be true. It couldn't...but it was. In the last

twenty-four hours his wife had caused an accident that could have killed herself and their two foster boys. She'd been hospitalized for a fall that still didn't make sense. She had lost custody of Casey and Cameron and written him a letter stating in no uncertain terms that she was finished with him and would divorce him soon. She had admitted that somewhere along the course of their life she had lied to him about something, apparently something crucial. And then she'd checked herself into a mental hospital where she was under—of all things—a suicide watch.

It was too much to bear.

"No! Help me, God…please!" He screamed the words, and they ricocheted against the textured walls of his empty home. When he didn't hear anything back from the Lord, he buried his head in his hands and did something he hadn't done since he was a little boy.

He wept.

What was Maggie doing? Did she intend to sever their vows, forget about him, push him aside? Why hadn't she shared any of this with him? *I'm your best friend, remember, Maggie? How could you do this? God, help me understand.* He remained unmoving, pain tearing through his body until slowly, carefully, he was able to accept one part of his new reality: Whatever her motivation, Maggie was very, very sick.

An hour later he still had no answers, no explanations. But he did have a single goal. Maggie was his partner, his confidante, his wife. He was closer to her than to anyone, anywhere. She was his Maggie girl. Whatever the problem was, he would help her. Even if he spent the rest of his life trying. Ben exhaled, pushing the pain from his lungs and realized it was the same way he'd felt back in 1991, the day he met her.

And just as he'd decided then, he would win Maggie over and prove his love, whatever it took.

Ben pulled himself to his feet and sat on the edge of the bed. He forced himself to think. Who would know Maggie well enough to shed light on the situation at hand? She had no siblings, no close friends since Tammy left the neighborhood the year before. Her father had died of a heart attack five years earlier, and that left...

A thought dawned on him.

Maybe his mother-in-law would be able to explain Maggie's behavior. Ben leaned back against the headboard. No, it wasn't possible. The old woman wouldn't know anything. Maggie and her mother had never been close, not really. Too different, Maggie always said. Her mother lived in Santa Maria, California, and was an upstanding, private person who wore her faith like a medal of honor.

Once every few years Ben and Maggie flew to the West Coast for a visit, and Ben would inevitably wonder how this woman could possibly be related to his wife. The older woman was wiry thin, with a rope of gray hair that she kept tightly knotted near the nape of her neck. Proud, private, and pinched. That was the feeling one got after spending ten minutes with Madeline Johnson. She was not a woman who hugged or cried easily, and from all Ben could tell she had struggled to understand her only child since Maggie was old enough to talk.

She said little and cared less, by Maggie's assessment, and Ben doubted she'd be any help.

Still, if this breakdown were somehow tied to something in Maggie's past, her mother was the only link Ben had, the only person who might help him understand whatever mistruth Maggie was talking about.

Lead me, Lord, that I might understand her. His vision grew blurred by tears again. *I can't live without her, God.*

The next morning Ben called his office and requested a two-week emergency leave. He'd rarely taken a sick day and he'd built up three months' time if he needed it. Four hours later, he was on a plane headed for Southern California.

The entire flight he prayed for one thing—that Maggie's

mother could somehow provide Ben with what he desperately needed: A key to unlock the secrets of Maggie Johnson's past.

Nine

THE FIRST SESSION WITH DR. CAMAS WENT BETTER THAN MAGGIE had expected. She stumbled over her words and hadn't gotten far in her story. She had the uncomfortable feeling that the things she said rarely made sense. But at least she'd kept her focus. And though the blanket of dark desperation still lay draped around her shoulders, she could somehow sense an occasional ray of light as she spoke. More than once during that initial conversation, Maggie was sure the light was coming from Dr. Camas's eyes.

If her life were an oversized ball of secret tangled knots, Maggie believed after one meeting that Dr. Camas was someone who had the patience to untie them. At the end of the session, Maggie felt more hope than she'd known in years. And though she battled unseen demons long into the night, she had a sense of urgency and excitement about meeting the doctor again.

Maggie spent her second day at Orchards, in the hours before her appointment with Dr. Camas, getting familiar with hospital layout and studying other patients as though she were going to write a column on the place. She had expected to see people with catatonic expressions head-butting walls or chanting single-syllable words for hours at a time. Instead, Orchards was filled with quiet people.

Quietly desperate people. People just like her.

Maggie wondered about their lives and what secrets they'd kept that caused them to break down and wind up in a psychiatric hospital. Was she the only one whose crisis was brought about by telling lies?

I haven't only told lies, I've lived them.

Breakfast and lunch could be eaten in the cafeteria, but the strange sense of not knowing what she was doing or who she was still hovered nearby, so Maggie thought she'd be safer eating in the chair near her bed. There was a sign on the wall of her room just above the desk that said Orchards Psychiatric Hospital. Maggie figured it was there for people like her. People who were inclined to forget even the most basic information.

When her mind was tempted to imagine Ben and the warmth of his smile, the security of his embrace, the pain he might be feeling, she forced herself to think of something else. Ben would get over it; after all, he had never really known her. If he had, he never would have married her. He deserved someone real, someone better. Someone holier. He would be better off without her.

The concentration it required to think correctly and only about certain things left Maggie exhausted by noon. She slept without ever touching her lunch tray.

The wake-up call came at five minutes before two, and Maggie jumped to her feet. She wasn't sure where she was or why she was there or what had caused her to sleep, but one thought was clear: Dr. Camas was waiting for her.

Moving through what felt like a fog, she ran a wet cloth over her face and tried to remember how she had gotten to the hospital. What had happened to her foster boys? Who was caring for them while she was here? The trip through the halls to Dr. Camas's office felt like it took an hour. When she took her seat across from him, her hands were sweaty and she was breathless, desperate for even a moment of fresh air.

"You feeling okay, Maggie?"

The calm in Dr. Camas's voice worked warmth through her and she settled back into the cushioned chair. "Not really."

Silence.

He must think I'm crazy. I am crazy…why am I here? Where are the boys? Where's Ben? She started to get up. "I think I better go since I'm supposed to—"

"Maggie." The doctor's voice halted her, and she fell back into the chair, her eyes locked on his.

"Yes?"

"This is our time. Remember?"

Our time? Our time...our time. That's right. They'd planned this meeting. She gritted her teeth and forced the clouds from her mind. "Our session, you mean?" Her voice was quiet and weak, nothing like she remembered herself sounding.

"Right. Our session. You were going to tell me more about your past...about what's happened to upset you."

Yes, that was it. She was upset. Very upset. She dug her fingertips into her temples and rubbed in small, tight circles. Then suddenly, almost as though she were seeing it played on a motion picture screen, her past began to appear right before her eyes.

As it did, she shared every detail with Dr. Camas.

It was the summer of 1991, the summer before Maggie's senior year in college, a season when she was standing on the edge of everything pure and good and hope-filled about the future, a time when the plans God had for her life seemed firmly in reach.

It was the summer she met Ben Stovall.

Maggie had grown up in Akron; Ben, in Cleveland. Once a year the church Ben attended staged an annual Prayer and Picnic. It was a time when neighboring churches from various denominations could gather and agree on two things: the sovereignty of Christ and the necessity of prayer. Over time, the celebration grew until by the late 1980s the event lasted through the weekend and was sometimes attended by thousands of people from more than a dozen churches. Games were held for various age groups, and revival-style preaching echoed across the grounds each evening.

The summer of '91 was the first time Maggie's church had

joined in. She was twenty-one and studying journalism at Akron University. There'd been nothing else going on that day so when her parents suggested the Cleveland picnic, Maggie agreed to go.

"Maybe I was trying to earn points with them," Maggie told the doctor. "I never…"

Dr. Camas waited. "Yes?"

"I never knew if my mother was proud of me or not. She was quiet, I guess."

Maggie drifted back again and explained that if one thing mattered to her parents, it was the importance of church family. After all, Maggie's family was very involved in their small congregation. If the elders had planned an event for the weekend, the Johnson family would be there. It was that simple.

Flyers were handed out to people as they parked their cars and headed for the open field where the event was set up, and Maggie's mother looked the information over carefully. "There seem to be events for young people too, dear. Why don't you run along and see if there's anyone you know? That way you won't be stuck with us."

Even now Maggie could hear the frown in her mother's voice, feel her cool, impersonal touch as she turned Maggie in the right direction and sent her off to find her peers. She took the flyer and found the sports events at the east end of the field, and as she arrived at the location she saw a dozen friends from her church in Akron.

"You came!" Susie Fouts ran up and pulled Maggie into a hug.

"Nothing better to do." Maggie linked arms with Susie and took in the scene. There were at least two hundred college kids milling about while a handful tried to organize games.

"They're doing a tug-of-war, but it has to be teams. Come on…" Susie grabbed Maggie's hand and pulled her into a full run. "We're next."

Maggie paused in her storytelling and stared at her hands.

"What is it?" Dr. Camas's words did not come out in a hurry; clearly they weren't demanding an explanation for her pause. Instead, they were gentle, carefully prodding, as though he were looking for the bruised area in an injury.

Tears flooded Maggie's eyes and she blinked them back, struggling to speak. "Susie...Susie..." She couldn't finish, and a sense of panic welled up in her. What if she started sounding crazy again? What if she couldn't force herself to remember? What if Susie hadn't gotten sick...

Dr. Camas folded his hands comfortably and waited. "Whenever you're ready, Maggie."

She had the feeling the doctor would be content to wait that way into the evening if necessary. After all, neither of them was going anywhere. She exhaled slowly. "Susie was my best friend growing up." She gulped and wiped a tear that had broken loose and tumbled down her cheek. "I...miss her."

"Yes."

Maggie looked up and again she saw that strange, comforting light in Dr. Camas's eyes. *Is that You, Lord? Beckoning me to Yourself?*

No one wants you, Maggie. You're not a Christian, you're an imposter.

She shifted her gaze back to her hands. "She died in childbirth a year after Ben and I were married." Maggie met the doctor's eyes once more and saw them fill with compassion.

"I'm sorry." His voice was warm, comforting.

"I...never told Ben."

Dr. Camas said nothing, but Maggie thought he wanted her to continue. "He would have asked too many questions."

Her mind drifted back again and the images returned. Susie running up to her, taking her hand. The two of them joining the group breathless and giggling. Maggie continued recounting the story.

Maggie's church youth group lined up on one side of the rope opposite Cleveland Community. Since the Cleveland group was hosting the Prayer and Picnic weekend, they had matching shirts and boastful attitudes.

"They think they're king of the tuggers, but not this time!" Susie shouted. "Come on everybody. Grab the rope and get ready."

Both teams took their places, and at the last possible moment a young man on the opposing team stuck his head out of line and made eye contact with Maggie. Something in his smile made her heart skip a beat, and Maggie couldn't help but grin at him.

"Pull!" A voice instructed loudly. The young man was still staring at her, and as the rope went taut, he lost his grip and was yanked forward where he fell face first in the dirt. Without his help, his team's momentum shifted badly, and Maggie and her teammates surged backward, landing on the ground in what was an unquestionable victory.

"We did it!" Susie had one fist in the air and the other around Maggie's neck. "I think it was the spinach I ate last night for dinner. Had to be good for something."

Maggie stood up and dusted off her jeans, her eyes still focused on the guy from Cleveland Community. Susie followed her gaze. "Whatcha looking at, Mag?"

"Nothing." Maggie turned away but it was too late.

"Don't lie to me. You're looking at that guy. The one who let go." She looked from Maggie to the young man and back. "Hey, I think he likes you, Mag…" She lowered her voice and took another look at him, and both girls saw that he was standing up, brushing himself off, and taking a fair amount of ribbing from his friends. Later Susie had told her that every few seconds he was glancing in Maggie's direction.

"Is he still looking at me?"

Susie nodded, her eyes wide. "He's gorgeous, Mag. I'm serious."

Maggie held her head high and kept her back to her apparent admirer. She hissed in a whisper barely loud enough for Susie to hear. "Stop staring at him. You'll scare him off."

Yanking Susie by the sleeve, the girls started to leave when the young man ran up. "Hey, wait!"

Maggie and Susie whirled around at the same time. Susie recovered first. "Did you want our autograph? We did just beat the host team, after all."

"No..." His gaze connected with Maggie's, and she felt an attraction that went to her very core, far beyond anything she'd ever known. "I'm Ben...Ben Stovall."

The girls nodded, and Susie looked from Ben to Maggie and back again. "Well, I'll be right back. My little sister's at the picnic tables and I promised her a snow cone.

"Yeah." Ben tore his eyes away from Maggie for a moment and glanced at Susie. "Nice to meet you."

Maggie tried to suppress a smile as Susie left. "You didn't even get her name."

A dimpled grin spread across his face. "I wasn't trying to get *her* name..." Maggie felt something inside her begin to melt under his unshakable gaze. "I was trying to get yours."

Susie's family had to leave early that day, so Maggie and Ben spent the rest of the afternoon and evening playing Frisbee and water balloon toss and sitting side by side as they waited for the prayer meeting to begin.

He was the son of missionaries and had spent the first fourteen years of his life in and out of Africa. His parents worked for the church now, helping with outreach programs in downtown Cleveland.

"Why'd you come back?"

"Sports. I'm the oldest, and my parents knew I wanted to go to high school in the States."

Over the next hour she learned that Ben had been quarterback of the Cleveland State University football team until he graduated the year before. Now he was about to begin his second year in the college's law school. Maggie felt like she'd fallen into a marvelous dream until he said the words she'd been fearing all day.

"You seeing anyone?" His eyes sparkled in the waning sunlight and Maggie felt her heart quicken.

"No. You?"

"Actually…" His gaze fell and he poked his toe at a chunk of Bermuda grass. "Yes. But it isn't serious."

Eventually he filled in the details and admitted that her name was Deirdre. Her parents and his had been family friends forever and now she worked as a loan officer at a bank in Cleveland.

"But you aren't…you know, serious?" Why was he paying her so much attention if he already had a girlfriend?

Ben shrugged. "Deirdre's a nice girl. We're definitely not serious physically, if that's what you mean." He caught Maggie's gaze. "I'm waiting 'till marriage for that. You too?"

Maggie remembered the hot feeling that had worked its way up her cheeks. She was completely taken by Ben, by everything about him—even his knack for being completely direct. "Yeah, I'm waiting."

He smiled at her, meeting her eyes in a way that made her insides melt like butter on hot bread. "Good." His voice was smooth and measured as his gaze lingered. "I like a girl who waits."

Her cheeks grew hotter still, and she fingered the ring on her right hand.

Ben noticed and took her fingers carefully in his, examining the silver band. "Pretty. Who's it from?"

Maggie's senses were entirely focused on the way their fingers felt together. *What is this? I barely know him.* No one had ever made her feel the way this man, this stranger, was making her feel. "A faith promise ring. My dad gave it to me."

Ben withdrew his hand and grinned at her again. "That's great, Maggie. Making a promise to wait until you're married to have sex, and knowing your father's praying for you. Not many girls around like you, you know that?"

"What about Deirdre?" Maggie was enjoying his attention, but if he had a girlfriend...

"I guess the trouble is I've never really felt any spark with her." Something about his tone of voice left Maggie no doubt that he was feeling sparks now. His smile faded, but his eyes welled with admiration for her. "Know what I mean?"

She swallowed and glanced down at her hands as they twisted nervously. "I think so."

The evening music and sermon were getting ready to start and Ben took her hand. "Come on, let's find somewhere to sit."

Maggie looked around. "Is she here?"

"Deirdre? No. Her cousin invited her to Detroit for the week."

Maggie silently blessed the girl's cousin and felt herself relax. If it wasn't serious and Ben wasn't in love with this other girl, then what was the harm of enjoying his company for one night?

Their conversation continued, and Ben told her about his plans to be a district attorney. He seemed intently interested when Maggie told him her dream of writing for a newspaper one day.

"This country needs people like you out there reporting the news, Mag." It was the first time he'd called her that, and Maggie felt her heart lurch. Somehow it seemed like the most natural thing in the world, sitting next to him, pretending he was her boyfriend and not some other girl's, hearing him call her *Mag.* A summer breeze danced over the dry field grass, and a praise band warmed up in the distance.

Maggie studied him while he talked. His words came out slow and deliberately, honey leaving a jar, and confidence was as much a part of his facial features as his chiseled chin and dancing blue eyes. In all the hundreds of college age guys at the picnic, clearly Ben was the most desirable.

With a sigh at the memory, Maggie stared sadly at Dr. Camas. "About that time I began having this, I don't know…a strange feeling, I guess. It made me remember something that happened when I was in seventh grade."

Dr. Camas shifted slightly, his eyes locked on hers. "Why don't you tell me about it, if you're comfortable."

Maggie nodded. "I was at Camp Kiloka, at a church retreat the fall I was thirteen. The first night of camp I stayed up late into the night talking to my counselor…"

The moment took shape in Maggie's mind, and she told the story, capturing every detail.

"Do you ever pray about the man you'll marry one day?" The older girl had asked. She was a college student, a volunteer who'd come along as a chaperone.

Maggie had shrugged. "Not really. I guess I'm too young to think about it."

The college girl looked surprised. "Your parents are Christians, right?"

"Right."

"I thought all Christian kids prayed about their spouses."

Loneliness stabbed at her. "My mom and dad are busy. We don't…pray together much."

Maggie and the girl were inseparable the rest of the weekend, and when Maggie came home she had a changed attitude toward prayer. From that point on she had done as the girl suggested and prayed for her future husband, that he would stay strong in the Lord and that she'd recognize him when she saw him.

Maggie was quiet.

"Did you feel that way then, when you met Ben?" Dr. Camas folded his hands together and angled his head thoughtfully.

Tears stung at Maggie's eyes. "Sitting beside Ben Stovall that warm summer night in 1991, listening to him talk about his faith and feeling him so strong beside me, I could almost hear God telling me he was the one."

Without further prompting from the doctor, Maggie continued her story.

As the evening wore on their conversation grew more personal. She told him how strict her parents had been and that she had never had a serious boyfriend.

"Come on, Mag, there must be a string of guys pounding down your door." The sky was growing darker, and the moonlight shone in his eyes, making a picture Maggie knew even back then she'd never forget.

She considered his statement. Boys had always been interested. But her parents hadn't allowed her to date until she was sixteen. And now that she was in college she was often too busy with her studies for serious boyfriends. Most of her social life was spent in group settings with friends from church. A gentle smile filled her face and she angled her head so their eyes met again. "No one special."

Ben grinned at her, and Maggie felt another rush of heat in her cheeks. "You know something? I knew from the beginning you were different." She felt herself grow shy under his unwavering stare. "Do you know how many girls call themselves Christians but act like everyone else? Most of the girls I know have already given in."

Maggie raised her eyebrows. "Deirdre?" *Was that why they weren't more serious?*

Ben's face filled with sadness and disappointment as he nodded. "She regrets it, but that doesn't change the fact. She gave in and now she'll never have that part of her back again."

"Is that why…" Maggie was afraid to ask the question that

welled in her heart, but she could tell by Ben's expression he understood.

"I don't know. Maybe." He stared up at the stars for a beat. "I care about her a lot. I just can't picture marrying her."

Though his statement sounded harsh, Maggie couldn't say she disagreed with him. There was nothing arrogant in his tone, but his words made her thankful she was a virgin. Thankful she would never be considered damaged goods by Ben or any other man. For a moment she imagined how she might feel if she had already had sex—and she couldn't help but wince. Ben's words would have felt like stones cast directly at her heart.

"You know what I mean?" He was waiting for her reaction.

"Definitely." Maggie nodded and thought of the friends she knew—some of whom attended various church college groups—who were having sex with their boyfriends. Since her junior high retreat she had believed what the college chaperone told her: *"God has a plan for you, Maggie, if only you'll follow His ways. Remember how special you are; God wouldn't want you to give yourself away to anyone but your husband."*

Maggie wasn't sure she had understood the words then, but she understood them that evening at the picnic, with Ben inches from her. In that moment she felt sure she'd achieved something great and honorable by staying pure.

The praise music was drawing to a close, the prayer meeting about to begin when Ben looked intently at her. "Maggie, do you believe in love at first sight, the kind of love that's meant to be?"

Maggie had felt her heart dissolving and she was thankful for the cover of night so that Ben couldn't see the way her hands trembled. "I guess I believe God's going to work things out for me. One day He'll introduce me to the right guy."

"Can I tell you something?" Ben lowered his head so that there was no way anyone but Maggie could hear him.

"Uh-huh." Maggie kept her eyes focused on his. She wanted

to shout out loud that yes, she believed in love at first sight, because she'd just experienced it. And that she would love him until the day she died. But all she said was, "I'm listening."

Ben hesitated, and Maggie could see how serious he'd become. "I feel something different with you, Mag. It's like I knew you the moment I saw you."

Maggie drew back a few inches and glanced around. Her parents would not think kindly of her sitting so close to a guy she'd only met that day—even if she was a junior in college. "What about your girlfriend?"

"I told you...she's not my girlfriend. It's nothing serious." For a moment she wondered if he might actually kiss her. Instead he sat straighter, and in his eyes she saw the attraction he felt for her. "Maggie, would you mind if I called you sometime?"

Even before she answered yes she knew that if she started dating Ben Stovall there would be no turning back. Her heart was drawn to him in every way that mattered, and whoever else she might meet in years to come would forever pale in comparison. The sermon lesson that night had been on fighting the good fight and persevering, on believing that God had a plan for His people, if they would only seek Him in love and truth.

Maggie felt like he was speaking directly to Ben and her.

Then why do you want to divorce him?

The voice came out of nowhere, breaking through her memories, and Maggie jerked backward, closing her eyes. She wasn't ready to return to reality, to psychiatric hospitals, and to seven long years of lies and a marriage that was supposed to last forever but was about to end.

She wanted to stay in that distant place for as long as possible, live again in that time when everything about the two of them was exactly what it should be, when plans God had for them were clearer than the evening summer sky over Cleveland.

There was silence in the doctor's office for a moment, and Dr. Camas finally cleared his throat. "Is this a stopping point for you, Maggie, or do you want to keep on? I have time."

If only that were where the story ended...

"No, that's enough."

Her heart was racing, and she gripped the edges of her seat so she wouldn't run out of the office, tear down the hallways, and burst out the doors to freedom. She didn't want to deal with the truth, the fact that she had done more than lie to Ben over the years. Sadly, she had lied to herself, too. Tears came hard and fast, making it difficult to breathe without sobbing.

Help me, God. Give me strength.

Weeping may remain for the night, but joy will come in the morning...

She caught her breath. *What was that last part? Joy?* In the surprisingly comfortable silence Maggie pondered the thought and realized something she hadn't before. That's what had been missing: joy. A sinking feeling lodged itself in her stomach. *It won't come in the morning, not for me. I'm stuck forever in the weeping night.*

Dr. Camas leaned over and slid a box of tissues closer to her. "There you go. It's okay to cry, Maggie. Crying is good. It means you're getting ready to deal with the issues at hand."

Crying? Had she been crying all this time? She ran her fingertips over her cheeks and found them dripping with tears. This was the second time she'd cried without knowing it. Even here, under the care of a kind and gentle psychiatrist and with antianxiety medicine coursing through her veins, Maggie was losing it.

The thought was discouraging and frightening, particularly because somehow she knew it meant she was closer to the truth than before. Terrifyingly close. Maggie took two tissues and dabbed at her face. "I can't do this anymore, doctor. I'm sorry."

"Nothing to be sorry about. It was a good session. I think we're headed in the right direction."

Maggie feared the direction they were headed, the direction of honesty. She had kept herself miles from the truth since the day she and Ben married—since before that even. And now here she was walking backward in time, hurtling toward the place where she would have to reckon with her past. And with it, every demon and monster and vestige of blackness that had tormented her over the years.

In that moment, it was all much more than Maggie was ready to take.

Ten

THE DRIVE FROM LOS ANGELES INTERNATIONAL AIRPORT TO Santa Maria was beautiful, oak trees draped in mild fall colors, foot-high grass blowing gently over the rolling hills. For most of the way, the Pacific Ocean lay sprawled on Ben's left and more than once he was tempted to pull over, to find a place alone on a rock and stare out to sea. He needed to talk with God but since he wanted to get to Santa Maria before nine o'clock, he held his conversation in the car.

Where had he gone wrong? He asked God over and over, and each time he felt the same thoughts fill his head: **Love deeply. Love covers a multitude of sins.**

Ben tried, but he could not make sense of the Scripture in light of what was happening. Who had sinned? Had Maggie done something crazy? Was she seeing someone else on the side? Ben almost laughed out loud. It was impossible. She was a committed Christian, a woman who had saved herself and been a virgin bride. A woman who had loved him the way he loved her—completely—since the day they first met.

Ben remembered that meeting and felt tears sting his eyes. He blinked hard and forced them back. He needed to concentrate, not fall apart. Of course Maggie wasn't having an affair. *So what is it, Lord? Why that Scripture?*

Love covers a multitude of sins, My son. Love deeply.

Ben stared ahead in the distance and barely noticed the way the sun shimmered on the ocean. It would be twilight soon, and again he was drawn to pull over and get out. Maybe rail at God for letting this happen or cry out loud at the top of his lungs. He *did* love deeply, and look where it got him! His wife was losing her mind, locked up in a mental hospital and refusing his phone calls and visits. What good had loving deeply ever done for him?

Love as I have loved you...

A twinge of something that resembled fear struck a chord on the keyboard of Ben's mind. Why did it feel like God had something against him? This was Maggie's fault, the whole mess. He would be patient, of course. If there were secrets, he was willing to uncover them and then forgive her, whatever it was. So what did God mean by implying he hadn't really loved Maggie?

He shifted uncomfortably in his seat, wrestling with the still small voice through Cambria and Lompoc and finally into Santa Maria. It was quarter to nine when Ben pulled up in front of the Johnson house.

Maggie's mother must have heard his car because she appeared at the door wearing wool slacks and a sweater, her hair pulled back severely in the familiar bun. Ben climbed out of the rented car and made his way up the walkway. The Johnson home was modest and the result of good planning on the part of Maggie's father. Since his death, Madeline Johnson had lived here alone with her memories, connected not to people but to a host of charitable organizations and busy work. Ben hadn't told her what was happening with Maggie, only that there was a problem and he needed to see her immediately.

"Good evening, Ben." She nodded curtly, making no effort to hug him. Instead she stepped back and gestured for him to come inside. When they were seated in the living room, she sat stiffly, her hands folded, and sighed. "I'm not sure I understand why you're here. But whatever it is it must be important." She hesitated, almost as if she did not want to ask the next question. "Is everything okay with Maggie?"

For the first time since meeting Maggie's mother, Ben wished they had a closer relationship. His parents had gone back to Africa after he and his brothers were grown, so they had little contact. It would have been comforting if only this one time he could break down in front of this woman and know he would have her care and support. But since that wasn't the case, he drew a deep breath and pondered how best to explain the situation. "Maggie's had a breakdown."

Madeline angled her head sharply and frowned. "A what? What type of breakdown?"

Weakness, perceived or otherwise, was something Maggie's mother hated. She wore the look of someone who had caught a whiff of week-old trash.

Help me here, Lord. I need to make her understand how important this is.

"What I mean is, Maggie's taken some time off work...she's at a facility...a place where they help people figure out what's wrong. Do you understand what I'm saying, Mrs. Johnson?"

Madeline's face lost some of its color, but otherwise there was not a flicker of emotion. "Maggie's at a psychiatric hospital? Is that what you mean?"

Ben nodded. "She's not been well. Things...they've been getting worse over the last few years."

"She never mentioned a word to me..." Madeline huffed softly, clearly indignant that her only child wouldn't have trusted her with such information.

"Well, Mrs. Johnson, she didn't say much to me about it either. A few days ago the state took the twin foster boys out of our home, and then yesterday Maggie checked herself into the hospital."

Ben thought about telling her how Maggie was refusing contact with him, but he decided against it. He didn't want to give her any reason to be less than honest with him about the questions he needed to ask.

"Is that why you've come?" Madeline leaned slightly back into the sofa as though it pained her to relax even a little.

"No...I mean, yes. The truth is Maggie keeps alluding to the fact that I don't really know her."

Ben was studying her closely, watching for signs that Maggie's mother might understand more about her daughter than she'd ever let on to him—and for a fraction of an instant there was a flicker in her eyes. A knowing look, as though Maggie's comment hadn't come as a surprise at all. Ben felt a surge of hope.

She knows something. Come on, Madeline, clue me in here.

"I'm sorry, Ben." Madeline's face softened some. "This must be very hard for both of you. I wish Maggie's father were still alive. He...he always knew how to talk to her."

They were veering off track. "Listen, I'm here because I think you can help me make sense of what Maggie's saying. She wrote me a letter, too...before she went to the hospital." A lump appeared in Ben's throat and he had to swallow hard before he could continue. "She said something about having lied to me."

Madeline Johnson sat perfectly still.

"So...I'm trying to find out the truth, whatever it is."

Madeline stood in a rush of motion and waved one hand in Ben's direction. "Well, young man, I'm afraid you've wasted your time. I don't have the slightest idea what Maggie's talking about." She made her way into the kitchen and returned with two cups of coffee. She handed one to Ben, black like he drank it. "Have you and Maggie prayed about this issue, whatever it is?"

Ben sighed and let his head fall gently into his hands. He rubbed his temples searching for the right words. "I think we're past that at this point."

"Past prayer?" Madeline shot him a disapproving look. "I didn't think there was such a thing."

Help me, Lord... "Of course not...not in that sense. It's just that Maggie's really hurting right now, and I have to find out what she means. What did she lie about?" He paused. "My guess is it's something relatively minor, like maybe she hasn't wanted to live in Cleveland all these years...or she doesn't

want to work for the paper anymore…something like that."
Liar! A voice in his mind taunted. *You think she's seeing another man. Admit it.* "Whatever it is, it's eating her up. It's destroying her, Mrs. Johnson, and if you can help me at all…"

The older woman set down her coffee cup, and again Ben thought he caught a hint of fear in her eyes. "It's destroying her?"

"Yes. To be perfectly honest, I think the hospital is worried she might kill herself."

This time Maggie's mother felt the blow. Her eyes filled with tears, and though she remained utterly still and dignified, Ben could see her heart breaking.

"Things have changed since I was a girl…"

Ben waited. Wherever she was headed, he had a feeling he was close…close to getting the information he so desperately needed.

"In my day, a young woman would never have allowed herself to become so self-absorbed. After all, God's given her a—" she motioned toward him and glanced his direction—"an upstanding Christian husband. In my day that would have been enough. A woman would have known to let dead dogs lay, not dredge up the past for strangers to sift through and analyze looking for answers. My goodness!" Madeline raised her voice a level. "Maggie has everything a girl could possibly hope for. And I'm sure one of these days God was planning to give her the babies she wants. Why can't she leave well enough alone?"

Ben didn't do or say anything to stop the woman. *Keep talking, Madeline. Keep talking.* "Maybe whatever it is seems too big to leave alone."

Madeline shook her head and stared into her coffee cup. "Times have changed."

"Mrs. Johnson, remember when Maggie and I fell out of touch there for a year or so? Before we were married?"

The expression on Madeline's face changed again, and Ben had the oddest feeling the older woman was steeling herself against something inevitable. She stared hard at him. "Yes…she was devastated."

Ben felt the dig. *Is this it, Lord? Did something happen while we were apart?* A ripple of fear skittered down his spine, and he felt almost sure they were treading on a hidden layer of information that would lend insight to Maggie's madness. After all, it had been the darkest year of his life, too.

"Maggie never said much about that time." Ben searched for the right words. "Do you know if—"

"His name was John." Her words spilled out, pouring forth information as if she couldn't bear to hold it in another minute. "John McFadden."

Ben felt his world tilt crazily. *"What?"*

At his whispered exclamation, Madeline lifted her coffee cup once more and took a long sip, leveling her gaze at Ben. "Maggie dated John quite seriously for several months that year. She didn't tell you?"

What is she talking about? Maggie hadn't dated anyone else, ever. Was this the lie? Had it been that easy to discover her secret? "No…she never mentioned him."

Whoever he was it couldn't have been serious. Maggie had been in love with Ben before meeting this John McFadden, and after Ben was finally able to work his life out, Maggie had married him, not the other man. Whoever John McFadden was, Maggie couldn't possibly have cared much for him. *But then why did she lie to me, Lord?*

Madeline seemed anxious to take control of the conversation. "Ben, you broke Maggie's heart when you stopped calling. John had been pursuing her for months and that summer the two of them spent…" She paused, clearly searching for the right words. "They spent a lot of time together. Her father and I did not approve."

Ben's head was still spinning. He could understand Maggie dating someone else, but someone her parents didn't approve of? "Was he a Christian?"

"Definitely not. He was popular and handsome, and in some ways he reminded us of you. Except that he made a mockery of Maggie's faith."

The truth settled heavily on Ben's heart. "I don't understand. Maggie would never have been attracted to someone who wasn't…" He let his voice drift.

"She wasn't exactly herself after you disappeared. Like I said, she was very hurt."

Obviously Maggie's mother blamed him. It had been Ben's fault back then, therefore it was Ben's fault now. He had made one bad decision in the spring of 1992 and as a result he had lost touch with Maggie for more than a year. Now, eight years later, he was supposed to believe Maggie's choice to date this John McFadden was the reason she had suffered a nervous breakdown?

The pieces didn't add up.

"Is that all? Did anything bad happen between them? I mean…" Ben couldn't bear to ask the questions that poked at his mind, but he had to know. "He didn't hurt her or do anything against her will, did he?" He knew Maggie well enough to know she would never have allowed John McFadden or any man to touch her before her wedding night.

But that didn't mean she hadn't been…

"She was not raped, if that's what you mean." Ben was shocked that Maggie's mother would speak so bluntly, but he was thankful all the same.

He exhaled slowly and realized he'd been holding his breath. "I guess I'm still a little confused."

Madeline crossed her legs and glanced nervously at her hands. "I'm not sure I should tell you this…but if Maggie is really that bad…" She folded her fingers together on her lap and Ben could see they were shaking. "Maybe you have a right to the information."

Not more lies. Lord, give me strength. "Go ahead, Mrs. Johnson, please."

"John McFadden still lives in Cleveland. Your area, actually. I believe he runs a bar on the south side. Topper's...something like that."

Ben struggled to make sense of all Madeline had told him. "Why would you still know that?"

"I could be wrong. But last time I was in Cleveland I saw an ad someplace and noticed his name. He's been there quite a while."

"Is there something else, anything you're not telling me?" Ben had the feeling there was. *Come on, Lord, make her talk to me.*

"I've told you all I know. Anything else you'd need to get from John. But I'm warning you...he's not a nice man. I think he's into some very nasty things, illegal things. Be careful."

Ben's mind raced. "How would you know that unless Maggie had told you?" Had she kept in touch with the man? And why hadn't she ever mentioned him? The whole thing was crazy.

"Maggie's father kept tabs on him. He threatened Maggie more than once, and Mr. Johnson liked to know where he was, what he was doing. Just in case."

"Just in case what?"

"I'm not sure. Maggie's father had a bad feeling about the man."

Ben wished there were some way he could blink and wind up back in Cleveland. He wanted to visit Maggie's old boyfriend before another fifteen minutes passed.

Patience, My son. Love covers a multitude of sins...

The voice that spoke to his heart calmed his trembling and helped him deal with the situation at hand. "That's all, then?"

Madeline drew a lengthy breath. "Yes. This thing Maggie's dealing with, I have a feeling it might be connected to John McFadden."

It had gotten late, and Ben accepted Madeline's offer of the guestroom and a full breakfast in the morning. Before he left, she studied his face. "Tell Maggie I'm praying for her. And whatever you find out, Ben...try to understand. Maggie would never have given John McFadden a second glance if you hadn't left her."

Ben bore the burden of the woman's comment every minute of the four-hour drive to the airport and on into his six-hour flight home. All the while his emotions took him in a dozen different directions—anger at Maggie for lying to him, guilt and regret for having broken up with her, anticipation and expectation for the moment when he could meet John McFadden and ask him about Maggie.

And, of course, overriding fear.

Because more than anything else, Ben was afraid of the meeting he was about to arrange. Afraid of what he might learn about the wife he loved more than life itself.

Terrified that the information might change his life forever.

Eleven

LAURA THOMPSON TOOK HER SEAT IN THE FOURTH ROW AT Cleveland Community Church and reached for her husband's hand. He winked warmly at her, and she leaned close, whispering even though the service hadn't started yet. "Have you seen Maggie Stovall?"

Larry frowned and glanced over his shoulder, scanning the congregation. "No. Whaddya want with the Stovall woman?"

Laura hesitated. She'd told him about the prayer mission her Bible study had taken on, but not the name of the woman she was praying for. Eventually she would tell him, when it became clearer why God had asked her to pray for Maggie Stovall in the first place. "Nothing. Just wondered if you'd seen her."

Laura settled back against the cold, wooden pew, occasionally checking over one shoulder or the other in search of the woman. Maggie hadn't missed a Sunday as far back as Laura could remember. She was always there, second row, middle of the aisle, smiling and greeting visitors as though she hadn't a care in the world.

Where is she, Lord? Is something happening to her? Is Maggie in trouble?

Pray, daughter. Pray diligently.

Laura was overcome by the gravity in the silent voice that resonated throughout her heart. It was true, then. Maggie must be having some kind of problem, and now Laura's prayers were needed quickly and desperately.

Without hesitating another moment or letting Larry in on the urgency that accompanied her thoughts, she closed her eyes, bowed her head only an inch or two, and prayed for Maggie Stovall as though her life depended on it.

On Maggie's third day at Orchards, Dr. Camas decided she needed to be on more medication. She had continued to take the antianxiety drugs, which seemed to help her heart beat normally, but now the doctor was bringing out the big guns. Along with breakfast that morning there were two additional pills on a small plate, and Maggie rang for the nurse.

She pointed to the pills when the nurse appeared. "What are these?"

"Oh, I'm sorry, Mrs. Stovall. I thought the doctor explained those. I guess he'll be in later to talk to you about it. You've heard of Prozac?"

Maggie's heart sank and she squeezed her eyes shut. *Prozac? Christians didn't go on Prozac. Lord, what am I doing here? Why did You let me build my whole life on a lie? I hate myself, God. Please…just take me now. I don't want to live…*

"Mrs. Stovall? Are you all right?" The nurse sat down on the edge of the bed and placed a hand on Maggie's arm. "It's okay, he didn't give you a high dosage. Just something to help you think more clearly."

None of it made any sense. She kept her eyes closed, ignoring the nurse's attempts at comfort. A week ago she'd been jogging around the park, enjoying Casey and Cameron, and writing a successful column for a major metropolitan newspaper. Now she was under watch and supervision by a staff of doctors and nurses at a psychiatric hospital. What had gone wrong?

"Does it bother you, having to take this type of drug?" The nurse's voice was gentle, but Maggie felt her anger rising to the surface. Her eyes flew open.

"Yes! It bothers me very much. I'm not a lunatic or something! I should be able to control my moods, my personality, the way I think…without taking some…some sort of *psych* medication."

A tender smile filled the nurse's face. "That isn't always so, Mrs. Stovall. There are many reasons why a person might need these types of medications. Here at Orchards we believe that God has allowed the development of drugs like this to help medical professionals restore us to the place we were before we were sick. Would it help you to think of it that way?"

Maggie sighed, then started when she realized there were tears streaming down her face. *Are You even there, God? Or did You check out at the door?*

It was possible. After all, God had a lot better things to do than baby-sit Christians who couldn't keep from falling apart, let alone live a joyful life. And other than the fact that it was based on a foundation of lies, Maggie knew her life should have been joyful.

"Fine." Maggie gulped down the pills with a single swallow of water. "What other drugs does he want me to take? Is there a happiness drug and a rational drug and a drug that'll make things right between me and my husband? Because I'm a candidate for those, too."

The nurse rose and headed toward the door. She still wore the trace of a smile, but Maggie could see she'd pushed her too far. "I'm sorry this is so hard for you, Mrs. Stovall. I'll be out at the nurse's station if you need anything."

Maggie crossed her arms furiously and pushed away her breakfast. She hated it here; hated being locked up and treated like a child. There was no point to it. The darkness still hung over her very being, lurking in the shadows of her room and following her down the hall to every meeting, every appointment. She still dreamed of the beautiful blond girl and still woke with arms aching from their emptiness.

That morning there were three physical examinations and two appointments with therapists who asked questions about how Maggie was feeling now that she was at Orchards.

"Honest." Maggie said the word with all the defiance she felt. She had never intended to be honest about any of this. She was being forced into it. She didn't want to revisit her past, to face the lifetime of hurt that lay ready to be discovered...but the medical staff at Orchards was leaving her no choice.

There was only one place where the feeling of impending doom seemed to lift, and that was in the quiet calm of Dr. Camas's office. Maggie took her lunch in her room again and dozed off and on until her two o'clock meeting. It was strange that she felt any peace at all heading toward the meeting with Dr. Camas. Especially since it was in his office that she was likely to come face to face with a past she'd been running from all her married life.

When she was situated in her chair, he gently recapped the things she had told him the day before. "Seems like you had very special feelings for Ben back then, is that right?"

Maggie thought for a moment and uttered a brief laugh. "Yes. I wanted to marry him from the moment I saw him."

The doctor nodded his understanding. When Maggie said nothing, he ventured forward. "Something happened to change that?"

Maggie felt a chill pass over her, the feeling of pure, cold, terror. The light in Dr. Camas's eyes caught her attention, and she felt compelled to tell the story, the complete story in all its frighteningly painful details.

She drew a deep breath and began to speak.

Ben placed the call to Topper's Pop Bar at just after noon that same day and immediately knew he had the right place. "I'm looking for John McFadden."

"Whaddya need?" The man on the other end was gruff, unwilling to share any more information than was absolutely necessary.

"I'm a friend of his from a few years ago. He owns the place, right?" Ben was guessing, and his heart sounded loudly as he waited for an answer.

"Yeah, okay, I guess so." His voice bore a thick New York accent, and Ben wondered if Maggie's mother was right. Maybe

John McFadden was into more than selling whiskey to the people who found their way to his bar. "Johnny's in after six. Call then."

Six hours. Ben thanked the man and hung up. No way was he going to wait six hours to call the man on the phone. If this was the same John McFadden who had dated Maggie that year, Ben wanted to see him. Now. In person.

He roamed aimlessly around the house wondering how he was going to pass the time. As he scanned the rooms, he realized their home had taken on a disheveled look. Maggie had always kept everything so neat. Laundry cleaned, clothes hung up, dinners on the table every evening. Of course, that was before things changed. In the past two years the house had been messy more often than not, and sometimes when she didn't have a column to write, he'd come home at six o'clock to find Maggie still in her pajamas.

Whatever it was that was eating at her, it had been a long time coming. *Why didn't I see it before?* Ben didn't like any of the answers that came to mind.

He made his way upstairs and started a load of towels. He guessed on the amount of laundry soap and hoped three scoops were enough. Then he grabbed his Bible off the nightstand near his bed. Everywhere he turned the message seemed the same...

Know the truth...the truth will set you free...worship in truth...

What are You trying to tell me, God? That You're glad I'm doing this, that You want me to find the truth out about Maggie? He finished reading and worked some more on the laundry, but still time passed slowly. Two-thirty, then three o'clock. Three hours before he would get in his car and head for a bar, three hours until he would come face to face with a man Maggie had cared for.

A man Ben hadn't known existed.

Maggie let her mind drift. She remembered the phone call like it was yesterday.

After meeting that summer, she and Ben talked to each other often, sometimes writing letters and making promises to be together. Maggie was busy with her school year, involved with her friends at church and working part time for the *Akron Beacon-Journal*. Ben was preoccupied with his toughest year of studies yet, in addition to studying for the bar exam and still, on occasion, seeing Deirdre.

One night, Ben invited Maggie to a party with some of his buddies from school. Before the night was over, Deirdre and a friend showed up, and Ben introduced them.

The girl barely spoke to Maggie, and though Ben seemed unaware of the tension, Maggie was certain of one thing from that moment on. No matter what Ben thought, Deirdre considered him more than just a friend. It couldn't have been any clearer if she'd written it in ink across her face. She was in love with Ben, and that gave Maggie an immediate feeling of insecurity.

"We'll be together more soon," Ben had promised Maggie a few weeks later. "Even this spring, after exams. That'll give us plenty of time to do stuff."

"What about Deirdre? I saw how she looked at you and I think you're wrong about her." Maggie wasn't sure if her words were meant as a warning to Ben or to herself. She knew only that he held the power to break both her heart and Deirdre's.

"Maggie, how many times do I have to tell you?" Ben's voice was kind and compassionate, filled with all the emotion she'd seen in his eyes that first time they met. "It's nothing serious." She tried to feel comforted, but something in the distant places of her heart warned her of danger where Ben was concerned.

Still, he would tell her the same thing over and over. "She's a friend. Kind of like she's always been there. I don't know…it's hard to explain."

No matter what Ben said, Maggie didn't understand. As far as she could see, there was no reason to spend any time with Deirdre if he felt so strongly about his budding relationship with Maggie.

Twice when she had a free weekend, Maggie drove up to Cleveland and spent the day with Ben, watching him play touch football with his law school buddies. He was a gifted athlete, hanging back in the pocket long enough to let his receivers find their right places on the field and then flinging the ball to them with uncanny accuracy. Maggie was proud of him and wished she'd seen him play for CSU. Even there, though, on the intramural field, she felt her heart nearly bursting with pride.

On one of her visits he took her to another party. Most of the people there had been part of the Cleveland Community College youth group and Maggie had the uncomfortable feeling she was being compared to Deirdre. About an hour later— once again—Deirdre and a friend arrived and made their way toward Ben and Maggie.

"Deirdre's here," Ben whispered, nodding toward the blond on the right.

"Hi, Ben." Deirdre put her arm comfortably on Ben's shoulder, leaned toward him, and kissed him squarely on the mouth. Although the kiss didn't last long, Ben's expression grew strained; he seemed to stumble over his words. When Deirdre and her friend wandered off to find something to eat, Maggie turned to face him.

"I thought it was only a friendship thing?" She was furious at him for lying to her and she had to fight the urge to walk out and never look back. If Deirdre was his girlfriend, she wasn't interested. "Good-bye, Ben. Call me when you're free."

Ben came after her. "Maggie, really. She never acts like that...that kiss thing. We aren't like that. Can't you believe me?"

Maggie stopped to face him again. "I'm not blind, Ben." She

whirled around and continued toward the door.

"What's that supposed to mean?" Ben moved in front of her and blocked her way.

"It means that Deirdre is in love with you. And as long as you two are seeing each other, I'm bowing out." In the distance she could see Deirdre watching them, whispering to her friends. Maggie leaned dramatically around Ben and made eye contact with the other girl. Then she smiled and waved with all the sweet, sticky sarcasm she could muster. When she was sure she had the girl's attention, Maggie leaned over and kissed Ben the same way Deirdre had. Only Maggie made sure her kiss lasted longer.

It was their first kiss, and even now, all these years later, Maggie felt a stab of regret that she had used it as a weapon of revenge.

Especially because it was a kiss she'd dreamed about for months.

Ben's face was layered in confusion and desire. "Hey, Mag...what was that all—"

Maggie interrupted him with a brief wave and an artificially sweet smile. "See ya, Ben." Then she turned and left.

There were phone calls after that, but Maggie kept them short. "Still seeing Deirdre?"

Ben would sigh in frustration. "You can't expect me to cut her out of my life overnight. We've known each other since we were kids."

"It's been nice talking with you, Ben. Gotta run." And she'd hang up.

By February, when Ben began studying more intensely for the bar exam, he had finally stopped seeing Deirdre except at college church functions. He called Maggie constantly, swearing his love and asking to see her more often. She took her time before accepting his offers, and finally they agreed that he would accompany Maggie to a dance at her university later that spring. They began dating every other weekend and often their good night kisses lingered for several minutes before Maggie would pull herself away.

"I love you, Mag…" Ben would tell her as she left.

"You, too." It was true. Maggie trusted Ben and believed that Deirdre was no longer an issue in their lives. Ben Stovall was the man God had chosen for her and she could see nothing but happy days ahead for both of them.

But that was before the phone call.

The news that would change her life forever, the words she would never forget, came one Monday in late March, four days before the big dance. Maggie was working on a term paper for investigative journalism when the phone rang.

"Hello?"

"Maggie…oh, Maggie, something awful's happened."

Even now she remembered how his tone had shot adrenaline racing through her body. She could see herself, the way she had dropped her pencil and leaned back in her chair. "What is it?"

On the other end, Ben drew a deep breath, and Maggie thought she could hear him crying. "Deirdre's mother was killed in a boating accident. They were out on Lake Michigan and…I don't know, something happened…a storm came up. I guess it was hard to see and another boat hit theirs head on. Deirdre broke her arm and fractured her hip. Everyone else was okay, but Deirdre's mother hit her head…"

"I'm sorry." An array of emotions assaulted her, and she had a sick feeling about where the conversation was headed.

"They radioed the Coast Guard and got Deirdre's mom to a local hospital…but it was too late. She was bleeding internally and…there was nothing anyone could do for her."

Maggie was silent for a moment, not sure what she should say. She remembered the party where Deirdre had gone out of her way to mark Ben as her own, and how Maggie had made sure to pay her back. "Deirdre must be devastated."

"Everyone is." She heard him stifle a sob. "Maggie… Deirdre's mother was my mom's best friend. She was like a second mom to me. I can't believe this is happening."

"Is Deirdre…" Maggie didn't want to sound jealous. Not at a time like this. "Is she at home or what?"

"She's in the hospital in traction. They transported her to Cleveland General this morning. They're going to operate on her hip first thing tomorrow and hopefully they'll let her out for the funeral."

"When is it?" Maggie knew the answer before she asked.

"Saturday. Same day as your dance." Ben hesitated, and Maggie squeezed her eyes shut. She was sorry for Deirdre, but something deep inside her heart desperately feared where all this could lead. Ben cleared his throat. "Maggie…you understand, don't you? Deirdre needs me with her at the service."

Maggie's hesitation lasted only a moment. "Absolutely, Ben. Definitely. It's just a dance." With all her heart she wanted to believe the words that so easily flowed from her mouth, wanted to trust Ben and not feel threatened by Deirdre's mother's death. But jealousy swelled deep inside her, leaving a lump in her throat and making it difficult to talk.

"I'm sorry, Mag, but I knew you'd understand." Ben sounded so relieved and deeply troubled at the same time that Maggie hated herself for being worried. She pictured Deirdre…and somehow the image of Ben comforting the blond in her greatest hour of need troubled Maggie to the point of tears.

"Hey, I gotta run, Maggie. I want to be there when Deirdre comes out of surgery. She needs me."

Maggie was silent, Ben's last words ringing through her head: *She needs me, she needs me, she needs me.*

Ben cut in quickly on her thoughts. "You know what I mean, right, Mag? She doesn't need me in *that* way. It's just that…well, she's lost so much." He paused as if he was searching for the right words. "And I'm still probably her best friend. You understand, right?"

Maggie stifled the tears that threatened to break loose at any moment. What choice did she have but to understand? "Sure, Ben. Call me later."

"Pray for her, okay?" She could hear in his voice that he was anxious to go.

"Sure."

When they hung up, Maggie dropped her head into her hands and muttered a sincere prayer that God show mercy to Deirdre in the days to come. Then she wept for Deirdre and the death of her mother and the sad fact that tragic things happen even to godly, Christian people. But most of all she wept for herself and the strange feeling that had come over her.

The feeling that she had just lost Ben Stovall forever.

Maggie fell silent and Dr. Camas shifted his position. "Is that all for today?"

The room was quiet except for the gentle whirring of heat circulating from a ceiling vent. That phone call from Ben had been the beginning of the darkest days in Maggie's life, the culmination of which made it hard for Maggie to think clearly eight years later.

Confess to one another...live in the light, daughter...

At that moment, the whispering of God did not seem intertwined with doom and desperation. Instead His words seemed the very seeds of hope. Her eyes met the doctor's and again she saw a wealth of warmth and light and somehow she knew she had to continue. Only by going back would she ever move forward toward the place of sunshine and hope that Dr. Camas—and God, Himself—were calling her to.

Fresh tears spilled from Maggie's eyes and she shook her head. "No, there's more."

"I've got time, Mrs. Stovall." His slight smile bathed the room in kindness. "Why don't you go ahead."

Maggie nodded and again allowed herself to drift back in

time, back to the place where Ben began spending every spare moment with Deirdre.

At first it had been out of necessity. There were details for Deirdre's father to handle, matters to be taken care of, and with Deirdre in the hospital, Ben was often the only person available to sit by her side. Maggie went to the dance by herself that weekend and spent the evening with a host of friends, including John McFadden, local baseball sensation and easily the most popular boy on campus.

"Hey, Maggie. I know you're one of those Christian girls, but what about you and me going out sometime, huh?"

Maggie felt herself blush. He was so good looking. In fact, in some ways he reminded her of Ben, with the exception of his eyes. Ben's eyes were filled with a love for God; John's were filled with something else...something dark and a little bit dangerous.

Though Maggie enjoyed every moment with John that evening, she knew about the rumors, how John used a girl and left her for another conquest. There was a significant trail of broken hearts lining the hallways of Akron University and a few guys even attested to the fact that John McFadden kept lists of the girls he'd been with.

So she looked at him that night and laughed lightly. "John, you and I are far better off as friends."

After the week of the funeral service, Deirdre had doctor appointments and physical therapy sessions, and much of the time Ben drove her around town or spent afternoons encouraging her to work her damaged hip so that she would get better. When she broke down, missing her mother and terrified of the future, Ben was the one who comforted her.

He explained all of it to Maggie, and though his reasons were good, Maggie could sense him pulling away from her. "She's a wreck, Mag," he told her once a few weeks after the accident. "Deirdre's never been like this before. It's like I'm all she has. She doesn't want me to leave her side."

His words seemed to imply something, but Maggie didn't question him. She was too busy comforting herself. Her gut told her clearly that her relationship with Ben was on shaky ground, and one month after Deirdre's mother's death, he called and confirmed her worst fears.

"Mag, I don't know how to say this…"

She closed her eyes and leaned against the hallway wall. *Say it, Ben. Tell me it's over.*

When she didn't say anything, Ben continued. "Deirdre needs me…"

"More doctor appointments?" Maggie hated the fact that she sounded bitter. It wasn't Deirdre's fault her mother had died, and Ben couldn't help the fact that he'd been friends with Deirdre all her life. Still the anger that boiled in Maggie's heart seeped out in her words, and there seemed nothing Maggie could do to stop it.

"No…I mean, yes, she has more doctor appointments, but that's not it." He sighed loud enough for her to hear. "I'm so confused right now, Mag. I think it'd be best if…"

The tears started then. They flooded her eyes and streamed down her face as though her heart had sprung a leak too severe for anyone to repair.

"Maggie? Are you okay?" He knew she was crying and she hated that fact. "Maggie girl, talk to me."

She swallowed and did her best to sound normal. "I'm fine."

"No, you're not. Listen, Maggie, I didn't plan any of this and neither did Deirdre. It happened. And now…"

"Now you're in love with her." It was a statement, not a question, and though the tears continued to pour from her eyes, her sinuses had not yet swollen so she sounded almost unaffected.

Ben moaned in frustration. "No, I'm not in love with her…I

mean, well…I don't know *what* I am."

"Ben, don't be afraid to admit the truth. You've spent a lot of time with her lately; it's only normal that you two would become closer."

"I don't want to lose you, Maggie. I love you. But…"

Here it came, the part where he would ask for time away and promise that maybe someday things would work out. From the beginning Maggie had done her best to avoid this. But here she was: completely in love with him, plans made in her mind to spend the rest of her life with him…and now he was pulling the plug. That was more than Maggie could bear.

She grabbed a tissue and wiped at her eyes as Ben mumbled the very things Maggie had known he would say. She caught the key words. *Time apart. Maybe later. Deirdre needs me.* None of it was important. The relationship she and Ben had started—the one she had believed God had brought about as an answer to years of prayer—was over before it had ever really begun.

Dr. Camas eyed Maggie thoughtfully. "You're married to him now; is that correct?"

"Not for long. I want a divorce."

There was no obvious change of expression on Dr. Camas's face. "Really?"

Maggie remembered the admitting nurse's information that Orchards was a Christian facility. She hadn't seen many overt signs of this, but there was a sense of God's Spirit everywhere. The doctor's question only added to that.

"There's more to the story. When Ben left, I figured God didn't have someone special for me, after all. I did—" Her voice broke and tears came harder. "I did some terrible things, Doctor. Things Ben doesn't know about."

Again there was no look of shock or condemnation. Instead, Dr. Camas gently patted Maggie's hand. "I think we've gotten through enough for today. Maybe you'd like to tell me about that time in your life when we meet tomorrow?"

A chill passed over Maggie and she forced back a sense of panic that suddenly threatened to overtake her. The session was over; nightfall was near. And the monsters that tortured her in the darkest hours were more tenacious than ever, reminding her exactly how worthless she was.

"Yes, that's fine." She wiped her eyes once more and stood to leave.

Outside Dr. Camas's office the desperation was waiting for her. *Help me, Lord…is this depression? What's wrong with me?* She'd heard a few of the nurses mention that she was being treated for depression and the thought appalled her. What did she have to be depressed about? She had a husband and a God who loved her. She should be filled with joy at all times, in all situations. Wasn't that what the Bible said?

She was halfway back to her room when she saw the little girl. The same one, with long, curly blond hair and questioning blue eyes. She was holding hands with a woman near the front desk, and Maggie stopped in her tracks. Resisting the impulse to run and take hold of the child, Maggie fell against the wall and froze in place.

Blink, Maggie. Blink until she disappears. It isn't her…it can't be.

The advice seemed simple enough, and she followed it willingly. Her eyes snapped shut once, twice, and on the third time the child became a dark-haired little boy. Maggie pulled in quick, short gulps of air and stared wide-eyed down the hallway toward her room. Despite the medicine and counseling and safety of Orchards Hospital, she was still out of her mind. Why else would the little girl have followed her here?

Her entire body trembled and she felt lightheaded as she forced herself to move. *You can do it, Maggie. One foot forward, another…another.* As she walked back to her bedroom, the place where the nightly battle with the forces of desperation would take place, she wondered for the hundredth time since coming to Orchards if there was anything anyone could do to help her escape the darkness. But even as the question came to mind she knew the answer.

It was as clear as the image of the little girl had been moments ago.

The feeling of doom had already consumed her, and the light—whatever light there had ever been—had been snuffed out long ago.

Twelve

IT WAS A FULL MOON THAT NIGHT AND BEN FIGURED HE COULD find Topper's Pop Bar without a map. It was in a rough part of Cleveland, where graffiti marked the vacant office buildings and convenience stores were operated by gun-toting clerks. A neighborhood where more than the usual number of homeless people milled about or lay on bus stop benches.

Ben spotted a used car lot that boasted, "All our cars run!" and he kept driving. Down another block he saw a cheap, 1970s-style neon sign blinking the words "Booze" and "Buds."

Ben took a steadying breath and pulled his car into the lot. He paused for a minute and hung his head. *It's now or never, God.* He climbed out, set his car alarm, and crossed the parking lot. Inside, the bar was nearly black with only a haze of light and swirling cigarette smoke, through which the silhouettes of people could be seen. Ben waited while his eyes adjusted, then made his way to the bar.

"Whaddya want?" The bartender was a short man with an attitude twice his size.

Ben figured the man must have failed the customer service aspect of his job training. *How does a dive like this stay open?* "Yeah. How 'bout a soda water with a squeeze of lemon." With his eyes adjusted to the light, Ben could clearly see the man's incredulous expression.

The bartender poked his coworker, who was also pouring drinks. "Get a load of this…rich guy here wants a *soda water with lemon.* Do you buy that? Soda water with lemon?" The short man turned his attention back to Ben. "What are ya, Mormon or something, pal? Need a break from the wifey—"

"Wifies," the second bartender interrupted. He leaned over

135

the bar and sized up Ben as though he were an alien. "Those Mormon boys have lots of wives."

"Listen, buddy," the short one said. "If you've got lots of wives you better have a double at least."

Ben was not afraid of the men, but he was growing tired of their noise. He stared at the short one first and then the one who had joined him. "Listen, I said I want a soda water with lemon. If that doesn't work for you, I'll take my business somewhere else." He thought he'd dressed down for the occasion but he could see that his tailor-made trousers and knit pullover still made him stand out among the patrons.

The taller bartender stuck out his hand and angled it back and forth. "Scare me, rich boy."

Ben was tempted to go behind the bar and get the drink himself when the bartenders suddenly stopped hassling him and returned to serving customers.

"Hey, sorry 'bout that…" A man in a pinstriped suit appeared at Ben's elbow. He was dark and handsome, and something told Ben he'd found the man he was looking for. "The boys think they're funny, but they get a little carried away sometimes. Did you, uh, come for anything else?"

Madeline Johnson's words flashed in Ben's mind. *He's into some nasty things, Ben…be careful.* Ben frowned. Wasn't there an article that appeared in the *Cleveland Gazette* not long ago? It had said that bars often were sites of heavy-duty drug smuggling. The sale of beer and other alcohol only helped the success of the cover-up. Shady characters frequented bars all the time, so if one showed up and left with a case of something, most people would assume it was alcohol.

Ben cleared his throat. He wouldn't be surprised at all to find out this was such a place.

"Actually, I'm looking for John McFadden."

"That's me. Did Bobby send you?"

"No…I'm here on my own." His soda water arrived and Ben took a sip. He noticed that the man in the suit was built like an athlete. Odd, but he even thought they resembled each other. *So this is the man, huh, Maggie? The one you hid from me all these years, the one who—*

"Good…good. What can I get for you?"

Again Ben had the sense that McFadden was offering more than alcoholic beverages, but none of that mattered now. He was here because of Maggie, not to uncover a drug smuggling ring. "This is going to seem a little strange, Mr. McFadden, but I need to ask you a few questions about Maggie Johnson."

Ben prided himself on being able to read people, and the moment he mentioned Maggie's name any doubts that he had the right man dissolved instantly. A look of recognition came across McFadden's dark face, followed quickly by deep suspicion. "What about her?"

"I'm married to her." He hesitated. "Maggie's…well, lately she's been having some trouble. Her mother told me the two of you used to see each other."

John held up his hands in mock surrender. "Hey, man, I don't have AIDS or nothing, if that's what you want to know. Me and Maggie only dated for a little while. Not like we were lovers for a year or none of that…"

Everything about Topper's Pop and John McFadden and the atmosphere in the bar felt like an assault on Ben's spirit. A dozen unspoken warnings told Ben to turn around and leave, but he was sure this man held part of the secret to Maggie's past. *Give me strength, God. Please.*

"I'm not here to get a health report on you." Ben paused and slid his hand into his pocket. "I need to know if there's anything you can tell me about Maggie, anything that happened during the time you two were together that she might still be troubled by now, eight years later."

McFadden leaned casually against the bar and sized up Ben much the way the bartenders had earlier. "What's it to you?"

Ben was confused at first. "She's my wife. I need to know."

"No…what I mean is what's it to you; how much you willing to pay?"

Anger flared through Ben, burning his chest and throat. He straightened to face the man, squaring his legs and crossing his arms. "I didn't come here to bribe you. I came here to find out about my wife."

John shrugged and a slow grin spread across his face. "Those are the kinds of things that sometimes go together." He held out his hands, palm up, raising and lowering them as if weighing something. "Information on Maggie, money; information on Maggie, money."

"All right, look. I'll give you a hundred dollars. It's here in my pocket. All you need to do is tell me what happened that year. Anything, any details you remember about Maggie."

Now it was the man's turn to stand straight and as he did he took a step closer so that he was only inches from Ben's face. "No deal, friend. Why don't you take your questions and your lousy hundred dollars and get lost." He spun around, shouted several orders to the bartenders, and disappeared into a backroom.

Ben watched him go, fighting the urge to chase the man down, tackle him to the floor and…

Instead, he pulled out a business card and set it on the bar with a five-dollar bill. "Here. For the soda." The short man took the five and started to get change but Ben stopped him. "Keep it. And give my card to your boss, will you?"

The bartender looked pleased with the tip and took the card gladly. "Hey, rich boy, you come on back anytime you want. We'll serve you up the best soda water in town."

There was a chorus of laughter behind the bar but Ben didn't bother to acknowledge it. *Cretins.* He left and headed back to the parking lot. *How do people have fun in places like that?* Outside, he spotted three or four men unloading a crate full of boxes from the back of an unmarked blue van. Ben recognized John McFadden as one of them, and at that instant their eyes met. McFadden whispered something to the other men and then vanished into the storage facility.

God, this place gives me the creeps. He knows something about Maggie and he won't tell me. Help me, Lord. At the last second, before reaching his car, Ben changed directions and headed toward the blue van and the men still working with the boxes.

"Get lost, buddy!" one of the men shouted as Ben approached. "This is private property."

"I'm looking for Mr. McFadden. We weren't finished talking." Ben continued toward the man but before he could ask another question something came crashing down on his head. His knees buckled and he fell to the ground, his body screaming, writhing in pain. Instinctively he reached for his head and felt a pulsating, warm, wetness in his hair.

Blood! I'm bleeding. Help me, God; I don't want to die here.

He covered his head protectively with his hands. "What do you want?" He shouted the question, but there was no answer. He couldn't move, couldn't see clearly. He thought of Maggie and how if he bled to death here in the parking lot of this bar she would never know why, never realize that he was only here because he loved her. At that instant a second blow connected with his skull and one of his hands, and he felt the searing pain of his fingers breaking. "Stop! I'll give you whatever you want…"

Ben had considered bringing his handgun with him tonight but he figured John McFadden wouldn't be antagonistic—certainly not to the point of harming him. Now as he lay there, two sets of feet walked past him. One foot kicked him in the head, and then the feet all walked toward the van and inside the warehouse.

In the distance he heard another set of footsteps, this time growing closer. *They're going to kill me. Lord, take me quickly. And please, God, let Maggie know I love her. Whatever it was she did or lied about I love her.*

His head was pounding and he felt himself losing consciousness. How much blood had he lost anyway? And how much longer would it be?

The steps were closer now, and he could make out the shoes. They stopped inches from his face. "Give me the hundred dollars."

Ben struggled to make sense of the words and realized they were coming from John McFadden. Apparently he had ordered the beating. Ben's reflexes were slow, and pain seemed to assault him from every part of his body. But he managed to slip his good hand into his pocket and retrieve the hundred-dollar bill. There was almost no strength left in his arms, but he held it out for him anyway.

"What...what do you want from me?"

"I want you to leave me alone and never come back." McFadden's words were more of a hiss and they held a threat Ben knew was worth taking seriously. If he lived long enough to worry about it. "Are you getting this, Ben Stovall, *attorney* at law?"

The man had Ben's business card. Whatever McFadden's staff was involved in, they communicated directly to the man leaning over Ben, and apparently he didn't take kindly to curious lawyers. Ben struggled to stay conscious.

"Now listen and listen good." McFadden jerked Ben to his feet and walked him across the parking lot to his car. The pain came in white-hot waves, and Ben was sure he'd lose consciousness soon. "You will get in your car and drive yourself to the hospital. You will report the news that you took a bad fall and you will never, ever set foot on my property again. Is that understood?"

Ben nodded. "Yes...let me go." He was woozy and his eyesight alternated between blurred and double vision. Something dangerous and secretive was going on at Topper's Pop Bar. Something much more secretive than whatever John McFadden knew about Maggie. Half expecting to be shot or beaten again, Ben pulled free of the man's grip. Was it possible? Was McFadden going to let him drive off the lot with his body still functioning?

Help me, God; get me to the hospital before I lose too much blood. I can't die without seeing Maggie one more time, without telling her I love her no matter what she's done...

The man shoved Ben into his car and hunched down so that Ben could see him as he spoke. "Oh yeah. Your information...I almost forgot." He smiled wickedly as if whatever he was about to tell Ben was going to bring him a great deal of satisfaction. "Maggie and I had a kid." He chuckled. "But you probably already knew that."

Ben's heart dropped, and his body was hit by a wave of pain far greater than any he'd received so far. His eyes grew wide and he stared at John McFadden in disbelief. "You...*what?*" It was impossible. Maggie was a virgin when they married...she couldn't have slept with...with this man. There couldn't have been a baby...not with his Maggie.

The man tossed his head back and laughed. "You mean she didn't tell you? Sweet little church girl like Maggie, and she didn't tell you she gave a kid away? Imagine that."

Someone called McFadden's name and he was suddenly on alert again. "Now get out of here. You come back, and I'll finish you off myself." He slammed the driver's door and kicked it hard with the heel of his boot before turning and walking away.

Ben did not hesitate. He started the engine, peeled out of the parking lot and headed immediately for Cleveland General. His head was still bleeding badly and his body was racked with pain. There were moments when he felt himself drifting, but still he drove on.

In the depth of his heart, he wasn't sure he was going to make it.

Not because of the beating he'd received, but because of the other blow. If John McFadden was telling the truth—and Ben had the unnerving sense he was—then Maggie truly had lied to him from the beginning.

Determined to hang on, Ben raised his eyelids and forced himself to remain conscious. As he drove, he changed his mind. It wasn't possible. If Maggie had given a child up for adoption, certainly her mother would have known about it. The woman had said nothing about any of that. Ben felt himself growing calmer.

It was a lie. Of course it was a lie. That creep McFadden knew Maggie was a Christian and a virgin. She had probably refused to sleep with him, and he was using this false information as a way of further punishing him for spying on whatever clandestine operation was taking place in the parking lot.

He pulled into the hospital parking lot and veered his car toward the front door. Halfway to the emergency room entrance, he collapsed.

"Maggie!" He shouted her name as loud as he could, and all around him he heard people responding, hurrying toward him, trying to help. Blood covered his face and hands now and he felt himself slipping away.

"Sir, sir, what happened? Can you talk to us, sir?" Someone in a white jacket bent over him as he was placed onto a stretcher and hurried into the emergency room. But the sounds and sights were growing dimmer, and Ben couldn't make his mouth work. *Tell Maggie I love her. Please tell her. Oh, God, please.*

Then everything disappeared and there was nothing but darkness.

Thirteen

DESPITE THE CHILL IN THE AIR THAT LATE SEPTEMBER AFTERNOON, Amanda Joy walked home from the bus stop slower than usual. Things had gotten worse at the Graystone house; two of the foster kids had even talked about running away. It wasn't that the old lady was always mean. But when chores weren't done just so, Mrs. Graystone would change into…well, a monster.

And then the beatings would begin.

Amanda pushed the thought away. She didn't want to think about that; she just knew she didn't want to be anywhere near the woman. Chores had been assigned that morning—fold a load of laundry, make her bed, clean her windows, and wash the walls in her bedroom—but Amanda's second-grade teacher had assigned a science project and much of her morning had gone toward finishing it.

Surely Mrs. Graystone wanted her to get her homework done, didn't she? She wouldn't punish Amanda this time, would she?

She slowed her pace even more, kicking up fallen leaves and stopping briefly to stare into the cloudy sky. *Are You there, God? Isn't there somewhere else I can live?* She waited, but the only sound was the rustling of leaves in the trees overhead. *I don't really need a mother, God. I'd be happy to live with Kathy and her family. Or just someone who liked me a little.*

There were no booming answers, no voices from heaven, but Amanda had the distinct feeling someone had hugged her close. The only one who hugged her now was Kathy, and Kathy hadn't seen her all week. So this hug, this feeling of being warm and safe in the arms of someone who loved her, must have come from God. She glanced once more toward the sky. *Thanks, God. I know You're working on it.*

By the time she walked through the door at the Graystone house, the other children were busy doing homework or cleaning. With her arrival, they stopped and stared at her, and the mixture of fear and warning she saw in their eyes made her heart pound.

"Hi." Amanda set her things down and heard heavy footsteps coming closer. Mrs. Graystone marched into the room and headed straight for her.

"I'm sorry about my chores…" Amanda took two steps backward until she was up against the wall. Her eyes were wide; her breathing was fast; and her arms and legs began to shake.

"You're a good for nothing, *brat!*"

"I'm s-s-sorry, I had to f-f-finish—"

"Shut up! You sound like an idiot when you stutter." Mrs. Graystone was upon her, yanking her by the hair and dragging her from the room. Amanda Joy knew better than to fight the old woman and she moved her feet in quick shuffling steps so the pain in her scalp would be less severe. Mrs. Graystone's breath was strong, sickening…like it sometimes was late at night, when her words didn't make sense. What was happening? Was Mrs. Graystone sick?

In the background Amanda Joy heard one of her foster sisters begin to cry. Chores had gone undone before, but Mrs. Graystone had never acted like this. Why did the other kids look so scared?

Mrs. Graystone flung her into her bedroom and closed the door behind them. Amanda regained her balance and then stood still, head down, waiting for her punishment.

"When I tell you to do something, I want you to *do* it, do you understand me?"

Before the girl could raise her head, the woman yanked her hair so she could see her face. "*Look* at me when I talk to you!"

Amanda winced. Mrs. Graystone seemed fine but her breath had that strong, funny smell. "Yes, m-m-ma'am." Amanda shook from head to toe. Whatever was wrong, it scared her to death.

"Oh, so you're gonna play scaredy-cat around me, is that it, missy? Well, I'll give you somethin' to be scared about."

Before Amanda could think or cover her face, Mrs. Graystone's palm hit her hard across the cheek.

"Stop!" Amanda froze, terror seizing her. She knew the moment she'd let the scream out that her punishment would—

A second slap hit her face so hard it knocked her to the ground. Mrs. Graystone looked furious—and crazy. She yanked Amanda's hair and pulled her to her feet.

"I will not have a brat under my roof who can't carry her own weight, am I making myself clear?"

Amanda felt dizzy, and her vision was fuzzy around the edges. She wanted to answer, but the words seemed stuck in her throat somewhere. Before she could make herself respond, she heard a hissing sound and felt a terrible burning sensation in her eyes. She screamed. "M-m-my eyes! Oh, my eyes…!"

At the same moment she smelled the fumes and realized that Mrs. Graystone had sprayed cleaner at her face. "Help m-m-me!"

The words came out loud and shrill, and Amanda prayed someone would come take her away before—

"You're a filthy excuse for a girl!" the woman shouted at her. "I'll clean you up and maybe you'll be worth something some-day."

"No, p-p-please! Stop!"

Another cloud of cleaner came at Amanda; the liquid and fumes filled her nose and throat and made her gag. "I can't b-b-breathe…"

"Shut up!" Amanda heard the bottle hit the wall, but before she could be grateful the cleaner was gone Mrs. Graystone slapped her across the face even harder than before. Amanda fell flat on the floor. There was something wet running from her nose and mouth, and she ran her fingers over it. Forcing her burning eyes open, she saw blood.

God, help…I'm bleeding.

"I hope you're ready!" Mrs. Graystone jerked her up from the floor by her hair again, and Amanda's entire head flamed in searing pain. She scrambled to her feet and realized she was crying. Big, gulping sobs. Her blood mixed with tears and bright red drops began to fall on the floor.

"Please, s-s-stop!" She continued to shout, terrified now that the only way out of the room alive was if someone heard her. "Help me!"

Mrs. Graystone's face grew hard and hateful, and her eyes blazed with something scary and evil. Amanda closed her eyes. Her entire body hurt and she was sick from the cleaner, struggling for every breath. The blows just kept coming, making her feel dizzy.

She was going to die.

Mrs. Graystone paused and glared at Amanda where she was huddled on the floor now. This time her voice was barely more than a whisper. "You better be ready, little girl, because it's time for your punishment to begin."

Carol Jenson stared out her window to the house next door.

Many times she had wondered about the goings-on there. Too many children under one roof for one thing. But she almost never saw them playing outside. She'd heard from other neighbors that the Graystones were foster parents. Well, what kind of parents kept their children indoors every day, even when the sun was shining?

And there was something else, a feeling or sense of some kind that she couldn't put her finger on. The children were sometimes bruised and withdrawn…

Carol was almost sure they'd been beaten, but she'd never

said anything. After all, bruises could be caused by a fall on the playground, a fight at school.

Still, whatever was happening at the Graystones, it had kept Carol up at nights on many occasions praying for the children who lived there.

Sometimes she would bring Mrs. Graystone baked goods or stop by with a piece of misdirected mail, hoping to catch her in the act if there was indeed abuse going on. That way she could report the situation and rest assured that the children would be taken care of.

If Carol had been concerned before, she was doubly worried now after reading the series of "Maggie's Mind" columns in the *Gazette*. Carol and her husband had one child, an infant, who at the moment was sleeping soundly in her crib. They were churchgoing folk, who lived a quiet, clean life and enjoyed the weekly wisdom in "Maggie's Mind." When Carol had caught the words "Children Sometimes Abused in Foster Homes" in a recent column headline, she had read it twice through. Foster homes, the article said, were often every bit as abusive as the homes children were taken from.

It was for that reason Carol was particularly sensitive to noises or actions or anything out of the ordinary coming from the Graystone house of late. Earlier, just after putting her baby down, Carol noticed a sad little girl making her way slowly to the house next door. She was fairly new, but Carol had seen her before.

This time something about the girl's walk caught Carol's eye. In that moment she'd had the desperate desire to intercept the sweet-faced little thing and ask her point-blank if there was someone hurting her or making her afraid of going home. But then Carol had to remind herself that it was none of her business—at least until she had more than suspicion to go on. Maybe the children didn't like playing outside. Maybe they were little couch potatoes who preferred video games and television programs to outdoor play.

With a sigh, Carol went to finish folding a load of laundry. But no sooner had she pulled a towel from the basket than she heard a sound that sent chills through her. It was a scream. She was sure of it. A muffled scream, coming from next door.

She dropped the towel in her hands and hurried to the nearest window. Unlatching the lock, she raised the glass pane and listened.

A woman was yelling, probably Mrs. Graystone. Carol couldn't hear everything but she was able to understand key words. "Shut up!" and "brat" sounded loud and clear. And in between the angry words Carol was sure she could hear the faint screams of a child. As she listened, the exchange grew more heated, the child's cries more desperate.

Should I call, Lord? Is this really what I think it is?

The response came with a sense of urgency unlike anything Carol had experienced.

Call now, daughter. Call!

Without hesitation or worrying about the ramifications if she were somehow mistaken, Carol grabbed her cordless telephone and dialed 911.

Officer Willy Parsons and his partner arrived at the home less than five minutes later. He had been investigating a nearby breaking-and-entering when the call came in: Suspected child abuse.

Parsons gritted his teeth, yelled to his partner, and ran for the patrol car. The idea that anyone would be deranged enough to harm a child was almost more than he could stomach. When he'd joined the police force ten years earlier it had been because of an article he'd read in the paper stating that child abuse was on the rise.

The two officers parked and ran to the front door. Parsons knocked sharply. "Police! Open up!"

A woman answered the door looking disheveled and

overexerted. "Whaddya want?" She ran her tongue nervously over her bottom lip, and Parsons noticed a layer of perspiration on her face and arms—and the strong smell of alcohol on her breath.

"We have a report from one of your neighbors of domestic violence, ma'am. We'd like to come in and take a look around."

Anger flashed in the woman's eyes, then faded as she laughed lightly. "It's just me and the children." She motioned to the dining room table, where four children sat quietly doing homework.

"Ma'am, our records show this is a foster home, is that right?"

The woman attempted a smile. "Why, yes. I like to help out whatever way I can. All my children are from the foster system."

Officer Parsons squeezed his way past her. "Then since you have wards of the state in your care, I'm sure you know the rules. We're able to check out your home environment whenever any concerns arise."

"Well, yes, but..." Her voice faded. "The children are all here."

At that moment, from the back of the house, there was a strange noise. Parsons cocked his head. What was it? The sound was a moan or a cry, like something from an animal. One that was wounded...

Or dying.

Chills passed over him and took up residence deep in his soul. There it was again. The sound echoed through the hallway, and suddenly Officer Parsons was propelled by a terrifying thought. He pushed past the woman and ran down the hallway, shoving bedroom doors open until he saw her.

"Dear God..."

At first glance, it looked like a bundle of red-stained rags lying in a heap on the floor, but then the bundle moved. And moaned. In that instant it became horrifyingly clear that what the officer was looking at was a child…a small, frail child in torn, blood-covered clothes.

He hurried to the little girl's side and looked intently into her eyes. "Hang on, little one. Everything's going to be okay." Then he turned around and yelled for his partner. "Get an ambulance here quick! And cuff the suspect! I don't want her to run."

He turned his attention back to the girl. She was six, maybe seven years old, and she lay in a pool of blood and vomit. Her face was swollen and cut beyond recognition, and grotesque, hand-shaped bruises covered her arms and upper torso. Wads of the girl's hair lay on the floor nearby, and the room reeked of household cleaner.

Parsons knelt over the girl, feeling for a pulse. It was rapid and shallow. She was in shock; each breath was labored. The child's left eye was swollen shut, but Parsons thought she could see something through her right eye. "How are you doing, sweetheart? Can you hear me?"

The girl groaned softly and muttered something about her head. She struggled for every breath.

"Your head hurts?" Parsons wanted to go back in the other room and tear the woman limb from limb. But right now the battered girl needed him, and he tried to keep his thoughts focused on her.

She moved her head slowly up and down, and Parsons could see fresh tears falling from her eyes. "Help me…" This time the girl's words were clearer. "I can't…breathe."

Parsons ran his fingers gently over her hair and leaned his face closer. "It's okay, honey, we're going to get you help real quick here." His eyes searched the room and spotted a bottle of cleaner on the floor near the bed. "Did someone spray cleaner at you, sweetheart?"

The girl coughed and winced in pain. "My head hurts."

"I know…it'll be better soon, I promise."

She moaned again, her breathing dangerously strained.

"She sprayed it…in my eyes…and mouth."

Parsons felt his heart constrict. *How could anyone…?* He couldn't finish the thought. There was no telling what horrific things the woman had done to this girl. She looked like she was suffering from a concussion, possibly several broken bones. Stitches would be needed to close the gashes on her cheek, forehead, and arm. On top of everything else, she was in dire need of oxygen, suffocating from the effects of being forced to inhale the cleaner.

Officer Parsons did not consider himself a religious man, but he liked to think God listened to him anyway. And now, as the sirens closed in and paramedics scrambled through the house with their equipment, he begged God to let the girl live. And to somehow help her find a real home.

"Sweetie, the medics are here now. They'll take care of you, okay?" He took her small hand in his and stroked her knuckles tenderly. "Hang in there for me, okay, honey?"

The girl was breathing too hard to answer him, but from somewhere in her battered body she summoned the strength to squeeze his hand. Parsons had to wipe tears off his cheeks as he left the bedroom and searched for his partner.

Now that the woman had been caught, she was belligerent as they led her to the patrol car. His partner informed him that the girl's social worker—a woman named Kathy Garrett—had been told of the girl's condition and would meet them at the hospital. If the girl lived, she would be placed in Kathy's home indefinitely.

Parsons helped his partner squeeze the woman into the patrol car, and then he stuck his face inches from hers. "You're lucky you get a trial in this country…" He spat the words, and she struggled to put distance between the two of them.

He studied her, this creature that was more beast than woman. "If I had my way, I'd—" He choked back the rest of what he wanted to say. His anger was getting the better of him. With a ragged draw of breath he shot her a final glare. "God have mercy on your rotten soul, lady."

They were loading the girl into the ambulance, and Officer Parsons left the patrol car to check on her.

In whispered tones, the lead medic told him the news. "She's in bad shape, but we're hopeful. If we can keep her heart rate steady and if she doesn't have too much bleeding in the brain she might make it."

A woman walked up, and Officer Parsons saw that she was crying.

"I'm Carol. I live next door."

"Are you the one who made the call?" Parsons stepped aside so they could talk.

"Yes...I feel awful. I should have called days ago, weeks ago. I always knew things weren't right here and that something bad was—"

He shook his head, placing a gentle hand on her arm. "You can't do that to yourself, ma'am. You called today; that's all that matters."

The woman nodded and looked wide-eyed into the ambulance, where the medics were still working to stabilize the girl. "Is she...will she be okay?"

There were tears in his eyes as he answered. Like most officers he did his best to stay detached from the crime scenes he worked. But this was more than a crime scene. It was a little girl clinging to life because of circumstances completely out of her control. He blinked back his tears and stared kindly at the woman. "If she lives, it'll be because of you."

A moaning sound came from the ambulance, and Officer Parsons was at the girl's side in an instant.

"Kathy...want Kathy..." The tiny voice quivered.

The medics shrugged and looked at Parsons as he nodded his understanding. The girl wanted her social worker. "Kathy Garrett? Is that who you want, honey?"

The girl moved her head up and down a few inches.

"Listen, sweetheart. Kathy's going to meet you at the hospital. She's there now, waiting for you, okay?"

Through the blood and bruises and swollen tissue, Parsons thought he saw the girl smile. There wasn't a reason in the world for this child to be happy, and yet she was smiling. Again she struggled to speak. "I'm okay…I know it." Her words were slow and deliberate, punctuated with pain and raspy breaths, but she continued to speak anyway, and the team of professionals around her listened intently. "I prayed to leave here…and so…" She took a deep breath and flinched from the pain. "Everything's okay…because now…" She moved her fingers to her face and lightly touched the broken areas. "I get to be with Kathy…"

There were tears streaming down the faces of the three men as they huddled around the child, the medics working furiously to hook up an intravenous line while Parsons did his best to keep her calm. She was trying to finish her thought when Parsons saw it again—a hint of a smile on the girl's broken face.

"I don't have a mommy. I have Kathy. If I can be with her…then God must have heard my prayers…" Fresh tears flowed from the girl's swollen eyes, and Parsons had the feeling they were almost tears of joy. "And if He heard my prayers, then maybe…maybe He loves me."

The three men were speechless.

Parsons squeezed the girl's hand in his. What could he say to a girl who'd been beaten to within a breath of her life, a girl who could still find it within her to smile—and beyond that…to feel loved by God? His throat was too thick to speak so he clung tightly to her small fingers—his tears falling softly on the girl's long blond hair—while the medics completed their work.

Less than a minute later, they were ready to transport her and one of them checked her vitals. "We're losing her," he whispered to his partner. "Let's get this thing out of here."

Parsons released the hold he had on the child's hand and pulled himself out of the ambulance, praying that the beaten little girl without a home or a mother or a chance in the world was somehow right.

That maybe God really did love her, after all.

Fourteen

THAT NIGHT, FOR THE FIRST TIME IN A LONG TIME, MAGGIE WASN'T tortured by demons spewing taunts of condemnation and blackest darkness. The doom and fear were gone, and in their place was a meadow with endless acres of summer grass and wildflowers. In the distance a child was frolicking about, chasing a butterfly or dandelion dust in the breeze.

Who are you, little girl?

Maggie squinted in the sunlight, and though her feet were not moving, her body was suddenly propelled to within feet of the girl. It was her! Of course it was! *Sweet child, why are you here? How can I help you?*

The little girl stopped what she was doing and turned. Her cotton dress danced on the gentle stir of wind in the air and she smiled at Maggie. "Hi."

Maggie wanted to get closer but her feet were stuck and she looked down. *What in the—? Who put shackles on my feet?* Thick, heavy iron cuffs held her legs in place and prevented her from getting closer. "Who are you, honey?"

The girl tilted her head, and Maggie was struck by her face, innocent and so much like… No, it couldn't be!

The girl opened her small mouth and said something, but Maggie couldn't hear her. "What, sweetheart? I can't hear you. I want to help…what can I do?" Maggie strained against the chains until she felt the skin on her shins shredding.

Again the girl spoke and though she couldn't hear her, Maggie could read her mouth. "I want my mommy…my mommy…my mommy." Then the girl began to cry.

Suddenly, Maggie was sure that the child's mother, or

maybe even—*It can't be…it's impossible.* "Don't cry, honey. I'm here…"

She shouted the words but they were lost on the breeze, and the image of the girl began to fade. *No…don't go. Not yet…I have to talk to you. I still don't know who you are…Wait!*

Then the scene changed.

She was in a hospital room and the air was filled with quiet strains of lullaby music. *Jesus loves me this I know, for the Bible tells me so…* Maggie cradled the infant girl tenderly, and around her the entire room was painted in soft pastels. Gently, quietly nuzzling the baby's cheek, Maggie rocked her back and forth, back and forth.

Then the music changed and became suspenseful, faster and faster giving Maggie the feeling something was about to overtake her and the infant, both. About that time someone burst into the room dressed in a black hooded gown. A quick glance told Maggie it was John McFadden, hidden by a cloak and carrying a hatchet in his hands. The music grew faster, more intense, more frightening as he moved closer.

In the dream, Maggie held the baby tighter and heard herself screaming. "I have to save her! Get away from me. Please! Someone help me!" But the figure moved closer still and raised the hatchet over his head. Maggie knew if it came down it would be on the baby in Maggie's arms.

Suddenly another figure entered from the other side of the room, and Maggie spun around to see a nurse. She stared at Maggie with vacant eyes, her face utterly expressionless. Then, in a slow, robotic manner, she made her way toward Maggie.

Again the music grew louder, and suddenly the baby began to speak. "Mommy, don't do it. Don't leave me, Mommy. I need you."

Her words were perfect and articulate, and Maggie felt herself flooded with confusion. The dark figure still loomed at her side while the nurse moved steadily closer, only now the face on the dark man beside her was not John's, but Ben's. Robed in midnight, her husband Ben held the hatchet over Maggie and the baby, but instead of John's sinister expression, Ben's face was filled with godliness, his eyes glowing with the light of the Lord.

"It's time to break the ties. For me, Maggie. It's time. Decide who you love more. Come on, it's time…"

Then she looked and saw a thick piece of twine tying her hand to the baby's. "Somebody stop that awful music!" But no one was listening to her. Before she could stop him, Ben brought the hatchet down on the center of the cord so that the baby and Maggie were no longer tied together. With that, the hatchet became a white dove that flew through an opening in the window.

The nurse tapped her on the shoulder. "Give her to me. Give her to me. Give her to me…"

That's when Maggie saw it wasn't a nurse at all, but a machine—an unfeeling, uncaring, cold-blooded machine with glowing electric eyes and a hinged mouth.

"Don't do it, Mommy, please!" The infant was speaking again, crying for Maggie to hold on, and she did so with all her strength. But Ben took her arm and began pulling her away.

"It's for the best, Maggie. Let her go." Without waiting for Maggie's response, he pulled harder. At the same time, the nurse grabbed the baby from her arms and spun in the other direction, moving mechanically toward a narrow door.

"Wait! Don't take her from me…" Maggie began sobbing hysterically, desperate for the feel of the baby in her arms once more. "Bring her back…please!"

But Ben was relentless. His eyes still glowing with faith and hope and love, his clothing black as the terrors of night, he tightened his grip on her arm and moved her from the room.

When they walked out the door, there was no longer a floor to step onto, but a sharp cliff leading to a deep, dark, deadly canyon. The music was almost deafening now, and in that instant she and Ben began to fall—

Maggie awoke with a start, sitting straight up in bed. The sheets were drenched in perspiration and she was trembling violently from the inside out. Where was she? Her eyes darted about the room and her breathing came fast and hard. Where was the baby? The little girl? Ben?

The fog began to clear and she forced herself to exhale. *Calm down. It was only a dream.* "Dear God, why?" The words escaped from her like the cry of a wounded animal. How could she have done it? Handed her baby over to the state's foster system all so she could...

Maggie climbed out of bed as her eyes darted around the room. The red glowing numbers on the clock told her it was five in the morning. Sweat continued to drip from her forehead, and she realized she was in the middle of a panic attack. She needed something, another pill or a doctor. Something.

Her eyes fell on the Bible sitting in the center of her bedside table. She had noticed it before but had never felt the need to open it. She could talk to God if she needed help. What more could His Word do for her at this point? After all, it hadn't brought her peace and joy and it hadn't prevented her from falling apart and being admitted to a mental hospital. No, she didn't need the Bible. She needed medication.

Her eyes searched the room again, focusing on a meal tray from last night. It lay on the floor, near her bed. Maggie rushed to it, rifling through the dirty items. Maybe she'd forgotten to take her antianxiety pill. She knocked over a glass of water in her haste and huffed in frustration. There were no pills on the tray. She pushed the nurse's call button.

After a beat, Maggie heard the nurse's voice. "Mrs. Stovall, can I help you?"

"Yes! I'm...uh, not doing very well here. I think I need...maybe you can get me one of those pills, okay?" Her voice shook from the fear raging through her.

"Mrs. Stovall, I'm afraid it's not time for that medication yet. It's very important that you don't take too much. Remember, the goal is to help you live without the medication if at all possible."

"It isn't possible!" she screamed. *What am I doing? Why can't I get a grip here, God?*

Joy will come in the morning. My word is a lamp unto your feet and a light unto your path...

The Bible. God wants me to read the Bible. Maggie's heart rate slowed considerably, and she stared at the intercom in her hand. "Never mind. I think I'll just...I'm sorry. Never mind."

Maggie dropped the device and moved slowly around the bed to the portable table. Was it still true, even after all the ways in which she'd failed everyone who mattered in her life? Could God's Word still light her path?

She remembered her father saying if people really wanted a friend in Jesus, they needed to get friendly with the Gospels. Flipping the pages gingerly, Maggie allowed herself to remember the thin, crinkly feel of them between her fingers—and the peace that spending time within them had once brought. She stopped at the book of Matthew and skimmed past the genealogy of Christ. Then she began to read in earnest.

Her sweating stopped and her trembling body stilled as she drew in the wonder of God's truth for the first time in months.

Nine hours later when she sat in Dr. Camas's office she was convinced there was still power in God's Word.

"I'm ready to finish the story." She sat straighter in the chair and though she had barely been at Orchards a week, Maggie had the faintest feeling that something inside her was learning to cope. If lies were like a wound to the soul, Maggie's had been festering for more than seven years. Only by exposing them to the light of day could the raw place inside her ever begin to heal.

Dr. Camas leaned back in his chair and his eyes offered encouragement. "Go ahead, Mrs. Stovall."

"Maggie. You can call me Maggie."

The corners of his mouth lifted slightly. "Very well. Go ahead, Maggie. Tell me the rest."

She closed her eyes, begging God for strength. Then she did what she hadn't ever wanted to do again. She allowed herself to drift back in time to the spring of 1992, to a place of reckless abandon.

To the season she dated John McFadden.

The worst part about dating John was that she'd known from the beginning what he was about, what he stood for. Her mother always said rumors were like smoke, and where there was smoke there was usually a fire or two; and that if it looked like a duck and walked like a duck and quacked like a duck, well, it probably *was* a duck.

After the dance—the one Ben couldn't go to because of Deirdre—John called Maggie several times a week and flirted mercilessly, doing his best to get her out on a date. Maggie enjoyed his attention but refused to take him seriously. Guys like John scared her. They were experienced and worldly and would want from her the one thing she intended to keep intact: her virginity.

But by the end of the third week, Maggie felt her defenses weakening. Ben hadn't contacted her once since his devastating phone call, and she figured he and Deirdre were probably spending much of their time together. *Forget him,* Maggie thought. *Let him go; I don't have to wait around until he's engaged to have fun. Besides, I'll be careful…*

Thoughts like that consumed her and they were dangerous, Maggie knew. But she no longer cared. Ben had broken up with her; how could she believe God had a plan for her life?

With that mind-set, she found herself giggling and blushing whenever John called; and finally, four weeks after the dance when he suggested they see a movie together she agreed to go.

Maggie remembered her father's reaction like it was yesterday.

"I've heard about him, Margaret." Her father only used her

given name whenever he was deeply troubled by her actions. "He's a womanizer…not the kind of young man suitable for a girl like yourself."

He was talking about Maggie's purity, but his upbringing wouldn't allow him to spell it out for her.

"Daddy, he's fun…" She couldn't think of anything else to say.

Instead of outlining the reasons John might be bad for her, Maggie's father raised his voice to a level he rarely used. "You will *not* date John McFadden!" He stood tall and stern, his posture symbolic of the way he felt on the issue. Maggie's mother waited quietly in the background, her head bowed. Clearly she was disgraced that Maggie had even considered dating such a one. "Hear me clearly on this, Margaret. You will not date him. I absolutely forbid it."

Maggie ran to her room and cried herself to sleep and for the first time since she could remember, she refused to pray. There no longer seemed any reason. If God had taken Ben from her, then obviously He didn't mind whom she dated. There wasn't one special person for her after all. And the gift she'd once held as precious and worthy only of her husband began to feel more like a burden.

On June 12 that year Maggie turned twenty-two, and the next week she used all her savings to buy an old Honda. Despite feelings of uncertainty she moved into an apartment with two girlfriends from college. She had secretly hoped her parents might try to stop her, maybe explain to her that God still had a plan for her life and that if only she would wait on Him things would fall into place. But they did nothing of the sort.

Instead, while Maggie packed her belongings into a borrowed van, her mother mended a pile of clothes and refused even to make eye contact with her. That day, her mother's single bit of advice to Maggie had been this: "If you must go, do it quickly. And be aware that you're breaking your father's heart."

Her father clearly disapproved also, but he helped her pack her things and hugged her before she left. "I am letting you go in the grace of God, trusting that by His mercy He will one day bring you safely home."

Maggie had always wondered how much her father loved her. He was so analytical in his thinking, so devoted to things of God. Often she figured he couldn't possibly have time for thoughts of her. But that afternoon, under clear, blue summer skies, she saw tears in her father's eyes—and every question she'd ever had about his love was answered in a single moment. Her father loved her, and he was willing to let her go so that she might find out for herself the weighty importance of one's choices in life.

After that, she and John began dating in earnest. At first it seemed to Maggie that she'd made a wonderful choice. John doted on her, bringing her jewelry and flowers for no reason other than to declare his love for her. Concerns about his character and intentions vanished like fog in the morning sun. But by the end of July, their relationship grew more physical.

They'd be sitting in the front seat of his car kissing and he'd move his mouth along her neck up toward her ear, begging in raspy whispers to come up to her room for a while, promising her it would be all right. "If you really love me, you'd trust me. I'll only stay an hour…come on, Maggie."

Twice she told him no, but on the third time, Maggie thought about her roommates and knew they wouldn't mind. They had been casual friends of Maggie's at Akron University, girls who hung out at beer keg parties while Maggie attended her church's college group and weekly Bible studies. They were thrilled to see Maggie "loosening up," as they called it, and Maggie knew they wouldn't pass judgment if she had John up to her room. Besides, guys had actually spent the night in their rooms several times since Maggie had moved in.

It was the first week of August and the air was hot and heavy. As she returned John's kisses in the stuffy car, Maggie finally caught her breath and smiled at him. "All right, come up. But you have to behave yourself."

Maggie had a television in her bedroom, and that first night John kept his promise. They talked and laughed and watched late night sports on TV. But two days later the scenario was wildly different. She and John had been talking about her plans for after college when he moved closer and began kissing her. The physical sensation of being close to John, kissing him, was something she had never experienced with Ben. She felt truly alive for the first time.

That night as their kisses grew more urgent she allowed him to ease her down onto the bed. At first she convinced herself they could stop if they wanted to. But his kisses built a fire in her that grew with each passing minute.

"Trust me, Maggie. It's okay..." His whispered words of reassurance convinced her that she had nothing to lose—nothing of any real value. Instead she might actually gain something: a closer relationship with John, a better understanding of what real love was about.

And so, with those thoughts in mind, she did the one thing she had promised since junior high never to do.

The changes in John did not happen overnight as she once had feared they would if she ever gave in to him. Instead, he seemed to love her more than ever. When they spent time together in her room at night, they no longer pretended to be interested in television. Instead they did the thing that made Maggie feel better with John than she'd ever felt with anyone in her life.

Including Ben.

Her feelings for John were never the intense longings she had felt for Ben, never the love she had imagined sharing with her husband one day. Rather it was a thrilling sort of sensation, as though she were flying above the masses of regular people and had been let in on a high only a privileged few might ever experience. Later she would remember a pastor telling his congregation that the fruit Eve took from the snake must have been delicious beyond belief because the lure of it was enough to make Eve turn her back on God.

It had been the same way with John, even if Maggie didn't recognize it at the time. She thought only about how complete and whole she felt being desired by someone like him, someone who could have had his pick of girls. John filled her senses until she was satisfied beyond anything she'd ever felt, and she hoped her days with him would never end.

As time passed, Maggie had done such a good job of convincing herself what she and John were doing was okay that she rarely suffered twinges of guilt while she lay in his arms. But in the light of day…that was another story. She often had moments of gut-wrenching conviction. From nine to five, Maggie worked at a nearby clothing store so she could pay her share of the rent. Sometimes the voices that haunted her during her shift were so distracting she could barely help the customers.

Flee immorality…be pure, daughter, as I am pure…

The memory of those holy warnings snapped Maggie back to the present.

"Are you okay?" There was concern in Dr. Camas's voice and he leaned slightly forward, resting his elbows on his oak desk. "Should we take a break, perhaps?"

Maggie shook her head. "No. I was just remembering something that happened before I came here. I almost…I was nearly arrested for talking to a little girl I didn't even know. She was…she was blond, and I've been seeing her everywhere…at the market, at the park, on my computer screen at work…" She stared at him and wondered what kind of terrible person he must think her. "It was part of what led up to this, to my coming here, I guess."

Dr. Camas cocked his head and frowned, but contrary to Maggie's fears, there was no contempt in his eyes. "You can't change the past, Maggie. It happened."

"But I lied. I'm the worst possible wife ever!" She choked the words off, aware she was yelling. Taking a breath, she went on, but more calmly. "And what about my column?" Maggie felt tears stinging at her eyes again. "Like I have any room to comment on society…"

He waited and after a beat Maggie lifted her head. "Now you see why my marriage is over."

"We can talk about that later."

"I hate him for making me—"

"Maggie, try not to blame when you're talking about yourself." It was the first time Dr. Camas had given any guidelines to their discussions.

His comment stung. *It is Ben's fault, all of it.* Maggie closed her eyes angrily, and two tears trickled down her cheeks even as the truth trickled into her heart, her mind.

Much of it may well be Ben's fault, but her behavior certainly wasn't. She sucked in a slow breath and stared at the doctor. "You're right. I have my reasons for hating Ben, but I hate myself more."

"Do you want to continue the story?"

Maggie sighed. "Eventually things changed between me and John…pretty fast, actually."

"It usually does."

Dr. Camas might not say much, but Maggie had found that what he did say was generally profound.

Two weeks after Maggie had given in to John, he called her and told her he'd be gone for a few days. "I've got things to do, love."

An alarm sounded in Maggie's gut, but she took him at his word. Five days later he called again. "Hey, Maggie…I've been thinking a lot…about us and…well…"

Fear coursed through her, and she told herself it wasn't

happening. He wasn't doing to her what he'd most certainly done to so many other girls. Not when she had trusted him implicitly. "What are you saying?"

"I guess I'm saying we need time apart. I'm not ready to settle down with just one person yet." He waited a beat. "I'm sorry, Maggie."

She and John spoke just once after that, when Maggie called to tell him she was pregnant. "What do you want me to do about it?" His voice no longer held any pretense. Instead he sounded like a stranger. An angry, agitated stranger.

"It's your baby, too." She held the results of the pregnancy test in her hand, terrified of what they meant to her life and her future. Desperate to think it all a mistake.

"Can you *prove* it's my baby?" His voice was mean, full of disregard for her and the child she carried.

"Of *course* it's your baby. When did I have time to be with anyone else?"

"Come on, Maggie. You gave up the goods too easy. What's to say you weren't doing some other guy at the same time?"

A flash of terror pierced her heart. Everything her parents had warned her about was true. She'd gone against God's Word and now she was left holding the apple core of sin. She remained silent, absorbing his callous tone, sorting through her options. Abortion was out of the question. There was no way she could take the tiny life inside her for the mistakes she herself had made. She could have the baby, maybe move into a less expensive apartment somewhere and try to raise the child on her own. That thought caused another flash of terror.

Maggie closed her eyes and resolved that however she might handle the situation, she would do so without his help. "Never mind, John. Forget I ever called."

In the days that followed, she halfway expected him to call and at least promise his support. But there were no phone calls, no promises.

She had done the math and figured she'd gotten pregnant

sometime that second week of August. Her last phone call with John took place in late October, and now she was nearly five months pregnant and still not showing. By that time, although much of what she would do in the future was still undecided, she had arrived at one conclusion.

She loved her baby.

Ben may have turned his back on her, and John might have seen her as little more than a conquest, but the life growing inside her was one she could love with all her heart. And she knew with absolute certainty she would be loved in return. It didn't matter that her parents would be disappointed or that she might have to walk a lonely road as a single parent. At least she and her baby would have each other.

But even the strongest love couldn't dispel the increasing doubts that nagged Maggie as the days wore on. Doubts about how she would care for her child, what means of support she would have. Time and again she found herself wondering what would have happened if she and Ben had stayed together, if this were his baby she was expecting under the marital umbrella of God's favor.

Although she still hadn't heard from Ben, her mind was consumed by memories of their conversations, the way he'd looked at her that first night at the picnic, his reaction when she'd kissed him that night at the party while Deirdre looked on.

Eventually Maggie made a plan. One of her roommates had family in Cincinnati. When Maggie confided her situation, the friend contacted her parents and made arrangements.

"You can live with them until you have the baby and stay there while you find a way to live on your own." The girl leveled her gaze at Maggie. "You know, you could always give the baby up for adoption."

Maggie's heart sank. She'd thought of that option and knew it was impossible. Not when she already felt the way she did for the child. "I...I couldn't."

Her friend took her hand and squeezed it gently. "You really want this baby, don't you?"

The question rattled around her empty heart. *If only Ben and I had...* "Yes," she finally answered. "With all my heart."

"Okay then, my parents' door is open."

After that it was just a matter of telling Maggie's parents. The holidays had come and gone by then and her parents were relieved about Maggie's apparent breakup with John McFadden. Of course, they had no idea how serious things had gotten.

"I always knew God would bring you back to your senses, Maggie," her father had told her when first she admitted they were no longer an item. "You're a very special girl, a girl who will save herself for her husband."

Between her father's sureness that Maggie was still a virgin and her mother's quiet disapproval of Maggie's recent choices, she could not bring herself to tell either of them the truth. Not yet. Maybe not until after the baby was born. They both were upset with her decision to move to Cincinnati; she could only imagine how they'd react if they knew she was pregnant.

"What's in Cincinnati?" her mother said, spewing the word as though it were an infectious disease.

Maggie sighed impatiently. "I'm tired of Akron, Mother. I need to get out and see the world and right now Cincinnati is the best I can do."

Her father watched from a distant chair and said nothing. Maggie had the unnerving sense he somehow knew she was in trouble, but she never revealed any details to him and he never asked.

The month before her move to Cincinnati she left her apartment and returned home to save money. She was searching her closet for pants with elastic waistbands one afternoon when the phone rang. She lifted the receiver.

"Hello?"

Silence. Maggie almost hung up, but then someone spoke. "Hi, Maggie girl."

It was Ben, and her heart swelled at the sound of his voice, the voice her heart had longed for every day since their last conversation. She was speechless.

"Maggie...it's so good to hear your voice."

For a while neither of them said anything. Maggie collapsed cross-legged on a pile of clothes, her hand firmly on her slightly rounded abdomen as tears streamed down her cheeks. *Why now? When it's too late?*

In the wake of her silence, Ben rushed ahead. "Maggie, I'm sorry...so sorry. I won't blame you if you hang up and never speak to me again. Really...but I had to call you, had to tell you...Maggie, I can't stop thinking about you. I never have."

Maggie swallowed several times, composing herself so that he wouldn't know she was crying. "Why, Ben? After all this time?" Whatever they might have had was lost forever now. She had thrown away the most precious gift God had given her, and in a few months she would be a single mother. She and Ben stood on separate continents now with no way to bridge the ocean between them.

He sighed and launched into an explanation of his choices that past spring. "Deirdre needed me...I don't know." He paused. "We thought...she thought if we were together maybe everything would be right with her world."

Maggie waited. Clearly Ben had felt the same way or he wouldn't have broken things off with her. Not that it mattered. The conversation was pointless. Everything about her life had changed, and if Ben knew the truth he'd hang up and never give her a second thought. He saw her as a precious virgin, the pure and wholly faithful girl she'd been back before their separation.

He released a rush of air. "Whew...this is harder than I thought it'd be."

"I guess I don't understand. You must have wanted to be with her, too."

"I loved her mother, Maggie. It seemed like the right thing

to do—like I owed it to her…to stay with her through that whole mess. I figured if we were supposed to be together, the way everyone always thought we would, then I'd know if we spent a few months with just us. With no distractions."

Maybe she should tell him the truth outright and stop the silly charade. But she couldn't. Instead she continued to listen.

"At first it seemed like maybe we'd made the right decision, but after a few months—when things settled down and Deirdre's hip healed—we both came to the same conclusion. What we have between us is more like a brother-sister thing. She started dating someone else two months ago."

Maggie closed her eyes, struggling to take a deep breath. If only he had called her sooner! Given her some hint that things weren't going well with Deirdre, that in fact his heart resided with her…

"I've thought about calling you every day, but I didn't want you to think I wasn't sure. So I waited. Maggie, I've never been more sure of anything in my life."

Her mind raced, searching for some way to make it all work out after all. "I've got plans now, Ben." She threw the comment out there, not sure what she was going to say next or what lie she might be willing to say to back it up.

"Plans?" He sounded nervous. "Have you…have you met someone?" When she was silent, he moaned out loud. "I should have called you sooner. Who is he? Where did you meet him?"

Suddenly a story appeared in Maggie's mind so tight and true she felt compelled to tell it. Maybe…just maybe… "I didn't meet anyone, Ben. I'm going away for a semester. I leave next week to get set up."

"Where?" Ben sounded crushed.

"Israel." Maggie spouted the word before she could stop herself. "As an exchange student."

"*What?*" Ben's shock was evident. "Maggie, why would you do that?"

She nestled both hands protectively over her belly and felt her anger rise. "Listen, Ben, until ten minutes ago I thought we'd never speak to each other again. Now you're asking me why I'm going to spend a semester abroad? I'll tell you why. Because you turned my world upside down when you left, and I had no choice but to make a way for myself without you."

He was silent, and her voice grew softer. "Maybe being out of the country for a month will give us both time to think."

"Okay...I'll give you that. You can take a semester or a year. Take whatever time you want. But when you're ready to give me a chance, I'll be here, Maggie. I'll wait as long as it takes—until you can look me in the eyes and tell me you don't love me."

Maggie wished she *could* tell him that, wished she could call him over to her parents' house and be honest about the past six months, then do just what he'd said—look him in the eyes and tell him she had no feelings left for him whatsoever. But it wasn't true. Her heart was pounding with the sound of his voice, and hope soared within her in a way it hadn't for far too long.

And yet, even as she celebrated inwardly, a small voice of concern sounded in her conscience: *What about the baby, Maggie? What about the baby?*

"Pray about us, will ya, Mag? I believe God will help you know what you want. And then...when you come back, let's get together and talk, okay?"

Her mind raced, trying to match the dates correctly. The baby was due in May. She'd have to figure out a way to leave the area until then and...

And then what? Ben would have to know about the baby sometime. Unless...

"You could always give the baby up for adoption...give the baby up for adoption..."

"I'll pray."

"Good."

Her mind was racing weeks and months ahead. Why

couldn't she give the baby up? There would be others with Ben, wouldn't there? Children who would be born into a loving home with both parents happily married. And what about the child she carried? If she really loved her baby, she would consider its future. No father, a mother who might have to work multiple jobs to keep them off the streets… What kind of life was that for a little one?

The idea began to take root, and she imagined holding the baby, giving her over to someone else…

She closed her eyes. *Don't think about it now.* If Ben was willing to have her, then giving her baby up might be the price she had to pay. A price that would bring about the best future for her *and* her child. Fresh tears formed in Maggie's eyes as raw pain settled over her heart.

Ben's voice interrupted her. "When do you get back?"

Maggie swallowed another sob. "I'll call you."

"Maggie, you're crying! What's wrong?"

Don't give it away, not now. "Nothing. I'm just…I wasn't expecting this, Ben. I thought you were gone forever."

"What about while you're gone? Will you write…just so I know what you're thinking?"

The threads of deceit worked their way around Maggie's throat, making it difficult to speak. "No…no, that won't be possible. I've got a lot planned and… Ben, I have a lot to think about."

"Your parents are okay with you leaving the country like that?"

"Of course." The threads tightened with every lie. "It's the Holy Land, after all."

"True…how are they, your parents, I mean?" Ben seemed suddenly desperate to catch up on all he'd missed over the past months.

"Fine."

"And what about you…what've you been doing since spring?"

Maggie exhaled slowly and forced herself to sound natural.

Why did she still love him, still picture him as clearly as if he were standing before her? How could she lie to keep him even after he had chosen Deirdre over her? Then it occurred to her that what he'd done for Deirdre was actually quite noble. Very Ben-like. And if Maggie hadn't been so personally involved she might even have thought it the right thing to do.

"Maggie?"

She answered quickly this time. Too much silence was bound to make him wonder. And the lies were too fresh, too newly thought up for him to start questioning her now. "I got a job at the mall, put some money away, and spent a lot of time thinking."

Ben considered that for a moment. "I'm sorry, Maggie. It's all my fault. I wish—"

"Don't!" Maggie's grip on her abdomen tightened, and she could no longer stop the tears from flowing freely. "Don't, Ben. The past is behind us."

She was suddenly desperate to finish the phone call. They had five months before they would see each other again, and in that time she had a million details to work out.

Most of all she had to find a way to let go of the only one she had loved these past months: her unborn child.

The memories faded, and Maggie was suddenly back in the doctor's office, trying to make sense of the nightmare that was her life. Inhaling, she filled her lungs with a deep, cleansing breath. She had told Dr. Camas the truth and still her heart was beating. The darkness had not completely consumed her; if anything, she felt somewhat lighter than before.

"So you moved to Cincinnati...is that right?" Dr. Camas crossed his legs casually, and Maggie felt nothing but empathy from him.

She nodded and wrung her hands nervously together. Then she forced herself to go back to the small farming town of

Woodland, Ohio, fifteen minutes out of Cincinnati. Back to Nancy and Dan Taylor and a four-bedroom house full of love and laughter and everything Maggie had never felt growing up as an only child with a busy salesman for a father.

Maggie moved out just before her seventh month, when the right clothing was still able to hide her pregnancy. Not wanting to alienate her parents again, she told them she'd be staying with a Christian family and that she'd be back sometime that summer. Maybe for good.

Maggie's parents were busy and, with John out of the picture, they trusted that what she said was true. They kept in touch by telephone once a week and never for a moment suspected that Maggie had gone away to give birth to a baby.

As the due date neared, Maggie began to have second thoughts.

The child inside her kicked and moved and had become so much a part of her she couldn't bear the thought of giving her up. A doctor in Woodland had discovered by ultrasound that the baby was a girl and that everything else about Maggie's pregnancy was proceeding normally.

Everything except the fact that upon birth, Maggie intended to give her daughter away.

She spent hours thinking about her own mother and how desperately she wished for a closer relationship with her. Sometimes whole days would pass while Maggie fantasized that she was keeping the baby and that she would certainly not be cold and militant as her mother had been. This daughter would be her heart's mirror image. They would sing silly songs together and hold sleepovers on the living room floor, complete with popcorn and root beer; they would giggle late into the night. Maggie would shop with her little girl and pray with her, and together they would share the very secrets of their hearts.

Then reality would hit her, and she would remember the truth: Someone else was going to have the joy of this child. She had chosen Ben over the tiny baby within her, and her decision would stand. How could she or the baby have any real life otherwise?

Because Maggie knew no other way, she made plans with Cincinnati Social Services office to give the baby up for adoption immediately upon birth. She signed a stack of paperwork and felt as if she were tearing away pieces of her daughter's heart with each stroke of the pen.

Once a social worker found Maggie going through the document that asked the birth mother's opinion on the type of family she would like to have adopt her baby. Tears were streaming down Maggie's face, and the concerned social worker put a hand on her shoulder. "Dear, are you sure this is the right decision for you?"

Maggie smiled through her tears. "Yes. I'm sure." But inside she wondered how she could spend her life with a man like Ben Stovall if she couldn't be honest with him. The mere thought of him—his strength and confidence, the presence he brought when he entered a room, the way he hungered after things of God—still made her heart soar, but what kind of man would demand absolute perfection of her? Worse, what kind of mother was she, willing to give her daughter away to strangers in an effort to appear perfect?

There were no answers, and tears flowed easily, especially in the final days before her due date. In some ways it was like the last part of a wonderful vacation with someone she could never see again, someone she'd come to love deeply.

Given the choice of dozens of home studies, families ready and waiting for the opportunity to adopt, Maggie chose a well-off couple in their late thirties with no other children and definite plans to stay in Woodland. Maggie thought them a perfect match and that Woodland—with all the conveniences of Cincinnati and all the charm of a small town—was the ideal place for a little girl to grow up. Since the couple planned to adopt other children, Maggie's daughter would be the oldest. A princess, of sorts.

Of course there was one other benefit of giving the baby to a couple who planned on staying in Woodland. If Maggie ever wanted to find her… *At least I'll know where she is.* The fact was the only comforting thought as each day brought her closer to delivering.

It was almost time to say good-bye, and the prospect nearly broke Maggie's heart.

Finally, three days after her due date, her water broke. Twelve hours later, just as the sun set on May 10, 1993, she gave birth to the most beautiful little girl she'd ever seen. The advice from Social Services was clear. Allow the baby to be taken by the nurses, sign the paperwork giving up rights to the child, and don't look back.

Don't ever look back.

Instead, Maggie watched every move the nurses made, allowing her eyes to follow her newborn daughter around the delivery room as a crew of people worked to clean her skin, check her heart rate, and cut her umbilical cord. *The first step toward taking her away from me forever.*

For the next fifteen hours Maggie held her daughter to her bosom, ignoring all requests by nurses to set the baby down or make a trip to the restroom or have a bite to eat. If this was all the time she would have with her daughter, she wasn't wasting a moment of it. She cooed at the infant, whispering words of love and praying a blessing over her that would have to last a lifetime. When the baby stirred, blinked, and made eye contact with Maggie, she felt a rush of emotion unlike anything she'd ever experienced.

Is this what joy feels like, little one?

She nuzzled and whispered to her daughter, and sometimes for hours at a stretch she bathed her infant with tears of guilt and regret and self-hatred. How could she call herself a

Christian and give away her own precious daughter? What kind of person was she to choose Ben Stovall and his expectations of purity over the bundle of love and hope and joy in her arms?

Maggie had no answers.

Finally, at just after nine the next morning, a pretty young woman from Social Services came to take the baby away. Maggie refused to look up as the woman entered the room. She kept her eyes on her baby's face, memorizing every feature, every detail in her cheeks and lips and chin because there would never be another chance.

"Mrs. Taylor?" The woman came closer and stood inches away at Maggie's bedside. At first Maggie thought they must have the wrong patient, but then she remembered. She'd used Nancy and Dan's last name so that no one could come back years later and find out that Maggie Johnson had given a baby away in Woodland.

The social worker put her hand gently on Maggie's shoulder. "The nurses said you're…having a hard time."

Maggie stared deeply into her baby's eyes and spoke without ever looking at the woman. "Please whisper…my daughter frightens easily."

The woman was speechless for a moment. When it seemed the room might burst from tension, she pulled up a chair, sat down, and softly stroked Maggie's arm. "Mrs. Taylor, if this isn't the right decision for you, we need to talk about it."

If only the woman had grabbed the baby and run! Then Maggie could blame someone else and not be forced to live with the fact that she alone was responsible for the decision. Maggie's tears landed erratically on the infant's face, and she gently lowered her head and kissed them off the silky, newborn cheek. "It's okay, sweetheart, Mommy's here."

The social worker crossed her legs and seemed to be waiting. "Mrs. Taylor, should I tell them you've changed your mind?"

Images of Ben swept her mind. He was the only man she'd ever loved, ever dreamed of marrying. Surely God would bless them with other babies. But if she kept this child now, there would be no future with Ben, no house full of babies raised in the loving light of godly parents. She would live her life as a single mother, and the baby would grow up most likely troubled and lonely. Probably repeating the very mistakes Maggie had made.

No, that was no life for the sweet angel in her arms, not when giving her away meant a secure future and two loving parents. Maggie snuggled the infant closer and squeezed her eyes shut. She had no choice.

The baby began to cry, and Maggie opened her eyes, turning to the social worker. "No, I haven't changed my mind." The words were so strained, so filled with desperation she barely recognized her own voice.

"Very well. I'll take her when you're ready. The adoption won't be official until the baby's adoptive parents complete the proper paperwork. But you should know, Mrs. Taylor: once you sign the papers, it's only forty-eight hours until your rights are severed."

Maggie nodded and her stomach began to tighten. Not the postpartum contractions the doctor had warned her about, but a terrible ache, like something inside her had slowly begun to die. *I can't do this, little girl. I'll remember you forever… God, help me know what to do…*

She nuzzled the baby close to her face and allowed herself to think the unthinkable. There would be no dresses bought for this tiny girl, no quiet moments to braid her hair or read her bedtime stories. Not for Maggie. *Maybe I'll die from the pain…then I won't have to spend a lifetime wondering.* She knew with utter certainty that the bond she felt in that moment would stay with her until the day she died. Giving her daughter up now felt almost as if she were about to drop the child off the edge of a cliff—it went against all the surprising maternal urges that had welled up in her over the past seven months.

Help me, God. There must be another way… But there simply were no other choices; not if she wanted to give them both a better life.

Maggie whispered into the infant's ear. "No matter where you go, little one…whatever you do…I will always be your mommy. And I will always—"

Her body was suddenly racked with a landslide of sobs so great she could only clutch the child in grief-stricken desperation and speak softly over and over, "I love you, honey…I'll always love you."

When it was more than she could bear, when she knew that if she waited one more minute she would change her mind and forget Ben Stovall entirely, she gave the baby a final kiss and handed her over to the social worker.

The woman—who had watched the scene quietly—had tears in her eyes as she took the infant. For a moment she held the baby and said nothing, only stared sadly at Maggie. When finally she could bring herself to speak, she said, "It's the right thing, Mrs. Taylor. I've met the couple…your daughter will have a wonderful life."

Maggie nodded, consumed by a feeling of longing for her baby, a feeling that was wild and desperate. *What could be more wonderful than being raised by your own mother?* How could the baby have a good life knowing that Maggie had given her away, hadn't wanted her?

She averted her gaze so that she wouldn't be tempted to let her eyes fall on the blanketed bundle in the social worker's arms. *She belongs to someone else now. Let her go. Let her go. Let her go.*

"I'll have someone bring in the paperwork." The social worker stood, and she and the baby left the room.

It was the last time Maggie had ever seen her daughter.

Dr. Camas shifted positions. "And you never told your husband about the child?"

Maggie shook her head. "How could I? He thought I was a virgin. Once I got back home, Ben and I started seeing each other right away. He asked me if I'd dated anyone, and I told him there'd been nothing serious. He assumed…well, that things hadn't changed."

"And physically he never doubted you?" Dr. Camas's voice held no accusation, only a desire to understand.

"Ben was a virgin. If there would have been a sign or something that might have told him I hadn't been sexually pure, he wouldn't have known it." She thought for a moment. "If he'd doubted me, I'm sure he would have said something."

Dr. Camas leaned back in his chair and looked at Maggie for a long moment. "So then, you've kept this a secret for eight years?"

Tears stung at Maggie's eyes, and the cloak of darkness was as heavy and threatening as if it had never lifted. "Yes."

Christ is light, and in Him is no darkness…

The Scripture came from nowhere and for several seconds the darkness eased. *Come back, God! Don't leave me now.*

Christ is light, and in Him—

"How do you feel about that?"

The holy whispers faded. Caught off guard, Maggie blinked and tried to remember what the conversation had been. "About what?"

There was not even a flicker of impatience on Dr. Camas's face. "Having lied about the baby for the past eight years. How do you feel?"

For an instant, Maggie wanted to scream at the doctor. How did she *feel* about it? Couldn't he see for himself? It had driven a wedge between her and Ben almost from the beginning of their marriage. Not a day passed when she didn't think about the daughter she had given away. And when they had been unable to have children, she was certain God was punishing her for trading a precious baby for a life of lies.

Adoption in and of itself was a good thing, Maggie knew. For many women it was a beautiful choice indeed. But not for her. Her reasons had been entirely self-centered, rooted in the soil of desire for a man who would not have wanted to share his life with her if he'd known the truth. So she lied and lost her daughter in the process.

All for selfish reasons.

How did she feel about it? "It's making me crazy. I hate Ben. I hate myself. I don't know what to think anymore."

Dr. Camas jotted something down on the clipboard in front of him and smiled softly at Maggie. "I think you're ready for the next step."

"Next step?" Maggie didn't want a next step. She wanted to keep meeting with Dr. Camas and going over her life. Searching for some reasonable explanation that would shed light on the choices she'd made and the desperate darkness attempting to consume her.

"Yes. Starting tomorrow we'll be adding group therapy to your daily program. You'll still meet with me; this will be in addition. Group therapy generally is where the most healing takes place. You'll be meeting with a group of people who have situations similar to yours."

Maggie's heart rate doubled. "Meaning what?"

Dr. Camas rested his forearms on his desk and angled his head in a gesture that reminded Maggie of her father. "Everyone in your group is here because of anger issues and severe depression."

He had to be kidding. "I'm not ready for that. I can't sit in a group and—"

"Maggie..." His voice was quiet, calm. He reached out and clasped his hand around hers, and although a great deal of fear and darkness remained, she felt the fight leave her. "Maggie, you're ready."

Her shoulders slumped forward, and she let her head fall as tears formed and spilled onto her lap. She didn't want to share her life with anyone else, especially with people who had troubles of their own. What if they recognized her? What if she forgot who she was or what she was saying and what if everyone in the group suddenly became blond, blue-eyed little girls looking for their mamas? "I can't…"

Dr. Camas waited until Maggie dried her eyes and met his gaze. "You can. Here's what will happen…"

They spoke several more minutes, Maggie asking questions about the group while she tried to calm her pounding heart. What if it wasn't time yet? There would be nowhere for her to run in a group setting. If he forced her to attend, she would refuse to speak, acting only as a silent observer. Nothing more.

By the time she stood to leave, she was so filled with panic her knees were knocking. She made her way to the door and as she set off down the hallway for her bedroom, she was filled with an overwhelming sense of doom.

Dr. Camas was wrong.

She would never be ready to bare her soul to a group of strangers. Much less tell them the truth. Even if her fight against the demons of depression or darkness or whatever it was lasted a lifetime.

The Depths

Trust in the LORD with all your heart and
lean not on your own understanding; in
all your ways acknowledge him, and
he will make your paths straight.

PROVERBS 3:5

Fifteen

WHEN BEN STOVALL REGAINED CONSCIOUSNESS IN A HOSPITAL BED at Cleveland General, his head swathed in gauze wrap, his entire body pulsating with a pain already dulled by medication, he was overwhelmed by two realizations—both of which rocked the foundations of his world.

First, he was alive. He was breathing; he could move each of his limbs; and he was thinking clearly enough to recognize both facts. Without a doubt he had been spared by God Almighty Himself.

The second realization was even stronger.

The events that had put Maggie in a psychiatric hospital and landed him near death in this one had come together in his head to form an undeniable sense, a deep and unfathomable longing that defied description. He was swept up in a protective feeling, one that made him want to swim oceans or leap mountains, whatever it took to get to Maggie.

He was in love.

Back when everything about his marriage came easily he had expected her devotion as absolutely as he expected morning. Now, with Maggie refusing his visits and phone calls—with their marriage hanging in the balance—he was madly, undeniably, head-over-heels in love with his wife. And determined to find a way to reach her.

What John McFadden had said wasn't true; it couldn't be. Maggie never would have slept with that…that man. She'd never gotten pregnant. And if she *had* been pregnant—if McFadden had raped her or forced her in some way—Maggie would have kept the baby. Ben was sure of that. Children were priceless by Maggie's standards. Certainly she would have felt comfortable enough at that age—what, twenty-two, twenty-three?—to tell Ben the truth. Rape was an awful thing, but it wouldn't have been Maggie's fault. Why would she have lied about such a thing?

The whole notion was ridiculous. She was a virgin when they were married; she had to be. Maggie was one of the most fine, upstanding women he knew. True, she was suffering from something terrible, something bigger than angry fan mail or failed attempts at pregnancy, something larger than anything she'd come up against before. But Maggie would never have given herself to a man like McFadden.

Still, in those first waking moments he realized that whatever was bothering Maggie it had to be worse than anything he'd previously guessed. He pictured her lifeless eyes and empty voice that last day, the day before she went to Orchards.

Whatever it is, honey, we'll work it out. I'll take some time off work, spend more time letting you talk, hearing you.

He sighed.

Why had it taken all of this for him to realize the depth of feelings he held for Maggie? His love for her was greater than life itself; he needed her more than the air he breathed. Without a doubt, if he hadn't been in the hospital—if somehow he could have walked out on his own volition, hailed a cab, and made his way to Orchards Psychiatric Hospital—he would have done so. He would have sought Maggie out, found her, and held her close so she would never again feel the need to lie to him about anything. So she would know exactly how he felt about her.

He gritted his teeth and tried to lift his arm over his head, but after a moment he let it drop again. Pain worked its way through every muscle in his body, seizing him in a vise grip. On his second try he found the strength to reach the telephone receiver. After getting the number from the operator again, he dialed the psychiatric hospital.

"Orchards, may I help you?"

This isn't going to work. Hope leaked from Ben like air from a damaged tire. *How can I get her to talk to me?* "Uh, yes, Maggie Stovall please."

The receptionist paused. "Who may I say is calling?"

Ben forced himself to think quickly. "Jay. From the *Gazette.*"

Seconds passed, and a phone began to ring. "Nurse's desk, just a moment. Maggie will be here in a minute."

Be here in a minute? She didn't even have a phone in her room? *How bad are you, Maggie? What happened to make you like this?*

"Hello?"

Maggie's voice took him by surprise. It had been over a week since he'd heard it. He basked in the sound.

"Maggie...it's me."

In the seconds that followed, Ben prayed she wouldn't hang up. Her anger was the first thing he heard. "That's a lousy thing to do, Ben."

He hesitated. "Maggie, we need to talk."

She drew several quick breaths, and Ben was struck by the nervousness in her voice. "No! There's nothing to say. We're finished. I told you in the note. I'll call you when I'm out of here." More quick breaths. "Now don't call back. Please. I...I can't take it, Ben."

She hung up before he could respond.

Stunned, Ben remained motionless, the receiver still in his hand. The woman he had just spoken to sounded like a stranger. *What's happened to you, Maggie?* He fought the urge to bolt from the room, the desperation to find a way to reach her and convince her she was wrong. Again only the intravenous tubing sewn into his arms held him in place.

Ben held his breath. The reality of the situation was becoming clear.

Whatever had happened in Maggie's past, whatever parts of McFadden's story were true or false, one thing was certain:

Maggie wanted nothing to do with Ben. She wanted to be left alone. And in the coming months she planned—unbelievably—to divorce him and move on with her life. Alone.

Ben felt tears stinging at his eyes, and he blinked them back. *Help me, Lord, there's got to be a way to reach her.*

You were saved for a purpose, My son. Follow Me.

Ben struggled to sit higher up in bed and allowed the reassuring holy whispers to wash over him. Somehow, even though his entire life had fallen apart in the past few weeks, God had a plan. God always had a plan for those who loved Him.

Ben tried to assess his injuries, but it wasn't until the doctor came in an hour later that he understood how grave his condition had been.

The emergency team had infused him with two units of blood and by the time they got him on an operating table his heart had all but given up. In addition, his skull had been fractured, and they were even now watching for signs of a blood clot in his brain.

"You're a lucky man, Mr. Stovall." The doctor was wrapping a fresh piece of gauze around his head injury. "A few minutes later, and you wouldn't have survived."

Ben was barely listening. He had the overpowering sense that God wanted him to continue searching. That somewhere—even if it had nothing to do with the lies McFadden told—there was truth where Maggie was concerned.

Love in wisdom and truth…love covers a multitude of sins.

The thoughts were enough to make Ben jump out of bed. His doctor was rambling on about resting and taking it easy, but when the man got to the part about filing police charges, Ben began to listen again.

"Police charges?"

"Yes. Do you know for certain who beat you up?"

He nodded. He could see as clearly as if he were watching it again the strange activity taking place near the van, the dozens of boxes being loaded from it into the bar storeroom. "I know everything. His name, where he works. All of it."

The doctor nodded. "How do you feel about filing charges?"

Love in wisdom and truth…

Ben frowned. How in the world did that Scripture fit his current situation? He inhaled slowly, grimacing at the pain in his ribs when he did so. He had no choice in this situation. Regardless of McFadden's threats, Ben would pursue charges because it was the right thing to do. "I'll do it. Whenever the officers are ready."

"Very good. Now, why don't you see if you can get some sleep."

Alone in his room, Ben stared hesitantly at the phone. Should he call Madeline Johnson again? Did Maggie's mother know more about her daughter's past than she let on? Reaching out, he rummaged through his bedside table and found his wallet. In it was Madeline's number and a calling card. In three minutes he had the woman on the line.

"You're calling me from work?" Maggie's mother sounded worried, and Ben was glad he'd left out the fact that he was in the hospital. "What sort of trouble is she in now?"

"Nothing new." Ben glanced at his bandaged shoulder and cleared his throat. "I talked to John McFadden."

A moment passed. "Was I right?"

Ben tried to shift positions and he winced. "Yes. He's not a very nice guy."

"He never was."

A dozen questions fought for position. *Why did Maggie date him if he was so rotten?* "He said something…I'm sure it's a lie. Still, I thought maybe there was something you might have missed—something that would help me understand Maggie's situation better."

There was a pause. "What did he say?" At the nervous edge to the woman's voice, Ben shifted, suddenly uncomfortable.

"He told me…" Ben sighed. "He said Maggie got pregnant

and that...that she gave the baby up for adoption."

The silence on the other end was enough to make Ben's heart skip a beat. "Mrs. Johnson?"

The shaky sound of shallow breathing filled the phone line. "That's absolutely false. Maggie would never have...they broke up after only a few months."

"So other than her semester in Israel, she was with you that whole year. I mean, she never left for a few months, nothing like that?" Ben was angry with himself for asking. Of course Maggie hadn't left. Why would she? The conversation was pointless because everything John McFadden had said was a lie, and the fact that Ben even toyed with the idea was—

"Israel?"

Ben's world tilted crazily. "Yeah, Israel...you know, Maggie's exchange program. Through the university?"

Another beat. "This isn't making sense."

His mind reeled, racing to understand the conversation. "What?"

Maggie's mother inhaled sharply. "Why would she have told you that?" Her voice sounded tired, as though it were all too much for a woman her age. "Maggie didn't study in Israel. She never spent a day outside the country."

Ben's head was spinning now. *Was this the lie? Why on earth would she have told me she was leaving the country if she wasn't?*

It was as though the foundations upon which he'd built his life were crumbling, as though he were scrambling to stay on solid ground....

He tried to swallow. He almost knew the answer to his next question before he asked it. "She was home the whole time, is that what you're saying?"

Madeline Johnson exhaled slowly. "No." The air eased out again. "Maybe this is the lie Maggie's running from."

Ben felt his head begin to spin. What was she talking about? "I'm listening." His heart stopped while he waited for her to continue.

"It was right after Maggie moved out of that apartment, the one she was sharing with those girls from—"

"Wait a minute." His heart thudded into a nervous rhythm. *Help me, God. What is this?* "What apartment? How come I didn't know about this?" Ben's insides felt like a ball of yarn that was free-falling, unraveling too fast to do anything but stand helplessly by and watch. How had they lived all their lives together and never discussed this? Why hadn't it come up sometime at a gathering with her family?

"Well…she did, Ben. She lived in an apartment with two friends from college. Girls that were wilder than she; girls her father and I didn't approve of. She dated John during that time." She sounded almost angry, and he wondered if it were because she didn't want to be saying these things, didn't want to think about it all…

As if she wanted to run from this as badly as he did.

"She and John broke things off sometime that fall. A few months later—early spring maybe—Maggie went to stay with some friends near Cincinnati."

A wave of nausea washed over Ben. Cincinnati? Why there? And more important, why hadn't she ever told him about it? "I…I didn't know."

"Her father and I thought it would be a good thing. Maggie was still broken up about you and that girl you were seeing. We wanted distance between her and John…" The woman paused, her implied accusation hitting its mark. "She was gone three months or so, I'm not sure. She came back the beginning of summer. About the same time you began calling again."

Ben's mind raced, and he tried to ignore the pounding in his temples, the tearing pain behind one eye…was he getting a migraine headache? "Did you see her during that time? Visit her?"

"We were busy, involved in the lay leadership of our church. Maggie's father was very much in demand, and I spent much of my time helping him."

Ben wanted to reach through the phone lines and shake her. They hadn't seen Maggie *once* during that time? Not even one time? "Did you talk to her?"

"Of course." Madeline Johnson snapped her answer. "We were in touch every week. She was living with her friend's family and she seemed to be doing very well." She sighed loudly. "Remember, she wouldn't have been there at all if you hadn't walked out on her the year before."

Anger surged through Ben like volcanic lava. He forced it down beneath the service. "We can't go back now. The only thing that matters anymore is Maggie, and whatever she went through that spring."

Maggie's mother seemed to concede that much because when she spoke again her voice was less defensive. "Are you thinking it's possible…I mean, do you think it could be true?"

Ben closed his eyes and loosed the possibility that lay coiled like a deadly snake on the pathway of his mind. "Do I think she went to Cincinnati to have a baby?" Ben massaged his temples and blinked his eyes open once more. "I don't know. I can't believe it, but…well, nothing's adding up like it should."

Madeline Johnson's tone became lighter. "Wait a minute…" Ben could hear her rifling through something. "I may still have the phone number and address."

Ben held his breath. *Help her find it, Lord. This may be our only chance to learn the truth.* "Here it is. Get a pencil."

A pencil? That's right, I'm supposed to be at work. Ben felt a stab of pain as he yanked on a drawer in the bureau next to him and found a hospital pen. Writing on a scrap of paper from his wallet, he jotted down the number Madeline Johnson read off.

"Their names are Nancy and Dan Taylor. Of course, they might have changed the number or moved by now."

Ben exhaled slowly and reminded himself to breathe. He thanked Maggie's mother and promised to call if he learned anything. Then he hung up and tried to get a grip on his emotions. He hated where this seemed to be going. After all, it wasn't even possible. Maggie was a good girl from a strong family. The idea of her having her own apartment and dating John McFadden, possibly even sleeping with a man like that and getting pregnant, was as foreign as if he'd seen his wife's face on the FBI's most wanted list.

Maggie simply wasn't that kind of girl. He wouldn't have married her if she...

As I have loved you, so you must love...love covers a multitude of sins, My son.

The Lord's words pierced the terrified place in his soul and he was engulfed by a different sort of anxiety. *Whose sins, Lord? What other lies has Maggie told?*

There was no shout from heaven in response, but the feeling—and the command to love unconditionally—remained. *I have loved Maggie that way, Lord. I'm still in love with her.*

But was he? Would he love her if her lies were as great as McFadden had said? Doubt, like the first pebble in a landslide, bounced down the rock wall of certainty in his mind.

Ben stared at the number he'd written and decided to call. He had to know if it was the same home, the same family who had once housed Maggie. He reached for the phone.

A mature-sounding woman answered on the third ring. "Yes, Taylors."

Taylors. That was the same name Madeline Johnson had given him. Nancy Taylor. "Yes, is Nancy or Stu there?" He threw the second name in to give himself an out. If it was the right number, he had no intention of having a conversation with them over the phone.

The woman sounded puzzled. "This is Nancy, but there's no Stu here."

Ben felt his heart thudding loudly in his chest. "Oh, never mind then. I must have the wrong number."

He hung up the phone and stared at his battered body again, willing it to heal. The moment he was well enough to walk out of the hospital and drive a car, he would set out for the place where he could find the next piece of the puzzle. Pieces he had not known existed…pieces that had been a part of Maggie all along.

Yes, he would go to Woodland, Ohio—just outside Cincinnati—to the home of Nancy and Dan Taylor.

What will you do if it's true, Ben?

For a fraction of an instant, he thought about how he might spend the rest of his life if what John McFadden had said about Maggie were true. Alone. Or possibly remarried. Because lying in the hospital bed, wrapped in layers of bandages and uncertainty, Ben couldn't imagine how their marriage might survive if McFadden had told the truth.

If the worst were true, then Maggie had kept crucial parts of her past from him for nearly eight years.

There's no way.

A nurse entered the room and gave him additional pain medication. When she was gone, he slid back down on the bed and closed his eyes, much of his body still throbbing from the beating.

He thought about their wedding—a beautiful ceremony in her home church—and later how they'd danced for hours at the reception, then taken off for their honeymoon. The week in Mexico's coastal Tenacatita Bay had been better than Ben had dared imagine. Maggie had been shy at first, tentative, very much the virgin, he thought. But in little time the two of them shared a bond that was only heightened by their physical intimacy.

McFadden's claims were ludicrous.

He closed his eyes, begging God to make sense of Maggie's struggles, to reveal what information might be missing from her past. Then he put all the questions about why she'd lied and gone to Cincinnati instead of Israel out of his mind, anchored himself to what he still believed to be true, and fell asleep.

Sixteen

THE MEETING BETWEEN KATHY GARRETT AND DR. SKYLER WILSON took place in a visiting lounge outside the girl's hospital room. Normally it was the type of meeting that would be conducted with a child's parents, but in this case Kathy was all the girl had.

In the days since Amanda had been beaten nearly to death, Kathy had visited the hospital each night, after her own children were fed and bathed. Now, with her husband at home putting them to bed, Kathy faced the doctor who had cared for Amanda.

"How is she? Really?"

Dr. Wilson wore a dark expression, his eyebrows knit together in concern. He flipped through the pages of Amanda's medical file and then glanced at Kathy. "Physically? She's healing. I don't expect any permanent damage. But the rest…"

Kathy looked down at her hands and nodded. Amanda might heal from her beating, but she would never be the same again. Her eyes rose to meet the doctor's once more. "Can she recover from it?"

"She's a very troubled little girl, Mrs. Garrett." Dr. Wilson sighed and opened the medical file. "Here. Take a look."

Kathy reached for the file and her eyes scanned the page. The notations were frightening: "Withdrawn and anxious… Severely depressed… Possibly suicidal… This child has little will to live and talks incessantly about her mother." Tears welled in Kathy's eyes and she passed the file back to the doctor. "Her mother isn't in the picture."

Dr. Wilson clutched the file and tilted his head. "Is there any effort being made to find her?"

"No. Amanda was given up at birth, Doctor. Even if there were a way to find the mother, I'm sure she's gone on with her life."

"What about a foster family?"

A soft rush of air escaped from Kathy's throat. "She was at a foster home when this happened."

Dr. Wilson's eyes narrowed and the muscles in his jaws flexed. "Are police pressing charges?"

"Oh, sure." Kathy's heart constricted at the mention of Mrs. Graystone. How had a woman like that slipped through the system and earned a license to provide foster care? Even if she spent the rest of her days in prison it wouldn't make up for what she'd done. What had happened to this precious child was enough to make Kathy plead with the Lord for His immediate return. "The woman will serve time, but it doesn't change what happened to Amanda."

The doctor held her gaze a moment longer. "She asks about you, also. Nearly every day. Sometimes I'm not sure if it's her mother she's wanting or you."

The tears that had been building spilled onto Kathy's face. "I love her like one of my own, but we can't take her. We have seven children, doctor. The state says any time she spends with us has to be temporary."

The doctor sighed. "I hate these situations." He glanced back at the open door to Amanda's room. "She's so…I don't know, vulnerable, I guess. She needs a home. Isn't there something the system can do?"

Kathy pulled a tissue from her purse and dried her tears. "I've been spending the past two years trying to answer that question. She's slipping through the cracks, and there doesn't seem to be anything any of us can do about it."

He shook his head and opened Amanda's file, discussing her physical injuries. Many of her bruises had begun to fade. Her young body was resilient and though she'd suffered a collapsed lung, three broken ribs, and multiple stitches from the beating, Amanda would heal.

"I expect she can go home with you in a few days, if that's all right." The doctor stood and held out his hand to Kathy. "Thank you for being here. It…well, I don't know if she'd have made it without you."

Kathy nodded. "Just give me a call. I'll be here the moment she's released."

When the doctor was gone, she headed for Amanda's room.

"Kathy! Hi!"

The girl's face lit up and Kathy felt her heart lurch. *This is the girl who's depressed? Suicidal?*

If only they could buy a bigger house, build on an additional room. *I love her, Lord. Isn't there anything I can do?* She stooped over the child and ran a hand along her small forehead. "Hi, honey. How're you feeling?"

The light faded from her young eyes. "I might have to stay two more days."

"Yeah…" Kathy wrinkled her nose. "But you have to get those ribs healed up."

"I'm going home with you, right?" There was such hope in the child's face. Kathy wanted to crawl in bed beside her, hold her close, and soothe away the pain like she would for her own children. *It isn't right, Lord, that this little one should be all alone. Help her, Father. Give her a miracle.*

That's what it would take at this point. People were not looking to adopt seven-year-old girls—especially those who had been abused almost to the point of death. Children like Amanda were marked with the failings of the system, considered damaged goods marred permanently by the very government agency designed to help them.

The newspaper column, "Maggie's Mind," had certainly been a true assessment in this child's case.

"Right, Kathy? I get to go home with you, right?" Amanda was waiting for an answer.

Kathy sat beside the girl, bent down, and gently kissed her

cheek, careful not to touch the area above her eye where the stitches remained. "For a little while, sweetie. We can take you in, but only until they find another foster family."

The child sighed and a lonely teardrop meandered down her cheek. "Kathy, do you think maybe it will happen soon?"

Kathy cocked her head and studied the child. "What, honey?"

"My mom. Do you think she'll find me soon? This year, maybe?"

"Oh, sweetie, I hope so." A weight settled in around Kathy's heart, and she leaned over, hugging Amanda. *God, please...hear her cries, Lord. I'm at the end of my abilities, Father.*

The girl was crying now, and Kathy could feel her small back shaking from the sobs that welled up inside her. "I...I just want to find my mommy. I know she's...she's somewhere."

"Ah, honey, it'll be all right. God loves you; I love you. He has a plan for you, even if it doesn't feel like it."

"So—" the child whimpered into Kathy's hair and she struggled to understand her—"Do you think maybe this is the year?"

Kathy felt her own tears making their way down her cheeks. "Sweetie, I hope so. I really hope so."

Long after Kathy was gone, Amanda sat wide-eyed in bed, staring at shadows on the ceiling...wondering about her mother.

She had to be somewhere, didn't she? And wherever she was, she had to remember she'd given a little baby girl up for adoption, didn't she?

Amanda studied the shadows, trying hard to imagine her mother's face, her eyes. She would be beautiful and kind and gentle, just like Kathy.

Amanda smiled. Just wait! When her mother found out about her and what had happened to her and how much she needed a family, she would come for her. She would take her home and love her forever. Amanda was sure of it.

Then, like they did every night since the beating, the shadows changed and began moving on the ceiling. Suddenly they became terrifying shapes, looming figures with pointed teeth and claws and horns. And in the midst of them was Mrs. Graystone's face. The woman was moving in closer, coming after her, trying to kill her.

"No!" Amanda clasped her hand over her mouth. She didn't want a pill or a shot like she'd gotten the other nights. She bit her lip and lay still, as quiet as she could. But she kept her eyes wide open, and felt her arms and legs tremble as the Graystone shadows came closer.

Please, God, make her go away! Suddenly the shadows were still again.

In the silent darkness, other thoughts began to take shape in her mind. She was seven years old, and no one wanted her. No one at all. Oh, Kathy loved her. She believed that with all her heart. But Kathy didn't have room for her.

Sometimes on nights like this she thought about all the people in the world—or just in Ohio—and how many families could take in a seven-year-old girl. There were lots of families. Lots of them! But no one had come forward to claim her.

Because no one wanted her.

There must be something in me that people hate. Especially people like Mrs. Graystone. It had been different when Amanda was little, when she lived with Mr. and Mrs. Brownell, before they went to heaven. But now that she was older, there must have been something in her smile or her eyes, something she couldn't see when she looked in the mirror, but something other people saw. Something that made people turn away from her.

Otherwise why had she spent time in so many different foster homes? People traded her in like a doll no one wanted to play with anymore. When they didn't get tired of her, they hurt her. Like the farmhouse boys and that awful Mrs. Graystone.

The girl squeezed her arms around her ribs and winced in pain. It still hurt, and that made her mad. She had something wrong with her for sure. Something other people wanted to beat out of her.

The girl thought about it long and hard. It was probably something deep inside her, maybe something that came from her heart. The longer she thought about it the more the shadows began to move again, taunting, threatening…

Mrs. Graystone was in the hospital somewhere. Amanda didn't know where—hiding in the corner, maybe—but she was sure the woman was there. Wherever she was, it was close. She was probably just waiting for the nurses to take a break so she could sneak into the room and finish Amanda off.

The shadows moved more quickly now, and Amanda put her hand over her mouth so no one would hear her scream. Screaming never stopped the shadows anyway. As the tears came stronger and harder, it dawned on her the reason people hated her. It all started back when she was born. Because if her own mother had been willing to leave her alone in the world, how could anyone else ever love her?

As quietly as she could, without being heard by the nurses or Mrs. Graystone—wherever she was hiding—the girl began to call for the one who could make a difference, the woman who could make everything right.

"Mommy, where are you? I need you, Mommy. I'm here. I love you. I'm not mad at you for giving me away. I just want to be with you. Please come and find me, Mommy. Please. Mommy…Mommy…I need you…"

Her whispered pleas continued until sometime in the early morning hours when, despite her tears, she fell asleep still afraid and drifted to a place where shadows prevailed and Mrs. Graystone ruled.

The place of Amanda's very existence.

Three hundred miles away, from inside an unmarked police car, two Cleveland officers watched a strange transaction taking place in the back of Topper's Pop Bar. A blue van had backed up to a storage unit, and now four men worked quickly to unload what seemed to be more than thirty boxes.

The officers were there for one reason: to arrest John McFadden for attempted murder in the beating of Ben Stovall the week before. But they had taken the unmarked squad car because of something the department had suspected for more than a year. Drugs had been infiltrating the south side of Cleveland for months—large quantities of marijuana and cocaine that were making their way into the hands of dozens of small-time dealers. On more than one occasion the bar had come up during questioning. But police never gained enough information to make a bust or even be granted a search warrant.

Officers routinely drove by the bar looking for suspicious activity. And though plenty of obvious criminal actions took place—public drunkenness, assault and battery, drunken driving—none of them had anything to do with drug smuggling.

But now, late on this dark Thursday evening in September, the officers were nearly certain they were witnessing a drug operation, and that raised an interesting dilemma. Should they carry out the arrest as planned and risk frightening away the proof of their longtime suspicions? Or would it be better to approach the men working around the van, guns raised, and then call for backup for what might amount to half a dozen arrests?

In minutes they both came to the same decision. Take care of the business at hand and bring the other information back to the office. If the men were drug dealers, then they were most likely armed. Heavily and to a man. By the time the officers might call for backup, the men would be finished unloading their cargo and long gone.

"Let's go get McFadden." The senior officer motioned to his partner, and a moment later they were inside the bar.

John McFadden was leaning against the counter, making small talk with two of the patrons when the officers approached him.

"What the—?" McFadden straightened. He hated cops. Why'd they have to come around at all? Especially tonight when the guys were delivering a shipment of—

"John McFadden?"

He scowled at the uniformed men. "Yeah, what's it to you?"

"We have a warrant for your arrest." The officer stepped forward and snapped handcuffs onto McFadden's wrist.

He jerked away, but the officer caught his loose hand and cuffed it, too. What was this? And what was happening outside? Had there been a bust, and now he was going down with his guys? Whatever it was, he would post bail before anyone would make him spend an hour in jail. He pulled his cuffed hands away from the officers and glared at them. "Isn't there a law against coming into someone's workplace and arresting them for no reason?"

"We're arresting you for the attempted murder of Ben Stovall. You have the right to remain silent. Anything you say or do can and will be..."

McFadden stopped listening. His mind was consumed with two all-invasive thoughts: Ben Stovall had lived, and more important, he'd been crazy enough to tell the cops what had happened. McFadden scowled. Stovall had seen his boys unload a shipment of marijuana. If the lawyer filed a police report on the beating, he probably mentioned the drugs, too. John gritted his teeth and allowed himself to be led away. Whatever the outcome of all of this, he had no intention of staying in jail. He would post bail and then take care of the business he'd failed to finish the first time.

Eliminating Ben Stovall from the face of the earth.

Seventeen

OF ALL THE HOURS IN A DAY, LAURA THOMPSON LOVED THE EARLY morning. Back when her children had flooded her home with noise and activity and constant conversation she had savored the predawn hour as the only time she and God could meet without interruption. How often had the Lord used those morning meetings to speak understanding to her heart or impart life-changing perspective from His Word? This fall morning was no different, and though her house was quieter now Laura couldn't imagine welcoming her day any other way.

For years she had enjoyed starting her quiet time with a psalm; today she was in chapter 30. Nearly every line seemed vibrantly alive and relevant to all that consumed Laura lately.

> O LORD my God, I called to you for help and you healed me.... You brought me up from the grave; you spared me from going down into the pit. Sing to the LORD...praise his holy name. For his anger lasts only a moment, but his favor lasts for a lifetime; weeping may remain for a night, but rejoicing comes in the morning.... You turned my wailing into dancing; you removed my sackcloth and clothed me with joy.

It was Maggie, of course. On the surface she looked bright and put together, but inside she was falling apart. Just like in the image she'd seen that first day, the image of a woman wearing a mask.

Pray, daughter. Maggie's in trouble...

Laura blinked back tears. Weeks had passed since Maggie had been to church, and though Laura had called the Stovall home twice since their initial conversation, no one had ever answered and she'd been forced to leave a message.

Help her, God...whatever she's going through. I can't reach her, but You can, Father.

Coffee brewed in the kitchen nearby and, as the words of prayer came, Laura's mind was filled with another picture. That of a little girl, alone and frightened.

What's this, Lord? Who is this little one?

Pray for her...trust Me; trust My Word. Anything you ask in My name will be given to you...

The words filled her heart with peace and Laura continued to pray for Maggie and the little girl and whatever secret lay behind the mask. Throughout the morning she held fast to the promise in the psalm: *Weeping may remain for the night, but rejoicing comes in the morning.*

She prayed the Scripture throughout her morning coffee and well past the folding of laundry and making of bread for dinner that night. By midday the urgency in Laura's soul was replaced with a deep-seated, peace-filled assurance. Somehow Laura knew the words to the psalm belonged especially to Maggie Stovall for this time in her life. And whatever dark place she was in, however the little girl fit into the picture, one day very soon there would come something from God Himself.

Great, abundant, overwhelming joy.

Only five minutes remained before Maggie's first group session, and she was trembling badly. Other patients filed in and took their places in the circle as Maggie gripped the edge of her chair and forced herself to stay put. She wanted desperately to flee the room, to sneak down the hospital corridor and climb back into bed.

Maggie wasn't sure if it was the medicine she was taking or the fact that in talking to Dr. Camas she'd finally told the truth about her life, but for some reason sleep no longer eluded her.

Instead it had become an escape, a way of numbing the pain that assaulted her when she stood in the glaring, harsh light of truthfulness.

The chairs were full except one, and Maggie remained motionless but for her eyes, which darted about the circle taking in something about each of the patients. There was a balding man whose polyester pants hung loosely on his skeletal frame. He leaned forward in his seat and studied the tops of his shoes rather than make eye contact with anyone. Across the circle a pretty girl of no more than twenty with fading bruises on her cheek bit her lower lip and rocked nervously.

Maggie wondered about the bruises as her gaze moved around the circle to a heavyset, middle-aged woman in an elegant cashmere sweater and wool pants. The woman's soft, leather shoes bore testimony to the fact that she had money, but the circles under her eyes proved that wealth had done little to ease her pain.

As far as Maggie could tell, the others were inconspicuously doing the same as she: checking out the circle and trying to decide what paths in life had led them here, as patients in a psychiatric hospital.

Maggie took in the group as a whole and noticed only a few that whispered casually among themselves. For the most part those seated in the circle were quiet, each person lost in his or her own ocean of stormy darkness. In some strange way, there was comfort in a roomful of people who were suffering like she was. Dr. Camas had said the others in the group had been meeting daily for the past week and that all of them were suffering from various stages of depression.

"You're not alone, Maggie," he'd told her at the end of their last session. "Many people hurt the way you have, but most do not seek help until it's too late. You're here. That tells me that deep inside you believe God will use this time to help you get better."

She would have loved nothing more than to walk away

from the group and find Dr. Camas now. He could make sense of her racing heart and shaking hands.

Peace I leave you, My peace I give you…

Maggie started to argue with the Scripture as it flashed across her mind, but she stopped as the words played again and again.

My peace I give you…My peace I give you…

Not me, Lord, I don't deserve peace. Not after what I did.

My peace I give you…

It wasn't a promise Maggie felt worthy of claiming, but for reasons she couldn't understand, her heart rate slowed, and she was able to draw a slow, deep breath. Before she could analyze her feelings further, a woman with a radiant complexion and twinkling eyes took her place in a nearby chair. On her pale blue sweater she wore a simple name badge, and once she was seated, she introduced herself as Dr. Lynn Baker.

"Welcome, everyone." Dr. Baker crossed her legs and smiled at the group. A glow of sincerity in her eyes put Maggie at ease, and she felt the muscles in her neck relax. "We have someone new with us today." She motioned to Maggie. "Why don't you introduce yourself to the group."

Instantly her muscles seized. What was she doing here, about to bare her soul to a group of perfect strangers? And what if they found out about her column? *I'll have no credibility at all once I'm finished here.* She cleared her throat hesitantly. "I'm Maggie."

Dr. Baker waited as though Maggie might want to expound on her introduction. When Maggie remained silent, the doctor continued. "Let's start with revelation." She looked at Maggie. "Revelation is a time early in group session when each of you has the opportunity to share something about your past, something about the reason you're here. It's an optional time."

The doctor looked around the room slowly, and there was an uncomfortable silence. The young girl in her twenties began twisting her hands together and shifting restlessly in her chair.

There were no sounds coming from her, but tears fell onto her jeans. Maggie guessed she was fighting some type of inner war, wanting to share with the group and terrified at the same time. Maggie could relate. She had no intentions of talking in front of these people. Not now or ever.

The group had focused its complete attention on the girl, and Dr. Baker took the initiative. "Sarah, do you have something to share?"

Sarah looked at Dr. Baker, and there was a well of deep desperation in her eyes. The girl opened her mouth and ran a hand self-consciously over her bruised cheek. "Y-y-yes. I think it's t-t-time." She glanced down at her hands again and Maggie saw that her fingernails were bitten down past the point of pain. The picture of Sarah sitting there, searching for a way to begin the journey into her darkest place, was so pitiful, Maggie forgot about her own fear.

Help her, God. Give her the words to speak her heart...

"C-c-can you tell them m-m-my name and stuff, you know, why I'm here?"

Dr. Baker smiled kindly and drew an easy breath. "Okay, everyone, this is Sarah. She's here by choice because she suffered a breakdown. Her parents have recently become part of her life again and are very supportive of the therapy she's receiving at Orchards." Dr. Baker looked at Sarah and waited until the girl nodded, apparently giving the doctor permission to continue. "Sarah's struggles come from having had three abortions." Dr. Baker paused. "Sarah, you want to tell them what you're feeling?"

Everyone in the group seemed to settle back in their chairs, and Maggie wondered if it was out of interest or because they were relieved to have the spotlight on Sarah.

Sarah ran the bony fingers of her right hand over her left forearm and kept her eyes trained on the floor. Seconds passed and her shoulders began to tremble as tears spilled onto her dime-store canvas tennis shoes.

"If you're not quite ready to share, we'll move—"

"No." Sarah looked up and wiped her shaking hand across her wet cheek. "It's time. If I don't talk about it now, I never will."

Maggie took in everything about Sarah and felt the unfamiliar stirrings of compassion in her heart. *Have I been so caught up in myself that I've forgotten how to feel for someone else?* Maggie didn't want to think about the answer. Not now, with Sarah about to bare her very soul.

"I never meant to get pregnant." Sarah exhaled loudly and tilted her head up so that her eyes fell on a Victorian print of a woman and child that hung on the wall. Fresh tears filled her eyes, but when she continued speaking, her voice was steadier than before. "I never meant to sleep with the guys I dated."

"Are you saying you wish you hadn't been sexually active with them?" Dr. Baker's question was soft, gentle.

Sarah nodded. "I was raised in a Christian home but, well, I didn't think it was what I wanted. All my friends were going to parties and drinking, sleeping with their boyfriends. I didn't want to be different. You know, Miss Goody Two-shoes." Sarah hung her head. "I stopped going to church and talking to my mom. She asked me stuff like always, but I wouldn't answer her. Just told her I was fine and to leave me alone. I deserved a life of my own."

Sarah stopped talking and wiped at her cheeks. Maggie's heart ached for the girl. How many others like Sarah were out there, suffering from a similar rebellion, with no one to talk to, to help them? No wonder there were so many hurting women in the church. Women like Sarah.

And like me, Maggie realized with a start. She'd been the same, hiding, in rebellion, not talking about her baby until...

"After that I ran with a wilder crowd. It was like I could do whatever I wanted for the first time. I broke curfew and snuck out my bedroom window in the middle of the night. The first time I got pregnant I was only fifteen."

Dr. Baker shifted her position. "Could you tell us how you felt when you found out?"

Sarah crossed her ankles and clenched her hands as the weight of tormenting regret filled her face. "At first I was a little excited. My aunt had a new baby at that time and I used to love to—"

She gave way to two quick sobs. The middle-aged woman beside her put an arm over Sarah's shoulders and hugged her close.

"Whenever you're ready, Sarah." Dr. Baker's voice was barely audible, more a verbal embrace than an urging to continue.

Sarah steadied herself, drew a deep breath, and leaned into the middle-aged woman's arm. "I love babies. I always have. So at first I dreamed about having it and what it would look like and what names I would choose. But after a few weeks my boyfriend broke up with me and all of a sudden I was terrified. He paid for the abortion and a year later I was pregnant again—this time by another guy."

"Sarah, help us understand something. Why did you choose to sleep with your next boyfriend after all the pain it caused you the first time around?"

Sarah's forehead creased. "That wasn't something I thought about much." Her eyes met Dr. Baker's. "I guess I figured I wasn't worth anything anymore. And that was the only way I could please the guy I was with. But since I've been here I've thought about it a lot and I think maybe…well, maybe I wasn't willing to be honest with myself."

"What do you mean?"

"Well, like I bought the lie."

"The lie about abortion."

Sarah nodded. "Right. I told myself everything the people at the clinic said was true. It wasn't really a baby, it was my choice. It was legal. There was nothing wrong with what I did. Those kinds of things."

"And you kept telling yourself those things after your second abortion?"

"Even after my third. The dreams didn't start 'till last year."

Dr. Baker nodded as if she was familiar with Sarah's dreams. "Are you comfortable talking about that?"

Sarah nodded and her face grew pale as she bit her lip. *I've been there, Sarah,* Maggie thought. "About a year ago, I started dreaming about my babies. All three of them. And there, in my hours of sleep, I began to really know them. There were two girls and a boy."

Silence echoed through the room for a moment, and Maggie felt a unified concern for this girl who had so clearly suffered for her choices. This time Sarah clenched her hands so tightly her knuckles turned white. "Of course I don't know if my babies really would have been two girls and a boy. But in my dreams they're the same each time. Three babies, each in a crib, and me in the middle. One by one I would take them in my arms and love them, snuggle them the way I never…never got to—" Sarah hung her head and wept.

Several group members went to her then, each placing a hand of support on Sarah's knees or shoulders.

Maggie wanted to join them, but she remained frozen in place.

"Do you want to stop, Sarah?"

The girl sniffed loudly and shook her head. "No, I've come this far. I want to finish if that's okay."

"Of course. Go ahead, whenever you're ready."

Sarah sat up straighter, and those who had surrounded her eased back to give her space. "The dream always changes then. After loving each of my babies, the room gets dark and a strong wind begins to blow. Then one at a time I'd take my little babies and walk them to the edge of a cliff. And…and throw them over the edge. I would look over and w-w-watch them until they disappeared. And I would know I was the most awful person in the world."

Sarah's body convulsed from the silent sobs that assaulted her. Maggie imagined living through such a dream, over and over and over again, and tears filled her own eyes. How had the girl survived such torment?

"Sarah, you know you don't have anything to fear anymore, right?" Dr. Baker leaned over her knees bringing her that much closer to Sarah.

"I know. The dreams stopped as soon as I confessed everything to Christ. He forgives me, and in my head I know I can go on without the guilt. But…" She swallowed thickly. "I can still hear their cries as they fall into the canyon. And somewhere in heaven there are three little babies that should be—" a single sob escaped—"five, four, and two years old."

Maggie felt her own tears turning into deep, desperate sobs. She wasn't alone. There were other mothers who had turned their backs on their babies to make their own lives easier. But there was one difference. She had actually held her baby and then tossed her over a canyon's edge. Or she might as well have done so. She had wanted to keep her little girl, but had instead given her away for the love of Ben Stovall. The wave of tears continued to wash over her.

The group uttered its support to Sarah, looking furtively at Maggie and the avalanche of pain that had been released. Dr. Baker took control. "Sarah, why don't you and the others take a ten-minute break, and then we'll meet back here. I think we've shared enough for this session, and I'd still like to spend some time looking at Scripture and talking about honesty."

Maggie remained in her seat, her head down, tears still flowing, as the others quietly filed out of the room. Dr. Baker moved to the chair next to Maggie's and placed a hand on her knee. "Touched a nerve?"

Maggie's head was spinning and she tried to remember what Dr. Camas had said. Would Dr. Baker know her entire history? Had he shared it with her before assigning Maggie to the woman doctor's group session? Maggie was, after all, a well-known personality. Dr. Baker would certainly know that much. The woman behind the "Maggie's Mind" column shouldn't be falling apart like this, in public, in group therapy, while a patient at a psychiatric hospital.

Let no deceit come from your lips…

No deceit? Maggie feared the thought. No deceit meant being transparent with people she'd never met. Her heart raced and a thin layer of perspiration broke out on her forehead. She couldn't tell the truth, could she?

"Maggie…do you want to talk before the others come back?" Dr. Baker's voice was patient, and suddenly Maggie knew the murmurs about avoiding deceit could only have come from a holy God. For the first time in longer than she could remember, Maggie chose to heed the counsel God had given her.

"Yes."

Dr. Baker crossed one leg over the other and Maggie silently thanked her for not seeming in a rush. She wasn't even sure she knew what to say. "How did it make you feel?"

Maggie thought about that for a moment. How did it make her feel? *Guilty, of course. And like an awful wretch.* "I…I guess I did the same thing she did. Only mine wasn't in a dream."

"I'm not sure I understand."

Maggie wiped her tears and tried to compose herself, but still the sobbing continued. "No. I…I gave my baby girl up for adoption and then lived as if I'd never…never had her. Like she'd never existed."

"Oh, Maggie." Dr. Baker stroked Maggie's back the way her mother had done when she was a child, before Maggie grew too old to warrant her attention. "Maggie, giving your baby up for adoption isn't the same as tossing her into a canyon. Many times it's the very kindest choice of all."

Maggie's tears came harder. *How could this stranger understand? Help me, God…the darkness is closing in quickly.* "I can't talk about it now." The others were returning without a word, careful not to interrupt her discussion with Dr. Baker.

"Very well. We can talk about it later. Perhaps you could

come to group twenty minutes early tomorrow?"

Maggie nodded and sat up straighter in her chair. She controlled her tears for the remaining hour of group time and barely registered the things Dr. Baker was saying about honesty and God's love. Something about a fictitious town named Grace where everyone lived in the sunshine and transparency of truth. A place completely motivated by the love of God.

Many of the others shared their thoughts on such a place, but Maggie kept silent. Every now and then a tear would slither down her cheek. Even later when she was in her room she couldn't shake the mantle of desperation that had settled over her.

There was a reason for feeling this way, and Maggie didn't believe any amount of counseling or talking to God could ever make it go away. The reason was a living, breathing child who was being raised by someone else. All because she was afraid of telling the truth to Ben Stovall.

As Maggie fell asleep, she couldn't decide which emotion burned stronger inside her: the aching loss for the child she'd never known or her hatred for the man who had demanded nothing less than perfection from her. The man for whom she'd lived a lie for the past eight years.

The man who had by his standards forced her to throw her tiny daughter over the edge of a canyon, then watch in agony until she disappeared forever.

Eighteen

NANCY TAYLOR PACED THE LIVING ROOM FLOOR OF HER MODEST ranch home and wished for the tenth time that hour that Dan were still alive. His lungs had never been strong, not really. So when he caught pneumonia three years back during one of the coldest weeks that winter, doctors said there wasn't much they could do. His body stopped working, pure and simple, and in two weeks time the illness claimed his life.

At first all there'd been were the memories—fond scrapbook pages that filled her mind and helped her pass the time. Nancy and Dan had been married a month shy of forty years, after all. But eventually time had a way of bringing to light the tasks at hand. Seasons changed, children and grandchildren filtered through the house, until one weekend the previous year Nancy woke up and realized she'd actually done it. She'd learned how to live life without her beloved Dan.

All that changed last night when she got the call.

Ben Stovall was his name, and Nancy had the uncanny feeling he was not some wacko from the big city, not some traveling salesman looking to sell a big-time insurance policy or a Kirby vacuum system. He'd said he was married to Maggie and really that was all he needed to say.

Though Nancy couldn't be sure of the young man's last name, back when Maggie lived with her and Dan she definitely was smitten by a boy named Ben. That much was certain. And thinking about Maggie brought every memory of Dan and the kids and that time in their lives back to mind.

Maggie Johnson.

Taking her in had been the Christian thing to do. Nancy and Dan had only discussed the idea for a few minutes before bowing in prayer and agreeing together that however crowded they might be, there was room for Maggie.

At first, the pale young woman hadn't opened up much. She'd been helpful and quiet and kept to herself. But as her due date neared she gravitated to Nancy, sharing the feelings in her heart and finally talking about Ben, the boy who made her blush at the mention of his name, the boy she loved so desperately.

Nancy stopped pacing and closed her eyes. For a moment she could see Maggie, lovely and radiant in her ninth month of pregnancy despite the emotional battle waging war in her heart. "Mrs. Taylor, this is the right thing, isn't it? Giving the baby up for adoption?"

Back then Nancy had been so certain of her answer. "Yes, dear. Of course it is. You have a lifetime of babies and marriage ahead of you. If this weren't the right thing, you wouldn't be here now, would you?"

In fact it was Dan who had first expressed doubts on the subject. Late one night while Maggie was sleeping he had pulled Nancy aside and frowned sadly. "I'm worried about her."

"Maggie?"

"Yes. I think she's getting herself too attached to that baby she's carrying." Dan struggled for a moment and doodled a design on the hardwood floor with the toe of his boot. "Ah, I don't know, Nancy. You and me understand how it is with babies. They're for keeps. Not something you can give away lightly."

"Dan, it's different with Maggie. She's not married, and she's not ready to be a mother. She said so herself. Adoption is a beautiful thing when the—"

"I know all that. For goodness sake, Nancy, my own two sisters were adopted. Adoption is wonderful for most people, but maybe not for Maggie. Watch her sometime. See how she holds her belly just so and strokes it when she thinks we ain't looking. She's getting attached, I tell you, and I think she might be making the mistake of her lifetime to give that baby up."

Nancy remembered the evening as though it were yesterday. She had considered her husband's words back then, but written them off. Besides, a woman knew more about these things than a man. Yes, Maggie was confused and anxious, but that was to be expected. Adoption still was the best possible choice. How could Maggie be ready for motherhood when she hadn't been willing to discuss her pregnancy with any of the people who mattered to her? Besides, there were so many childless couples desperate to have a baby. Certainly Maggie's child would be cared for and loved, nurtured in a way that Maggie never could have done at her age.

Nancy sighed. Eventually the baby was born, and Maggie had given her up. But far from the relief Nancy had expected, almost overnight a light burned out in Maggie's eyes. For the next month—until she returned home to Akron—Maggie would cry herself to sleep. Even now Nancy could hear the muffled sound of that sweet girl weeping for her baby.

Why didn't I do something back then? Nancy gazed out the window, watching for the car Ben had described. In the years since Maggie left she hadn't stayed in touch…but Nancy had come to believe that Dan's whispered words late that night so long ago had been right all along.

It had been a mistake for Maggie to give up her baby.

The awful truth about the whole thing was that there'd been nothing any of them could do about it after the fact. Dan never brought it up again the way he had that night in the kitchen. But every now and then, when a television program would end and they'd turn off the set and make their way up the stairs to bed, he'd pause at the landing and mutter out loud, "I wonder how Maggie's doing…"

It was a statement that hadn't demanded an answer, and Nancy generally said nothing in response. Still the image hung in their home—and in their hearts—a moment. As it always would. And that was when Nancy would wonder why she hadn't seen it the way Dan had back when Maggie was nine months pregnant.

Why hadn't she asked more questions? Made Maggie call her parents and come clean about her pregnancy, or tell Ben— whoever he was—that there was a baby in the picture? She could have encouraged Maggie to keep the baby, but she had done nothing of the sort. Why?

Nancy had no answers for herself. Not years ago when Dan was alive, and not now.

She opened her eyes, glanced out the window, and searched for the navy blue Pathfinder. Nothing yet. It was 2:45 and, according to Ben's call, he'd arrive sometime in the next fifteen minutes. Her feet propelled her from one side of the room to the other as she considered the situation.

She still couldn't imagine why he'd contacted her.

The man had been polite. He'd introduced himself as Ben Stovall and asked permission to visit the following day. How in the world had he found their number? Nancy stopped pacing and thought about that for a moment. There was only one answer. Somehow Maggie's mother must have held onto it all these years and now Maggie was in trouble. If that were the case, then Ben Stovall—the same Ben, Nancy guessed, that had caused Maggie to blush eight years ago—needed help.

Nancy began moving again, and this time she paced herself into the kitchen where two envelopes lay on the freshly wiped Formica countertop. The first held a slip of paper on which she'd written the name of the social worker who had handled Maggie's adoption case. Though Nancy hadn't doubted Maggie's choice those long years ago, she had always felt it wise to tuck away that information. After all, if Maggie hadn't held onto it—and Nancy doubted that she had, as confused and distraught as she had been after her baby's birth—there might be no one else who would know how to link Maggie with the baby she'd given up.

The second envelope was sealed, and inside was a letter for

Maggie. Nancy had written it a few months after Dan's death, on a sunny morning with the house absolutely silent…that was the moment she first realized Dan had been right.

In part the handwritten letter was an apology from Nancy for not encouraging Maggie to follow her heart. But it was also a prayer to almighty God. For though Nancy had not kept in touch with Maggie, and though she might never know what happened to Maggie's baby, God knew. He knew as surely as He knew the number of hairs on her head.

And so the letter was part prayer, asking God to keep special watch over Maggie's little one and begging Him to reunite them one day, should His will warrant such a meeting.

Nancy wasn't sure what Ben Stovall wanted to talk about or what could be so important that he would drive straight from Cleveland to meet with her in person. But whatever it was, he would leave her house with the two envelopes.

After so many years of doubting her actions during Maggie's pregnancy, this one act was the least she could do for the girl who'd been so dear to Dan and her. The only thing she could do.

Nineteen

BY HIS ESTIMATION, BEN STOVALL WAS TEN MINUTES FROM NANCY Taylor's house and he pushed the accelerator as far down as he safely could.

Why, Maggie? Why are you doing this to us? Did you really have to lie to me about Israel?

He asked the questions countless times on the five-hour drive from Cleveland to Woodland, and still he had no answers. There were other questions, too…horrible concerns about the things McFadden had said, but Ben refused to think those things through. He couldn't stand doing so.

Besides, after today he would probably have more answers than he wanted.

He felt the familiar thickening in his throat and blinked back tears. *Why, God? What did I ever do to make her lie to me? We did everything right, didn't we? Followed Your plan, sought You at every turn? Why has it come to this?* Ben was baffled at what had become of his life. Two weeks ago he and Maggie were happily married, their foster boys were flourishing in their care, and he had never had a run-in with the law in any way, from any angle. Now…

He gave a humorless laugh. Now his wife was in a mental hospital refusing to see him, while her former boyfriend—a drug-dealing street thug, no less—had told who knew how many lies about his relationship with Maggie. A relationship that happened the year before she and Ben had married.

On top of that, the man had very nearly beaten him to death, and now Ben had signed a criminal complaint in a case that would likely drag through court for two years. The foster boys were gone, his job at the office was on hold, and he had driven three hundred miles south on a crazy search for a woman he'd never heard of before to see if she knew whether his wife had ever had a baby out of wedlock.

It sounded like a soap opera, not the kind of life a man of faith should be living. *How did we end up here? What terrible thing did my Maggie girl do when she dated—*

Judge not, or you, too, will be judged…

The advice filtered through his mind, and Ben dismissed it. He wasn't judging anyone. He was defending Maggie's honor. He knew her better than that…that *criminal* ever had. Nothing could have forced Maggie to give a baby up for adoption. And if that part of what John McFadden had said was false, Ben guessed the rest was false, too.

Whatever time and energy he might spend on his trip to Woodland, it was worth every minute. He would defend his wife and perhaps, in the process, help her come to her senses so that when she did, they could resume their lives.

Ben followed the directions Nancy Taylor had given him and turned a corner, which put him in the heart of a middle-class neighborhood with 1970s-style ranch homes. He drove past four houses, then pulled over in front of the largest one on the block. Ben turned off the car and studied the house for a moment.

So this was where Maggie had lived. *Definitely not Israel.*

He paused. Maybe Maggie had lied because she was trying to impress him. Maybe the whole story about Israel was designed to make her look well traveled and educated. The truth—that she'd spent the semester in Woodland with the Taylor family—wasn't nearly as appealing. But would such a lie cause Maggie to reject him completely, to look him in the eyes and tell him he had never really known her?

Ben doubted it and for a moment he was pierced with fear of the unknown.

What if Maggie—

He shook his head and climbed out of the car, slipping on a

pullover sweater. He wouldn't consider the idea. It was impossible.

He walked up a brick pathway to the front door and rang the buzzer.

A woman in her midsixties answered the door and offered him a smile that never quite reached her eyes. *Help me here, God. Please.*

"Hello, I'm Nancy Taylor. You must be Ben?"

"Yes, thanks for letting me come."

The woman opened the door wider and extended her hand. "Come in. Have a seat, and I'll be there in a minute."

Ben followed her into a front room and sat down while Mrs. Taylor disappeared into the kitchen. The smell of fresh-baked bread filled the air. At the far end of the sitting area a cheery blaze danced in the fireplace beneath a mantle lined with framed photographs of smiling teenagers. Ben had the feeling he'd come home somehow, and he felt himself relax.

No wonder Maggie wanted to spend a semester here.

The place was as warm and inviting as anywhere Ben had ever been. Mrs. Taylor brought him a mug of coffee and a plate of cookies and then settled down across from him. She was weathered and white-haired, but she had an amazing energy and a light in her eyes that seemed to come straight from her soul.

"One question first…" Nancy set her cup down and leveled her gaze at Ben. "Are you the Ben Maggie talked about when she stayed with us?"

Ben thought back to that summer those eight years earlier and his fears faded almost completely. Maggie had talked about him to the Taylors, even though they hadn't officially gotten back together at that point. "Yes. Maggie and I talked before she moved here. She knew I was waiting for her back in Cleveland."

Nancy nodded thoughtfully and stared at the cast on Ben's arm. "Were you in an accident?"

Ben knew the visible bruises had faded now so he didn't feel the need to explain. "Nothing serious."

Relief filled Nancy's eyes. "I thought…I was worried Maggie might have been in an accident…"

Ben understood the woman's concerns. "No, nothing like that."

Situating herself more comfortably, Nancy cocked her head. "Okay, I'm ready. Tell me what's happening with Maggie."

Ben sighed and combed his fingers along the length of his cast and noticed that the pain was not as intense as before. "She's not doing very well, Mrs. Taylor."

"Nancy. Call me Nancy."

"Okay. She's in a psychiatric hospital and…well, she doesn't want to talk to me."

This was harder than he'd thought. How did he tell a woman he didn't even know that his life was suddenly in disarray? Ben studied Nancy Taylor's face and felt encompassed by her quiet spirit. "I guess I need to start at the beginning."

He took a fortifying swig of coffee and set the mug down while Nancy waited. He was no longer afraid of what he might find out. Maggie wouldn't have spent the semester talking about him if she'd been hiding a pregnancy by McFadden.

"For the past few months she's been saying strange things to me, telling me I never knew her and acting weird, out of character. I guess it was part of the buildup. Then one day she forgot our foster boys at the—"

"Foster boys?" Nancy sat up straighter. For some reason she seemed concerned by this bit of information.

Ben hesitated. "Yes. We've tried but…well, we can't seem to have children of our own. We were actually considering adoption when Maggie had her breakdown."

Nancy sighed and shifted positions. He couldn't tell for sure, but it looked like the weight of the world had just taken up residence on the woman's shoulders.

"No children?" The question was low, heavy.

"No, ma'am."

"Maggie very badly wanted babies. But, of course, you know that, I'm sure."

Ben felt like a man waiting for the other shoe to fall. Why was the woman stuck on this subject? "Yes. She still feels that way, I'm sure. But since she accused me of not knowing her, I decided to do some research into her background. Figure out what she's been hiding."

"Maybe her breakdown has nothing to do with not knowing you…"

Ben decided to let Nancy continue.

"Maybe this is about the baby."

Ben felt the blood leave his face. *Baby? No, God, it can't be true…* If there had been a rewind function on the tape player of life, Ben would have hit it immediately, excused himself from the room, and never returned to the Taylor house. Instead, he remained glued to his seat, motionless but for his heart, which had skidded into a wild, unrecognizable rhythm.

"Ben? Are you okay?" Nancy leaned forward in her seat, her face etched with grave concern. "I'm assuming you never connected the two?"

Ben swallowed hard and tried to keep his mind from spinning. "I'm not sure I follow you. What baby?"

A look of realization came over Nancy's face and a shadow of guilt filled her eyes, as if she'd accidentally done or said something that she only now understood to be taboo. "Why, Maggie's baby of course. The baby she had when she was staying with us."

Ben couldn't have felt worse if someone had walked up and sent a hammer deep into his gut. So, it was true. The horrible things John McFadden had said about Maggie had actually happened. And the foundation of everything she'd ever told him was a lie.

The realization was more than Ben could bear.

He stood and moved across the room to the front window.

There, turning his back on Nancy Taylor, Ben stared at the cloudless sky and tried to absorb the pain. *Say something, do something! Scream or cry or run back to the car.* But he was completely paralyzed by the truth.

Maggie had lied to him for eight years.

The woman he had married was none of the things she had pretended to be.

From behind him, Ben heard Nancy set her coffee cup down on the saucer. "Ben, I'm so sorry. I always thought you knew. Maggie told us you were…"

Ben spun around, hot anger coursing through his veins. "The *father?*" He turned back toward the window. "Don't believe it, Nancy. That was a lie, like a lot of other things Maggie said back then."

"So…the baby wasn't yours? You're sure?"

Ben clenched his fists and faced the older woman once more. This time he returned to the overstuffed chair and sat perched on the edge, his gaze leveled at her. "Maggie and I waited until we were married to become…intimate. There is no way on earth that baby was mine."

Shock settled over Nancy's features and then sorrow. "It all makes sense, then."

Ben was too angry to care. He dug his elbows into his knees and planted his head in his hands. "How could she lie about that? Make me believe she was a virgin? Keep me in the dark about this for *eight years?*" His voice was seething with rage and when he fell silent, Nancy cleared her throat.

"I don't know the answers to your questions, Ben, and maybe this is none of my business. But you're here, and I believe the Lord would have me say this. Maggie agonized over giving that baby up for adoption. When we talked about it, the only thing she would say was that the two of you weren't ready for children yet. She loved that baby, but clearly she loved you more."

What was this now? Was Nancy fighting Maggie's cause for her? How could anyone calling herself a Christian defend Maggie's decision to sleep with a man like John McFadden, to lie about the fact, and then to give her child up for adoption all to marry another man. And all under the guise of false virginity?

It was an indefensible crime.

For all have sinned and fall short of the glory of God...forgive, My son, forgive.

Ben squeezed his eyes shut. This was no time for Scripture. He'd just been dealt the most devastating blow of his life. Everything about the past eight years, the woman he'd married and all she'd represented, had been a lie. All might have fallen short, but what Maggie had done crossed a line, and Ben wasn't about to forgive her. His heart filled with the image of Maggie in her wedding dress, her eyes aglow.

How could she have...?

His emotions warred within him, and he knew that the undying love he'd felt for her the day before was now rivaled only by the intensity of his hatred.

When Ben remained silent, Nancy continued. "Do you blame her?"

For an instant he started to raise his voice, then he remembered that Nancy wasn't his enemy. Maggie was. "Of course, I blame her. This is all about her."

Nancy settled back into the sofa and leveled a curious gaze at him. "Listen to you, Ben. You're furious with her. If this is how you react now—with your wife suffering a breakdown at a psychiatric hospital—perhaps she felt she had no choice but to lie to you back then."

Ben glared at Nancy. "With all due respect, Nancy, you don't know the whole story. Maggie did more than tell a simple lie. She slept with an awful man, got pregnant, gave the baby up for adoption, and never told me a word of it."

Nancy was silent, but there was a maddening calm and compassion in her eyes—feelings Ben was certain were not derived from any pity for him. The woman was sympathizing with Maggie!

Why couldn't she understand Maggie's fault in this? "Oh, never mind. You don't understand." Ben stood to leave. "Listen, I gotta get out of here and do some thinking, get a hotel or something."

The woman remained seated and said nothing.

"Thanks for your time." Ben moved quickly across the room and was halfway out the front door, when she spoke up.

"Ben?"

He paused, tempted to ignore her, to leave and never look back, to forget everything she'd said…or that he was ever married to a woman named Maggie in the first place.

His insides seemed to be deflating and his sense of balance was off. *How could she? All those years of marriage and never, not once, did she tell me the truth! And then her boyfriend nearly killed me—*

He turned and stepped backward into the Taylors' front room. With his back to Nancy, he braced himself against the door frame. "Why?" He shouted the word and it hung in the air. Struggling to find his composure once more, he turned abruptly and found Nancy still on the sofa, her watery eyes locked on his.

"Listen carefully to what I'm going to tell you, Ben. I don't know if it'll make a difference between you and Maggie, but maybe it'll help you understand."

Ben didn't know what to do, what to feel. *I don't want to listen; I need to think, Lord. Get me as far away from this as…as…it can't be true, Lord. No…not my Maggie!*

His blood was hot with the intensity of his anger. The muscles in his hand twitched and he craved the relief of crashing his fist through a wall. Anything to relieve the rage and sorrow that warred in his heart. Helpless to act on any of these feelings, he stood motionless, his shoulders slumped, utter defeat washing over him.

Nancy continued. "In this world there is no shortage of phonies, of people who come at you with one line or another never intending to make good on their word. Maggie wasn't one of those. She never could have been. Maggie Johnson was a scared young woman desperately in love with you. And in the midst of the most terrifying time in her life, she made a decision to give her baby up for adoption—from the sounds of it, the only baby Maggie's ever had—all because of her love for you."

Nancy wiped an errant tear off her cheek and cleared her throat. "But Maggie couldn't live a lie like that forever. So gradually, year after year, the truth must have been eating away at her. Not only the truth about the lies she told you, but the truth about her baby, that she gave that child up when everything in her screamed not to do so."

Ben closed his eyes and crossed his arms; the woman was romanticizing the entire situation. There was nothing sentimental about what Maggie had done. She had lied, plain and simple, and then lived that lie every day for too many years. She was no longer someone Ben could—

"I don't know what thoughts are rambling through that self-righteous head of yours, Ben, and forgive me for being so forward. But in a world full of people who say what they want, when they want, and never look back, Maggie is genuine. The fact that she's lived these past years never knowing her child's love, never certain of that baby's welfare, never telling you the truth about her past—those facts have obviously become more than she can bear."

Ben raised his head and stared at Nancy. "The whole thing could have been solved up front—" he pushed the words out through clenched teeth—"if only she'd been honest with me. Don't you see that? Maggie's right. We have no marriage now because I can't be married to someone I don't know. And this...this Maggie who would do these things...is someone I don't know at all."

Nancy sat back into the sofa and cocked her head thoughtfully. "Is that right? A Maggie who would go to whatever extremes necessary to win your love? You don't recognize that woman?"

Ben sighed. Nancy was twisting everything around. It wasn't only the lies Maggie had told. It was the reality. The fact that she'd been with another man—a man like John McFadden—before they were married. It was something Ben couldn't stomach even if he—

"Ask yourself this, Ben. Would you have married Maggie if she'd told you the truth? Would you have married her if she'd confessed she wasn't a virgin on your wedding night?"

Ben twisted his face in confusion. "I don't know...I'd saved myself for Maggie, and she was supposed to do the same thing. I always thought I'd marry a—"

"A virgin." Nancy finished his sentence. "Exactly." She paused a moment and studied Ben through disappointed eyes. When she spoke again her voice was barely more than a whisper. "And you wonder why she lied?"

Forgive, My son, as I have forgiven you...

No, Lord, I don't want to. None of this was how I planned it and now my whole life is ruined, changed forever—

For I know the plans I have for you...plans to give you a hope and a future and not to harm you.

Ben pushed out the quiet whisperings in his soul so that he could think about his next step. Where in the world did he go from here? Should he call Maggie and tell her he knew the truth? Tell her he was in agreement with her plans for a quick divorce? Maybe initiate the proceedings himself before—

"I'll be right back." Nancy stood and slipped into the kitchen. When she returned she handed Ben two white envelopes. One looked slightly yellowed, as though it had been sealed years earlier. The other was bright and new. "I think you should have these before you go, in case I never see you again."

His anger subsided briefly as he studied the envelopes. "What's this?"

Nancy pointed to the older envelope. "That's a letter I wrote

Maggie years ago when my husband died. I didn't know where to send it so I held on to it."

Ben was confused. What was he supposed to do with it? Especially now, with Maggie refusing his visits. Was he supposed to wait until they were in divorce court and then hand them to her? In Nancy's presence he felt like the villain, as though she unconditionally accepted Maggie and her choices and somehow blamed *him* in the process. It was easy for her to stand in judgment of him, assuming he had driven Maggie not only to lie but also to give up her child.

She doesn't know me, Lord. What's happened isn't my fault.

Nancy reached out and ran her finger over the yellowed envelope, then brought her eyes up to Ben's. "After my husband died, I realized Maggie never should have given that baby up for adoption. She loved that little girl more than life itself. But somehow she was bent on making you happy."

Ben's head reeled once more. *Girl? Maggie's baby had been a girl?* "Did you say the baby was a…"

Ben checked his heart and wondered at the strange sensations coursing through him. He chided himself for his reaction. It didn't matter whether Maggie's baby was a girl or boy. The child belonged to another man. Besides, she was adopted more than seven years ago. She might live in another country by now for all he knew.

So why was the knowledge of her existence, and the fact that she'd just been made more real by the identification of her gender, causing a lump in his throat?

"Yes, Maggie had a girl. Which brings me to the information in the second envelope. The name of Maggie's social worker in Cincinnati. I don't know what your intentions are, Ben, but while you're here it wouldn't hurt to look that woman up."

Ben clutched the envelopes tightly and jammed them inside his jacket. For a moment he hung his head, not sure what more he could say.

Forgive…as I have forgiven you, so you must forgive…

This time the quiet whispering sparked a twinge of compassion in his soul. He was still angry, but somehow the image of Maggie all those years ago, missing her little girl...not knowing where she was... *Poor Maggie, hiding the truth all these years...giving up a baby girl...all because she loved me.*

His anger sounded loudly once more. *No matter what happened, she didn't have to lie. Year after year after—*

He met Nancy's gaze once more wishing only for the solitude to sort through his feelings. "I'm sorry about my reaction. I guess I...I thought Maggie was...I believed her. It makes me feel like I really don't know her."

Nancy leaned toward Ben and patted him firmly on the shoulder, her eyes wet with tears. "Maggie's a good girl, Ben. She loves you more than you know. But you're going to need to pray hard this time, because if she's set on divorcing you...well...if I know Maggie, it's going to take a miracle to change her mind."

Maybe I don't want her to change it. Maybe it'd be best to let it... Ben pushed his thoughts back, thanked the woman again, and left.

He walked in a haze, feeling as though his life had been decimated by an atom bomb. Everything he knew to be right and real and true had been obliterated in the time it took Nancy to say four words: *"Maybe it's the baby."*

Shuffling, Ben made it to the car, slid inside, and pulled the newer envelope from his pocket. The one with the information on Maggie's social worker...the information that could lead him to Maggie's illegitimate daughter. He stared at it for a minute, then tossed it on the seat beside him. As he started his car, Nancy's words came back to him, taking up residence in his mind and taunting him as he drove across town to the local motel, checked in, and climbed wearily into bed.

Through every action, the woman's words remained:

"I don't know what your intentions are, Ben, but while you're here it wouldn't hurt to look that woman up...look her up...look her up. It wouldn't hurt to look her up."

Ben had no intention of contacting the social worker. He wanted only to get home, return to work and sign whatever divorce papers Maggie was having prepared from the hospital.

It wasn't until three o'clock that morning—while Nancy's words rattled around in his head refusing him any sleep—that he realized maybe the woman was right. After all, his office wasn't expecting him back for another week. Why not do some checking?

He flipped on the bedside light, climbed out of bed, and found the crisp, white envelope where he'd set it on the table. Fine. He'd open it and find out what was inside. Working his finger under the seal, he ripped the flap and pulled out a single slip from inside. Scrawled neatly across the middle it said: "Social worker Kathy Garrett handled the adoption of Maggie's baby girl. Kathy works out of the Cincinnati County Courthouse."

Ben let his eyes linger on the words. *Maggie's baby girl. Maggie's baby girl? How could it be possible?* The whole ordeal was unimaginable, like something from a terrible nightmare. He rubbed his eyes and stared once more at the slip of paper.

Nancy Taylor was right. If he didn't want to lie awake all night tossing and turning while her words haunted him, he'd take the next day and do some research. What could it possibly hurt?

Ben leaned back with a sigh. How many times over the years had he wanted a little girl of his own? A child who was part Maggie, part princess...one who would look to him with adoring eyes knowing he would protect her, cherish her to the end of time.

A little girl. Maggie's daughter. I can't believe it, Lord.

He tried to imagine what Maggie's little girl might look like.

Blond hair, probably, like Maggie's when she was a child. Big, cornflower blue eyes in a face that—

He sat up with a jerk. *Forget about it! She's McFadden's daughter, too. Besides, she probably has a wonderful life with her adoptive parents. His interference now would do nothing but harm her.* His emotions warring within him, he lay back down and sometime later that night fell asleep, dreaming about little girls who looked like Maggie and a social worker named Kathy Garrett.

Twenty

IN THE WEEK SINCE JOHN MCFADDEN HAD POSTED BAIL HE'D HAD plenty of time to reconsider his earlier vow and decide that killing Ben Stovall might not be necessary. The guy should have died from the beating, but since he hadn't, John had come up with an alternative plan. One that involved the kid.

Of course, killing Stovall would be the most satisfying solution. And the easiest. No one to testify against him in court, nobody pressing charges for assault. No witnesses to the drug trafficking taking place at the bar. But after thinking it through, John recognized several drawbacks.

The worst was the chance of getting caught. If John acted alone, he'd get the death penalty should the police catch him. And more often these days, police seemed to do just that. Not more than a month ago a regular at the bar had been nailed for knocking off an...associate. Took the guy out nice and clean with a simple car bomb. The bum deserved it. If he'd tampered with one of John's laundering operations, he'd have gotten the same thing. Dead. The guy who did the killing had been careful. No fingerprints, nothing. But the police still figured it out.

No, the chance of being caught where murder was concerned was very real. As real as the gas chamber.

The whole idea of the death penalty had forced John to examine his reasons for wanting Stovall dead in the first place. Yeah, the guy had seen them handling drugs, and being a lawyer, he was sure to blow the whistle on them. John gritted his teeth. His whole operation could come down around his ears if Stovall talked. Still, time in prison for drug smuggling—however long that might be—beat a death penalty conviction.

Then there was the chance that Stovall didn't know what

he'd seen. Could be the upright, uptight lawyer-man didn't know John and his boys were unloading drugs. If he did Stovall, took him out like he itched to, it was a sure bet the cops would be on his doorstep. He'd be a suspect, no doubt. And a murder investigation would have blue uniforms swarming around the bar looking for any information they could find. And that would also kill his operation.

He uttered a curse and went to pour himself a drink. Why did the guy have to show up anyway? Why didn't he have the sense to die from the beating?

John took a slow sip of his drink. Maggie's husband, huh? Figures she'd marry a straight-and-narrow like that. He sneered at his reflection in the bar mirror. Yeah, it would feel good to kill Stovall…problem was, there was really no clean way to kill the guy. If there was one thing John couldn't stand it was a messy crime scene. Bloody fingerprints and murder weapons and signs of struggle…any of it could lead police to his front door. And then it would be all over but the switch pulling.

Which meant he needed another plan. He thought of the little girl again, and his face twisted into a satisfied smile.

No, he wouldn't kill Ben Stovall, he'd drive him crazy instead.

And if the kid got hurt in the process, so be it.

Twenty-one

LATE THAT NIGHT, AMANDA ROLLED ONTO HER SIDE AND INHALED sharply. It still hurt. She'd looked in the mirror before going to bed—the bruises were starting to go away. Ugly, yellow-brown streaks still showed on her face and arms and ribs. And her eyes were still that icky red, even after two weeks. Broken capill…capill…

What was that word? She couldn't remember. Broken something.

She gently touched the place over her eyebrow where she'd been cut, and traced the scar across her forehead to the place where her hair began. Forty-two stitches, the doctor said. And it still hurt to take a deep breath, but the doctor said broken ribs were like that. Sometimes it took months before you could breathe without pain.

But the happiest thing was that none of it mattered. Not the pain or the scars or the scary memory of Mrs. Graystone.

The only thing that made any difference at all was that she was back with the Garrett family. And as long as they couldn't find a foster home for her, she'd stay right there, sleeping on the couch and doing her best not to be a nuisance.

Sometimes on nights like this, she would lie awake and thank God over and over and over again for letting her live with the Garretts.

"You love me, don't you, God? I can tell." The whispered words slipped out into the empty room, and Amanda smiled at the darkness. The Garretts were sleeping, and she didn't want to wake them even if she wasn't the slightest bit tired. Wonderful thoughts danced in her head. Maybe they'd never

237

find another foster home for her. Maybe the Garretts would build that thing, whatever it was called, so that there'd be an extra bedroom and she could live with them forever.

She thought of Kathy Garrett, so kind and gentle and loving. Even when Kathy was busy with the other children she would draw Amanda close, stroking her hair and arms and promising her everything would turn out okay. When Amanda's ribs hurt and she couldn't help crying, Kathy would lie next to her and rub her back, asking Jesus to find the right home for Amanda and help her heal up real quick.

But most of all, the thought that kept Amanda awake at nights was one she hadn't shared with anyone else. It was a crazy thought, maybe, but it was so wonderful it was worth thinking about for hours and hours. Even if it meant lying awake on the couch under a pile of blankets while everyone else was sleeping...

Amanda smiled. What if, somehow, just maybe, Kathy was actually her real mother? Amanda hugged herself and let out a soft giggle. She bet it was true. She bet, maybe, a long time ago, Kathy gave up a little girl and maybe she'd been looking secretly all these years trying to find her. Maybe she hadn't said anything about her missing little girl because she had given up any hope of finding her.

It was possible. Maybe that's why Kathy took in foster kids and even adopted some of them. Because she had given up Amanda and didn't know where to find her, didn't know that living right there on her very own sofa was the little girl she'd been searching for. After all, Kathy had said she'd known Amanda all her life. So maybe...just maybe...

"Amanda?" She heard the soft padding of Kathy's slippered feet and watched as she came around the corner in her bathrobe, a worried look on her face.

"Hi." Amanda remembered to whisper. It was a lot of work for Kathy when the other kids woke up too soon.

Kathy sat down on the edge of the sofa and smoothed back

Amanda's bangs. Amanda loved the way Kathy's hand felt on her skin…cool and gentle.

"Sweetie, why're you still awake? You went to bed five hours ago. Are you feeling okay?"

"Mmm-hmm." Should she tell her?

Kathy ran her fingers over Amanda's cheek. "Then what is it, honey? You need your rest, just like the other kids."

Tell her. Go on, tell her and maybe it'll be true after all.

Amanda squirmed under the covers and rolled partially on her side so she could see Kathy better. "I got a thought the other day and it won't go away."

"A thought?"

"Mmm-hmm."

"You wanna tell me?"

Kathy wasn't mad at her for still being awake. It seemed to Amanda like she never got angry, not when you spilled your milk or asked too many questions or waited until morning to do your homework. Amanda wasn't worried that her secret thoughts would make Kathy mad, just that…well, what if she said them out loud and they weren't true?

"Amanda?" Kathy eyes got that soft look, like they did whenever she had a question. "What is it, sweetie?"

"I'm not sure I can tell you."

Kathy smiled that favorite smile. The one that made Amanda sure she was safe and warm and loved. The one that made her think that somehow, Kathy might be her real—

"Honey, you can tell me anything. You know that. We've had some great talks since you've been here."

Amanda bit her lower lip. *Why not? If it was true, it would be the happiest day of her life.* "Well, okay." She waited, trying to think of the best words to explain. "You know how me and you have known each other ever since I was a baby?"

"Yes. Ever since you were placed with the Brownells."

"Well, I was wondering… Kathy, did *you* ever give a baby up for adoption?"

Kathy's face clouded. "Why, no, honey, I never did. What makes you ask that?"

Amanda felt her smile fade. Maybe Kathy had trouble remembering...maybe it was something she'd tried to forget, like the months Amanda had spent with Mrs. Graystone. "Think real hard, Kathy. Don't you remember?"

"Sweetheart, why do you ask?" Kathy was sitting up straighter and now she wore that confused look.

Amanda sighed. "I was thinking maybe you gave a baby up, you know, maybe seven years ago, and maybe you work with adoptions 'cause you wanted to help kids. So you wouldn't feel so bad about the little girl you gave up. And I was thinking maybe if you did give a little girl up, then maybe that's why God let you be in my life."

Kathy's eyebrows moved closer together, and her mouth opened and closed a few times. "God let me be in your life because I had a little girl I'd given up? That's what you thought?"

Amanda shook her head. "No." Her voice got quiet, and there was a deep aching in her chest that had nothing to do with her broken ribs. "I thought if you gave up a little girl, maybe I was her. And maybe all these years you'd been searching for your own little girl and the whole time it's been me. Right here." Amanda felt two tears trickling down her cheeks and she wiped them with her pajama sleeve.

"Oh, honey, I'm so sorry." Kathy leaned over her and pulled her into a hug that lasted a long, long time. "I love you like you're my own little girl. That much will always be true."

Amanda's tears were coming faster now, and her body trembled with sadness. "S-s-so...you never gave a little girl up for adoption?"

Kathy's arms tightened around her. "No, sweetie. But that doesn't mean I don't love you. I couldn't love you more even if you were my own little girl."

"But you'd let me live with you forever if I was, right?"

Kathy was quiet, and Amanda pulled back enough to see that she was crying.

"Oh, Amanda, of course. I'd let you live with us now, but it isn't up to me. You know that. The state says our house is too small for another child."

Amanda knew. She didn't understand, but she knew. It wasn't like she was that big, like she took up that much space...

They both were quiet for a long time while they dried their tears and remained locked in a hug. "I have a mother somewhere, don't I, Kathy?"

"Yes, dear."

"Tell me about her again. Please." Amanda lay back down on the sofa as Kathy sat up once more and sniffed back her tears.

"Your mother was very young when you were born, Amanda. Too young to take care of you or give you a nice home. So instead, because she loved you very much, she decided to give you to the Brownells. The Brownells couldn't have their own children, so you were their little princess. They were wonderful people and would have been your forever family if it hadn't been for the accident."

Amanda squeezed her eyes shut. She had loved the Brownells, but they were gone and she didn't want to talk about them. Not now, when there was nothing they could do to help her. "What about my mother? What happened to her?"

Kathy angled her head thoughtfully. "I imagine she returned home, wherever that was, and grew up. Probably got married, that sort of thing."

"Do you think she misses me?"

"Sweetheart—" Kathy swallowed hard and her voice sounded funny—"I'll bet there isn't a day that goes by when she doesn't think of you."

Amanda thought about that. Her mother was out there somewhere, and wherever she was, she spent time each day thinking about the little girl she gave away. If that was true, then there was a chance her mother might actually try to find her. And if she did, then it was possible that one day—maybe even one day soon—her mother would show up and take her home forever.

The ache in her chest faded a bit. "Really, Kathy? You really think she remembers me like that?"

Kathy bent down and kissed Amanda's cheek. "Really and honestly and truly. For all we know, she might be thinking about you right now."

With a soft good night Kathy stood and left Amanda to fall asleep. And as Kathy—who wasn't her real mother after all—padded up the stairs, Amanda prayed harder than she'd ever prayed before that God might move mountains or send angels or do whatever He needed to do.

As long as He helped her find her mommy.

IT WAS TIME TO TELL THE GROUP.

After that first session the previous week, Maggie had taken to coming twenty minutes early every day. Combined with her time with Dr. Camas, Maggie was finally able to move beyond the past and begin unraveling her current thoughts and emotions. The conversations with Dr. Baker had helped Maggie feel more comfortable with the group as a whole.

In the past week she had learned all of their names. She had listened while—one at a time—they each had bared their hearts to the others. There was the bone-thin man who had trouble making eye contact. Harold was his name, and six months ago his wife and daughter were killed in a car accident. He had stopped eating. That was his way of checking out, of expressing his lack of will to live. In group discussion he realized that his depression centered around a very real feeling of abandonment. Not only by his family, but by God, as well.

The well-dressed woman in her late forties was Betty, a homemaker whose husband had left her ten years earlier. Now her children were raised and gone and she was desperately afraid of being alone. Her fears had built over the previous year so that now she was battling anxiety so great she was terrified of leaving her house. Being homebound had left her with little to do but eat and now, in addition to her fears, she was fifty pounds overweight and suffering from clinical depression. After much discussion it seemed clear both to Betty and the others that she had developed a dependence on everything but the Lord she claimed to serve. First her husband, then her children, and now her fleeting image.

Sarah, the sweet young girl who had been through three

abortions, began to recognize the consequences of living for self, with no regard for others. Although her missing babies still left a deep ache in her heart, her depression seemed to have lifted.

And there were others who Maggie thought were smiling more, talking more easily, making eye contact where once they could only hang their heads. The solution seemed to have everything to do with honesty. As they each were able to share more of their heart, the desperation faded. In fact, the darkness that initially seemed to cloak all of them seemed to be lifting for almost everyone.

Everyone, Maggie thought, but her.

She considered this as she made her way to the group session room. *Is it my pride, Lord? Is that the problem? Is it because I haven't been honest with them?* The group was still unaware of Maggie's professional identity, but was that the only reason she'd kept silent every day while one group member or another bared his or her soul?

Maggie had no answers, only a realization: If she was going to get better, she needed to talk about what was in her heart. And that meant finding the strength—somehow—to tell the group about her past. She rounded a corner and opened the first door on the left.

"Hi, Maggie." Dr. Baker smiled up from a small stack of papers.

"Hi." She made her way across the room and sat down next to the doctor. "Today's the day."

Dr. Baker raised an eyebrow. "Revelation time?"

Maggie nodded. "I've waited long enough."

There was silence. That was something Maggie had grown to enjoy about Orchards Psychiatric Hospital. The silence. None of the people who worked here seemed to feel the need to fill holes in the conversation with meaningless chatter. Instead it was almost as though they encouraged moments of reflection. "I see they've decreased your medication again."

"Yes, but…"

"That worries you?"

Maggie nodded. "I…I'm still having the nightmares, still feel the darkness dragging me down at different times throughout the day."

Dr. Baker flipped through a few sheets of paper and paused as she studied what was written there. "Dr. Camas hasn't reduced the Prozac, Maggie. Just the antianxiety medication." She looked up. "Are you still feeling anxiety?"

Maggie sighed. "I'm a believer trapped in a fog of darkness, Dr. Baker. I'm a conservative, God-fearing woman about to divorce my husband after seven years of lying to him about a child he knows nothing about. On top of that, I'm a columnist who writes about the need for morality and returning to godly standards in our world." Maggie planted her elbows into her knees and let her head fall into her hands. "Yes. I still feel anxious."

"Try to understand, Maggie. The medication you were on was very strong. And now that you're not—"

She raised her head and stared sadly at the doctor. "Now that I'm not suicidal? Is that what you mean?" Her gaze fell to the floor. "Maybe I still am."

Dr. Baker leaned back in her chair and set her clipboard and paperwork down beside her. "Okay, Maggie. Tell me the truth then. Do you still want to die?"

Maggie closed her eyes and there, standing before her, was the little girl. Seven, almost eight years old, dressed in blue jeans and a sweatshirt, her blond hair pulled into a simple ponytail. She was waving sweetly, mouthing the same words she mouthed every time she appeared this way: *Mommy? Where's my mommy? Do you know where my mommy is?*

Maggie reached out for the girl but suddenly, in her place, there was nothing but a wisp of fog that evaporated without a trace.

"I have to find her." Maggie's voice sounded desperately sad, even to her.

"Your daughter?"

Maggie nodded. "I can see her, hear her, imagine her in my arms. But when I reach out for her, she…"

"She isn't there, is that right? Like it always happens?"

"Yes."

"Then I guess your answer is simple, isn't it?"

Maggie looked up and saw a holy glow in Dr. Baker's eyes. "What do you mean?"

"I mean you can't possibly be suicidal. You don't want your life to end, Maggie. You just want to find your daughter."

Tears spilled from Maggie's eyes onto her cheeks and she nodded again and again. "She already has a home, of course. A mother and father and people who love her. But…"

Dr. Baker waited until Maggie could find her voice and the strength to continue.

She sniffled loudly and reached for the tissue box at the center of the circle. Blowing her nose, she turned once more to Dr. Baker. "No matter who has her, she's still my baby and nothing will be right, nothing…until I can see for myself that she's okay. Maybe then I can tell her I'm so—" Maggie's voice halted.

No, Lord, don't take me down that path. It isn't my fault. I never would have given her up if it weren't for Ben. It's his fault, God. Don't make me tell her I'm sorry…

"Tell her what, Maggie?"

"Nothing."

Dr. Baker hesitated, but when the silence remained, she stood and stretched. "The group will be here any minute. I'll let you decide if you're ready to talk. If you are, I'll do whatever I can to help."

"Okay." A heavy feeling settled over her shoulders and Maggie moved them up and down, trying to rid herself of the oppressive weight. When it would not leave, she went to pour herself a cup of herbal tea, found her regular seat, and nervously waited for the others.

Sarah opened up revelation time by announcing that she had received her discharge orders.

"Next Monday I'll be going home with my parents." She smiled, and Maggie noticed that the bruises on her cheeks were gone now. Sarah had explained to the group several sessions ago that her last boyfriend had beaten her regularly. Her breakdown had come when she feared she was pregnant for a fourth time and had suffered the worst blows of all when she'd told him the news. She had been considering suicide, but went home instead and shared everything with her parents. With their help, she'd gotten through her time at Orchards more quickly than many people. She would be expected to continue treatment on an outpatient basis for the next three months.

"How do you feel?" Dr. Baker leaned back in her seat and focused her attention on Sarah.

"Most of the time great, like a truck has been lifted off my shoulders."

"Most of the time?"

Sarah's face clouded. "There're still times when I think of my babies, Dr. Baker. But I've learned something here at Orchards." She looked at the others and for a moment her eyes caught Maggie's and held them. There was compassion there, and Maggie wished she had taken the time to get to know Sarah better. "I've learned there's nothing I can do to change the past, but I can take responsibility for today. By doing so, I can grasp onto tomorrow, too. My babies are safe in the arms of Jesus. When I think of them now, I think of them that way. And I look forward to the day—in God's timing—when I'll join them there."

Dr. Baker smiled at Sarah and looked around the room. Maggie had the uncomfortable feeling that everyone was looking at her, that they were all thinking how she was the only one in their midst who hadn't shared yet. "Anyone else?"

Say something, Maggie. It's time you talked it through. She gritted her teeth…and suddenly the words were out before she could stop them. "I hate my husband."

Every member in the group was suddenly focused on Maggie. Dr. Baker cleared her throat. "Do you want to talk about it, Maggie?"

Normally this was when the doctor would step in—especially if it was a person's first time to share in front of the other group members. But Maggie didn't want someone else summarizing her situation. *She* wanted to tell them. They had shared their hearts with her, their lives and losses. Now it was her turn. She nodded to Dr. Baker, then turned to face the group.

"I'm here because I had a…well, a breakdown, I guess. All because of something that happened nearly eight years ago."

Maggie glanced from face to face and saw she had their undivided attention—and more than that, their empathy. They had each journeyed back in time at one point or another and found it almost unbearably painful. Now Maggie could see that they were there for her, ready to hold her up or hug her close or cry with her should her journey backwards become too difficult.

She drew a deep breath and told them about falling in love with Ben, and how young and pure and ideal her intentions had been. How Ben had—for a time—chosen Deidre over her, and how she had taken up with John McFadden. She shared with them the fact that she'd gotten pregnant and how, for a brief while, she had considered keeping the baby.

"I dreamed about her even then." Maggie had come this far without tears, but now her eyes filled quickly. "I imagined what she'd wear, and how she'd look, and how it would feel to hold her in my arms. I was her mommy and even if everything else was falling apart I knew I'd be the best mother in the world. I l-l-loved her so much."

Sarah fell to her knees, shuffled across the circle, and took Maggie's hand in hers. *Dear God, how could I choose Ben over my very own baby?* She closed her eyes tight, clinging to Sarah's hand, and allowed the sobs to wash over her.

After several minutes, Harold handed her a tissue and patted her back. "We're here for you, Maggie. Whenever you're ready."

Maggie blew her nose again and forced herself to continue her story. She told them about hiding the pregnancy from her parents while she thought about her options, how just when she was going to tell them the truth, she received the call from Ben.

"He was a perfect man, at least I thought he was." Maggie sniffled, and Sarah squeezed her hand. "When he told me he still loved me, I knew there was only one thing to do."

Dr. Baker had been quiet through most of the story, but she interrupted now. "Can you explain yourself, Maggie?"

She nodded. "I lied to him. Told him I was going to Israel for a semester as an exchange student. Instead I went to Woodland, Ohio, moved in with a wonderful family, and finished my pregnancy."

More tears fell onto Maggie's cheeks. "She had this tiny, perfect face. The most beautiful little girl I'd ever seen. And…"

Sarah leaned her head on Maggie's knees.

"Oh, God, how *could* I?"

Dr. Baker waited while Maggie's sobs subsided again. "You gave your baby up for adoption, is that right, Maggie?"

"Everyone said adoption was the best choice…"

"It's a wonderful choice for a vast number of women, young and old."

"But not for me! I loved her so much it killed me…handing her over to the social worker and watching her disappear from my life." She sniffed loudly. "I gave her away for one reason only—so I could convince Ben I was the sweet, young virgin he'd always wanted to marry."

The room had grown quiet. "Is that why you feel so strongly about him now?"

"Yes!" Maggie could hear the anger in her voice. *Where's this rage coming from, Lord? What's happening to me?* She drew a steadying breath. "I don't ever want to see him again."

"So you blame him for having to give up your daughter, is that right?" Dr. Baker's voice was calm, without accusation or judgment. Still Maggie felt a piercing sense of conviction.

What? It is his fault. I would never have given her up, never have lied if it hadn't been for him.

"Definitely. He forced me to lie and made me give up my baby girl. I hate him." Maggie's voice rose. "I'll hate him till the day I die. And when I'm out of here, the first thing I'm doing is filing for divorce."

Sarah made her way back to her seat and an uncomfortable quiet echoed through the room in the wake of Maggie's statement.

What was everyone's problem? Wasn't this where they were supposed to circle her and cry with her and help her get through it? Weren't they supposed to agree with her and empathize with her? The familiar fog of darkness began to settle once more over Maggie's mind and soul, and she fought the urge to dart from the room.

Make them understand, God. Come on. I need Your help here.

"Maggie? Can I say something?" It was Howard, and although Maggie had always seen him as floundering and pathetic, today he was sitting straight in his chair and his eyes held a serenity that Maggie hadn't known since before her daughter's birth.

All eyes were on Howard, and Maggie nodded in his direction. "Sure."

Although he'd filled out somewhat during his stay at Orchards, Howard was still painfully thin, and he shoved the sleeves of his sweater up past his elbows as he prepared to speak. "Don't take this wrong, Maggie. But after losing my family I've become certain of one thing—" he glanced at the others and Maggie saw them giving him silent encouragement to continue—"God wants families to last forever. Or until He takes one of you home. Have you—you know—have you ever explained any of this to your husband?"

Suddenly, as though someone had thrown up a window blind, Maggie had a glimpse of the situation from Ben's perspective. It was the first time since coming to Orchards that she'd even considered his side. Obviously he knew by now that she wasn't receiving his calls or visits. But otherwise he knew nothing. Not about the lies she'd told or the baby she'd given up. Not even about how she blamed him for all that had gone wrong in the past eight years.

She could picture him, see the worry on his face, in his eyes…the care and concern for her. She closed her eyes and pictured him, still loving her even as he struggled to figure out what had happened to them, to her. The image caused her burning hatred to cool some. For a moment.

Then she blinked hard, and the images of Ben disappeared.

She didn't owe him an explanation! He didn't love her, not really. He loved an image, someone he'd created in his mind— the perfect godly wife; the chosen virgin bride. But that wasn't Maggie.

No, she wouldn't feel sorry for him. All of this was Ben's fault.

"That's ridiculous, Howard." The anger in Maggie's voice was gone, but she felt the tension between her and the rest of the group.

Dr. Baker looked at her watch. "Well, Maggie, maybe you can finish tomorrow. For now we better move on. I've got a passage in the book of Romans I'd like us all to take a look at…"

Bile was rising in Maggie's stomach, and she was suddenly engulfed in a closet of anxiety. *I can't breathe in here, Lord. Get me out.*

Repent, My daughter. Come into the light of honesty and repentance.

No! It's not my fault! None of this would have happened if only—

Everyone else had their Bibles open, but Maggie could no longer understand what they were saying. The darkness that had pursued her for so long was back and it was demanding something of her—something Maggie couldn't understand. No, wait. This was different. This time it wasn't really darkness at all, it was ominous, but not in an evil way...

It was like the hand of God.

Maggie tried to breathe but couldn't, and in that moment she knew she had mere seconds before her entire breakfast would be on the floor. She stood quickly and grabbed her things. "I have to go now..."

Her words jumbled together and she couldn't decide whether to run to the nearest bathroom or down the hall and out into the courtyard for the air she so desperately craved.

As she ran out of the room she felt her stomach heave, and she barely made it to the bathroom before the first wave of vomit shot from her body. She remained there, huddled on the floor, her face hanging over the edge of the toilet, while her stomach convulsed again and again. She might have stayed there longer, but when she was finally finished, she felt a gentle hand on her shoulder.

"Maggie, are you okay?" She looked up and saw Dr. Baker.

"I need air."

"Come on, let's get you cleaned up. Dr. Camas wants to see you."

Something about the doctor's tone made Maggie feel like a naughty child. She struggled to her feet and once more felt the familiar heaviness on her shoulders and back. She should never have talked to the group. Now she'd blown it for sure. They'd probably kick her out and tell her to find help somewhere else. Anger singed the edges of her heart.

"Oh, I get it!" Maggie snatched a paper towel and wiped her face. "This is a *Christian* hospital, and I made the mistake of mentioning the fact that I hate my husband and can't wait to divorce him." She stared at herself in the mirror, then turned around slowly to face Dr. Baker. "They're going to kick me out, right?"

"Not at all." Dr. Baker's face broke into the most genuine smile Maggie had ever seen. "Dr. Camas heard about our session. He thinks you've reached a breakthrough."

Twenty-three

AFTER WRESTLING WITH HIS DECISION MOST OF THE NIGHT, BEN chose to sleep in. Whoever Kathy Garrett was and whatever information she might hold, it would simply have to wait. By the time he showered and made his way across the street to Hap's Diner for the Wednesday morning omelette special, Ben began doubting his decision to visit the Cincinnati courthouse at all.

Ben set down his fork and from his seat along the counter he stared out the window through a layer of greasy residue, the same residue that seemed to cover nearly everything in the diner.

So this was where Maggie went? Not Israel, but Woodland, Ohio.

He let his eyes fall on a horse and rider making their way down Main Street. Woodland was little more than a glorified farm town, too close to Cincinnati to warrant any industry of its own and too far away for most commuters.

Still, there was a sort of old-fashioned charm about it. Ben sighed, picked up his fork, and poked around the omelette again. The melted cheese had grown cold, and grease had begun to harden along the edges of the egg, turning Ben's stomach. Was it possible that somewhere between this sleepy little place and downtown Cincinnati there lived a seven-year-old child who was Maggie's very own daughter?

He shoved his plate back and clenched his jaw. What did it matter? Even if the girl did live here, she was probably part of some wonderful family, happily getting on with her life. Possibly even unaware that she had been adopted. What good could come from digging up a situation that had been sealed and buried so long ago?

A grisly old man sat down on the stool beside Ben and took off a threadbare baseball cap. The man's plaid lumber jacket smelled faintly of old motor oil and cow manure and as he leaned onto the counter, Ben caught an offensive stench of body odor. Wringing his hands together nervously, the old guy turned to slap Ben on the back so hard Ben had to use his feet to stop from falling off the stool.

"Mornin'! Y'must be new around here."

For a moment, Ben wondered if he was the brunt of some kind of practical joke. He glanced over his shoulder but throughout the diner people were minding their own business. Looking back at the man, Ben snorted softly. *Just my luck...*

"See ya ate the special." He laughed out loud, and Ben felt suddenly self-conscious. The guy was probably homeless—a bum or something—and now he was going to attract the attention of everyone in the diner. He tossed the old man a sideways glance and figured him to be in his late eighties. At least. *Probably half deaf, too.*

"Uh—" Ben looked down at his plate—"Yeah. The special. Sure." He signaled the girl behind the counter and asked for his bill. Quaint or not, he'd had enough of Woodland. It was time to go home and face Maggie, time to hire a divorce attorney so both of them could get past this nightmare and go on with their lives. A flash of gnawing emptiness filled his heart at the thought of losing Maggie. She was his best friend, his...well, his everything. Wasn't she the one—other than God—who made his life complete? Or had he never really known her? Had the woman he'd loved only existed in his imagination?

Either way, this was no time to be sentimental. After all, Maggie was the one who wanted the div—

"You remind me of me at your age."

Ben faced the old man, trying to find a balance between being polite and discouraging the conversation. He'd spent enough time in Woodland; it was time to get home. "Do I know you?"

"Nope." The man stroked his whiskered face. "But I've seen your type. All sure 'o yourself, thinking you're better 'n everyone else."

Ben clenched his jaw. Where was the old man going with this? If only he'd skipped breakfast; he'd be halfway back to Cleveland by now. "Listen, I have to get—"

"Just finished up a mighty fine Bible study, I did." The man's interruption forced Ben back into his seat. Maybe he needed a handout. In that case Ben was more than willing to pick up the old guy's breakfast tab or help him out some. As long as Ben could get back to his car in the next five minutes.

"Look, do you need something. Money for breakfast, a few—"

He waved a gnarled hand in Ben's direction. "Got everything I need in the Good Book. Yes, siree."

The man rubbed his eyebrows and his smile disappeared. "I was young once, too. Had me a pretty wife, children." He gazed straight ahead and Ben saw that there were tears in the man's eyes. "They wouldn't recognize me now."

Ben glanced at his watch. *What would Maggie's little girl look like? How was life in her adoptive home?*

Ridiculous, he silently chided himself. *Forget about her.* Better to listen to the old man's story and be on his way. It was getting too late to see the social worker anyway. He angled his head at the old man. "Did they move away; your family, I mean?"

The man stared down at his weathered hands and shook his head. "Nope. Died in a car wreck back in the fifties. Started drinking a week later and, well…here I am." He locked his hands together. "Know something?" He brought his gaze up again and this time his tears were unmistakable. "I miss 'em like it was yesterday." He kept his eyes on Ben's. "You got a family, young man?"

Ben thought of Maggie locked in a psychiatric hospital across the state, and of her little girl…whatever her name was…

He swallowed hard. "I…uh…yeah. I have a family."

The man took a swig of coffee and put a hand on Ben's shoulders. "Do something for me, will you?"

In light of the old guy's sad story, Ben no longer cared about the other customers in the diner or how it might look if he was fraternizing with a homeless man. He resisted the urge to pull away. "Sure you don't need some money or a meal or something?"

The man shook his head. "Nah, I get by." He aimed his gaze at Ben, and a single tear navigated its way down the creases and crevices of his worn face. "I want you to love that family of yours, you hear?" The man brushed at the tear and tightened his grip on Ben. "Don't let even a minute go by without loving 'em and telling 'em so. Not a minute, understand?"

A strange sense of knowing came across Ben's entire being, as though God Himself had sent the man. *Don't let a minute go by…a minute go by…a minute go by.* The old man's wisdom rattled around in Ben's broken heart, and suddenly his throat was thick with sorrow and longing for the only woman he'd ever loved. He stared hard at the old guy and nodded. *Maggie girl, where are you? I love you, I do…if only I could tell you.* He pictured the child, Maggie's little daughter, and felt an overwhelming desire to see the social worker. Wherever it might lead, he would do at least that.

The man dropped his hand and his expression softened. "You won't be young forever…and take it from me, you can't go back. Not ever."

With that, the man finished his coffee, took two quarters from his pocket and laid them on the counter, then stood to leave. Before heading for the door he cast a final glance at Ben. "Do it now, you hear? Make every minute count."

Ben tipped his head at the man. They were the exact words he'd needed to hear. *God, did You send him to talk to me?* The question hung in the rafters of his mind. "Thanks." Then the man took off down the street before Ben could give more thought as to how he might help the man or how grateful he was for the unexpected insight.

As Ben climbed into his car he had no idea what the future held, but one thing seemed clear. Whatever else he didn't understand about his meeting with the old man, however dismal the situation between he and Maggie, the old guy was right. Time really was fleeting; every moment did matter. Because of that he would not leave town without doing a very important task, one that was quite possibly an errand sent from heaven.

Looking up Kathy Garrett.

IT WAS ONE OF THOSE DAYS AT THE DEPARTMENT OF SOCIAL Services, a time when it was difficult even for someone like Kathy Garrett to see the good in what she was doing. There were children needing foster homes, foster parents needing relief, and an hour ago a judge had ordered a two-year-old crack baby—born addicted to heroin—back into her mother's house because the woman was finally out of prison.

Kathy huffed out loud as she sifted through a mountain of case folders, all of which needed her attention in one way or another. If only she weren't so tired. Poor Amanda, up half the night wondering if maybe by some God-ordained miracle Kathy might actually be her real mother. Tears welled up in Kathy's eyes again and she dabbed at them angrily. *Why, God? Why isn't there someone for her?*

There was a knock at the door, and she sighed. She needed time alone, a chance to sort through the foster home files and maybe find a placement for Amanda that would last longer than a few months. One where she would fit in, maybe even find some happiness.

Kathy moved easily across her office and opened the door to find a man standing there, a man she'd never seen before. He was young—early thirties, maybe—dressed in expensive slacks and a slightly rumpled, button-down shirt. "May I help you?"

The man shifted his position awkwardly and glanced back at the front door. Then he met her eyes and forced a smile. "Uh…yeah, I guess. I'm looking for Kathy Garrett."

If this was a potential foster applicant, Kathy wished one of the clerks had helped him. *Make me more patient, Lord.* "That's me. What can I do for you?"

The man squirmed again, and Kathy had the distinct feeling that this wasn't about a foster application. He was nice looking, a little over six feet tall, good build. But his eyes were shadowy and they seemed to bear a reservoir of pain or anger, some deeply intense emotion that Kathy couldn't quite read.

"I...my name is Ben Stovall. I'm from Cleveland, visiting for the day." He ran his fingers through his hair. "I need to talk to you. In private, if possible."

Kathy thought about the myriad of cases that needed her attention. "I'm sorry, I'm very—"

Talk to him, daughter.

The voice was so clear she wondered if the man had heard it, too. *Fine, God. I'll talk to him.* She opened the door and motioned to a chair near her desk. "I have a few minutes. Come in."

"Thanks." The man didn't hesitate. "I'll keep it brief. I know you're busy."

She glanced at her desk and smiled, the weary feeling lifting a bit. "Just a little."

When they were both seated, the man ran his hands along his pant legs and drew a deep breath. "Seven years ago my wife moved to Woodland and had a baby." The man must have seen her puzzled expression because he hurried to explain. "We weren't married at the time. I thought she was out of the country on an exchange student program." He stared at his hands a moment, then his eyes met hers again. "I didn't know about the baby until...until recently."

"Mr. Stovall, I'd like to help you, but if your wife had an open adoption, the paperwork can be found by filing a request at the county courthouse. If it was closed—"

"It was." There was desperation in his eyes now, as if she held information that he absolutely had to have. "I already checked."

"Well, then I'm sorry. I'm afraid there's nothing I can do." Except get back to work so some of these kids have a safe house to sleep in tonight. *Please, Lord, make him leave so I can get on with my day.*

"Actually, I think there is something." He bit his lower lip and leaned over his knees. "I spoke yesterday with Nancy Taylor; she was the woman my wife lived with before the baby was born…"

Nancy Taylor. Nancy Taylor… The name ran through Kathy's mind a handful of times. She recognized it from somewhere, but with the number of cases she saw each day the connection might have been any one of a hundred possibilities. "The name sounds familiar, but I can't place it. I'm sorry, I—"

"Wait!" He held up his hand. "Forgive me for interrupting you, Ms. Garrett, but my wife's name was Maggie Johnson at the time. According to Nancy, you were the one who arranged the adoption. She said she thought you…"

"I what?"

"You were a believer."

Listen to him, Kathy.

The holy request came gentler this time, and Kathy leaned back in her chair. Where was this going? "Yes…I'm a Christian."

The man exhaled as though he'd been holding his breath. "See…my wife and I are believers, too. And right now she's…" He let his head fall a few inches and for a moment he seemed too overwhelmed to speak. His focus remained on his hands as he cleared his throat. "She's in a psychiatric hospital. They're treating her for depression."

The pieces were still not coming together. "Does she regret the adoption, Mr. Stovall? Is that what you're saying?"

The man rested his elbows on his knees and clasped his hands. "I don't know; we haven't talked since she was admitted. But Mrs. Taylor seems to think I need to find out about the baby—the girl, actually, since she'd be seven now—and make sure she's okay. At least then I could tell Maggie she'd made the right decision."

A wave of compassion came over Kathy, and she resisted the urge to walk around her desk and take the man's hands in hers. He was here for that? To give his hurting wife some small ray of hope? Something to assure her that her unknown child was doing well and that adoption had been the kindest thing she could have done at the time?

Kathy pushed aside her emotions. Rules were not meant to be played with. It was a state-run agency after all, and adoption files could not be pulled without her having to account for her reason in doing so.

She sighed softly. "Sir, I'm very sorry about your wife. But I'm not at liberty to check the files of closed adoptions."

The man drew a deep breath and stood to leave. "Okay, then. I guess I did everything I could."

He shook Kathy's hand and left the office without any further request. Kathy watched him go, sitting motionless in her chair, her eyes glued to the door. Something about the man's request didn't sit right.

Seven years ago…seven years ago…

Kathy had the unnerving feeling that she'd just missed a God-given opportunity. Her mind raced backward in time, trying to make sense of her overwhelming desire to catch the man before he left the building.

Seven years…

Then it hit her. Kathy caught her breath sharply. Seven years ago…there was only one little girl she could clearly remember having been given up for adoption at about that time. But it couldn't be…

Kathy worked thousands of cases from Cincinnati and the surrounding suburbs. There might have been a dozen baby girls given up for adoption that year. Still…what if it *was* her? What if this Maggie Johnson, Maggie Stovall, now receiving treatment for depression was actually…

Kathy was on her feet, pushing around her desk and tearing down the hallway, then out into the parking lot. Frantically she looked around and she saw him, about to climb into a Pathfinder. "Mr. Stovall!"

Her feet carried her quickly to where he stood. Breathless, she met his questioning gaze and smiled. "If you can come back in for a minute, there's something I'd like to look into."

Minutes later they were both seated at her desk again, Mr. Stovall staring strangely at her, waiting for her to explain.

"Sorry about that, but I just thought of something, and I didn't want you to leave before I could check it out." *Be calm, Kathy. Oh dear Lord, could it be that these are the people? Could it possibly be that this man sitting here is the answer to my prayers?*

Suddenly she wanted to know more about him, his wife, and everything that made up their lives. "Do you have other children, Mr. Stovall?"

The man angled his head and his eyes bore an expression that was just short of hope. "No. We…we haven't been able to."

A vision filled Kathy's mind, images of this man and his wife healed and whole taking Amanda into their home and loving her for a lifetime. Just as quickly, Kathy chided herself for romanticizing the situation. The woman was in a mental hospital, after all, and probably wasn't even Amanda's mother. Still, it was worth pursuing if only she could justify looking up the file. She pictured Amanda's teary eyes last night, heard again her small voice hoping and praying that somewhere her real mom was thinking about her.

A child's life was at stake here. That was justification enough.

"Mr. Stovall, I'm going to see if there's a way to check the file. Wait here a minute, will you?"

The man's eyes implored her again. "Listen, you don't know me, but I wouldn't be here right now if I didn't believe God Himself had sent me. Please…" He swallowed hard, again nearly overcome by emotion. "Please look it up for me. Tell me she's well adjusted and enjoying life, tell me she has a wonderful family here or somewhere else. Just tell me something, so I can finally understand all the missing pieces."

Kathy frowned. "Missing pieces?"

"It's a long story. Just please, please look it up."

She refused to promise him anything. "I'll be back in a few minutes."

Adoption records were all in computerized files now, so Kathy knew it wouldn't take long to find what she was looking for. Alone in the dimly lit archives room she found the correct screen. Under "birth mother" she typed in, Maggie Johnson; date: 1991. Then she clicked the search button, and three seconds later she had her answer: *No matches for that search.* Disappointment rocked her back in her chair and brought tears to her eyes.

Lord, I wanted her to be the one.

Keep searching, My daughter…

The prompting made no sense. Maggie Johnson—whoever she was—obviously hadn't given her baby up for adoption in Cincinnati. Kathy thought of how disappointed the man in her office would be. Maybe he had his facts wrong or maybe his wife hadn't given a baby away. Or if she had…

Kathy let out a shout and her hand flew to her mouth. That was it! Of course! There was no reason Maggie had to use her real name. Kathy frowned, trying to remember. What was the name of the woman Ben Stovall had mentioned, the woman his wife had stayed with?

Tanner…Trumbell…*Taylor!* There it was. This Maggie woman had been living with a family named Taylor.

Without hesitating, Kathy typed in two words: M-a-g-g-i-e T-a-y-l-o-r. Maggie Taylor. The name was suddenly very familiar. An hourglass appeared indicating the search was underway. Seconds passed.

Come on, give me something. Please, God…

Suddenly a file appeared. As Kathy scanned the information she felt herself sliding off the chair, falling to her knees on the cold linoleum flooring.

It was her; it had to be. The woman Amanda had been praying about for years. It was all coming back now, the frightened girl living with the Taylors, saying all the right words, making them believe she wanted nothing more than to give her baby up for adoption. Kathy remembered a scene from seven years ago and it hit her as strongly as if she'd been slapped in the face.

The young mother had not wanted to let go of her baby.

It had been at the hospital, the day Maggie delivered. She'd been sad, despondent even. Kathy choked back her tears and closed her eyes as the memory grew clearer. She could see the images clearly in her mind…

Kathy had approached the girl and asked her if she was sure. "You don't have to do this, Maggie," she remembered saying. "Adoption isn't for everyone." But the girl had gritted her teeth with determination and promised that this was the choice she needed to make.

Kathy's tears fell freely now and she wondered why she hadn't pushed the girl for more answers. Certainly if she interviewed a birth mother now and found her ambivalent, she would ask a host of questions. If only she'd had it to do over again, she would ask Maggie why she hadn't felt up to keeping the baby herself.

God, I've made a terrible mistake. Everything that's happened to Amanda…all of it could have been avoided if only I'd been more aware, more thorough with her mother. A thick sob worked its way up from her heart and echoed against the particleboard in the archives room. *What have I done, Lord? How different Amanda's life would have been if only I'd talked her mother out of the adoption. And what of Maggie, Lord? Is she beyond caring? Does she even wonder about her little girl?*

Kathy remembered the well-dressed, clearly distraught man waiting in her office. They were childless, after all. Was he the baby's father? If so, then Amanda was their only child. A child who had nearly died from abuse while waiting year after year for someone to give her a home.

Trust with all your heart and lean not on your own under-standing.

A rush of peace passed over Kathy, and she felt physically comforted by the Holy Spirit. Amanda's life had been miserable, but maybe…

Trust Me, daughter.

Kathy exhaled. She wiped her eyes with her sweater sleeve and worked herself back to a sitting position. Closing out the computer screen, it was all she could do to stop the accusations that threatened to consume her. *If only…*

Trust Me.

Kathy closed her eyes. *Lord, I want to trust You. Really, I do. But all these years. What if—*

Trust.

Okay, give me wisdom then, God. Wisdom and strength to go back in there and face that man with the truth about Amanda Joy.

Fifteen minutes had passed, and Ben was getting restless. Maybe it was a crazy idea. First Nancy Taylor, then the old man at the diner. How could they possibly know what God wanted from him? Here he sat, in some tiny social services office, wasting the time of an obviously busy woman over an adoption that was sealed from the public. Ms. Garrett had been clear on the matter: The records were not available.

He scanned her desk for a piece of paper. He'd just write her a note, explain that he'd left town, and thank her for her help. He spotted a notepad, but as he reached out, she returned. The tearstained look on her face made Ben's breath catch in his throat.

"I found her, Mr. Stovall."

Ben's heart pounded in his chest. *What? She'd found her? The child? Maggie's daughter?*

The social worker sat back in her desk chair and faced him squarely. She opened her mouth to say something but no words came out. She paused, then tried again. "She lives very near here."

Until that moment it had been easy for Ben to blame Maggie, to find fault with her for sleeping with John McFadden and giving a baby up for adoption without ever saying anything about it. Ben's attention had been mainly on the way Maggie had betrayed him. But now…now there was a living, breathing child involved, and not just any child. This little girl was the daughter of the woman who still meant more to him than he could admit or understand. Maggie's flesh and blood.

His eyes were wet, and Ben hung his head, unable to speak. *Maggie girl, you have a child. A daughter. After all these years…* If only she were here beside him, holding his hand, hearing this news with him. *I've found your little girl, Maggie…* He closed his eyes for a moment. *Dear God, what does it all mean?*

He swallowed, trying to squeeze words through a throat thick with emotion. "She's…she's okay, then? Adopted by a family somewhere nearby?"

Kathy Garrett shook her head and brought her clasped hands up to her chin. "Her name is Amanda…she's living with me, Mr. Stovall."

Ben's thoughts were instantly jumbled. *Amanda…Amanda…* The name seemed to work its way into his heart. So it was true. Maggie's daughter was alive and well and growing up. Her name was Amanda.

"You mean, you adopted her? I thought…Nancy Taylor told me you were the social worker, not the adoptive—"

"No." The social worker closed her eyes, and Ben wondered if perhaps she were praying. "I've been Amanda's social worker from the beginning." She hesitated. "Mr. Stovall, normally it is not ethical to give out information about a private adoption. But I've prayed about this situation for years and I believe with all my heart that God would have me tell you about Amanda."

Ben sat up, suddenly alert. *What was there to tell? Had something happened to the girl?* Feelings of love—amazingly strong and protective—assaulted Ben until his heart seemed to lodge tightly in his throat. "What about her?"

Ms. Garrett sighed. "It's a long story. To begin with, Amanda was adopted by a childless couple—the Brownells. They were not well off, but they were kind and loving and good parents for Amanda."

Ben couldn't stop himself. "Were? They were? Isn't she with them anymore?"

The sadness in Ms. Garrett's eyes pierced Ben with deep concern. "They died, Mr. Stovall. When Amanda was five. It was an awful ice storm, and best we can tell they were headed to the school to find Amanda. A branch fell on their car moments after they left home." She paused. "They were both killed."

Ben settled heavily back into his seat, his heart breaking for Maggie's little girl. What an awful thing for her to have suffered through. The death of her adoptive parents, and at an age when they would have been everything in the world to her. He crossed his arms against the pit that had formed in his stomach. "Amanda went to live with you then, is that it?"

"No." Ms. Garrett's expression grew dark. "The Brownells had no extended family. Amanda was made a ward of the state and put back into the Social Services system."

Ben frowned, trying to sort through it all. "But she's with you now…"

Fresh tears filled Ms. Garrett's eyes. "She's lived with us off and on since her adoptive parents' deaths. She's been in several foster homes for the most part. The last one…"

Her voice trailed off and she covered her eyes with her fingers. As she did, panic rose in Ben. What happened to Amanda? "Was there trouble?" Maybe the girl was violent or given to tantrums. Or worse.

Ben couldn't bring himself to imagine anything worse. *Please…no…* Not Maggie's little girl.

The social worker lowered her fingers and the pain in her eyes was almost more than Ben could bear. "Amanda was beaten, Mr. Stovall. She nearly died."

The words hit his heart squarely, but that impact was nothing compared to the rage that suddenly pulsed through his body. The state had assigned Maggie's seven-year-old daughter to a foster parent, to be cared for and nurtured, and that monster had nearly beaten the girl to death?

Ms. Garrett sighed. "Amanda's been with us since being released from the hospital."

No, God, it can't be true. He hung his head and imagined a child so young and helpless hurt to the point of...

In that heartbeat, Ben knew with every fiber in his being that he had to see this child, had to hold her in his arms if only one time, and love her the way Maggie surely would have loved her if she'd ever had the chance. She was Maggie's daughter.

Maggie. The thought of his wife caused him to close his eyes. His feelings for her seemed to change daily. Before her breakdown—if that's what it was—Ben had loved her in a way he thought was unconditional. Then he'd learned the truth and before this meeting with Kathy Garrett he knew he'd have willingly accepted a divorce from her. Now he wanted nothing more than to sit down beside her and hold her, rock away the pain and pretense and...and what? Ben wasn't sure how to feel anymore.

Was he supposed to forgive her and act like none of it had ever happened? Like she hadn't spent their lifetime together lying to him? Like she hadn't refused his calls and visits and threatened divorce from the moment she left their home?

His heart was so heavy it nearly forced him to the floor. With his eyes still closed, Ben willed his racing heart to slow down. Whatever the future held for him and Maggie, dwelling on it would have to wait. There was something more important at hand now. "I'd like to meet her, Ms. Garrett. Is that possible?"

"I assume you're her biological father? Is that right?"

Here it was. The question of the hour. How many more

times in his life would he have to address the fact that his wife had gotten pregnant by another man the year before they were married? He sighed and tugged on his chin, running his thumb and forefinger over his day-old beard. "No. I didn't know about the baby until recently."

There was a pause. "I thought—"

"She…Maggie saw someone else before we got engaged."

The woman's eyes widened a fraction, and she seemed at a loss for words. Ben inhaled deeply. He no longer cared what Maggie had done or about any of the lies she'd told. He cared only for this little girl, battered and without a home, the daughter of his wife.

And of a man who nearly killed you…

He shook his head. Even that didn't matter. He could hardly contain the sudden, inexplicable love he felt for the child, love that had no reason except that it was. "Does it matter? Can I see her anyway, for a few minutes?"

The woman's eyes twinkled. "If you only knew her, Mr. Stovall; she's the sweetest child I've ever worked with."

Again his heart swelled. "Well, then…"

Ms. Garrett shifted uneasily in her chair and her face fell. "I don't think it's possible, not legally anyway. Now, if you were a licensed foster parent interested in an interview so that—"

"Wait a minute!" Ben's heart was instantly light in a way it hadn't been since he'd found Maggie's note in their bedroom. "I *am* a licensed foster parent. Since we couldn't have our own kids, Maggie and I have been taking in foster kids for the past two years."

"In Ohio?"

"Yes, in Cleveland." Maybe he would get to meet the girl after all. And then maybe… He forced his thoughts not to race ahead. This wasn't the time to be planning the girl's future. She might not even want to meet him or care to know the whereabouts of her real mother. It was all so overwhelming, yet the thought of meeting her—holding her the way he had dreamed of holding his own children one day—filled him with hope.

Kathy Garrett's grin worked its way across her entire face. "Are you serious?"

"Check the computer." He pulled out his wallet, ripped his driver's license from inside, and tossed it to the social worker. As he did so he remembered the old guy at the breakfast bar an hour earlier. *"Make every moment count...every moment..."*

He was trying. God help him, he was trying.

Another smile flashed across Kathy's face. "You're in!"

Hope washed over Ben. Not that it made any sense. Not that the situation with Maggie was any less real or true or devastating now. But he welcomed the hope all the same. "Well?"

Ms. Garrett rested her forearms on her desk and turned to face him with a mock businesslike expression. "All right then, Mr. Stovall...about that foster child you'd like to meet." She grinned again. "How about this afternoon?"

Twenty-five

LESS THAN TWO HOURS AFTER BEN STOVALL WALKED INTO THE Cincinnati County Courthouse, the phone rang in John McFadden's suburban, middle-class home.

"He's here, just like you said."

It was Alfie; John recognized his buddy's voice immediately and felt a surge of vengeful relief. He could always count on the boys; any time he needed a favor they came through.

"You sure it's him?"

"You bet, boss. Everything lines up. Signed his name on the information request form and everything."

So, Stovall wanted the kid after all. John chuckled softly; his plan was taking shape nicely. "Who talked? The curvaceous redhead?"

Alfie chuckled long and hard. "Is that what Mikey told you?" His laugh grew until he sounded like an excited donkey. "She was curvaceous all right. Sixty extra pounds curvaceous."

John enjoyed these lighter moments with the boys. Dealing was so tense sometimes, what with worrying about authorities, guarding the stash so no one took more than the right amount along the way, making sure the goods were as pure as promised. Too many details. But this was more enjoyable than John had expected. "What'd you do, promise her a date?"

"Nah, Mike went in a few days ago and flashed a hundred. Dame about wet her pants. Got all secretive, looking both ways, making sure no one was watching. Mikey slipped her his cell phone number, told her to call if a Ben Stovall came to the courthouse for any reason at all." Alfie stopped laughing and struggled to catch his breath. "I think she liked the attention,

275

boss, know what I mean? I bet she'da done it for ten bucks, you know?"

John smiled. If Ben Stovall intended to shut down his operation, the bribe was money well spent. He'd reimburse the boys with cash from the next shipment. "She took the money?"

"Right. Mikey promised another hundred if she delivered the information. We got the call just after noon today."

"Nice work. Tell Mikey there'll be two loads for him, free, in the next shipment and—"

Alfie hooted loudly. *"Two* loads, boss? Free? Hey, Mike'll like that. We thought we was doin' this just for the—"

"I'm not finished." John paused. He liked the boys, but sometimes they tested his patience—especially Alfie, who had never been the sharpest knife in the drawer. "I was about to say all I need from you boys is a little surveillance work. Grab a pen and write this down."

"Surveillance?" Alfie's tone went blank.

"Yeah, you know, follow the social worker—Kathy Garrett's her name. Find out who she is; watch the parking lot and follow her home. And look out for Ben Stovall. You writing this down, Alfie?"

"Sure boss, yeah. I'm writing. How'm I gonna know what Stovall looks like?"

"He's dark-haired, tall, good build, I guess. Looks like Mr. Corporate America. Clean cut, harmless face. My guess is he'll be with the social worker."

"Social worker..." Alfie hesitated. "Oh, right. Kathy Garrett. Okay, I got it."

"Pass the information on to Mikey, will ya?"

"Sure, boss, we're on it."

McFadden's heart pounded as he calculated how little time he had to face the judge and make a plea as the child's long-lost father. "Call me when you find Stovall and then update me every time they go anywhere."

"Like driving, you mean?"

John sighed. "Right, Alfie. In the car, on foot. Anytime they go anywhere let me know." His mind raced ahead. "Oh, and one more thing. They might have a little girl with them. Seven or eight years old, something like that."

There was a pause, but Alfie didn't ask for any details. That was one of the things John liked best about Alfie and Mike: They never asked questions when they shouldn't. "Okay, boss. A little girl. What's she look like?"

John thought a moment and again a chuckle sifted up from his gut. "Like me, Alfie, okay? Watch for a kid that looks like me."

Alfie thought that was even funnier than the bit about the redhead. He guffawed so loudly John had to move the receiver away from his ear.

"Hey, boss. Really, now. What's she look like?"

"She looks like a little girl, Alfie. Never mind. Just call me, will ya?"

"Cell phone, right?"

"Right. I'm leaving in an hour, and I'll check into a room somewhere in town when I get there."

John moved to open the suitcase on his bed and began tossing in socks and underwear and T-shirts. Enough to last a week, at least. If it took longer than that, something definitely would have gone wrong. In that case, he didn't want to think about what clothes he'd be wearing, since they'd probably be issued by the local jail.

"Understand?"

"Right o, boss. Got it all down on paper right in front of me. Uh, hey boss...two loads? You sure about that?"

"Absolutely. You and Mike just make sure you get hold of Kathy Garrett before she takes off early and we miss her altogether. I want her followed today, got it?"

"Got it."

McFadden hung up the phone and made a mental list of the things he would need. At least one nice pair of pants and a dressy shirt—one of the silk deals he'd picked up in Vegas last year would work. Just right for showing the judge he was the fatherly type.

He'd get to town, request an emergency hearing, and explain the situation to the judge. The suitcase already held the results of a quick but pricey DNA test done the previous week. Of course, the results would match those on the adoption papers—there was no doubt he was the kid's father. He'd present the test and give the court a teary-eyed report on how he'd looked high and low for the girl with no luck until now.

Oh, yeah, and that he'd absolutely begged Maggie Johnson to keep the child, but Maggie had tricked him, moved to another part of the state and handed off the baby without his having any say in the matter. All he'd ever wanted was to claim his rightful spot as the baby's father.

And now here he was, prepared to do just that.

Yes, that's exactly what he'd tell the judge. And with the kid stuck in Social Services, what better timing?

Another chuckle slithered to the surface as John shut his suitcase. He figured he'd get a meeting with the judge by tomorrow. Matters involving children tended to get precedence. At least that's what the redhead had told Mikey. Then it'd be just a matter of hours before John and Ben Stovall met again. The do-good lawyer could have the brat for all he cared, but first he'd have to pay up.

McFadden ambled across his expansive bedroom, pulled open the top drawer of a mahogany chest, and grabbed the loaded revolver. If Plan A worked, he wouldn't need it. Stovall would give him the cash and make the call to Cleveland police withdrawing the assault charges. That done, John would happily make his way back home.

If Plan A failed, though, he was prepared.

One way or another, Stovall was going to cooperate. Even if it meant taking the kid by force.

Twenty-six

IN THE TEN MINUTES MAGGIE HAD TO CLEAN UP BEFORE MEETING with Dr. Camas, she went to her private room and locked herself in the bathroom. She brushed her teeth to rid her mouth of the stale smell of vomit, and when she was finished, she leaned forward against the countertop and stared at her face in the mirror.

Nothing.

Not a single thing about her face or her eyes resembled the tenderhearted young girl who had attended that picnic so many years ago, when she first fell in love with Ben Stovall. Back then her dark blond hair and lithe, attractive figure were only added benefits. Her real beauty had come from somewhere deep within. It was something that burst through her smile and radiated from her eyes, something that made her face alive with the vibrancy of hope and the expectant promise of her future.

Maggie studied herself. How different would she look now if she'd told Ben the truth? Okay, so she'd made a mistake. She'd done the one thing a good Christian girl is never supposed to do: She'd had sex. But wasn't Ben supposed to forgive her?

She let the question dangle in her mind for a moment, and the answer was clear. They'd only been friends back then. Ben might have forgiven her, but he wouldn't have had any obligation to marry her. He very simply would have offered his condolences and moved on with his life. Without Maggie. He'd made it clear: He was looking to marry a woman of virtue, a virgin, plain and simple. Girls who gave up their purity were a dime a dozen, and Ben planned to hold out for someone like himself.

Someone with a modicum of self-control when it came to things of the flesh.

She drew back from the mirror, taking in her lifeless lip-line and the hardness around her eyes. She was still pretty, she knew. Fit, polished, store-bought. But no amount of money could undo the years of lies and the poison they'd bled into her system. No, the light that once burned inside her, the flame of youth and faith and hope and promise, had been extinguished long ago.

And it was all Ben's fault.

I hate him, God… He never loved me, not a single moment. Not for me, anyway.

Let no deceit come from you.

Maggie squeezed her eyes shut, and the Scripture faded. Just as well. She didn't have time to think about it. She needed to be in Dr. Camas's office in two minutes.

He was waiting as usual when she entered the room, calmly, coolly, so that the peace and confidence than ran through him fairly filled the air. Being in his presence made Maggie feel safe and warm, and as she sat down she exhaled slowly.

"You wanted to see me?"

Dr. Camas smiled, and Maggie knew this conversation would be slow and meaningful, like all her discussions with him. "Yes." He shifted his position so that he faced her squarely, crossing one leg over the other knee, clearly relaxed. "It was something you said in group."

"I figured."

The doctor cocked his head curiously. "Figured what?"

"The part about wanting a divorce. I figured that'd get a rise out of somebody in a Christian hospital like Orchards."

Doctor Camas's expression remained the same. "Actually it wasn't that at all. You should know by now, Maggie, we aren't here to force morality on you. That's a choice you have to make, something between you and God. We're here to help you unravel your feelings because the knot you brought into this place was making you sick, remember?"

She felt like a petulant junior high student, and her cheeks grew hot under his gaze. "Yes. I'm sorry."

Dr. Camas picked up a pencil and tapped the eraser a few times on his desk, his gaze still on Maggie. "No need to apologize. I just want to make sure you're clear on our roles."

If they aren't pushing me to do the right thing, then what was I feeling in the bathroom before I was sick? Maggie struggled with the question, but realized Dr. Camas was waiting for her response. "Okay. I'm clear. So what'd I tell group that made you think I was making progress?"

He caught his chin in his forefinger and thumb in a gesture that had become strangely comforting to Maggie. "You said you hate your husband."

Maggie's defenses rose and anger burned in her gut. "Don't I have a right? After all he expected of me and all it's caused me in my life, don't I have a—"

"Maggie…" He waited until he had her attention. "Did I put a judgment on your statement?"

She thought back a moment. It had to be wrong, making a statement like that about her husband. Didn't it? "No. I guess not. But it isn't exactly godly, telling a group of strangers that you hate your husband."

A faint smile turned the corners of the doctor's lips upward. "No, it isn't. But it means you're willing to talk about more than what happened."

Her heart filled with uncertainty, and she blinked twice, waiting for the doctor to continue. "Meaning?"

"Meaning in the past you've talked about what happened between you and Ben. You talked about your pregnancy and how it felt to give your daughter up for adoption." Dr. Camas paused, and Maggie dropped her gaze to her hands and felt the familiar pit in her stomach. *Where are you, precious baby girl?*

She couldn't take much discussion about the adoption now, not when she was dying to get out of Orchards and begin taking steps to find the child.

The doctor cleared his throat and she looked up again. "What you seldom talked about was how you felt about Ben. Until now." He leveled his gaze at her. "Okay, Maggie, go along with me for a minute here, will you?"

She nodded.

"Why do you hate your husband?"

"Because he expected me to be perfect." There was anger in her voice again, but she didn't care. There would never be a better time or place to talk about this.

"He thought you were a virgin."

"No, he *expected* me to be one. There's a difference." Maggie could feel her cheeks growing hot again.

"And since you weren't, you lied to him."

"I *loved* him! I had no choice."

The room filled with the ticking sound of Dr. Camas's wristwatch. "What if you'd told him the truth?" The question was calm and measured and unquestionably reasonable.

Maggie huffed and crossed her legs in a blur of motion. "He'd have moved on to someone else."

"Are you sure?"

"Of course." Who did Dr. Camas think he was, second-guessing her and acting like he knew Ben better than she did? "He was going to marry a virgin, no matter what."

Dr. Camas leaned back in his chair. "Let's try something for a minute."

A sigh escaped and Maggie resisted the urge to roll her eyes. This entire line of questioning was pointless. What was done was done. She hated Ben for forcing her hand, forcing her to give up her baby girl and to live nearly eight years of lies in order to appease his appetite for perfection.

The doctor was waiting and Maggie knew she had no choice but to go along. "Fine."

"Think back, Maggie. What was it about Ben that first made you love him?"

She didn't like the question. At this point in her life and treatment, she was finally getting over Ben, feeling strong enough to stand up to him, preparing for the day when she would face him with the truth and hand him the divorce papers. This was no time to muddle her emotions with a trip back to where and when and why she first loved her husband. She crossed her arms in front of her and clenched her jaw. "I think we're past that, doctor."

"Perhaps. But humor me, will you? What was it? Come on, Maggie, think."

"Oh, okay." She cast her gaze upward and studied the pattern of tiles on the ceiling. This was pointless, but…well, he was the doctor. She thought back to the picnic, to the way so many of her friends had been there that day. "He was different."

"What do you mean? Go deeper, Maggie."

She squirmed in her seat. "He knew what he wanted in life. When he talked about his faith it was like…a real thing, a real relationship. Stronger than mine, even; stronger than my parents'. And they'd been Christians all their lives."

Dr. Camas nodded slowly. "But he said he wouldn't marry a girl unless she was a virgin, is that right?"

Wasn't it? Hadn't he said it that way? Maggie thought hard…

She could feel the humid, night air on her skin, hear the worship band playing in the background. And suddenly it was as though Ben were sitting beside her again, the way he had been that night on the grass at the picnic. She closed her eyes and she could almost hear his voice…

She shook her head. "I don't think he mentioned it that night, honestly. He said he knew God had a plan for his life and he…he wanted to obey so the plan would happen one day. Something like that."

"Okay, so sometime in the next few weeks, then. He must

have told you he wouldn't marry a girl who wasn't a virgin, right? Think back, Maggie."

She sighed and her vision blurred as tears filled her eyes. He had said that several times. At least, that's how she'd always remembered it. She shut her eyes again, squeezing out several tears that fell onto her cheeks. "He...we didn't see each other that much, but we talked on the phone..."

Memories flooded her mind. Ben sharing his heart with her, and she with him. Snapshots of laughter and innocence and promises that lay ahead. But none of the memories was the one she'd hung onto these past years. Her eyes flew open as frustration swept her. "I can't remember. Can we be done with this?"

Dr. Camas remained still, his eyes connected with hers. "I think you remember more than you're willing to admit. Try harder, Maggie. Let's lay it out so we can take it apart and figure out where the hate comes from."

A gnawing feeling ate at Maggie's gut, and she wondered if she'd be sick again before this session was finished. She did hate Ben, she had every right. But until she finished this...this *game* or whatever it was, she couldn't move on. Gritting her teeth, she thought back once more—and this time she could hear her voice.

"How come you always talk about God's plans for your life, Ben? How do you know He has plans for you?" She'd been playing with him, baiting him to see what he was really made of.

"It's true, Maggie. The Bible says so right in Jeremiah and probably a dozen other places, too. That's why I've never wanted to get too serious with anyone."

"I don't get it."

Maggie could hear her response as clearly as if she had tape-recorded the conversation years ago and now had the opportunity to play it back over loud speakers.

She remembered the words...heard them again...and froze. *No...no! That's not how it was.* Maggie squeezed her eyes shut. Her heart and mind went blank...and cold. "I'm finished,

Dr. Camas." She rose, wringing her hands and biting fiercely on her lower lip. "I need some air."

Before Dr. Camas could speak, Maggie rushed out of the room, slamming the door behind her, certain that if she'd stayed in the office another moment she would have suffocated and died.

Twenty-seven

ALFIE AND MIKE WERE IN A PANEL VAN LOOKING VERY MUCH LIKE repairmen resting between calls. It was the perfect cover. Earlier, Mike had gone into the office asking for Kathy Garrett, just like the boss wanted. When the clerk returned with a gentle-looking woman in her forties, Mike stood and approached her. "My name's Harry Bedford. We have a four o'clock appointment."

The Garrett woman had looked at him strangely. "Bedford? There's nothing on my calendar about it. Are you sure you made it with me?"

Mike forced a grimace. "I thought so. Wife and I are interested in adopting a child from the inner city. That's your specialty, right?"

A knowing look filled the woman's face. "No, I handle foster children. I think you're probably looking for the downtown office." She scribbled something on a slip of paper. "Do you know that area?"

Mike took the piece of paper and began backing away. "Like the back of my hand. Thanks a lot."

Now he was sitting in the parking lot with Alfie, frustrated that the job was taking longer than he thought. They had business to do back at the warehouse and women lined up for later that night.

"I'm hungry." Alfie had finished off a bag of chips and two sodas.

"You're always hun—"

"Hey," Alfie cut him off. "Is that her?" He nodded toward a woman leaving the building. She was alone and headed for a blue sedan.

"Bingo." Mike started the engine. *Good. We'll follow her home, get the news to the boss, and be home in time for the party.*

In the seat next to him, Alfie picked up the cell phone and tapped in a series of numbers. There was a pause. "Boss, we got her." Alfie gazed through the windshield at the woman as she climbed into the sedan. "Yep. She's getting in her car right now. We'll let you know where she lives as soon as we get there."

Kathy Garrett made her way home more quickly than usual. So much had happened, she could hardly wait to tell Amanda. *God, You are faithful beyond anything, beyond anyone.*

The fact that she had just located Amanda's mother by means of a man who stopped in her office on a whim was nothing less than an answer to the child's prayer. Kathy was sure of it. She pulled into her driveway minutes later and bounded lightly up the steps. "Kids, I'm home."

A chorus of voices greeted her from various parts of the house. The older children were always so good with the younger ones, and Amanda was no exception. She was probably caught up in a checkers match with Jenika, their oldest.

Kathy hung up her coat and unwrapped her scarf. It wasn't quite Thanksgiving and already it felt cold enough to snow, but no chill could dispel the warmth that radiated through Kathy at that moment. She made her way into the den and found the girls. For the first time her heart ached at the news she was about to share…it might mean saying good-bye to Amanda for good. She swallowed a lump in her throat and smiled at the child, sitting cross-legged on the floor with Jenika. "You girls have a good day at school?"

"I need help with my math." Jenika made the announcement and then looked up and grinned. "Other than that it was great."

"Betsy didn't sit by me today because she said she's going to Elle's sleepover on Friday and I can't come." Amanda's eyes looked sad.

"Did you work it out?" Kathy was impatient to get past the small talk. *None of it's going to matter in a minute, Amanda. Your prayers have been answered! I've found your mommy!*

Amanda shrugged and the corners of her lips turned slightly upward. "We played together at second recess, so I guess so."

"That's good." She paused. *Give me the right words, Lord. Please...* What she was about to tell Amanda would change her life forever. The smallest part of her wanted to wait and keep Amanda to herself a little longer. But that wouldn't have been fair. Besides, Amanda had been waiting too long already. "Amanda, may I talk to you for a minute?"

Jenika was five years older, but Amanda was far more intuitive in matters dealing with Social Services. Her eyes fell and she cast a knowing look at Jenika. Kathy understood the exchange. Whenever she came home from work and needed to talk to Amanda it usually meant one thing: They'd found a foster home for her. And it was painfully obvious that Amanda hated the thought of ever leaving the Garrett home.

But this was different. So different Kathy could hardly wait to talk to the child. She took Amanda's hand, helping her to her feet. "Come on, honey. It's good news. Really."

The two moved into the dining room and sat side by side at the kitchen table, their chairs angled slightly so that they could see each other. "I met someone very interesting today."

Concern creased the corners of Amanda's eyes and she reached instinctively for Kathy's fingers. The child's gaze fell and she seemed to study the way her hand fit in Kathy's. After a moment a small tear splashed on her pant leg and when she spoke, her voice was barely audible. "I don't wanna leave."

"Oh, sweetie, I know." Kathy stared sadly at the child. If only Maggie Stovall had kept Amanda from the beginning. And if Kathy had listened to her heart all those years—

"Can't I stay with you, Kathy, please?" Amanda's eyes begged through a pool of tears as she reached out and placed her other hand in Kathy's, so that they both nestled in Kathy's palms.

"Come here, honey." Kathy felt tears in her own eyes as she pulled the child into her arms, stroking her hair and whispering, "It's okay, baby. Everything's going to be all right."

Amanda paused, then pulled back, studying Kathy's eyes. "It's true then? You found me a foster home?"

A single tear spilled onto Kathy's face, and she wiped it quickly with the back of her hand. "Well, actually…" She forced herself to sound upbeat. "Actually, it's good news."

"Good news?" Again Amanda tilted her head. She was such a darling girl, peachy skin with only the faintest smattering of freckles across the bridge of her nose, and long hair that looked spun by the hands of angels. For all that Amanda had gone through, something innocent still sparkled in her eyes, and the effect only made her more beautiful.

Looking at her now, it was hard to believe that scant weeks ago she was in the hospital fighting for her life. Kathy let out a single, soft chuckle at the lovely picture Amanda made.

All right, here goes, sweetheart. "Yes, good news. A man came into the office today very interested in you. He said he thinks he and his wife would like to be your foster parents and…" Kathy tried to read Amanda's reaction, and since she saw nothing that resembled excitement, she gently took the girl's shoulders in her hands and stared deeply into her eyes. "And one day they might even want to adopt you. Forever, Amanda."

Panic worked its way across Amanda's face. "B-b-b…" She exhaled in a huff. "B-b-but…" Amanda crossed her arms, and focused her attention on her feet. "Kathy, I c-c-can't make my words right."

Kathy's heart melted. "Oh, sweetie, it's okay. Lots of people have trouble making words when they're upset. Just take your time." She ran a hand down the back of Amanda's head.

When Amanda's eyes lifted they were filled with tears. "I d-d-don't even know him…"

Kathy swallowed back a lump in her throat. *Poor little dar-*

ling, *Lord. Help me say the right thing.* "Honey, I know that. But he's a very nice man. He said you were exactly the type of child he and his wife were looking for." Kathy hated keeping the facts from her, but Ben Stovall had asked that she do so. Besides, Kathy wasn't at all sure it would be wise to tell Amanda she'd been found by her birth mother. Not when the woman was in a psychiatric hospital being treated for depression, unaware that her husband had even located the child.

Momentary worry washed over Kathy. What if Maggie Stovall refused contact with Amanda, let alone a foster or adoption arrangement? That would be too great a heartbreak for Amanda to take. It was better to keep the details simple, at least for now.

"W-w-why would he w-w-want an old girl like me? Most p-p-people want little kids...b-b-babies."

Kathy felt the girl's shoulders trembling and she moved her hands slowly down the thin arms to take hold of Amanda's small fingers again. "That's true." She lowered herself so that she could see directly into Amanda's eyes. "But this man is different. He said they were looking for a girl like *you*. They don't want a baby who cries all night or a toddler who hasn't learned to read. They want a girl just exactly like you, Amanda."

She shook her head and fresh tears filled her eyes. "I don't wanna go, Kathy. P-p-please. Don't m-m-make me."

"Baby, we've been through this before. The state won't let me keep you. Not unless there's no foster homes available."

"Yeah, but I...l-l-love you guys. I don't wanna leave."

"Oh, Amanda..." Kathy pulled the girl to her and held her close. The enthusiasm she'd felt earlier was all but gone. *How am I ever going to let her go, Lord? She doesn't even know these people. They could be awful for all any of us know. How can I—*

Trust Me, daughter.

But...

Trust Me.

There it was again, the soothing reassurance Kathy knew

came from the Lord. She exhaled slowly, forcing herself not to get caught up in her selfish feelings. If God had brought Amanda's mother back into her life there had to be a reason. Besides, Amanda was pretty well out of options in the Social Services system.

Kathy just needed to do all she could to help make the transition as smooth as possible. Amanda remained nestled in her arms, her head against Kathy's chest. What was she thinking? How does it feel to know your life could change at any moment, that you have no control over where you might be sleeping on any given night? *Help her, God. Please shut the door on this if it isn't from You. And give me wisdom to know what's best for Amanda.*

The girl pulled back and studied Kathy's eyes nervously. "Am I going with him tonight?"

Kathy smiled. "No, silly. Of course not. You need to meet him first."

Another look of terror flashed in Amanda's eyes. "By m-m-myself?"

"No, sweetie, I'll be with you." Kathy reached out and smoothed her hand over Amanda's hair. "How 'bout we all meet at Party Pizza tomorrow for lunch?"

The fear was gone for the moment, but in its place was resignation. Amanda had been this route before; she knew the protocol. "So I leave tomorrow night?"

Kathy shook her head. "The man's wife is in the hospital right now. We'll have to see what happens, but I think it could take a few days to get everything lined up." She hesitated. "Are we on then? For tomorrow, I mean?"

"Okay." The girl's eyes glistened with unshed tears, and Kathy was struck again by how tender yet tough this child was. Tender to all that was good and right with God and the world, yet tough enough not to break down sobbing when her very existence was being turned upside down.

Kathy hugged her close. "I wish you could stay. You know that, right?"

Then Amanda did something she'd never done before. She reached out a single finger and softly traced a heart on the back of Kathy's hand. "Know what that means?"

Kathy fought back tears. "No, honey, what?"

"It means that even if I go, you'll always have my heart."

Amanda tried to sleep, but it was hard. She wasn't sure what to feel. Kathy had said the man's name was Mr. Stovall and that he was good and kind and that he and his wife were probably an answer to prayer. Amanda turned onto her side and tried to keep her eyes shut. It was possible, wasn't it? That God had heard her prayers for a forever family and brought the Stovalls as an answer?

But why hadn't God given Kathy a bigger house instead? That would have been the best answer.

She didn't want to meet this man tomorrow. Because if things went well, she'd be leaving Kathy's house very, very soon. She blinked and stared about the shadowy room. What if Mr. Stovall really was a nice man? The kind of friendly-looking man that Amanda had seen on television shows. Maybe he went off to work in the morning and came home at night, and he'd play with his kids—with her—on the living room floor like Mr. Garrett. Maybe he and his wife were sent by God to take her home and love her forever.

Amanda closed her eyes again. Of course she'd thought that about Mrs. Graystone, too.

No, there could only ever be one, true answer to prayer where her life was concerned. If God wasn't going to give Kathy a bigger home so Amanda could stay with her, there was only one person who would qualify as an answer to prayer. And it wasn't Mr. Stovall.

It was her mother. Her real mother. The one who somewhere, somehow must still remember the baby she gave away. The one who surely one day would do whatever it took to find her.

Twenty-eight

JUDGE CALEB "HUTCH" HUTCHISON HATED EMERGENCY HEARINGS and he rarely granted them. Especially first thing in the morning. But that brisk November day a week before Thanksgiving, he had examined the circumstances and decided there was no other choice.

The situation seemed on its surface an open and shut case. Long-lost father shows up to claim a child caught in the Social Services system. Judge Hutch's job was merely to make sure the facts matched up and send the father and daughter on their way. Still, something about the man and the little girl he claimed to want for his own troubled Hutch. Deeply.

Alone in his chambers, five minutes before the meeting was to take place, the judge reviewed the situation for the fifth time. One John McFadden waltzes into the courthouse, fills out an emergency request form saying he only recently learned he had a child in Cincinnati, and then produces enough information to convince the clerk he's the real father. The child is a girl named Amanda Joy Brownell, a ward of the Social Services system who's been wasting away in a series of foster homes for the past three years.

Judge Hutchison had worked as a jurist in that same courthouse for more than twenty years. He knew his peers considered him both brilliant and tough—a judge criminals feared, whose sentences brought a sense of justice to the people of Cincinnati and the surrounding area. But criminals weren't the only group Hutch detested. There was one other group of citizens he was loathe to waste time on: deadbeat dads.

Therefore, his decision to meet with the man today had nothing to do with any generosity of spirit. If this McFadden had truly been concerned with the welfare of his daughter, why hadn't he come forward before now? The possibilities as to what had motivated him—after so many years—to seek custody of the child now were less than encouraging.

So the only reason Judge Hutchison was giving the man five minutes of his time was pure and simple: Hutch loved children. He had five grandchildren of his own and often found himself fighting back tears when the victims in his cases were kids too young to help themselves. Amanda Brownell's file had made his eyes watery after only the first page.

If there was even a remote chance that this McFadden character really was an upstanding citizen who only recently realized he'd fathered a child and who truly wanted to give this hapless little child a permanent, loving home, Judge Hutchison did not want anything to stand in the way.

He checked his watch. The man should be there by now, sitting in his courtroom waiting the judge's decision, which could go one of two ways: a temporary grant of custody rights—one day, for instance, so the two could become acquainted—or a refusal until the situation could be further examined.

Judge Hutchison had long ago learned to trust his instincts, and they were telling him that McFadden was almost certainly not the type of father who would give little Amanda a happy, loving home.

The man was in too great a hurry.

No, McFadden was more the kind of man Hutch would subject to intense scrutiny; the kind that might not only be false, but perhaps even dangerous.

He opened the door and walked from his chambers into the courtroom. A dark-haired man with a falsely humble expression rose to his feet. "Your honor, my name is John McFadden, and I'm—"

"Sit down, Mr. McFadden." Hutch glowered at the man, more certain than ever that something wasn't right. Something about the flashy cheap suit and the depth of darkness in McFadden's eyes made him look more like a Las Vegas pit boss than a loving father who had only recently stumbled onto his long-lost daughter.

Hutch took his seat and sorted through his docket. Several minutes passed before he looked up and rapped his gavel twice. He nodded to a court reporter sitting nearby. "I will now hear the emergency matter of John McFadden regarding his request to be granted custody of his seven-year-old daughter, Amanda Brownell, who is currently a ward of this court." He peered down and found the man watching him with great expectancy. "You may present your information, Mr. McFadden."

As he stood, the man glanced behind him, then side to side. *Nervous sort,* Judge Hutch thought. McFadden took a handful of documents and presented them to the judge. "Here. I believe this is everything you need."

The judge sifted through the papers. A notarized DNA test, a request form asking the judge to check McFadden's DNA against that of the child's, a request form for temporary custody, and another request form for a hearing that would give him permanent custody. Everything was in order...but the gnawing feeling that something was wrong remained.

"All right, Mr. McFadden, why don't you give me your driver's license, and I'll go back to my chambers, make a copy of it, and check out the DNA with the child's birth certificate. It shouldn't take long to pull up the information on the computer."

McFadden's shoulders relaxed and his face seemed to sag with relief. "Thanks, Judge, you don't know what this means to me. I can't wait to see her. I mean, after all these years and such, you know how it is. This is really amazing..."

The man was still rambling as Hutch took his identification and slipped back into his chambers. Before he checked the computers for matching DNA; before he contacted Kathy

Garrett, the social worker listed on the girl's file; before he did anything else for that matter, he was going to run the man's information by someone else. Just in case.

He picked up the phone and was immediately connected with the court clerk.

"Yes, your honor?"

"Get me the police department, please."

John McFadden tapped his foot, anxiously awaiting Judge Hutchison's return. With each passing minute, his heart rate increased. Finally, when the eighth minute passed, John clenched his teeth, cursing under his breath. No DNA match should take this long. That judge must have discovered more than whether or not John was the kid's father.

He stood and took three quick steps toward the court reporter. "Tell the judge...uh, I had to use the restroom."

The court reporter looked up briefly. "Sure."

In three minutes, McFadden was in his gold Acura, pulling out of the courthouse parking lot. He steered into the first alley he saw and dialed Alfie's cell phone.

"Yah, buddy." Alfie's words were muffled; the lug was probably eating again. Alfie was always stuffing his face.

"It's me."

"Oh...hey, boss, what's up?"

John gritted his teeth. They'd forced his hand. He had no choice now but to—

"You follow the girl this morning?"

"Sure thing, boss. Walked to a bus stop a block from her house. Waited, oh, maybe five minutes." He paused. "We didn't follow the bus. Was we supposed to?"

"Nah, you did good. What was the name on the bus?"

"Wood-something."

This guy was the limit. "Ask Mike, will ya?" John tried not to get impatient with Alfie, but there were times...

In the background he heard Mike's voice. "Woodland Elementary, I wrote it down."

"Hey, boss, he wrote it down. It was—"

"I heard him. Never mind. Do me a favor and put Mike on. I need to know exactly where the bus stop is."

When John had the directions, he hung up and called the operator. "Yeah, I need the number for Woodland Elementary."

A minute later he was on the phone to the school secretary. "Hi, my son told me school's out at 2:15 today, is that right?"

"No, sir, 3:10, like usual."

"I thought so. I tell ya, that boy has an active imagination. Thanks."

He looked at his watch as he hung up the phone. 10:15. Smiling, he started the engine and headed for his motel. As he drove he fingered the loaded handgun beside him, running over the plan again in his mind. In less than six hours he would meet his daughter for the first time.

Then he would take care of business his way.

The demons were still taunting her, hissing at her, reminding her of the doubts that had first taken shape in Dr. Camas's office the day before.

Had Ben really been to blame?

Maggie rolled over, caught in the layer of reality somewhere between sleep and consciousness.

It's your fault, Maggie. Everything that's happened. Your fault. The hissing became louder until it became a ringing that grew more and more persistent.

The alarm clock! Maggie shot up in bed and hit the buzzer on the machine beside her. It was 9:30 in the morning, and though Dr. Camas had honored her request for solitude the day before, he had insisted on today's early appointment. She had thirty minutes until their meeting, and she flipped onto her back, staring at the ceiling.

Ben must have been to blame, God. Tell me I'm right.

Silence.

I can't think about it, won't. Then, moving like a woman late for the last bus out of town, Maggie showered, dressed, and ate a blueberry muffin from her breakfast tray. Through the routine, a thought occurred to her.

For the first time since entering Orchards, she had awakened filled with energy. By ten o'clock she was sitting across from Dr. Camas.

"I've talked with Dr. Baker. We're excited for you, Maggie."

Her heart pounded. How could there be anything exciting about the confusion she was feeling? She was awful, sick in the head, the worst wife anyone could possibly—

"Maggie…you okay?"

She twisted in her chair and struggled to maintain eye contact with the doctor. "I, well…I keep thinking about our talk yesterday."

"Yes, me too." He smiled gently and reached out, patting her hand the way her father used to do when she was a little girl. "It's all right, Maggie. You can finish the story whenever you're ready. We were talking about what Ben said to you back in your early days together."

Maggie nodded and forced her fingertips into her temples. *Go back, Maggie…remember it right this time.*

Be truthful, Maggie…come into the light. My grace is sufficient for you, daughter.

Maggie felt herself relax. Wherever it went, whatever happened afterward, she had to remember the truth about her past. The truth about Ben.

"I'm trying to remember what he said…" She let her hands drop to her lap, and this time she caught Dr. Camas's gaze and held it. "And I'm…not sure he ever really demanded that I be—"

She stopped short as Ben's long-ago words came back in a rush: *"I wanna be pure, Maggie. My wife—whoever she is—*

deserves that. I wanna be pure...I wanna be pure..."

Dear God, was it true? The reality nearly knocked her to the floor. The idea of purity hadn't come as a directive from him, but rather a promise. He had wanted to offer himself pure, as a precious gift. The notion that she—in turn—could be nothing less than a virgin had come from—

"No! It can't be..." Her voice was a hoarse whisper; a piece of her heart felt as though it had been ripped open.

Dr. Camas leaned slightly forward. "Go on, Maggie. What do you remember?"

Sobs welled up in her chest. There had to be other conversations! Times when he had pompously demanded perfection from anyone who might grace his arm down the aisle of a church, anyone who would wear his ring and take his name...

She was weeping now, and still the doctor waited. She knew there was no choice but to tell him what she remembered. "I...I think he said he wanted to...be pure. S-S-something like, h-h-his wife deserved that." She gulped and her shoulders shook from the sobs that washed over her. She didn't know how long it took to compose herself enough to speak. "Then I asked him..." She squeezed her eyes shut, horrified she hadn't remembered things correctly until now. "I asked him if that meant he wouldn't marry a girl who wasn't a virgin."

The only sound in the room was that of Maggie crying as she forced herself to remember the rest of the conversation. How could she have hung on to a memory that had never existed? How fair had that been?

The questions weighed on her heart as she found her voice. "He told me he thought God had a girl for him, someone like him...someone who loved the Lord and had s-s-saved herself the way he had. H-H-e told me he thought she had hair like mine, and a smile like mine, and a laugh like..."

The memory of her husband and all he'd been back then lay in front of her, like an innocent child about to receive a punishment for something he hadn't done. Ben hadn't demanded perfection from her after all. He had merely been teasing, baring his heart and telling her in his own, shy way that he could picture the two of them marrying one day. Somehow…sometime, she had twisted the truth, convincing herself Ben had started the conversation, that he'd stated his expectations up front: He'd only marry a girl who was as pure and wholesome as he was.

"I convinced myself it was something he demanded, a requirement." She grabbed a tissue and blew her nose. Trembling from her fingers to her knees, Maggie stared at Dr. Camas, desperate for answers. "Why did I do that?"

The doctor considered her for a long moment. "You tell me."

The answer danced on the tip of her tongue, but it was so bitter she hated to speak it. Her voice grew quiet, and she felt regret like a millstone around her neck. "So I wouldn't have to…" She drew two quick breaths and stifled another wave of sobs. "So I'd have someone to blame…someone whose fault it was that I gave my baby away." Maggie covered her face with her hands and sobbed.

She had been running from the truth all this time, refusing her part in what happened. By blaming Ben every time she thought of her baby, her little girl growing up somewhere else, with some other mother, she had eventually…

She looked up, her sight blurred from the tears. "I taught myself to hate him, didn't I?"

"What do you think?" Dr. Camas's tone and gaze were filled with compassion.

"Yes. I did. So I wouldn't have to blame myself."

"Maggie, depression often comes from lies we tell ourselves. When we're willing to lie to those we love—the way you did when you married Ben—then it's quite normal to lie to ourselves, as well. That's at least part of why you're here, wouldn't you agree?"

Maggie nodded, feeling as though she were falling into a

dark hole. *What have I done, God? Help me, please…help me find a way back out.*

"How do you feel, Maggie?" The doctor wasn't pushing, but his question stabbed at her all the same. How was she feeling? Like she was suffocating under the weight of her bad decisions. Like there would never again be hope for her. Like she was the worst mother, the worst wife in the world…

"Like I made a lot of mistakes."

"And…"

Suddenly it dawned on her. All she'd ever wanted from God was deep, genuine joy. The kind that would remind her in the darkest days how close and real God was, and that somehow hope was at hand. But every bit of joy she'd ever felt had vanished that terrible day, the morning she gave her daughter up for adoption. She had always thought it was because she'd been forced into it. Backed into an emotional corner.

Now she knew different.

Not only had she walked away from her child, she'd walked away from God as well. Hadn't she heard His quietly urging voice that day telling her not to let go, to hold tight to her tiny daughter whatever the cost? It had taken every ounce of strength to fight against the screaming inside her soul, her desperate longing to stop the social worker from taking her baby. Back then she'd thought she was fighting against herself, her selfish desires. But the situation was clearer now. She'd gone against the prompting of the Holy Spirit, choosing to take matters into her own hands—and every day since then she'd blamed Ben for having expected perfection from her.

But no one had forced her to give her baby up for adoption or to lie about it all these years. The lies were hers and hers alone.

And never, not once since then, had she ever repented. Maggie fought back the sobs that caught in her throat.

I'm here, daughter, turn to Me…

Slowly, finally—after all this time, all her pain, the quiet prodding of the Holy Spirit felt like balm to her soul. She exhaled and forced herself to remain steady, for her entire being ached to do the thing God had always wanted of her.

Okay, Lord, I will…I'll repent. She made the promise silently, but she meant it as much as if she'd broadcast it throughout the hospital.

"What're you feeling, Maggie?" Dr. Camas waited patiently.

She drew a deep breath and allowed herself to be comforted by the kindness in his eyes. *Where do I start, Lord?* "I need to make things right with a lot of people."

"Such as?"

"Well, Ben most of all." How cold she'd been to him, how unbending and hard-hearted. Could he ever forgive her for all she'd done? Even if he could, would he still want her?

The questions were staggering; Maggie would have to deal with most of them later.

"Are you ready to talk about it in group?"

Maggie nodded. "In some ways I've never felt worse than I feel right now." She wrung her hands together and blinked back fresh tears. "But I also feel hope; it doesn't make sense."

A warm smile filled the doctor's face. "God promises us joy in the morning, Maggie, and I believe for you the darkness is beginning to lift." He paused. "It's all about being honest. First, with God; second, with ourselves."

The words washed over Maggie, easing the anxiety within her. He was right, and even in the fading darkness it felt wonderful to finally be truthful with the Lord and herself.

Now it was time to be honest with everyone else. The group, her parents, her daughter. And of course Ben.

Him more than anyone.

Early the next morning as she slept, Maggie dreamed of a hospital in Woodland, Ohio, and a beautiful baby girl sleeping in her arms. A nurse entered the room and made an announcement. "Liars can never be suitable mothers." Then the woman walked up to Maggie's bed, snatched the baby from her arms, turned, and disappeared through the door.

Maggie screamed for the nurse to stop. "I won't lie. I'll tell the truth, I promise. I love my baby. Please, bring her back. Please!"

But the nurse was gone, and a strange aching developed and grew stronger until finally it woke Maggie at four o'clock in the morning. Drenched in sweat, tears running down her face, she realized the aching was the emptiness she felt without her baby.

"Where is she, God?" Maggie whispered the question through her tears. "I only want to know that she's okay."

Is that all?

The startling question seemed to come from the Lord Himself, and it echoed quietly in her heart.

Yes, God, that's all. Even as she thought it, Maggie knew she was lying again. She wanted more. Much more. She wanted her daughter back, wanted a chance to undo what she'd done that day at Woodland Hospital, wanted to hold her daughter close and take her home and raise her the way she'd imagined in those early days of her pregnancy.

"Why can't I stop lying, Lord?"

Repent, My daughter. Now. While your heart is right. My grace is sufficient for you...

Maggie's breath caught. She had realized her need to repent, but she'd never actually done it. The day had slipped by, and still she hadn't met with the Lord, asked His forgiveness. Quietly, reverently, she slipped out of bed and landed on the cold, linoleum hospital floor. There was no time to wait.

Forgive me, Father. Forgive me...

She hung her head, pouring her heart out to the Lord, begging His forgiveness and promising to be honest with Him and herself and everyone else as long as she drew breath.

Then, one at a time, she confessed the lies she'd told—lies

to herself, lies to Ben, and lies to the Lord—until finally she repented of the one she'd just told. And then, just before breakfast, she did something else...something she'd been wanting to do since she checked herself in at Orchards.

She pulled a small phone book from her purse and turned to the T section. There it was. Laura Thompson. Wrapping her robe tightly around her waist, Maggie carried the book into the hall, toward the community phone, and made the call.

"Hello?"

Maggie closed her eyes, squeezing back tears. *Help me find the words, Lord.* "Laura...this is Maggie Stovall. I should have called you sooner..."

"Maggie, dear! I've been praying." The woman's voice was pure and filled with such love that Maggie almost went to her knees again.

She's been praying for me all along, hasn't she, Lord? His love, His provision, overwhelmed her. "If you have a minute, Laura, I have some things to tell you...things I'd like you to pray about..."

"I'm listening, honey. Tell me whatever's on your heart."

Maggie poured out the entire story, amazed that there was cleansing in every word she spoke. Laura listened and Maggie could feel her concern and understanding through the phone lines.

"So that's why I needed prayer." Maggie was grateful for the older woman, certain that along with everything else God had done, He'd blessed her with a lifelong friend in Laura Thompson.

"Well, I finally understand the mask."

"The mask?"

"Yes, dear." There was no condemnation in Laura's voice. "The Lord gave me a picture that first day, the day I drew your name. A woman in a mask."

Goose bumps rose on Maggie's arms. "Me?"

"Yes. And the image of a little girl, too. Your little girl, I'm guessing. When I pray for you, I pray for her, too."

"Oh, Laura...I don't know what to say..." Maggie closed her eyes briefly. *It's all coming together, Lord.* Was the arm of God that far-reaching? His love that persistent? Had He cared so much that He'd put Maggie's deepest needs in the heart of Laura Thompson? *I stand in awe, Father.*

Maggie made plans to talk with Laura again soon. And after she hung up, Maggie was engulfed by a peace so vivid she could almost feel it wiping away what remained of the darkness. The older woman's words of hope and encouragement rang clear in her mind.

I'm sorry, Lord...so sorry. I want to be close to You again, clean and right and ready to do Your will.

Daughter, I have loved you with an everlasting love...I will remember your sins no more.

"Oh, Lord, you're so faithful." Maggie hung her head as the words flooded her heart with peace—and with the beginning of what Maggie knew was joy. Joy of knowing she was a daughter of the King of kings, joy of being saved by His precious blood, joy of being certain that one day she would live with Him in heaven, eternally. Deep, abiding, genuine joy. And once it had taken root in her heart, Maggie knew it would continue growing until the darkness was gone forever.

Forgiveness, wholeness, restoration...they all were hers. Even if she ached a lifetime for the daughter she would almost certainly never know.

IT WAS NOON, AND THE COMMOTION AT PARTY PIZZA WAS AT A fever pitch. Picnic tables lined the dining room where mothers, preschoolers, and the occasional older child gathered for lunch.

Ben ordered a large Hawaiian pizza as he took in the scene and tried not to be nervous. Kathy was picking Amanda up at school fifteen minutes before lunch, so the two would be there any moment.

He'd been thinking about Amanda Joy since the moment he'd learned of her existence. Would she look like Maggie? Would her eyes twinkle when she laughed? What would her personality be like? *Probably jaded from years in the Social Services system...*

For what had to be the hundredth time in the past twenty hours, he wondered how different all of their lives might have been if only Maggie had been honest.

Judge not, lest you be judged.... Love covers a multitude of sins.

The sting of conviction came, as it always did lately, every time he tried to blame Maggie for what happened. He planted his forearms on the table and exhaled slowly. The Lord was right. Back then he would never have understood. He would have written Maggie off, broken up with her without looking back. There would have been no getting together again, no engagement, no marriage.

But even if he and Maggie had parted ways, at least one little girl might have been spared a beating, one child might have known a lifetime of love rather than sorrow.

Ben pushed the thoughts from his head. *It wasn't my fault she got together with John McFadden.*

Love covers a multitude of sins...

A sigh escaped him, and Ben massaged his eyebrows with his thumb and forefinger. That same Scripture had haunted him for days now. Weeks, even. Ever since Maggie left, it seemed. *What does it mean, Lord? I loved Maggie; I treated her right.*

Silence.

Fine. Leave me wondering. But one of these days, Lord, I'm going to need You to make it clear to me.

A blur of motion near the front door caught his eye, and he turned and stared. It was Kathy. And clutching her hand tightly was a beautiful, wide-eyed, blond-haired child, whose face...

Ben sucked in his breath. *Oh, man...she looks just like Maggie.*

He watched them weave their way closer until they were standing before him. If the girl had come by herself and stood among a throng of children, Ben would have recognized her without any trouble. He'd have known her anywhere. The shape of her eyes, the way she held herself—stiffly, wanting him to think she was tough even though her eyes showed her fear—she was the image of her mother.

Maggie, if you could only see her. Ben had an overwhelming desire to take the child in his arms and soothe away a lifetime of pain and hurt and abandonment. Instead he held out his hand. "Hi, I'm Ben."

Amanda nodded curtly and gave him a polite smile. "I'm Amanda." The child still held tightly to the hand of her social worker and after several seconds, Ben pulled his back. It hit him then. Amanda loved this woman, this social worker. In a world of uncertainty, Kathy Garrett had always been there for Maggie's little girl. Now the child would see him as the intruder, the man who wanted to take her away, maybe forever.

What am I doing, Lord? She's got a life already. Give me wisdom, please; the child's been hurt enough.

Kathy had been watching the brief exchange between Ben and Amanda, and now she opened her purse. "Well, you two sit here and get acquainted. I'm going to order pizzas and—"

"No, sit down." Ben motioned to her. "I ordered a few minutes ago. It'll be up any minute."

Amanda and Kathy took their seats beside each other, across from Ben. He noticed how the girl snuggled close to Kathy, how her small eyes had softened just a bit. She looked at Ben with a gaze that didn't waver. "I like pizza."

He was taken aback at how her comment made him feel. His heart soared at the small concession—it seemed a white flag of sorts, her way of saying she was going to try to like him. He smiled at her. "Me too."

Kathy slipped an arm around Amanda's shoulders and squeezed once. "Listen, I have to use the ladies' room."

"Me too! I—"

"Amanda…" Kathy's tone was part warning, part reminder. Ben wondered if the two had talked about the child needing time alone with him.

Amanda's face fell and she nodded a slight smile in Kathy's direction. "Okay. I'll go later."

Great. Kathy's leaving. What am I supposed to say? What do seven-year-old girls like to talk about? He studied her face, and the image of Maggie was so vivid he had to blink to focus his thoughts. "So, tell me about school."

"It's fine." Amanda's gaze followed Kathy until she was out of sight. Then she turned to him, her eyes veiled in uncertainty.

Off to a good start… Fine. If she wasn't in the mood to talk, he'd make up for both of them. And maybe, just maybe… "Okay, so tell me about the class pet. I mean, everyone in second grade has a class pet, right?" Before Amanda could answer, Ben cocked his head. "Let's see, I think our class had a monkey when I was in school. No, wait. That was the teacher. She just looked like a monkey…"

Amanda giggled and a twinkle—Maggie's twinkle—brought a spark of life to her eyes. "We have a goldfish."

"A *goldfish?*" Ben's voice was filled with mock indignation, and Amanda giggled again. "That's not the right kind of pet for second grade. You need something like a muskrat or a house of rabbits or a giant python. Something the boys can let out of the cage to scare the class half to death, isn't that right?"

"We have a lizard, too, named Frank."

"Frank the lizard? Sounds like a very old lizard to me; does he do tricks? Read newspapers, work the computers, that kind of thing?" Ben made his eyes wide, as though he actually suspected Amanda might say yes. This time she let her head fall back and the laughter that spilled from her throat sounded so like Maggie a lump formed in his throat and a wave of sadness washed over Ben. It was Maggie back in the days when they first met…back when she still had something to laugh at. He worked hard to keep his face from reflecting what he was feeling.

"Are you always this goofy?" Amanda leaned forward, resting her thin arms on the table and meeting his gaze.

"What day is it?"

"Wednesday."

"Yes. On Wednesdays I'm always this goofy. Now Thursdays are my days to sleep a lot, and on Fridays I'm serious nearly all the time. But on the weekend…well, then I'm actually extra-goofy. Sometimes I tell knock-knock jokes for an hour straight. Especially on Saturday."

Amanda's eyes danced with laughter. "Tell me one."

"A knock-knock joke?" Ben made his eyes wide again. "On Wednesday?"

"Yes!" Amanda's laughter made him smile. "Please…"

"Well, since we just met and you've never been with me for a Saturday knock-knock joke hour, I guess just this one time…" He thought a moment. "Knock-knock."

"Who's there?"

"Boo."

"Boo who?"

The silliness faded from Ben's voice. "Ah, that's okay, Amanda. Don't cry." He paused, hoping with all his heart that she could see he was no longer joking. "Everything's going to be okay, Amanda Joy. I promise you."

Her eyes clouded, and her expression grew serious. "Why do you want me, Mr. Stovall?"

She wasn't afraid to ask the big questions, that much was certain. But then, there wasn't enough time to make small talk, really. Not if he was going to take over as her foster parent in the next day or so. Ben sighed. How best to answer her? He didn't want to tell her about Maggie, not yet…not when he had no idea how that news would affect her. *Lord…help me.*

"Kathy showed me your file and…well, I knew I was going to love you." That was true, anyway. "I guess it felt like my wife and I have known you all our lives."

Amanda's eyes softened again and the hint of a smile played on her lips. "Really?"

"Yep. Kind of like there was always a missing piece before. And now it seems like…" Ben felt his eyes grow watery and he blinked. This was no time to be emotional; Amanda would not understand the significance of the moment. "It seems like we've waited all our lives for you."

The child thought about that for a moment, her small face pensive and earnest. "But you don't even know me."

Ben looked into her eyes and saw Maggie looking back at him. His heart swelled with love for this child he'd known only ten minutes, and a smile covered his face. "I know you, Amanda Joy. Better than you think."

Concern flashed across her face as if she were recalling an awful memory. "I d-d-don't clean my room very w-w-well, though. Sometimes that gets me in trouble. P-p-people send me back when that happens."

Ben ached to climb around the booth and take her in his

arms. The poor child. What had she suffered over the years? Unable to resist any longer, he reached across the table and wrapped his fingers around hers. Suddenly he knew with everything in him that he could never, ever let this child go. He wanted to promise her that nothing could make him send her back, but he still needed to talk to Maggie.

He drew a deep breath. How could he help her understand his feelings for her? "Amanda, love—the kind of love God wants us to have—doesn't change because of a messy room. Do you believe me?"

Amanda nodded. "Kathy loves me that way."

"Did I hear my name?" Kathy walked up, a pizza in one hand and a pitcher of root beer in the other. She grinned as she set both in the center of the table, next to three plastic cups and plates. "Didn't either of you talkers hear the order come up?"

Ben and Amanda shared a conspiratorial glance, and then the threesome dug into the food. Amanda chattered about different pizzas and knock-knock jokes and classroom pets, while Ben and Kathy exchanged occasional smiles. When the girl was finished eating, she pointed toward the video games and gasped. "Hey, I can't believe it. Kristen's here! She must be on lunch break, too." Amanda flashed a questioning look at Kathy. "Please? Can I go play with her? Just for a few minutes?"

"Well—" Kathy looked at the child's plate—"I guess so. But hurry. You have to get back to school soon."

When Amanda was out of earshot, Ben leaned back in the booth and shook his head. "She looks exactly like her mother." He watched the child talking animatedly with her friend across the dining hall. "I mean, exactly. Nearly took my breath away."

Kathy folded her hands neatly on the tabletop and studied him. "She likes you."

"Yeah." He met Kathy's gaze again. "The feeling's mutual. She's...after all she's been through, she's something else."

"I know." The social worker's eyes fell for a moment, then found Ben's again. "Believe me."

Ben angled his head. "She loves you very much."

Kathy looked away and took a sip of her drink.

Something had bothered Ben since he first recognized the attachment Kathy had for Amanda and he figured it was time to ask. "How come you never..."

"How come I didn't adopt her a long time ago?" Kathy's smile didn't reach her eyes. "We have seven children living with us—five by birth, two by adoption. I've tried to take Amanda in as a foster child, but every time I petition for her, the court says I'm at my limit. No more children unless we get a bigger house. My husband is in construction, so money isn't always regular. Moving is out of the question. Any time Amanda is with us is strictly temporary according to court records until a more suitable arrangement can be made."

The irony of Amanda's predicament hit him hard. The only reason he and Maggie had a chance to make the girl their own was because the state was unwilling to let Kathy Garrett have her—even after Kathy had invested so much in her. "I'd like to bring Amanda home, short term, anyway. For the weekend, say. That way she wouldn't miss any school."

Kathy looked at him thoughtfully. "Will you tell her? About her mother, I mean?"

"I'd like to. In fact, I'd like to introduce them this weekend, if everything works out." His voice softened. "It's a long shot, I'm afraid."

"I know it's none of my business, Mr. Stovall, but what happened?"

"With Maggie?" Ben braced his arms on the bench beside him and took a deep breath. It was such a hard story, especially when he had only learned the details so recently himself. "There's a lot to it. Basically, back before we were married, we were apart for a year or so, and she got pregnant. By the time we got back together, she'd already given Amanda up. She told me she was a virgin, and until a month ago I didn't know anything about the baby."

"How'd you find out?" Kathy asked.

"When Maggie checked herself into the hospital she left me a note saying we were finished, that she wanted a divorce. She...they were worried she might be suicidal." He clenched his teeth, not sure if he was saying too much. Her eyes caught his and the compassion there encouraged him to continue. "She told me I never really knew her. Since then she's refused my letters, phone calls. Everything."

Kathy's eyebrows lowered in concern. "A psychiatric hospital?"

Ben sighed. "Doesn't sound very Christian, does it?"

He caught a momentary flash of concern in her eyes. When she spoke, her tone was firm. "Do you know how many Christians suffer from depression, Mr....Ben? We've all convinced ourselves that believers aren't supposed to wrestle with darkness or hard times. And nothing—absolutely nothing—could be further from the truth."

Ben leaned back, frowning. *Is it true, God? Are there other women like Maggie? Women in the church?* "No one ever knew...she didn't...she always seemed so happy."

The expression on Kathy's face softened. "They all do, especially when they know the rejection they'd face otherwise." She stirred the straw in her soft drink. "You'd be surprised how many people wear masks to church."

What was she saying? "So you mean it's a good thing, this hospital stay?"

Kathy smiled. "I know it's hard to understand, but many times depression comes from a chemical imbalance. Stress, other factors in life become too hard to handle and the body's chemistry is thrown off. When that happens, nothing but medication will set things right again. Even if it's only temporary."

Medication? Ben hadn't thought of that—his Maggie being on drugs to get through life. "It seems so...I don't know, worldly, I guess. Shouldn't prayer be enough?"

Kathy's shoulders lifted in a gentle shrug. "Lots of people

would say the medicine available today is an *answer* to prayer." She paused. "It seems your Maggie is where she needs to be. The bigger question is whether she'll want to see Amanda."

Ben made a fist and gripped it with his other hand. Before all this happened he would have known the answer—of *course* Maggie would want her daughter. But now…now he had no idea what might be going on in his wife's mind, what her reaction to Amanda would be. "You're right." He stared across the room at Amanda and her friend. "That's why I'm afraid of telling her anything yet."

He sighed. The question had haunted him since the moment he laid eyes on the child. Now that he'd found her, there was something deep within him that couldn't imagine ever letting her go. "I haven't worked through all the details and, well, I know Amanda needs a mother figure." His feelings for Amanda were greater than he'd thought possible. And if Maggie wasn't interested…

Does it matter, God…what Maggie decides about this? Aren't children sometimes raised by single fathers?

He searched for the right words. "What I'm trying to say is, I want to give her a home, Ms. Garrett. No matter what Maggie decides."

Kathy studied him and an understanding smile worked its way across her face. "I hoped you might feel that way." Kathy glanced at her watch. "We can talk about it later. Let's get Amanda back to school, then head back to the office so we can file the right paperwork."

He hesitated. "I've been a foster parent but…I can't believe it's this easy to take custody of a child in the foster system." The idea worried Ben. What if he'd been the type of foster parent Amanda had had before?

"The moment a licensed foster parent breaks the law or is arrested, that type of thing, a red flag shows up in the computer and the license is automatically revoked. But…" Her shoulders settled forward a bit, as though the weight of the matter were almost more than she could bear. "Obviously it's not a fool proof system."

She looked at him intently. "I've prayed about you, Mr. Stovall. I know you're a licensed foster parent in the state of Ohio; and I believe you're married to Amanda's birth mother. I also believe you know the same Lord I do. Because of that, I'm ready, if you are, to arrange a short-term agreement. I trust God to make the other details fall into place later." She smiled, even as her eyes filled with fresh tears. "Much as I'll miss her, you should know one thing, Mr. Stovall."

"What's that?"

"I'll be praying that your wife will get the help she needs…so she can see the chance God's giving her. And that one day very soon—" Kathy's eyes sparkled with hope—"the three of you will be a family."

The paperwork was easier than Ben was used to. Short-term care—especially for a foster parent already licensed by the state—was by nature designed to be an expeditious process, so that the child could be transported as soon as possible into the foster home. In this case, he and Kathy had talked to Amanda before taking her back to class. They'd agreed Amanda would go with him after school tomorrow. She could miss Friday and spend a three-day weekend with him.

Now it was just after two o'clock, and Ben lay on his bed, sorting through the feelings assaulting him. Sometime tomorrow he and Amanda would drive the five hours back to Cleveland. Then, on Friday morning he would call and—by the grace of God—get a report on Maggie. As long as she was making progress and nearing the end of her treatment, he would do what some might consider the craziest thing of all: He would take Amanda to Orchards Hospital, where he wouldn't leave unless Maggie refused not just him, but her daughter as well.

How should I feel about Maggie, God? Part of me still can't believe it, can't imagine that she lied to me all those years, that she hid something as serious as this. But part of me feels guilty, Lord.

For the life of him, Ben couldn't understand why. What had he done to drive Maggie into John McFadden's arms? How had he pressured her to give up her daughter and lie to him all these years?

Love covers a multitude of sins, My son.

Ben flipped onto his stomach and breathed in the sterile scent of hotel bedding. "What's that mean? Tell me, God. Please." He voiced the request through clenched teeth.

Nothing came to him, and he closed his eyes. But as the minutes passed he drifted back in time through a series of memories, times that until then, he had completely forgotten.

The first one took shape…he and Maggie were fishing on the edge of a dock along a small lake, hidden away from the main road. It was seven, maybe eight years ago. They heard something and turned to see a teenage couple walking hand in hand, heading into the woods. The girl looked nervous; she checked over her shoulder more than once. The boy had a thick blanket under his arm, and his steps were sure and steady.

"Looks like trouble," Maggie had whispered.

He could see the concern on her face as clearly as he had seen it that day.

Ben snorted softly. "She doesn't look too worried."

Maggie's eyes had widened, her eyebrows set in frustration. "What's that supposed to mean?"

Ben remembered being taken aback. "It means whatever happens out there in the woods today, she asked for it."

He could still see the indignation that had flashed in Maggie's eyes. "That girl isn't asking for anything."

"Look, Maggie, when a girl sneaks off into the woods with a guy and a blanket, she's asking for it." He placed an arm around her and smoothed his thumb over her troubled brow.

"Look at you and me. We didn't get in trouble because we held ourselves to a higher standard, a godly standard. I'm not saying it's easy to stay pure, Maggie. But we did it, didn't we?"

In the memory, Maggie's response was something Ben hadn't recognized before: A shadow crossed her face and she let her gaze fall to the water without answering him. Ask her what's bothering her! He screamed silently at the image of himself in the memory, but it did no good. Years had passed since then, and the moment was obviously gone. Instead there was only the same verse that had plagued him too often.

Love covers a multitude of sins…love covers a multitude of…

Another image took shape. He and Maggie were sitting across from each other in a restaurant just after church one Sunday a handful of years earlier. It was a day when one of the elders had shared news of his fifteen-year-old daughter's unplanned pregnancy.

"Maybe I'll give her a call," Maggie had said. She was staring out the window.

"I guess, if you want to." Ben kept his eyes trained on the menu, but in the memory he could see the hurt expression on Maggie's face.

"What's that supposed to mean?"

Ben looked up. "Nothing against you, Maggie. But she made her choice when she slept with the guy. I mean, don't get me wrong. I feel badly for her, but she never should have let herself get in that situation."

Like with the previous memory, Ben saw the veil of shame cover Maggie's face. But at the time he'd been too involved in whether to order grilled swordfish or chicken alfredo. He hadn't really thought much about her silence, her expression.

Maggie, I'm so sorry, honey. The signs were all there. How could I have been so blind? The questions tore at him, making him wish for a way back in time so he could look deep into her soul and gently pull the truth from her, talk with her so he wouldn't have to wait until now to understand her pain.

Love covers a multitude of sins…love covers a multitude…

Memory after memory filled his mind. Each time the conversation was about immorality or fleshly weakness. And each time, as Maggie expressed compassion, Ben had silenced her with righteous indignation. Finally at the end of the last conversation Maggie had tears streaming down her face—and again Ben had missed the opportunity to connect with her.

Love covers a multitude of sins.

Ben lay in bed wrestling with himself and with the Scripture that refused to let him sleep. He rolled onto one side, then flipped onto the other until finally he lay on his back, his heart pounding, his eyes wide open. "I might have been kinder back then, God…but I loved her. This isn't about me; it's about Maggie. It's her fault she…"

A new image took shape in his mind. The image of a man, nailed to a cross that was anchored on a hill and surrounded by a throng of people. But rather than weep for the crucified man, the people mocked and jeered and held their heads high. "You brought it on Yourself! You asked for it!" Suddenly Ben heard himself gasp out loud. Among the faces in the crowd, he had spotted his own. Then at the same moment, he caught the eyes of the one on the cross. Jesus' eyes, calm and merciful and full of lovingkindness.

Forgive them, for they know not what they do.

Jesus' words washed over him, and he blinked back the image. "Oh, God, what have I done?" Tears gave way to gut-wrenching sobs that tore at his heart and threatened to consume him. "What have I *done?*"

He had asked for a sign, hadn't he? Well, the Lord Himself had given one. He could deny the truth no longer. The same way the crowd had mocked Jesus, Ben had mocked those around him who were in pain. By believing himself somehow superior or invincible to the destructive reality of sin and temptation, he had missed dozens of opportunities to get to know Maggie, to really love her.

Suddenly Ben knew with certainty that had he seen her back then the way he'd seen her tonight, in his memories, he would have pulled her close and asked her what was wrong. Had he seen her that way even a few years ago…a few *weeks* ago, maybe they could have unraveled the ball of lies that had become their life and prevented Maggie's breakdown.

Maybe Amanda would never have been forced into a foster home where people hurt her.

And maybe the Lord wouldn't have had to show Ben's face among the crowd of people mocking Jesus.

"Forgive me, God. Please, forgive me." Ben wept, and as tear after tear coursed down his face, his heart grew softer than it had been in years. A hundred times over he apologized to Jesus, begging Him to prepare Maggie's heart for the moment when he could finally tell her how sorry he was. When he was finished, he felt drained of every wrong emotion he'd ever experienced. What's more, he no longer even considered Maggie's role in all they'd been through. He forgave her completely and wanted only for her to be able to say the same about him.

"Let her love me again, Lord. Make her believe me." Ben did love Maggie. He knew that now more than ever, more than at any point since their first meeting on that long-ago summer's night. Maggie was the only woman he would ever love, and Ben wanted nothing more than to take her in his arms and soothe away the years of hurt and lies and anger. The years when she must have thought daily about her child, yet was unable to share those feelings with him because of her desire to meet his standards.

And now where were they?

The reality of their situation hit him harder than ever before. Maggie wanted a divorce. Having kept her feelings locked away for so long, she was no longer willing even to consider working things out with him. The thought terrified him until he realized something else. He loved Maggie's child. If

Maggie refused to come home, if she no longer wanted anything to do with her daughter, he would continue to pursue Amanda's adoption.

"I love that little girl, God," he whispered into the still, night air. "Like she was my own flesh and blood."

As his tears eased, he begged God to work a miracle in the situation...pleaded that somehow, when this nightmare was over, the three of them could be something none of them had ever been before.

A family.

Thirty

THE TIME HAD FINALLY COME.

Now that it was here, Maggie noticed something that made her heart soar. It happened while she sat stiffly in a padded folding chair with the members of the group forming a protective circle around her. There, in the midst of them, she realized the darkness was gone.

She closed her eyes and they filled with tears of gratitude.

"Most of you know why we're here." Dr. Baker stood in the center of the circle, her hand on Maggie's shoulder. Maggie felt the presence of the Holy Spirit as tangibly as if God Himself were standing there beside her. "Maggie has had a significant change of heart, and this afternoon she asked if we could meet here and pray for her." Dr. Baker turned to Maggie. "Do you want to say anything to the group?"

She nodded and wiped the tears from her face with the back of her hand. "I want to thank you for…for being honest with me." She sniffed once and then took a tissue from Sarah, who knelt at her side. "Sarah and Betty and…" Maggie looked at Howard and smiled, "and you, Howard, for being bold enough to be honest with me even when you knew it might make me too mad to ever come back."

Her watery eyes made their way around the group until she had connected with each of them. "You've taught me that depression isn't something strange or unusual, that people who love God very much can suffer in the pit of darkness and still be believers."

There were gentle smiles from the group members; Sarah wiped at the tears that were now running down her face.

Maggie knew she might not have another chance to say all

that was on her heart, so she continued. "I used to think believers couldn't be depressed. Or shouldn't be. If a person trusted God and prayed and read the Bible and really had faith, then there was no room for things like depression, right? Christians who were depressed must have something wrong with them, or they didn't trust God enough. That sort of thing."

Maggie couldn't stop the small, sad laugh that escaped her. "Then I found *myself* fighting depression…and losing. So I was sure there was something wrong with me, that I just needed to trust more." She firmed her shoulders. "But I know now that was all wrong. The problem is something else entirely. Too many of us have been afraid to be honest, afraid that by being honest, our spouse or daughter or sister wouldn't love us. God wouldn't love us. We haven't felt able to walk and live and love in the abundant sunshine of God's honesty and grace. I know *I* didn't feel able…until now."

Dr. Baker squeezed Maggie's shoulder, encouraging her. "So, I wanted to ask you to come here, to pray for me. Pray I'll find a way to be honest with the people who matter in my life." Her throat tightened with emotion, and she looked down at her hands. "It'll take a miracle to save my marriage…"

She looked up, met the eyes watching her again, and went on in a whisper. "But then, God's done far greater things. I only have to look at the cross to remember that." She hesitated as a fresh wave of tears slid down her face. "I know you'll be okay when you leave here. We all will be so long as we remember how very big our God is, and how unconditional His love is. Even if we never see each other after this, I know we'll meet again. Because I believe God will see us through. Thank you, each of you."

Maggie's words faded into silence, but she didn't mind. It was true…she would survive. God had brought her, as He'd brought so many others, out of the darkness into the sunlight of His grace and joy.

Before they started to pray, Maggie remembered something else. "You know some of the specifics of my situation, but I need you to pray for something else."

"Whatever it is, just tell us, Maggie." Sarah handed her another tissue and waited expectantly. "We'll pray daily, you know we will."

Maggie nodded. "Somewhere out there, outside the safe walls of Orchards, I have a daughter I've never met. She's probably doing fine, living with her adoptive family. But when I'm finished here, if I feel it's really what God wants, I'll do whatever I can to find her. I'm not sure I can have peace about that part of my life until I know she's okay."

Then the group of downtrodden, desperate people, many of whom had only recently escaped the throes of desperation and found hope again, formed a chorus of voices and lifted Maggie and her needs straight to the hallways of heaven.

Thirty-one

AT 2:55 THAT AFTERNOON, KATHY GARRETT WAS WORKING AS diligently as possible on the stack of files that had gone unattended that day. She knew with everything in her that the decision to let Amanda go with Ben Stovall for the long weekend was a good one. And, true to her word, she prayed that he would be successful in meeting with his wife and introducing her for the first time to her daughter.

Kathy had no doubt that Amanda had made a connection with Mr. Stovall at their lunch. The child had an uncanny ability to recognize a genuine person, and from everything Amanda had said, she was hopeful things would work out with the Stovalls.

Amanda was good that way, not given to long bouts of sadness when she had to leave the Garrett family. It had happened often, and she understood.

But this time—if things worked out—Amanda's absence would be for more than a few days...and the idea of saying good-bye to the child caused Kathy's mind to wander, making it nearly impossible to concentrate on the files in front of her.

Kathy took a sip of lukewarm coffee and reached for the top folder on the stack. As she did, the phone rang.

She sighed. *It never stops, does it?* "Hello?"

"Ms. Garrett?"

Kathy didn't recognize the voice. "Yes, this is she." Something in the man's firm tone sent an unexplainable ripple of alarm through Kathy's veins.

"This is Judge Hutchison. I'm worried about one of your charges, Amanda Joy Brownell. Earlier today I heard an emergency session for a man by the name of John McFadden. He appeared with documentation proving he was Amanda's biological father. Before he got much—"

Kathy's heart skipped a beat. Amanda's biological father? What was the judge talking about? "Wait a minute…why didn't you call me?"

"It never got that far. I doubted the man from the beginning—something about his eyes or his look…I couldn't put my finger on it. Anyway, I went into my chambers and ran a rap on him." The judge hesitated. "DNA matches. He's the girl's father, all right. But he's a bad man, Ms. Garrett. I've left you a few messages since then."

Kathy hadn't had time to check her answering machine since lunch. Her mind raced in a dozen directions. "What'd you tell him?"

"That's just it. He left the courtroom before I could make my decision."

Kathy's heart rate doubled. "You aren't worried, are you?"

"Actually, I am. He wanted custody of Amanda immediately. He knew she was a ward of the court and that she was between foster homes. He hadn't found out about her until recently, but he wanted full custody."

A pit formed in Kathy's stomach. What could this mean? What could the man possibly want with Amanda? "So, where is he now?"

"He could be anywhere, I guess. But if he wants the child…"

"What do you mean?" Panic rose and Kathy's hands began to tremble. Who was this John McFadden and why was he here in town now? Was he somehow connected with Ben Stovall? Kathy glanced at her watch. Three P.M. Amanda would be getting out of school in ten minutes.

"It took a little while to run the check on him. My guess is he panicked and ran before I could call the police."

Kathy worked her fingers through her hair and tried to calm her pounding heart. "What's his rap sheet say?" She closed her eyes, not wanting to hear the judge's answer.

"Officers are investigating him for drug trafficking, and he's currently facing charges on attempted murder of a man in Cleveland. A Ben Stovall."

The room began to spin, and Kathy fought to maintain her balance. "Ben...Stovall?"

Judge Hutchison hesitated. "Stovall pressed charges. The report says the beating nearly killed him."

"Oh no!" Kathy forced herself to concentrate. "This can't be happening. Judge, listen, thanks for the information. I've got to go meet Amanda at the bus."

"If you see anything out of the ordinary, I want you to call the police immediately. I already notified them that McFadden's in town. I hate to say it, Ms. Garrett, but my instincts tell me the guy could be dangerous."

Seconds after hanging up, Kathy called the motel where Ben Stovall was staying. When he answered, she didn't mince words. "I don't have much time here, Ben. There's a man in town by the name of John McFadden. He came before the judge today and wanted immediate custody of Amanda. What do you know about him?"

"He *what?*"

"I'm serious. We don't have much time. What do you know?"

"The guy's dangerous. He's Amanda's father, but there's no good reason why he'd be here unless it's somehow about me."

"You remember where I live?"

"Sure, I'm a mile away."

"Amanda's bus stop is a block up the street. Meet me there."

Kathy hung up and raced out of her office, praying desperately that she had nothing to worry about.

And if she did, that she would reach the bus stop in time.

Thirty-two

JOHN MCFADDEN HUNKERED DOWN IN THE FRONT SEAT OF HIS car and watched as the weathered, yellow school bus screeched to a stop.

Deciding which child was his would be the trickiest part. Of course, it would get trickier when police got wind the kid was missing. By then, though, he would have made contact with Stovall and presented his demands. If things went right, he could be done with the kid in an hour or so.

But then, things hadn't gone great so far.

He fingered his gun and tapped his thumb on the steering wheel. Maybe this wasn't the best plan, after all. If the police arrested him, he'd have to prove the girl was his daughter. They couldn't arrest him for kidnapping his own kid, could they? A gnawing pain ate at the pit of his stomach, and he tried not to think about it.

The bus pulled away, leaving two boys and a girl, who immediately began walking in different directions. John squinted through his sunglasses. *So that's her.* He stared at the girl, surprised to feel a twinge of regret. What if he'd stayed with Maggie, worked things out? What would his life be like today if they'd moved in together and raised the kid? Whatever it would have been like, it probably wouldn't involve him running from the police.

You're weak, McFadden! Forget the brat! This was no time to be thinking fatherly thoughts. The girl was moving quickly along the shaded, residential street, and he had to get her. He looked around—no signs of cars coming in any direction. It was now or never. He started the engine and moved the car slowly toward the girl. "Let's get it done with…"

As his car pulled up alongside the kid, she glanced at him over her shoulder and picked up her pace. John was struck by how pretty she was. Just like Maggie had been that summer…

He hit the automatic button and rolled down the passenger window. "Hi, Amanda." She started, but kept walking, holding her books more tightly to her body. Great. She probably knew about not talking to strangers. He gave the car just enough gas to keep even with her. "I'm a friend of Ben Stovall's. He asked me to meet you at the bus stop and drive you to the park."

Hurry, kid. It was only a matter of minutes before she reached that social worker's house or a car drove up and thought something suspicious was happening. "Ben and Kathy Garrett are going to meet you there. At the park."

The girl stopped and turned to face him. Fear showed clearly in her eyes, and the feeling in his gut intensified. She bit her lip. "Kathy sent you?"

Thatta girl. Come on, get in the car. "She wanted you to come with me." He'd have to thank Mike and Alfie later for giving him the right details.

Amanda moved closer to the car. "I'm not supposed to go with strangers."

That was it; he couldn't wait another moment. He drove up a few feet ahead of her, slammed on the brakes, and pushed open the passenger door. Before she could get past him, he pointed the gun at her. "Don't make me shoot you, Amanda." His friendly tone was gone. "Get in the car. Now!"

She looked ready to run, so John pulled out his final card. "You leave now, and I'll kill Kathy Garrett. I know where she lives *and* when she gets home." Amanda froze, her eyes wide. "I'll do it, Amanda. Now get in the car."

The girl clenched her jaw and hesitated only a moment before walking briskly toward the car and climbing inside. She barely had the door shut when he jerked the vehicle away from the curb and sped out of the neighborhood.

He had expected her to cry or scream or carry on. Instead

she sat there, staring out the windshield. Then she broke the silence by humming something. It was the same tune over and over and over again.

"Don't you wanna know where I'm takin' you, Amanda?"

The girl kept her eyes straight ahead. "How do you know Mr. Stovall?"

Her voice was a strange combination of jaded maturity and tender innocence. Again he wondered why he was doing this. To blackmail Stovall into dropping the charges against him? It didn't even make sense anymore. Not when he was driving his own daughter at gunpoint back to his hotel. What if he really did want to have custody rights at some point? She was his kid, after all.

Maybe so, he mocked himself, *but no judge in his right mind would grant you a stinkin' thing after this. Not even visitation.*

The girl's question about Stovall hung in the air. Stovall. This was all *his* fault. "Well, Amanda, your old daddy knows a lot of things."

At that she stopped humming and spun around, eyes wide, mouth open. "You're not my daddy."

He grinned at her. Sassy little thing…just like he'd been as a kid. "Well, actually, I *am* your daddy. No time like the present to get acquainted, eh?"

She turned to stare out the windshield, and the dratted humming started up again.

Fine.

If she wasn't interested in getting to know him, forget her. He ran his finger over the gun in his hand. She wasn't his daughter. She was just a kid with DNA that matched his. And if she pulled anything funny or caused too much trouble, he'd waste her and hide her body. He wouldn't have any trouble getting away with it. After all, she was just a lonely Social Services brat; the system wouldn't even miss her.

The humming was getting on his nerves. "Would you shut up, already! I hate that song."

"'Jesus Loves Me'?" There was no fear, no anger in her soft voice. It was weird. Like she was in some kind of safe place, all by herself. She started humming again.

"Listen, kid, you're with me now. Jesus ain't exactly in the picture."

She just smiled. "Jesus loves me and whoever you are, He loves you, too."

Of all the—

"You're crazy, kid. I could shoot you right now, and no one would know the difference. And all you can do is sit there humming some stupid song about Jesus?"

She turned and leveled her gaze at him. "That's not all I'm doing."

Why wasn't she scared? The uncanny calm in her eyes was enough to make his skin crawl. If he hadn't regretted his decision to take her before, he sure did now. Of course, she *was* his daughter—so it made sense that she was tough even in the face of a gun. He turned onto a busier street. "Okay, smart mouth, what else are you doing besides staring out the window humming some stupid song about Jesus and getting on my nerves?"

She bit her lip and studied him. "I'm praying for you."

Ben had a sick feeling in his stomach.

He and Kathy arrived at Amanda's bus stop at almost exactly the same moment, and there was no sign of Amanda. Ever since receiving the call from Kathy he'd been in a panic, but now he was hit with genuine terror.

He pulled his car up alongside Kathy's and motioned for her to roll her window down. "Where *is* she?"

"The bus should have come by now." Kathy's face was ashen, and though Ben had only met her that week, he was sure she was feeling the same jolts of raw fear he was.

"So she's at your house, right? Wouldn't that make sense?"

Kathy nodded, and the stiff way she held her mouth made

336   KAREN KINGSBURY

Ben think she couldn't talk if she'd wanted to.

Ben looked around and spotted an older woman across the street. She was hanging a Thanksgiving wreath on her front door, then she turned and stared at them. Ben motioned to Kathy to follow him as he jumped from his car. "Excuse me, has the school bus come already?"

The woman walked the few steps to meet them and her face knit into a mass of wrinkled concern as she considered the question. "A while ago."

Kathy smiled politely, but Ben noticed her hands were trembling at her sides. "I'm Kathy Garrett. I live down the street; I don't think we've met."

"Polly. Polly Russell. Me and Grandpa been living here thirty years now. Watch the school bus come by same time every day."

Ben jumped in. "Mrs. Russell, there's a little blond girl that gets off at this stop…did you see her today?"

Again concern filled the older woman's eyes. "I always notice the girl. Reminds me of my own sweet babies; same hair, eyes, and coloring. That kind of thing."

Kathy shifted anxiously, speaking in quick, choppy sentences. "The girl lives with me and my family. She's waiting for a foster home. Did you see her? Maybe talking to someone when she got off the bus?"

"Matter of fact, I did. A man pulled up in a big ol' car and talked to her while she was walking. After a minute or so, she climbed in with him." The woman looked from Ben to Kathy and back to Ben. "I figured he was her daddy, since she went so willingly."

"Thanks…thank you, Mrs…" Kathy's face was white, and Ben thought she might pass out.

"The child's okay, isn't she?" Alarm filled the woman's features at the thought that something may have happened to the little blond girl. Ben knew how she felt.

"It's fine. We'll take care of it. Thanks." He nodded at the woman and led Kathy by the arm back to his car. "Pray. Start and don't stop."

"That's all I've been doing." Kathy's voice was shaky.

Father, how can this be happening? I've just found Amanda, Maggie's very own daughter, and now she's been kidnapped by…by… He remembered McFadden's blows as he lay on the pavement, the merciless kicks to the—

No. Ben couldn't bring himself to think of Amanda with that man. It was too horrible to imagine. She'd already been through so much…

Dear God, let her be home by now. Protect her. Please!

He helped Kathy into his car and—leaving her car parked at the bus stop—they sped down the street to the Garrett home.

"What if…?" Kathy's question hung in the air as he parked the car.

"Don't! That woman might be wrong. Maybe Amanda's already here." He followed Kathy as she raced inside, but she stood frozen in the entry and hugged herself tightly. "Hey, kids, I'm home." Each word was an effort. "Is…is Amanda here?"

"Not yet, Mom. How was your day?" It was the voice of a teenager from a room across the house.

Ben forced himself to breathe as the hurried exchange went on. *No, God. No! Let her be okay. Please…*

Amanda wasn't there. Kathy sat down on the sofa and leaned over her knees, rocking slightly. "He took her. McFadden took her. I feel it in my heart." A sob caught in her throat and she pointed to the phone. "Hurry, please. You make the call."

Without hesitating another moment, Ben picked up the phone and dialed 911. The dispatcher barely got two words out before he blurted, "My daughter's been kidnapped."

Officers Aaron Hisel and Buddy Reed deeply enjoyed their work as Cincinnati police officers. As partners they had seen each other through ten years of arrests and criminal investigations—not to mention the births of their combined seven children. They were family men, dedicated to keeping the streets safe.

It was just before four o'clock, when the two would normally have been making their way back to the office and checking out for the day. But they were working on a case they were close to breaking, a case that put them squarely in the heart of Woodland, a suburb just east of the city.

They had spent much of the day interviewing witnesses and were making more progress than they'd hoped when the call came in. An APB to be on the lookout for a white male suspect named John McFadden, driving a gold Acura. McFadden was already facing charges of assault and attempted murder and now he was running from the law.

Hisel glanced at Reed. "Didn't we get that call a few hours ago?"

Reed nodded as he turned the wheel. "I thought so, too. Check with dispatch, will you?"

Hisel picked up the radio and called headquarters. "This McFadden APB, is that an old call? We got word about him earlier. Something about him leaving the courthouse in the middle of a meeting with Judge Hutch. Hutch ran the rap and found an attempted murder charge. Are we talking about the same call?"

The radio crackled as dispatch answered. "Negative. You must have missed the first part of the call."

"What else do you have on him?" Hisel grabbed a pen and a pad of paper from where it was clipped on the dashboard.

"He just kidnapped a seven-year-old girl. She's got long blond hair, blue eyes. Took her from her bus stop approximately thirty minutes ago. There's reason to believe he's armed and dangerous." The dispatch provided the location of the bus stop and repeated the license plate number of the Acura McFadden was driving.

Hisel's stomach clenched and he exchanged a glance with Reed just as his partner flipped the squad car around and headed toward the address.

"Let's go get him." Hisel thought of his own children, safe at home with their mother. Then he thought of all the unspeakable things a child might suffer in the course of a kidnapping.

He and Reed had discussed it a hundred times over the years and each time their consensus was the same. High on the list of crimes that were the worst, most atrocious, horrific actions a person could commit were those that caused the blood of both officers to boil.

Crimes against children.

Thirty-three

THE MEAN MAN WAS DRIVING VERY FAST. DEEP INSIDE IT MADE Amanda nervous, but she wouldn't let him see that.

She wondered where he was taking her. Would he really kill her when they got there? *Jesus, help me be safe, please.*

She knew God would answer. After all, He'd saved her from the boys and their baling twine; He'd rescued her from Mrs. Graystone. No matter what happened to her, God always brought her through okay, and Amanda knew there was a reason. The Lord had a forever home for her and somehow He would find a way to get her there.

She glanced at the man. His face was all sweaty. Shivers ran down her arms and she was glad he wasn't her father. What a terrible lie. She turned to stare straight ahead. *Help that man know about You, God. He needs to change and love You more.*

The few times the man had talked to her, he'd been grouchy and scary, but Amanda wasn't frightened. God wouldn't let him hurt her.

"Whatcha looking at, brat?" The man's face twisted up in an angry look.

"I'm p-p-praying for you."

"Praying? What're you doing *that* for?" The man's voice was growly and hard.

"It's what I always d-d-do when someone's mean."

She could hear Mrs. Brownell's kind, caring voice: *"That's a good girl, Amanda. You pray for them. And make sure to tell them you're praying, just so they know."*

Most of the time when she told someone mean she was praying, he stopped being mean and walked away. Mrs. Brownell had said being nice and praying for someone made it hard for them to be mean anymore. Something about putting coals on their heads.

Amanda had never noticed coals on the heads of the mean kids at school. And they hadn't shown up on the boys' heads in the barn, either, or on Mrs. Graystone's head. She glanced again at the man beside her. There were no coals on his head, either. Maybe the coals thing meant something else. Like about how hearing something nice can make you hurt all over. Especially if all you've been is mean.

Praying was the right thing to do, though, because it was the only thing that absolutely worked every time. God wouldn't let her down. He would see that she stayed safe and found a way back to Kathy Garrett and that nice Mr. Stovall. Maybe he would be her forever dad and take her to live in an always, ever-after family.

Dear God, help the police find us so I can go home with Mr. Stovall. Please let them catch this mean man and take him to jail. The car turned suddenly, and Amanda struggled to keep her balance.

"I prayed that the police would c-c-catch you."

The man squinted his eyes at her. "If they catch us, I'll tell them you're my kid." He laughed at her, and his loud voice hurt her ears. "Or maybe I'll just shoot you and them, too. You don't want that do you?"

"I'll k-k-keep praying for you. Did you know that Jesus loves you, mister?"

A strange, sad look came across the man's face…maybe he was feeling the burning coals after all. *Make him change, Lord, please.*

She didn't know where they were driving. Where was he taking her? She sank back in the seat. Maybe he really would shoot her. Maybe that was God's plan for her. She considered that and realized she was not afraid. If he killed her, she'd be with Jesus right away. And then she'd have the best forever home of all.

The only sad part was that if she went to be with Jesus,

she'd never find her real mom, never hug her or touch her face or ask her if she'd been looking all her life for the little girl she gave up.

And Amanda still wanted to do all that. Very, very much.

Hisel and Reed were cruising Broadway, checking side streets and scanning the horizon for any hint of a gold Acura. Ten minutes had passed since the APB went out, and both men were feeling a sense of urgency. Statistically, the odds of finding her alive decreased with each passing minute.

"I'm worried about her." Hisel clenched his jaw and kept searching the road.

His partner cocked his head to the left and pressed his foot down on the gas pedal. "Wait! I think I see him."

Almost two city blocks ahead of them was a gold car! Within seconds, Reed maneuvered their police car directly behind it. "Gold Acura, all right. Run the plates."

Hope surged through Hisel as he grabbed the radio and checked the number with the one scribbled on his notepad. "It matches!"

"Notify dispatch; request multiple backup units." Reed kept his eyes trained straight ahead. "I'm afraid the guy's going to take off if he sees us."

Hisel picked up the radio and made the request. "I can't believe he hasn't noticed us yet." The man was driving the speed limit and seemed almost oblivious to his surroundings.

"Looks like he's talking to the little girl."

"Come on, let's get this thing over with. Hit the siren."

Reed shook his head. "No. Not yet. I'd rather have backup, just in case. We'll follow him until he sees us or until other units show up. I don't want him panicking and hurting the child. A few more squad cars and he'll know he doesn't have a chance. Just stay on the radio and let dispatch know which way we're headed."

The strange feeling that everything was falling apart had taken root the moment John laid eyes on the child. And now the feeling was so strong it was making his chest hurt. His face was cool and clammy and his left arm ached.

Probably a heart attack.

He kept driving. Something about the girl's quiet calm, the serenity in her eyes, and the way she insisted on talking about Jesus was making him crazy.

Look at me. I'm a loser! After this I'll spend most of my life in jail. I must have been nuts to take the kid and think it could make things better. He stroked his chin. *Now what do I do? Kill her? Leave her in an alley somewhere? Go back to the warehouse and pick up business where I left off?*

The pain in his arm intensified. None of it made sense anymore. *No wonder the kid doesn't want me as her father. Look at me. Drug dealer, wanted by the police. Yes, sir, a real Mr. Good Guy.*

He thought about his home and the three used sports cars parked in his garage and he felt…dirty. Go figure! Almost like someone had walked up and plastered him with layer after layer of pure crud. His language, his friendships, his business dealings—everything he was had been bought with dirty money.

And now it had come to this.

He and his very own daughter were outrunning police so that he could blackmail an attorney into dropping charges against him. The whole situation was so rotten it stunk. And it was all for nothing. John had the unnerving feeling that the foundation of his reputation and his drug empire were crumbling as quickly as it had taken Amanda to say, "I'm praying for you."

He tapped the steering wheel and glanced in his rear and side mirrors. *No cops; not yet.* If he heard another word about prayer or God or Jesus loving him, he would explode! It was stupid. No God would ever love him now. He'd made his choice long ago, sealed his fate. All he could do was find ways to make the path he'd chosen stretch out as long as possible, because one day…

John shut the thoughts out of his mind. Death wasn't something he had to think about for decades, so why was it on his mind now? He shifted positions to ease the discomfort in his chest. If only he could forget his kid's innocent eyes or her words about Jesus…

Let her go…turn to Me and let her go.

The voice was almost audible, and John spun his head around and checked the backseat. No one. He wiped the sweat from his forehead. His heart pounded through the wall of his chest. *I'm losing it. Five days off work, and already I'm going crazy. That's all this is. Stress. Too much going on back at the warehouse for me to be driving around Cincinnati with some wise-mouth brat.*

Let the child go…

He gripped the steering wheel tightly to prevent his hands from shaking. It wasn't a real voice, not one that sounded through the car. It was more like a silent echo in his mind, his soul—

The girl's prayers! Maybe this was some kind of answer to Amanda's prayers. The thought sent chills down John's arms, and suddenly the pain in his heart eased. He had to let her go; it was that simple. Otherwise that God of hers would make his heart explode inside him, and he'd be left with nothing. No estate, no cars, no dirty money…

No life.

"You still praying?" He heard the fear in his voice as he let the gun drop to the floor of the car.

Amanda turned to him and nodded. "Yes, very hard."

There was a gas station up ahead, and John jerked the wheel of his car, turned into the lot and pulled to an abrupt stop. He stared straight ahead. "Get outta here, kid. Go on, get!"

But just as Amanda was opening her car door, a siren sounded behind them, and in his rearview mirror John saw the flashing lights of a police car.

Kathy's confession came as soon as Ben Stovall hung up the phone after calling the police: She had a terrible feeling in her gut that she was about to lose Amanda. The woman's tears came slowly at first, and then as the minutes passed they came in silent torrents. Ben positioned himself beside her as if by doing so he could stop her body from shaking.

"It's okay, everything's going to be fine. The police will find them." He heard how his voice lacked confidence, and he knew he was trying to convince himself as much as her.

"What if I lose her? She's the sweetest, most trusting child I know. After all she's been through, I couldn't bear it if—"

"Shhh. Don't!" She was scaring him, making him picture terrifying scenarios where Amanda was being hurt or worse. The love that gripped his very soul was so strong it stunned him. He had only met the girl once, but he loved her like his own daughter. And now she might be gone forever.

No, he couldn't think that way. Without saying another word, he closed his eyes and reached for Kathy's hands. "Come on now, let's pray. God knows where she is; He'll get her back safely."

Kathy's quiet weeping continued while Ben begged God for mercy, asking that the police find McFadden and Amanda, that no harm be done to the child. "God, we know that where two or more are gathered, there You are also. Please, Lord, save Amanda from harm. Bring her back safely. We beg You. In Jesus' name, amen."

"I'm so afraid…" Kathy collapsed against Ben, seeming too distraught to do anything more. They remained that way as Ben's eyes fell onto a framed picture on the wall of Amanda and Kathy, smiling and holding hands. Suddenly he was struck by the realization that Kathy had been the closest thing to a mother Amanda had ever known. Even if the police were able to rescue the girl from McFadden, and if somehow Maggie was willing to meet her daughter and take them both back...no matter what happened, Kathy Garrett would come out the loser.

She remained in his arms, crying for several minutes until finally she pulled away and reached for a tissue. "We have to hear something soon. This is driving me—"

The phone rang. Immediately she lunged for it. "Hello?"

Ben waited breathlessly. *Please, God, let it be good news. Please.*

"Yes. Okay." Kathy's swollen, tearstained face lit up, and her smile made Ben's heart soar with relief. "We'll be right there."

Then she pulled him into a tight hug, exhaling as if she hadn't done so all afternoon. "She's okay."

Ben drove, and along the way Kathy cleared her throat and turned to face him. "I think you should tell Amanda the truth about your wife."

His heart skipped a beat. "Don't you think I should wait? Until I've talked with Maggie? I mean, what if she—"

"It doesn't matter." Kathy's voice was sure and strong, as though she'd given this careful consideration. "Amanda is seven, almost eight. That's old enough to know the truth, and the truth is she's been praying that she'd find her real mother for as many years as I've known her. No matter what Maggie does, Amanda deserves to know the truth."

There was something so final about telling Amanda. And what if Maggie didn't take him back, didn't want to meet her daughter?

Lean not on your own understanding, but in all your ways acknowledge Me and I will make your paths straight.

The verse from Proverbs stopped him cold. That was it. He

needed to trust God, because once he told Amanda the truth, he'd be in way too deep to find any other way out.

They pulled into the gas station and parked behind six police cars. McFadden was there, sitting in one of them, cuffed and looking—of all things—strangely sad. A distance away on the sidewalk, Amanda stood beside two of the officers, her eyes searching the road anxiously.

"She's looking for us." Kathy led the way, and in a moment Amanda saw her.

"Kathy!" The child ran the remaining steps that separated them and flung herself into Kathy's arms. Ben stood beside them and placed his hand protectively on Amanda's shoulder.

"I prayed and Jesus s-s-saved me."

"I know, honey. He always does." There were fresh tears in Kathy's voice, and Amanda pulled away and kissed her on the cheek. At the same instant, she looked up and spotted Ben.

"Mr. Stovall! You're here!" She moved away from Kathy and wrapped her arms around Ben's waist—and he thought his heart would burst with joy. "I knew you'd come. I thought if God was going to let me live with you, and if maybe you and your wife were going to be my for always family, then of course He'd bring you here to find me." She leaned back and beamed at him. "And here you are."

Ben caught a look of unfathomable pain in Kathy Garrett's eyes as she took in the scene, but it only lasted a moment. Then the woman smiled and put her arms around both of them. "I have a feeling God's going to answer all your prayers, Amanda." She met Ben's gaze with a wink. "Every single one of them."

Kathy moved away and motioned to the police. "I need to check on the arrest report and make sure they've contacted Social Services. That'll give you two time to talk."

Despite all the bad that had come from Amanda's time in the Social Services system, at least she'd had Kathy Garrett. Ben watched the woman go and knew without a doubt that losing

Amanda was breaking the woman's heart. He respected her deeply for the job she'd done with the girl, for allowing herself to love Amanda like one of her own, all the while knowing that someday she'd most likely have to say good-bye.

Ben pulled Amanda close and knelt down on one knee so they were eye to eye. He studied her eyes and saw the light of God there. No matter what happened, this child would always be his. Maggie might not forgive him, but, God willing, he would hold tight to Amanda as long as he lived.

Right now, though, he needed to tell this wonderful little girl about her mother. *Help me, God. I'm trusting You on this.*

"Amanda, there's something I want to tell you."

Kathy Garrett checked with the officers, making sure her department had been notified of Amanda's status.

"Sweet little girl," one of the officers said, nodding toward Ben and Amanda.

Kathy followed his lead and looked at them. "Yes, she is. She's something."

For a moment her gaze lingered, and she saw that Ben was having a serious discussion with Amanda. *He's telling her the truth about her mother.* She watched Amanda nod several times, then saw how her face burst into the biggest smile Kathy had ever seen.

Her sweet Amanda knew the truth now: God had answered her prayers and brought her together with her real mother.

Kathy watched the two hug for a long while, but the happiness she felt for Amanda was no match for the pain she felt deep in her heart. The premonition she'd felt earlier had been right after all.

She was going to lose Amanda. And even though she was sure it would be good and right and the greatest answer to prayer Amanda would ever know, the thought of living life without her was enough to break Kathy's heart in half.

Thirty-four

AFTER MOVING FROM HOUSE TO HOUSE IN THE FOSTER SYSTEM, Amanda had precious few belongings to pack. There was the photograph of her and the Brownells taken on Amanda's first day of kindergarten.

She wrapped the photograph inside a T-shirt and stuck it in her suitcase. Then she gingerly took hold of a scrapbook Kathy had made for her. The first part held pictures of Amanda as a baby and a little girl, of happy times with the Brownells. The rest of the book was pictures of her and the Garretts.

Amanda sat cross-legged on the floor and opened the book, flipping quickly to the back. She smiled at the memories in the pictures. Kathy's family gathered around, celebrating Amanda's seventh birthday; she and Kathy on the back of a horse at the stable two blocks from the Garrett house; the two of them roller-skating at the park across the street.

The foster homes she'd been forced to live in didn't matter—she had always belonged to Kathy. But now God had answered Amanda's prayer about finding her mother, and Amanda was going to have to say good-bye.

She closed the book and felt the sting of tears. For several minutes she held it close to her heart and let the tears come. Then she set the album carefully into her suitcase alongside her few clothes and things. So much had happened the last few days. Now Kathy said a whole new world was waiting for her.

Amanda wondered what that world would be like.

Mr. Stovall said that her mother was sick right now. That she was in a hospital, and that they would need to pray very hard for her. But Amanda was sure that one day very soon her mother would be well again. Then they would meet.

And Amanda's life would truly begin.

But even though she knew it was all going to be okay, Amanda just couldn't imagine her life without Kathy and the Garretts.

She could hear Kathy in the other room, talking with Mr. Stovall. After today she wouldn't hear Kathy at all. Amanda closed her eyes and it was suddenly hard to swallow. She always knew God would answer her prayers.

She just didn't know it would hurt so much when He did.

The children were playing kickball in the front yard so the house was quiet as Kathy and Ben sat at the kitchen table and talked about the coming week. Sitting across from Ben, Kathy felt a peace that ran deep in her veins. There was something in the way this man was so willing to rearrange his life for Amanda that made Kathy know it was the right thing for the child to be with him.

He must love his wife very much.

Ben grew quiet, his eyebrows lowered. "Have you ever worked around people with depression?"

Kathy thought of the number of times she'd been forced to place a child in foster care because one or more parents was paralyzed by the effects of that illness. "Yes. But usually the people I work with have other problems, too. Drugs, alcohol addiction, criminal behavior."

"Okay." Ben set the mug down and looked at Kathy. "Tell me what you know about depression. I know we talked about it a little at the pizza place, but how can someone be a believer all her life, then wake up one morning and check herself into a psychiatric hospital?"

Kathy drew a steadying breath. "I'm not an expert, but from what I know depression is pervasive. People like to think it only happens to weak individuals, those without faith or character or inner strength. But nothing could be further from the truth."

Ben ran his thumb around the rim of his still-warm mug. "Someone like Maggie, for instance. I loved her all those years. We had fun, we laughed, we prayed together. I thought our life was good. So how does it happen?" Ben braced his forearms on the table and his eyes grew watery.

"Lots of reasons. Our faith can help us *through* the valley, but it won't always give us a way around it."

Ben shook his head and stared at the table for a moment. When he raised his eyes, the pain there took Kathy by surprise. "What about the Bible? 'I can do all things through Christ who gives me strength.' Or giving your burdens to God? Why wasn't that enough for Maggie?"

Kathy folded her hands in front of her and thought for a moment. "I don't know your wife, Ben. But from what you've told me, my guess is Maggie never allowed herself to really believe those verses. She was too busy pretending to be someone she wasn't. At least in her mind." Kathy leaned back in her chair. "Imagine living nearly eight years with the kind of secret she kept from you. The pressure of that grew until she couldn't take it anymore."

Ben let his head drop. "She couldn't take me anymore, either." He glanced up. "I've had some long talks with God about this. He's done a good job of showing me how I held Maggie—everyone really—to an almost unattainable standard. But still...if only she'd told me."

"Do you think there's hope? For your marriage, I mean?" Kathy reached for her coffee and took a slow sip.

Ben rubbed the back of his neck, then sat straighter in his chair. "Realistically, I don't know. But I believe Scripture is true and that with God all things are possible, Kathy. Even this."

Amanda walked into the room carrying her tattered, beige suitcase. "I'm ready."

Kathy felt a surge of panic. *Not yet, Lord. I don't want to say good-bye.* She steadied herself and forced a smile. "Okay, honey. Come on, let's load up the car."

The three of them walked outside, and Ben lifted the suit-case into the trunk as Kathy waved to her other children. "Come on, say good-bye to Amanda."

One by one they bid her good-bye, promising to see her soon and talk on the phone. This was a familiar scene for them, but only the older ones knew the finality of the situation this time. As far back as they could remember, Amanda came and went from their lives. There were no tears among them, and Kathy could tell by their faces that even the older children believed somehow she'd be back. Probably sooner than later.

Sometime in the next few days she'd have to explain that this time was different.

"We'll see you all the time, right?" Jenika was the only one who looked concerned.

"Yes, Cleveland's only five hours away." She smiled at Ben. They had discussed the different scenarios—whether Maggie would want to take custody of Amanda or whether she might prefer a trial extended foster care period—either way, they would need to work with the Cincinnati court and Kathy in order to keep the paperwork straight.

There would be visits, but Amanda's time with the Garretts would never be what it had been before.

The other children returned to their game, leaving Kathy and Ben and Amanda huddled in a small circle. "I'll be back next week, right?" Amanda peered up at Kathy and bit her lip.

"Right, sweetheart. Mr. Stovall will have to file some papers to determine what type of arrangement you'll have with their family." *Please, Lord, let me be right. Don't let them reject her after all she's been through.* The one possibility none of them had dared consider was that Maggie might be willing to take Ben back, but not Amanda. *If that happened…* Kathy refused to think about it. God was in control, and He knew there was only so much a child could take.

Ben put his hand on the girl's shoulder and smiled warmly at her. "Once things get settled we can come back and visit

Kathy any time you like, okay? We have a lot to do next week, introducing you to your mom and all of us getting to know each other. But we'll be back."

Amanda's eyes fell, and she studied her feet for a moment. Then in a burst of motion she threw her arms around Kathy. Dropping to her knees, Kathy held Amanda close and whispered into her hair, praying the child couldn't hear the tears in her voice. "This is what you've always wanted, Amanda. It's okay. It's a good thing."

"I-I-I'm going to m-m-miss you so much, Kathy. Who will t-t-tuck me in and talk to me at night when I'm s-s-scared?" Amanda rarely cried, a trait Kathy recognized all too well among children who'd survived year after year in the foster system. But the pain Amanda was feeling now was terrible, and Kathy wiped the child's tears as they streamed down her face.

"Mr. Stovall will." *Please, God, let it be true…* "And your real mother will, too, one day. I believe that with all my heart."

Those final words seemed to comfort her and she pulled back, studied Kathy for a minute, then leaned over and kissed her on the cheek. "I'll always love you, Kathy."

The lump in Kathy's throat was so big she couldn't speak. Instead she nodded and pulled Amanda to her one more time. "I'll always love you, too, honey." Her voice was hoarse with sorrow. "Now go on and don't forget to pray. God has a plan for you, Amanda." She stood up and gently presented the child to Ben. In a whispered voice intended for him alone she said, "I'll be praying for you."

He studied her for an instant and then shook his head slightly. "You're amazing, Kathy."

"Call me when you know how it's going, okay?" She could feel tears falling from her eyes and wiped at them self-consciously. "Now go on and see what God has for you."

The two of them climbed into the car.

Kathy remained on her driveway until she could no longer

see the sadness in Amanda's eyes or the way she reached out her hand toward Kathy from the side window.

When the car was gone, she let the tears come. Waves and torrents of them, washing the pain from her heart and causing her to remain firmly in place, unable to walk or move or do anything but miss the ray of sunshine that had just been taken from her life.

"What is it, Mom? What's wrong?"

She looked up to find Bobby, her youngest, beside her, his eyes wide. He must have seen her crying and left his game to come to her.

She swallowed and tried to find her voice as she put her arm around his small shoulders. "Nothing, honey. Mommy's just happy, that's all. Very, very happy."

It was eight o'clock on Saturday morning, and Amanda was still sleeping. Ben's heart raced and he couldn't still his shaking hands.

Would Maggie refuse his request like every time before? Or would she understand that at some point they needed to talk? *Lord, speak to her heart. Make her understand that we need this time, and if she'll let me see her, please open her heart.*

As Ben picked up the phone, a knot formed in his stomach. *It's like a first date,* he thought. Then he dialed Orchards Psychiatric Hospital and held his breath. "This is Ben Stovall." He closed his eyes and exhaled. "My wife, Maggie, is a patient there, and I'd like to make an appointment to see her, please."

"Mr. Stovall?" The nurse sounded like she was about to end the conversation, and Ben clenched his fists.

Come on, God. I need Your help. "Yes. My wife's been there for quite some time…"

He heard the nurse sigh. "Yes, Mr. Stovall, I'm aware of that. Your wife has requested no visits, no phone—"

"Wait! I know that's how it was before. But I thought now

that she's been there a while…just ask her, will you? This is…it means a lot. Please."

There was a hesitation. "All right. I'll ask her. Hold for a minute."

While the seconds passed, Ben thought of how far he and Amanda had come over the past couple of days. She was cautious about giving her heart, but they had forged a bond over Scrabble games and picnics at the park and knock-knock jokes that would make a foundation for the future. *If there is a future. Come on, Maggie. Meet with me.*

Two nerve-racking minutes passed before the woman returned to the phone. "You were right." There was apology in her voice. "Mrs. Stovall said she'll meet with you this afternoon at two o'clock."

Ben felt relief surge through his body. He had so much to tell her, so much ground to make up. To think that she'd loved him enough to let Amanda go…

"Thank you. Please tell her I'll be there."

He could barely wait to tell Amanda, but before that, before anything else might distract him, he clasped his hands, bowed his head, and thanked God. Of all the pain and discovery he'd been through in the past month, the most incredible lesson of all was this: He'd finally gotten a glimpse of the real Maggie, the woman beneath the mask…the woman he'd married. What he'd seen there was flawed and real, warm and caring.

And more beautiful than anything she had ever pretended to be.

Thirty-five

THE DISCHARGE PAPERS CAME LESS THAN AN HOUR BEFORE BEN'S
call, and Maggie wondered if Dr. Camas or Dr. Baker or one of
the well-meaning Christian attendants at the hospital hadn't
tipped Ben off. The doctors had agreed the day before that
Maggie was ready to live life on her own again. She had come
face to face with clinical depression and by God's grace she had
not been consumed. Instead she had explored the darkness
and analyzed the desperation until finally she was coming to
understand it, willing to be honest with herself and God and
everyone else.

Even Ben.

Her anger and resentment toward him had been replaced
with a sorrow deeper than anything Maggie had ever known.
She would apologize to him, though she knew it wouldn't
make any difference. Their marriage still seemed like a pretense—a way to manage the passing of the years—rather than
anything real and intimate the way God had intended.

That doesn't mean the Lord wants you to go your separate ways.

Maggie nodded at the thought. They were, after all, still
legally married. Even if nothing about their marriage had ever
been true.

She sighed. The point was probably moot, anyway. Once
Ben learned the truth he would hire a divorce attorney quicker
than she could ask for forgiveness.

Maggie, open your heart to Me, to My ways…

The call came from deep within, and tears filled Maggie's
eyes as she recognized the still, small voice. *Lord, if You want me
to stay with Ben You'll have to change us both. I'm willing, Lord. But
he has to forgive me.* A sob escaped and bounced off the walls of

her hospital room. *Oh, if only he could forgive me…*

The tears came harder until Maggie closed her eyes and forced herself to regain control. Ben would be there any moment; there would be time for tears later. Now she needed to think about what she would say, how things would go, and what she might do if he turned and walked out of her life forever.

She sat on the edge of her bed and looked around the room. It looked more like a luxury hotel accommodation than part of a hospital. After weeks of living here, the subdued, striped wallpaper was beginning to feel like home—the only home where she'd been able to be herself for too many years. Although she still had much to work out about her life outside Orchards, she would always be grateful for their intervention.

And for leading her back to a place of freedom in Christ.

She would stay through the weekend, but by Monday morning she needed a place to go, to live. Maggie looked at the clock on the wall. Ten minutes, and Ben would be there. Her heart raced, and the anxiety that had welled up within her would not go away, but the darkness was gone. There was no doubt about that.

Maggie noticed her palms were sweaty and she wiped them on her pants. A combination of God's grace, her willingness to be honest, and the medications and counseling had set Maggie free in a way she had never imagined possible.

But the questions loomed.

Where did she go from here? Would she and Ben be able to salvage their life together, to go on together in truth and honesty?

She didn't know. She could always rent an apartment until she figured out what to do.

The idea of returning to the paper ratcheted Maggie's anxiety up a notch. Did her coworkers know where she'd been? What would they think? Worse, what would her editors think? Yes, they'd told her in the beginning to take her time, that no matter what happened her job would be there when she returned. But how could she resume writing a conservative, morally minded column when she had pretended to be something she wasn't?

Trust in Me with all your heart and lean not on your own understanding.

As soon as the Scripture flashed in her mind, Maggie's heart rate slowed and she felt infused with strength. She could do this; she could face Ben and, with God's help, she could deal with whatever the outcome was. She hung her head and wove her fingers tightly together. *God, You've been so good to me. Your words are nothing less than a healing oil to my spirit.*

In all your ways acknowledge Me and I will make your paths straight.

There it was again, absolute truth, the very words that had so often provided her a safe tower—and they would do so again in the coming minutes with Ben. Those words were a road map that she could safely follow the rest of her days. And somewhere along the journey she knew she'd find the daughter she gave up. That certainty pulsed within her as strongly as her renewed desire to live. With her mind fixed on God, and thoughts of her child filling her head, Maggie was reminded that although the next hour might be one of the saddest of all, she had every reason to be excited about the future.

The only question was whether Ben wanted to travel it with her or not.

Although Thanksgiving was just four days away, the weather was unseasonably warm and sunshine filtered through a hazy layer of clouds as Ben parked his car and he and Amanda headed, hand in hand, for the front door of Orchards Psychiatric Hospital.

He'd explained to Amanda that her mother was not sick in the way some people get sick, with coughs and high fevers. But she was sick all the same—it had more to do with her heart, where feelings and thoughts can get all tangled up.

"She's been very sad, Amanda."

"Sad enough to be in the hospital for a long time?" Ben was pleased that the girl's stuttering had disappeared after the first day with him. He'd purchased a pink-flowered bedspread for the guestroom to make Amanda feel more comfortable, and she'd loved it. She talked to Kathy every night and seemed to be adjusting well.

"Yes, sad enough for that."

Amanda had smiled a little, empathy dimming the usual glow in her eyes. "Then I'll have to pray extra hard for her."

The fact that Maggie had agreed to the meeting at all proved that God was, indeed, at work answering their prayers. Ben opened the front door and he and Amanda entered the lobby.

"Looks like a rich person's house," Amanda whispered to him. Her eyes were wide as she took in the velvet upholstery and elegant curves of the carved mahogany furniture. She moved closer to him.

Ben's mouth was dry from the raw terror that ran through his veins. *What if Maggie turns me away? What if she doesn't want to meet Amanda? What if she's mad at me for finding her? What if she—*

Trust in Me with all your heart and lean not on your own understanding…

I'm trying, Lord, really I am. I can't even believe I'm here. Open her heart, God…I love her so much more than ever before. He swallowed hard before leading Amanda to a chair near the reception desk. "Stay here, sweetie. I'll talk to Maggie first and then…then you can come in and meet her."

She sat quickly in the chair, gripping the armrests firmly and keeping her eyes trained on him. Her hair looked like the palest spun gold, and she wore a new pink dress that they'd picked out together for the occasion. Ben could see how Amanda's knees trembled beneath the skirt, and for a moment he forgot his own fears at the realization of how frightened the child must be.

Meeting her mother for the first time had to be the most overwhelming moment of Amanda's life. He stooped and put his hands on her shoulders. "It's going to be okay, Amanda. God wants us to trust Him."

Her eyes were locked on his, absorbing his words and every ounce of strength they might offer. She nodded quickly. "Okay."

Ben grinned and squeezed her hand. "Thatta girl."

He checked in with the receptionist and was given directions to Maggie's room.

"Could you keep an eye on her?" He motioned to Amanda. "I don't want to bring her in just yet."

"No problem." The woman behind the counter smiled warmly at Amanda as Ben winked at the child and headed down the hall toward Maggie's room. With each step he felt more and more like a giddy, nervous schoolboy, as though he were about to find the angel of his dreams and ask her to be his steady girl. *Make her say yes, God, please.* Although his heart moved along twice as fast as his feet, he was suddenly just outside Maggie's door.

Whatever happened now Ben knew this much: The rest of his life depended on the next few minutes.

The gentle knock at the door made Maggie jump, and she stared at the handle for several seconds before standing. *Give me the right words, Lord...*

"Coming." She opened the door and there he was. Ben Stovall, the man of her childhood dreams, the one for whom she had been willing to sacrifice everything: her honesty, her heart, even her daughter.

Like the first time she saw him, she felt her breath catch in her throat. Ben's conservative, darkly handsome looks were so striking they could stop women at a busy supermarket—which they had done a number of times.

"Maggie…" His eyes were tender and filled with teary forgiveness, and she felt herself flinch. *If he knew what was coming he'd look different…*

They stood there, drinking in the sight of each other—and Maggie realized how long she'd been away and how much she'd missed the nearness of this man. Without saying another word, Ben moved to her and pulled her close. They came together the way two people do at a funeral, when someone they both love has passed on. His embrace told her everything she could ever want to know, that he loved her and missed her and wanted her home.

With all her heart she wanted to let him hold her that way forever and never tell him the things he needed to hear.

But finally she could bear it no longer and, tears pricking her eyes, she pulled away. "I need to tell you something." Her words were so heavy with sorrow Maggie expected to hear them hitting the floor.

Ben searched her eyes. "No…me first. Please, Maggie, I—"

"We both need to talk; I realize that. But there's something you need to know first. Something I should have told you years ago. Before we were married."

The weight of what she'd done to him, to their marriage, to her child was almost too much to bear. Ben sat down on the edge of her bed, and though her feet felt like they were dragging through syrup she pulled up a chair and sat across from him, her eyes trained on the floor. After a moment she looked up and spoke in what sounded like barely a whisper. "I'm not even sure where to begin."

There was an energy exuding from Ben, and suddenly his eyes flashed with realization. "Maggie, you don't have to." He looked like he wanted to close the gap between them and take her in his arms again, but was too nervous to do so. "I already know."

She stared at him numbly and her mind went blank. *What did he mean?* "I'm not talking about my breakdown; I'm talking about my past. The year before we got married."

Tears filled Ben's eyes and the subtle lines on his face smoothed into a reflection of serenity. "I know all about it, Maggie. All of it."

Her stomach was suddenly in her throat, as though she'd fallen down a forty-two-story elevator shaft. *What is he talking about? There's no way he could have found out about…* "I don't know what you mean, but there's something you don't—"

"Maggie, please, listen to me." He wiped his palms on his black jeans and held her with his gaze. "I know. About McFadden and the baby and everything that happened that summer."

A faint feeling came over her, and her cheeks felt like they were on fire. If he knew, then he probably had come with divorce papers. "How…how long have you…"

Ben reached out and slowly, tenderly took her hand in his. "A lot's happened these past few weeks, Mag."

Her arms and legs were trembling now, and she hugged herself tightly. She hadn't even had time to apologize, and already the tombstone of truth stood on the table, marking the death of their marriage. "So you want a divorce, is that it? You came here wanting my signature? Because before we talk about—"

Ben closed his eyes and shook his head, but there was not even a hint of condemnation in his expression. "Maggie, stop." He pulled an envelope from his pocket and handed it to her. "This isn't from my attorney, it's from me. Read it, will ya, Mag? Before we go any further."

Maggie tried to remember to breathe as she stared first at Ben, then at the envelope. Finally she slid her finger under the flap, pulled out the letter, and froze. "Ben, don't tell me good-bye in a letter…I want to talk face to—"

"Just read it, Mag. I'll sit right here and wait." He planted his elbows on his knees and cupped his fist with his right hand. "Go on."

Her heart was pounding so loudly she figured the patient next door could hear it. Whatever Ben had written, it was time to face it and move ahead. She opened the letter and began reading.

My precious Maggie...

She paused. *He called me his Maggie! Maybe it isn't too late, maybe...* No, it wasn't possible. Not after what she'd done. She forced her eyes to continue.

So much has happened since you checked into Orchards, I hardly know where to begin except at the beginning. You said something to me before you left, something that has stayed with me daily since then. You told me I didn't even know you, and at different times over the past month those words have taken on two very different meanings.

The letter went on to say how he had learned about John McFadden and then taken it upon himself to look the man up.

I caught him in the middle of what looked like a drug deal, so he beat me up pretty good...

Maggie gasped and her eyes flew to meet Ben's. "John beat you up?"

"I lived. Keep reading." There were still pools of tears in his eyes, and for a moment Maggie wished more than anything she could forget the letter and just take him in her arms so she could love the hurt away. She let her eyes fall back to the letter.

I learned about the baby from McFadden, and that led me to Woodland where I found your old friend, Nancy Taylor.

Maggie blinked hard. Ben had found Nancy Taylor? It didn't seem possible.

"You met Nancy?" She couldn't believe any of this was happening.

"Yes. That reminds me, she gave me a letter for you. I have it in the car. She said to tell you she tried to find you but couldn't. She blames herself for not telling you her real thoughts sooner."

Maggie's mind raced. What did all of this mean? "What real thoughts?"

"How she never should have encouraged you to give your daughter up for adoption, how badly she regretted not telling you so at the time. Before it was too late."

"You...you know my baby was a girl?"

Ben squeezed Maggie's knee and whispered. "Keep reading."

A wave of sorrow washed over Maggie and threatened to drown her. So Nancy knew the adoption had been a mistake. It was one more sad affirmation that she had made the wrong choice. But it was too late to change the past. What was done was done, and it hadn't been Nancy's fault, it had been Maggie's. And wherever Maggie's little girl was now, she had a life of her own, and nothing Nancy or Ben or any of them could say would ever change that.

"I can't believe you already know." Maggie's voice was heavy with regret, and she was stunned by the way Ben was handling the situation. "Why didn't you say something sooner?"

Ben said nothing, just held her gaze and smiled sadly. The answer to her question was suddenly obvious. Ben couldn't have said anything if he'd wanted to. Until that afternoon, she had refused his phone calls and visits. She returned to the pages in her hands.

When I first learned you'd been with John McFadden, gotten pregnant by him, I was angry with you, Maggie. I believed you were right, that I never really knew you and now that I did it was probably better that we stay clear of each other. It seemed like you said that our marriage was over. But then I found Amanda.

If the first free-fall was enough to make her dizzy, this one turned Maggie's stomach and made the blood drain from her face. She was terrified to ask the question, because deep in her soul she already knew the answer. "Who…who is Amanda?" Her fingers twisted together and she couldn't still her shaking.

"She's your daughter, Mag." Ben's words were slow and steady, measured by the calm of a man controlled by the Holy Spirit. "She'll be eight in six months or so."

The tears came then, and Maggie moved into Ben's arms where she collapsed against him, sobbing, desperately trying to make sense of what he was telling her. How was it possible? Ben had learned the sordid truth about her past and instead of finding an attorney and being done with her, he had continued his search until he'd found her daughter. *Amanda. Amanda…Amanda, Amanda, Amanda.*

She ran the name over and over again in her mind.

"It's okay, Mag. She's fine and she…she looks just like you." He spoke softly, into her hair. "You should see her. She's beautiful."

"Y-y-you've *seen* her?" Maggie couldn't control her weeping. *Lord, what is all this? Why didn't You let me know this was happening?* She exhaled, and when she could speak more clearly she leaned back and searched Ben's eyes. "You found her? Is she…is she okay?"

"She's wonderful." He took the letter from her hands and finished reading. "After I found Amanda, I knew what you'd told me was truer than I could ever have imagined. I never knew you. And now that I do, Maggie, now that I know how much you gave up to be my wife, I feel like I know you for the first time."

He studied her eyes. "I love you, Maggie. I just—" His voice was choked with emotion. "I think of all the times I seemed unforgiving, like I expected you and everyone else to be perfect." He sighed and shook his head. "What that must have done to you, Mag. I'm so sorry."

She was having a crazy dream. That had to be it. Or maybe someone had slipped her some psychiatric medication. Every hour since her moment of reckoning, she had dreaded facing Ben with the truth and apologizing for the sins of her past. But here he was, already aware of all she'd done—and he'd found her daughter. Now he was asking her forgiveness. None of it made sense…

Trust in Me with all your heart and lean not on your own understanding…

She closed her eyes briefly. Of course it made sense—God had been working on Ben behind the scenes at the same time He was working on her here at Orchards. There could be no other explanation. That's why Ben had come, why he was here now, of all things, apologizing to her.

Her eyes locked on his again, and she shook her head. "I'm the one who's sorry. I should have given you a chance, told you the truth from the beginning."

"It doesn't matter." Ben pulled her close again and stroked her hair. "We're here now and we have a future to figure out."

"There's still something you don't know, Ben."

He waited, his eyes only mildly curious, as though nothing she might say could change the way he felt about her. "I'm listening."

Maggie drew a deep breath. "I've ached for that child since…" Her voice cracked with emotion. "Since I gave her up. I've seen her in supermarkets and at church functions and looked for her on milk cartons. I've dreamed about her nearly every night and in the past week I decided to do whatever I could to find her." Maggie gulped back a sob. "I don't know what the future holds for us, Ben. But she's my daughter. I can't deny that another day."

He smiled at her and despite the tears in his eyes she caught a glimpse of the familiar twinkle, the one that always appeared when he was keeping a secret or about to surprise her with flowers or a night out. "I'm not *asking* you to deny it, Mag."

The questions hung around her heart like a heavy curtain, and she was terrified to ask even one, but she couldn't wait any longer. In some ways, she'd been searching for her daughter since the moment she'd let her go back in the hospital room in Woodland. And now the man she'd thought would turn his back on her had found her little girl. She had to have answers. Just knowing Ben had found her, seen her, made Maggie's arms ache from missing her. She could still remember the way her daughter felt as a swaddled newborn safe in her embrace.

God, I want to hold her again. Just one more time…

"About Amanda…is she…are her adoptive parents good people?"

Ben pulled back slowly and helped Maggie back to the bed. "Her adoptive parents died nearly three years ago, Maggie." He held both her hands and she was sure he was looking straight into her soul. "She's been in the foster system, up for adoption ever since."

Maggie gasped and her hands flew free of his to cover her mouth. Three years ago? For three years her daughter had been in the foster system? And though Maggie and Ben had been licensed foster parents they hadn't even known about her. How could that be? It was devastating. But at the same time it offered the slightest ray of hope. If she was still up for adoption…

Ben framed Maggie's face with his hands. "She's in the lobby, Mag. I didn't know if you'd want to see her today or not."

This final shock was greater than the other two combined. Every day since determining she would find her daughter, she'd prayed that God would make the way clear. And now, here was Ben, offering not only sorrow and forgiveness without reservation, but also the moment she'd dreamed of every day since letting her daughter go.

Maggie let loose a laugh that was half cry, half triumphant shout. "Are you serious?"

"She wants to meet you. She's been wanting to find you as badly as you've wanted to find her."

"But why do you have her—? I don't understand." Again she wondered if she were dreaming. *God, I can't believe this... You're so good...*

"Her social worker assigned me as her temporary foster parent. We didn't know if you'd...how you'd feel about meeting her."

Fresh tears stung at Maggie's eyes. *Was it really possible? Was her daughter actually waiting in a room just down the hall...waiting to meet her?* "Oh, Ben, please go get her." She was on her feet, hugging him as her heart filled with the greatest anticipation she had ever known. "Hurry, Ben. Please."

At first Amanda had made time go by with watching the people who passed the reception desk. But after a while her stomach grew nervous, so she closed her eyes and prayed. *Make my mama happy again, dear God. She's been here a long time because she's sad. And I know You don't want her sad anymore.*

Just then Mr. Stovall walked around the corner and smiled at her. "You ready?"

Her heart jumped inside her and she was on her feet at his side in an instant, her hand safely in his. "Yep." She grinned up at him. The butterflies weren't because she was worried; they were because she was happier than she'd ever been in her entire life. She was actually going to get to meet her mother!

Amanda could hardly wait.

Thirty-six

THE MOMENT MAGGIE SAW HER, SHE INHALED SHARPLY.

Lord, she's exactly the same girl… The precious, blond child I've seen so often over the past year.

And now she was suddenly standing there for real, hand in hand with Ben, looking so like Maggie at that age that she wondered again if it weren't all part of some marvelous, imaginary moment.

"Hi, honey." Maggie held her distance, not wanting to frighten her. **She's beautiful, Lord. I can't believe she's here…**

With eyes that glowed, the child smiled sweetly at Maggie and stepped forward, one hand outstretched. "Hi, I'm Amanda."

It was actually her, the daughter Maggie had held only a few hours, the child she'd loved every moment these past eight years. She reached out to shake the girl's hand, then caught herself. What was she doing? This was the daughter she'd dreamed of holding as far back as she could remember.

"Oh, Amanda! Honey, come here." Maggie felt tears in her eyes as she slid to the edge of the bed and held out her arms. Amanda ran to her, and they joined in a way that only mother and child can. Ben moved into the room but allowed them this time. Maggie's heart was nearly bursting with gratitude for him and a love that seemed to be blossoming by the moment, a love far more intense than anything they'd shared in the past.

The details about Ben and Maggie would have to wait. Right now she had Amanda, and that was all that mattered. She held onto her little girl and allowed her tears to mingle with her daughter's long blond hair. "I've wanted to find you since the day I gave you up."

Her daughter's arms were locked around her and she could feel her small body convulsing with sobs. "I've p-p-prayed for this f-f-forever."

Maggie couldn't tell which emotion was stronger: the heartache for the years they'd lost or the joy at having found her now. She pulled back a bit and gently moved Amanda's bangs out of her eyes and wiped her daughter's tears with her thumb. "So who are you, Amanda? Tell me about yourself."

Amanda looked at Ben and a grin flashed on her tearstained face. "I'm braver than the Crocodile Hunter, that's what Mr. Stovall says."

Maggie laughed. "You mean you've been watching that crazy crocodile guy on TV?"

Ben and Amanda exchanged a smile, and Amanda's laughter rang across the room. "Mr. Stovall says there's nothing like the freshwater crocodile gallop and that the Crocodile Hunter is the only guy who thinks rattlesnakes are beautiful."

"He's got that right." Maggie beamed at the girl in her arms and cupped her face tenderly in her hands. "I can't believe you're here, Amanda. And you've been in foster care how long?"

In the background, Ben shook his head and mouthed the word, "Later." A sick knot formed in Maggie's stomach, and she remembered the columns she'd written on the Social Services department before going to Orchards. She flashed him a questioning look, but he only shook his head and something pained in his eyes told her that Amanda's time in foster care had not been good.

"A l-l-long time. But I had Kathy, so it was okay."

"Kathy?"

Ben cleared his throat and cut into the conversation. "Kathy's the wonderful social worker I was telling you about."

Amanda nodded. "Kathy was going to adopt me, but the state said her house was too small. So I had to keep going to foster homes. Whenever things didn't work out there, I stayed with Kathy."

Whoever this Kathy was she had found a special place in Amanda's heart, and Maggie couldn't wait to fit the pieces together and meet the woman. Whatever had happened during her years of foster care, they could talk about it later. Now was the time to hold her and laugh with her and help her understand that even though they barely knew each other she would always be safe and loved with them.

Is this a forever thing, Lord?

She ran her hands down Amanda's arms as she studied her daughter again. It was utterly unreal that she was here—a living, breathing little girl standing before her, and that she was indeed the child she'd wondered about for so long.

She wanted to ask Amanda never to leave, to consider staying in Cleveland and live with them for always. But that, too, could wait.

Amanda hugged her again and this time when she pulled back, she looked sad. "Mr. Stovall says you're here because you're sick. And that you've been sad. Are you getting better?"

Maggie caught Ben's eye in the background and tried to convey to him the love that was bursting in her heart. "Actually, I'm not sad anymore at all. In fact, I can probably go home today if I want."

Ben's eyebrows raised and he started toward her, then stopped. She understood and again she was grateful. This was Amanda's moment not his, and he obviously wasn't going to do anything to interfere.

She grinned at Ben, then back at Amanda. "So what do you think of old Mr. Stovall?"

"He's great. We got to do all kinds of things the last couple of days. He even bought me a new bedspread—it's pink with flowers on it." Amanda cast Ben a look of trust and admiration. "Best of all, he prays with me whenever I feel like it. No one ever did that before except for Kathy."

Ben shrugged and returned a smile to Amanda.

Maggie's jaw dropped as she watched the exchange. The situation grew more amazing by the moment. Her husband had clearly been captivated by Amanda's beguiling charm and was now so smitten by her little-girl love for him that he was looking every bit the proud father.

"Can you believe it, Maggie?" Ben's eyes said the things his words didn't.

"I keep pinching myself…"

All her life she'd feared Ben might refuse contact with her daughter if Maggie ever found her. **I didn't really know him, either.**

Trust in Me with all your heart, My daughter.

Maggie chuckled. "I guess God must be smiling pretty big right now."

Amanda clung to Maggie again, and she could feel the girl nodding in agreement. "I'm so glad you've been thinking about me, Mrs…"

She let the word hang there for a moment, and Maggie leaned back far enough to see her daughter's questioning eyes. "What's wrong, honey?"

"I guess I d-d-don't know what to call you yet." Amanda's face was a mixture of fear and anticipation, and Maggie felt a wave of protective love more powerful than she'd known could exist.

"Sweetheart, what do you want to call me?"

"Well…Mrs. Stovall seems kind of funny."

Maggie glanced at Ben and saw tears form in his eyes as he watched the scene unfold. "Yeah, it is kind of funny, isn't it? You could call me Maggie, I guess. If you want."

Amanda cocked her head and seemed to wrestle with the idea for a moment. "No…not Maggie. That's kind of like a sister or something."

I don't want to push her, Lord. "Is there something you'd like to call me?"

A single tear spilled onto Amanda's cheek, but her gaze was unwavering as she looked deeply into Maggie's eyes. "C-C-Can

I call you Mommy?"

Maggie knew she wasn't dreaming now, because as she pulled Amanda close again, her heart soared with a love that couldn't be contrived even by her own imagination. "Yes, honey, yes. Call me Mommy, little girl. I've prayed for you every day, Amanda. Thought of you and wondered about you. I am your mommy, I'll always be your mommy, and it would be the greatest gift in the world to have you call me that."

Ben came closer and wrapped his arms around them both so that they were clustered in a group hug that seemed to need no words. When he straightened again Maggie saw him nudge Amanda and send her a lopsided grin. "I think I'm the only one with no name."

Amanda laughed. "That's silly. If she's my mom, that makes you my dad." A troubled look settled over her face. "You know that mean guy, the one who took me from the school bus?"

"Yes…"

Alarm sliced through the warmth of the moment and Maggie flashed a wide-eyed look at Ben. He held up a hand and shook his head as if to tell her this, too, could wait until they had time to talk alone.

"He said he was my dad. Is that true?"

Maggie felt her heart lurch and she gulped back the questions she was frantic to ask. Then she reached for Ben's hand and pulled him close. "Honey, I think you already answered that question a minute ago when you said if I'm Mom, Mr. Stovall must be Dad."

Amanda sighed and nodded her head. "Good. That's what I thought."

Maggie smoothed a hand over Amanda's hair. "What's your middle name, Amanda?"

"Joy. Amanda Joy Brownell…unless I get adopted." She grinned at Ben again, and Maggie wondered what they'd been talking about the past few days. She had so much to catch up on; she could barely wait to hear the weeks of details she'd missed out on.

Then it hit her.

"Joy? Your middle name is Joy, honey?"

Amanda nodded. "Isn't it pretty? The Brownells told me they gave me that name because I brought so much joy to their lives."

Maggie caught her breath. Joy was what she'd been missing all these years and now, when she finally had been set free from the darkness, joy had come to stay. Homeless, full-hearted, lonely little Amanda Joy.

"Well, it's almost dinnertime…" Ben met Maggie's gaze and held it, his question clear.

She smiled at him. Dear, sweet Ben. How had she ever for a moment thought he'd turn his back on her for telling the truth? **God, You were right again…I had only to trust You and everything has fallen in place.** She directed her gaze at Amanda again. "If you guys'll help me pack, I'd like to join you for dinner. We have a lot to catch up on, don't you think?"

At the thought of Maggie coming home with them, Amanda was back in her arms, her hands clasped tightly around Maggie.

Maggie smiled. "I love you, honey. I've always loved you."

There was silence for a moment and then the muffled sound of Amanda's voice, ringing with sincerity. "I love you…Mommy."

In that moment Maggie knew she was blessed beyond anything she'd ever known or imagined, and that no matter what happened from that point on, she would be thankful for this time with Amanda as long as she lived.

That same afternoon a hearing was wrapping up in Judge Hutchison's courtroom.

"Mr. McFadden, do you understand that you are being charged with felony kidnapping, and that the sentence for this crime—should you be found guilty—is a possible life in prison?"

John McFadden stood upright, his shoulders straight, and met the judge's gaze head on. "Yes, your honor."

"Very well then, how do you plead?"

"Not guilty, your honor."

The judge wrote something on his pad of paper and checked a thick book at his side. "This case will be handed over for judgment and will be given a preliminary trial to be scheduled the third week of January. Your attorney will inform you of the exact date as the time draws closer. Until that time you will remain in the…"

John tuned him out. The fact that he was the girl's father should get him a lighter sentence. It was what his attorney had suggested, and it sounded all right to him.

But it didn't matter, really.

All that had mattered since that day was the way his little girl's faith had been unwavering, even in the face of extreme danger. **Jesus loves you…I'm praying for you…** He might never see her again, but her words had come back to him over and over—and with them, he felt a certain…peace. They could do what they wanted with him now; his drug-dealing days were behind him for good.

Somehow he'd come to believe his daughter's words, and that belief made his heart light with a hope that was as foreign to him as the message she'd given him that day.

Jesus loves you…Jesus loves you…Jesus loves you.

It didn't make sense, not by a long shot, but John felt freed by those words. And if Jesus loved him, he was going to spend the rest of his life trying to figure out why.

GRADUALLY THE PHONE CALLS GREW LESS FREQUENT, AND KATHY took that as a good sign. In fact, the letter was the first she'd heard from Amanda in two weeks.

Kathy waited until she was alone with a cup of coffee before reading it. She studied Amanda's painstakingly neat printing—Amanda must have been doing better in school, penmanship was never her strong point. On the back of the envelope, Amanda had drawn two hearts and written underneath, "Love and kisses."

Kathy slit open the envelope and took out the folded note inside. The carefully written sentences took up the top half of the page, and at the bottom was a picture of Amanda and the Stovalls with a caption underneath that read, "Mommy, Daddy, and me."

The picture spoke volumes, and Kathy smiled and shook her head. *Lord, You're amazing. Who'd have ever thought this would happen to Amanda Joy?* She moved her eyes to the top of the page and began reading.

Dear Kathy,

I just got legally adopted and I'm so happy. God has answered every one of my prayers. We went into court and Mr. Stovall told the judge he wanted to be my dad forever. Then my mommy told the judge she wanted me for always and ever. And the judge asked me what I thought and I said I wanted to be with them, too. So he made us a family. But really the truth is God did that, right? I miss you and the kids. But mostly you. I love you always.

Love, Amanda Joy Stovall.

Amanda Joy Stovall. Kathy's heart swelled with gratitude for all God had done for the child. Thousands of kids were wasting away in state-run foster systems across the country, but Amanda had found a way out because her faith had never once wavered. She read the letter again and let her eyes settle on Amanda's drawing. Kathy studied it and noticed something she hadn't before. In the past, Amanda's hand-drawn people had straight lines where the mouth should be. They weren't dark or sad or odd-looking. Just adorned with straight-line mouths. But this picture was different.

All three people were smiling.

For just a moment there was a familiar stinging in Kathy's eyes and a single teardrop landed on the picture. She would never forget Amanda, not ever. Her situation had seemed utterly hopeless to everyone—everyone but a little girl with a heart as good and big as her future had suddenly become.

And to her God—who in the end had been bigger than all of them put together.

The church service was under way and Amanda—wearing her pale pink chiffon dress—sat nestled between Maggie and Ben. It was her big day, and they had bought the new dress to mark the occasion. Maggie glanced down at Amanda and savored the way her daughter's small fingers felt linked with her own. Amanda loved to hold Maggie's hand, and although Maggie still felt deep sorrow for the years she'd missed with her daughter, she was too busy cherishing the current days to dwell long on the past.

The music that Sunday was particularly moving, and it allowed Maggie a moment to reflect on all she'd learned over the last three months. She'd worked through the feelings of shock and anger over the truth about Amanda's time in foster care, and though she was grateful her daughter had survived, a part of her would always hurt over what had happened. She tried not to play the "what if" game, but now and then she'd catch herself wondering how different things might have been if she'd followed her heart all those years ago.

Then there were the details of Ben's search for who she was; why she'd succumbed to the darkness of depression; his dangerous encounter with John McFadden; and the man's eventual kidnapping of Amanda. Never had she imagined Ben would love her like that, without standards or expectations, but just because she was his wife. His other half. He was so much more a godly man than she'd ever believed possible, and she was struck daily by how horribly different things might have been if he hadn't been devoted to God's will through it all.

The music played on, and Maggie's heart soared as she recalled the several meetings they'd had with Kathy Garrett, a woman for whom Maggie would be forever grateful. Kathy was a living example of why one could never generalize about the pitfalls of the state-run foster system. After all, without the system, Amanda never would have known the love of that one, very dedicated and devoted woman.

Maggie could still hardly believe all that had happened while she was at Orchards. She went once a week now for follow-up counseling, but the darkness was so far gone it felt as though it had happened to a different person altogether.

What she'd learned at Orchards had given her perhaps the most amazing truths of all—that in Christ there is only honesty, no matter how grave or wrong or desperate life becomes. That only in that truthful place can the sunshine of God's grace and joy and forgiveness find its way through the darkness.

The music stopped, and the worship leader opened his Bible and began to read. Beside Maggie, Amanda looked up and smiled first at her, then at Ben. *Oh, Lord, I can't believe she's really here. Thank you…thank you.* It was a prayer that was constantly on Maggie's heart.

The worship leader was saying, "Proverbs tells us there are times when our lives take a wrong turn, for whatever reason, and when that happens there is one thing we must remember. Trust in God with all your heart and lean not on your own understanding. In all your ways acknowledge Him and He will make your paths straight."

Maggie's eyes flew open. It was the verse! The very one that had spoken to her heart whenever things seemed desperate and hopeless. Of all the days to have it read in church… Out of the corner of her eye she caught Ben motioning to her as if he had something important to say. They leaned close, forming a shelter over Amanda.

"That's the Scripture," he whispered so quietly that Maggie knew Amanda couldn't hear him. "Whenever I thought things were hopeless, that verse came to me."

Maggie felt goose bumps rise along her arms and neck. "Me too!"

Ben gave her a look of amazement. "The same verse?"

She nodded, and they exchanged a look that said they'd probably spend hours on the subject later, like they did on so many topics these days, almost as though they were newlyweds again. Only this time they had nothing to hide, and the intimacy of their hearts was greater than Maggie had ever imagined.

As they returned their focus on the worship leader, Maggie was overwhelmed by God's faithfulness. *Lord, how could it be? You were speaking the same promise to each of us? During the darkest time in our lives?* Peace washed over her at the mercy they'd both been shown. *Everything I have is because of You…my marriage, my life*—she glanced at Amanda beside her—*especially my daughter.*

The worship leader moved from the piano to center stage and interrupted Maggie's thoughts. "We have something special we'd like to do before the sermon today." He smiled, and Maggie thought there were tears in his eyes. "If the Stovall family will please come up."

Maggie and Ben rose, each taking one of Amanda's hands as

they made their way up front. When they had turned to face the congregation, the worship leader explained that the couple wanted to dedicate their newly adopted daughter, Amanda Joy. While he was talking, Maggie saw someone near the back of the church that made her heart swell.

Laura Thompson.

The two women caught each other's gaze over the crowd. Maggie could still hear Laura's tearful voice. *"I've been praying for you night and day, dear…night and day…night and day…"*

God had been faithful in so many things! Laura had been down with the flu for two weeks, but here she was, well enough to be part of Amanda's dedication service. *God, You are good beyond words.*

Maggie glanced down at Amanda and caught the love in her daughter's eyes as she looked from her to Ben and back again, squeezing their hands.

Maggie focused her attention on what the minister was saying. "Is it your desire to raise this child in a Christian home, in the love and knowledge of Jesus Christ?"

I've never known any greater desire, Lord. Ben and Maggie nodded in unison. They had planned ahead that Ben would speak at this point, so the worship leader handed him the microphone.

"Some of you know what Maggie and I have been through these past few months." He scanned the people before him. "I just want to tell you that whatever you're going through, whatever thing you're up against today, give it to God. Seek Him with all your heart, because the Scripture we heard a few moments ago is a promise straight from heaven." He looked from Maggie to Amanda and smiled. "The three of us are here today as living proof."

Maggie watched him with a full heart, amazed at how totally and completely she had fallen in love with him since returning home. *I never would have believed it, Lord…* He was wonderful with Amanda, and Maggie knew he loved her unconditionally, the way she had only dreamed of being loved.

The worship leader took the microphone back. "Why don't some of you come up and surround this family as we pray for them."

Led by Laura Thompson, people—many of whom were now familiar with their story—came and circled them in a wreath of support that brought tears to Maggie's eyes. Laura laid her hand on Maggie's shoulder and bowed her head, eyes closed. While the worship leader prayed aloud, the overwhelming presence of the Holy Spirit surrounded them and Maggie was washed in the light of God's love and kindness. Suddenly she had the strangest sensation that Laura was sick, sicker than any of them knew. And that praying for her these past months had been her last earthly task.

No, Lord, don't let it be so…

Lean not on your own understanding, but in all your ways acknowledge Him…

Maggie felt her eyes sting with the beginning of tears. Whatever Laura's future, she would forever be part of the Stovall family, and if it would soon be Maggie's turn to pray for a season, she would welcome the task. *The way a family should.*

The music started again, and Maggie recognized the tune: "Great Is Thy Faithfulness."

They huddled close, with Ben's arms around Maggie and Amanda, and Laura praying beside them. Together they sang as one.

"Great is Thy faithfulness, O God my Father. There is no shadow of turning with Thee…"

Maggie felt the tears fall onto her face as she clung to her husband and daughter. This was a hymn that had brought pains of conviction in the past, conviction because she, herself, had lived in the shadows far too long, blind to the faithfulness of her God. But the conviction was gone now, and in its place was unspeakable joy. Their three voices rang together and it was the sweetest sound Maggie could remember hearing.

"Morning by morning new mercies I see. All I have needed Thy hand hath provided…"

With Amanda snuggled closely between them, Maggie and Ben looked at each other. Their eyes met and held for the remainder of the song, and what she saw there was a love she knew would last through the years. God had given her real, lasting joy and along with it, an understanding that in Christ alone there is victory over the darkness—whatever trials might come.

They held tight to each other and finished the song together as if they were the only three people on earth.

"Great is Thy faithfulness, great is Thy faithfulness, great is Thy faithfulness, Lord, unto me."

Dear Reader,

I believe with all my heart that God gave me this story for such a time as this. Around us, throughout our country, the spiritual battle is heating up in more ways than we know. Scripture tells us the enemy comes to steal, kill, and destroy. To that end, I've seen him try two common tactics: distraction and discouragement.

Distraction often happens first. We start off meaning well, reading our Bibles and viewing life with spiritual eyes. But over time complacency veils our enthusiasm until we wake up and lie down with thoughts that have nothing to do with our Savior. We opt for a cup of coffee instead of a chapter of Scripture to get us going, and we become so caught up in the here and now we forget that our focus, that our entire lives must be directed at the ever-after if we are to live free, effective, joyful godly lives.

When we are fully distracted, we no longer tap into the greatest resource given mankind—the Holy Spirit. Instead we walk by a compass of our own design, and in very little time end up lost and confused. This is when discouragement hits.

Depression, then, is the combination of the two: distraction and discouragement, multiplied to whatever degree the enemy is seeking to destroy us.

Although I have never personally dealt with clinical depression, I know what it is to be buried in discouragement. I remember driving to Northern California on a family vacation and taking in the beauty of the Lake Shasta area. The trip followed a lengthy period of warfare and spiritual attack—a season of discouragement. As my husband drove through the mountains that day, tears fell from my eyes as though a dam had broken in my heart.

The Lord, in all His lovingkindness, reminded me of some basic truths as we made our way through the pines. First, He is bigger than any problem I have. Second, everything in this life—absolutely everything—is temporary. And God's Word says we are to fix our eyes not on the temporary but the eternal. Finally, He adjusted my perspective so that I no longer hurt for things that had taken place that past year. Instead, I knew that somehow they would work to the Lord's glory. My eternal perspective was back in place.

Now I know that a season of discouragement pales in comparison to depression, but over the past year, God let me understand pain in this area. Pain that is being buried, masked by thousands, perhaps even millions of women today—both in and outside the church.

If you are one who is suffering this way, please seek professional help without shame, and know that God loves you just as you are. He is beckoning you even now to come into the sunshine of His grace and truth. Come in honesty and never look back.

Some of you have no idea what it means to have a relationship with the Lord. To you I pray that you please make a decision to accept God's gift of salvation. Tell Him you can't live any longer without Him. Buy a Bible, find a Bible-believing, Christ-centered church near your home, and get connected.

If you're already there and are silently suffering, it's time to be honest with your church family. If news of your depression isn't received well, continue to seek those who will listen with an open heart, and pray for your church. I believe the time has come for all of us to recognize the enemy's hand in this pervasive illness and come together the way Christ would have us do.

If you have never dealt with serious depression, thank God sincerely and ask Him to make you compassionate. Someone—probably someone closer than you think—may be hiding in the darkness even now. Ask Him to show you how you can help, how you can care for others and be a light in the darkness.

Thank you for journeying these pages with me. I look forward to hearing from you, especially from those of you who have faithfully read each of my novels. You can still write me at my e-mail address: rtnbykk@aol.com.

Blessings abundant to you and yours and grace as you seek to walk in His light.

Sincerely,

NOVELS BY KAREN KINGSBURY

Where Yesterday Lives
When Joy Came to Stay
On Every Side
A Time to Dance
A Time to Embrace
One Tuesday Morning
Beyond Tuesday Morning
Oceans Apart

THE FOREVER FAITHFUL SERIES
Waiting for Morning
A Moment of Weakness
Halfway to Forever

THE REDEMPTION SERIES
(co-written with Gary Smalley)
Redemption
Remember
Return
Rejoice
Reunion

THE RED GLOVES CHRISTMAS SERIES
Gideon's Gift
Maggie's Miracle
Sarah's Song

www.karenkingsbury.com

OTHER NOVELS BY
KAREN KINGSBURY

WHERE YESTERDAY LIVES
In the wake of her father's sudden death, Ellen Barrett must journey back to the small town where she grew up and spend a week with antagonistic siblings. In the process, she must reckon with a man who once meant everything to her.

WHEN JOY CAME TO STAY
Maggie Stovall is trapped inside a person she's spent years carefully crafting. Now the truth about who she is—and what she's done—is revealed, sending Maggie into a spiral of despair. Will Maggie walk away from her marriage and her foster child in her desperation to escape the mantle of depression cloaking her? Or will she allow God to take her to a place of ultimate honesty before it's too late?

ON EVERY SIDE
Jordan Riley, an embittered lawyer, sues his hometown to have a public statue of Jesus removed. The conflict causes him to cross paths with a spirited young newscaster named Faith, who opposes Jordan's suit in surprising ways. Perhaps most amazing of all is how Faith begins to disassemble the walls around Jordan's heart. Will love be enough when the battle rages on every side?

THE
FOREVER FAITHFUL SERIES

WAITING FOR MORNING—*Book One*
A drunk driver...a deadly accident...a dream destroyed. When Hannah Ryan loses her husband and oldest daughter to a drunk driver, she is consumed with hate and revenge. Ultimately, it is a kind prosecutor, a wise widow, and her husband's dying words that bring her the peace that will set her free and let her live again.

A MOMENT OF WEAKNESS—*Book Two*
When childhood friends Jade and Tanner reunite as adults, they share their hearts, souls, and dreams of forever—until a fateful decision tears them apart. Now, nearly a decade later, Jade's unfaithful husband wants to destroy her in a custody battle that is about to send shock waves across the United States. Only one man can help Jade in her darkest hour. And only one old woman knows the truth that can set them all free.

HALFWAY TO FOREVER—*Book Three*
Matt and Hannah...Jade and Tanner—after already surviving much, these couples now face the greatest struggles of their lives: Parental losses and life-threatening illness threaten to derail their faith and sideline their futures. Can Hannah survive the loss of an adopted daughter? Will Tanner come through decades of loneliness only to face losing Jade one final time?

ABOUT THE AUTHOR...
Karen Kingsbury is an award-winning author and former reporter for the *Los Angeles Times* and *Los Angeles Daily News*. She is also a recognized author with the Women of Faith Fiction Club. Kingsbury lives with her husband and six children in Washington.

KAREN KINGSBURY

AND PRISM COFOUNDER TONI VOGT

THE PRISM WEIGHT LOSS PROGRAM

The PRISM® Weight Loss Program, founded in 1990, has helped more than 60,000 people transform their eating behaviors with a sensible, lifestyle-change approach. Now available in *The Prism Weight Loss Program* by bestselling author Karen Kingsbury and PRISM cofounder Toni Vogt, the book shows readers how to not just "tame the monster" of food addiction, but destroy it through simple eating strategies and biblical principles. It includes testimonials, descriptions of the authors' personal struggles with food addiction, details of the program, and a fabulous recipe section that will help readers become the fit people God created them to be.

"Karen Ball has penned a modern classic and given us two unforgettable characters to root for. This is an author to watch!"

—ROBIN LEE HATCHER, bestselling author of *Firstborn* and *Promised to Me*

Gabe and Renee Roman are on the edge—relationally and spiritually. But after years of struggling in their marriage, their greatest test comes in the most unexpected of forms: a blizzard in the Oregon wilderness. Their truck hurtles down the side of a mountain, and suddenly they are forced to fight for survival by relying on each other. But both must surrender their last defenses if they are to come home at last—to God and to each other. Only then will they learn the most important truths of all: God is sufficient, and only through obedience to His call can we find true joy. Can the Romans overcome their greatest obstacle—themselves—in time?

www.multnomahbooks.com

From Bestselling Author

KAREN BALL

Her daughter Faith is the answer to Ann's lifelong prayer to be a mother. But her dream is shattered when the teenager rejects Ann's love and the love of God. After years pass, and God heals their relationship, Ann falls seriously ill. Faith watches her mother weaken, struggling with role reversals and leaning on God as never before. Through all the intricacies of their relationship, all the joys and trials, they are reminded that God is with them. He brings them peace in the darkness, joy in the midst of sorrow, and hope in the face of death.